STEPHANIE LAURENS
KASEY MICHAELS
DELILAH MARVELLE

Rules of Engagement

HARLEQUIN® BESTSELLERS

ISBN-13: 978-0-373-60584-2

RULES OF ENGAGEMENT

Copyright © 2012 by Harlequin Books S.A.

The publisher acknowledges the copyright holders of the individual works as follows:

THE REASONS FOR MARRIAGE
Copyright © 1995 by Stephanie Laurens

THE WEDDING PARTY
Copyright © 2012 by Kathryn Seidick

UNLACED
Copyright © 2012 by Delilah Marvelle

Recycling programs for this product may not exist in your area.

Printed in U.S.A.

CONTENTS

THE REASONS
FOR MARRIAGE

Stephanie chats with her readers on Facebook
(https://www.facebook.com/authorstephanielaurens)
and via her website at www.stephanielaurens.com.

CHAPTER ONE

THE DOOR OF THE Duke of Eversleigh's library clicked shut. From his chair behind the huge mahogany desk, Jason Montgomery, fifth Duke of Eversleigh, eyed the oak panels with marked disfavour.

"Impossible!" he muttered, the word heavy with contemptuous disdain laced with an odd reluctance. As the sound of his cousin Hector's retreating footsteps dwindled, Jason's gaze left the door, travelling across the laden bookcases to the large canvas mounted on a nearby wall.

Expression bleak, he studied the features of the young man depicted there, the impudent, devil-may-care smile and mischievous grey eyes topped by wind-tousled dark brown hair. Broad shoulders were clad in the scarlet of regimentals, a lance stood to one side, all evidence of the subject's occupation. A muscle twitched at the corner of Jason's mouth. He quelled it, his austere, chiselled features hardening into a mask of chilly reserve.

The door opened to admit a gentleman, elegantly garbed and smiling amiably. He paused with his hand on the knob and raised a brow enquiringly.

"I saw your cousin depart. Are you safe?"

With the confidence of one sure of his welcome, Frederick Marshall did not wait for an answer but, shutting the door, strolled towards the desk between the long windows.

His Grace of Eversleigh let out an explosive sigh. "Damn it, Frederick, this is no laughing matter! Hector Montgomery is a *man-milliner*! It would be the height of irresponsibility for me to allow him to step into the ducal shoes. Even *I* can't stomach the thought—and I wouldn't be here to see it."

Pushing back his chair, Jason swung to face his friend as he sank into an armchair nearby. "More to the point," he continued, stretching his long legs before him, a somewhat grim smile twisting his lips, "tempting though the idea might be, if I introduced *cher* Hector to the family as my heir, there'd be a riot—a mutiny in the Montgomery ranks. Knowing my aunts, they would press for incarceration until such time as I capitulated and wed."

"I dare say your aunts would be delighted to know you see the problem—and its solution—so clearly."

At that, Jason's piercing gaze focused on his friend's face. "Just whose side are you on, Frederick?"

Frederick smiled. "Need you ask? But there's no sense in ducking the facts. Now Ricky's gone, you'll have to wed. And the sooner you make up your mind to it, the less likely it will be that your aunts, dear ladies, think to take a hand themselves—don't you think?"

Having delivered himself of this eminently sound piece of advice, Frederick sat back and watched his friend digest it. Sunshine shone through the windows at Jason's back, burnishing the famous chestnut locks cut short in the prevailing mode. Broad shoulders did justice to one of Schultz's more severe designs, executed in grey superfine, worn over tightly fitting pantaloons. The waistcoat Frederick espied beneath the grey coat, a subtle thing in shades of deeper grey and muted lavender, elicited a twinge of envy. There was one man in all of England who could effortlessly make Frederick Marshall feel less than elegant and that man was seated behind the desk, sunk in unaccustomed gloom.

Both bachelors, their association was bound by many common interests, but in all their endeavours it was Jason who excelled. A consummate sportsman, a noted whip, a hardened gamester and acknowledged rake, dangerous with pistols—and even more dangerous with women. Unused to acknowledging any authority beyond his own whims, the fifth Duke of Eversleigh had lived a hedonistic existence that few, in this hedonistic age, could match.

Which, of course, made the solution to his present predicament that much harder to swallow.

Seeing Jason's gaze, pensive yet stubborn, rise to the portrait of his younger brother, known to all as Ricky, Frederick stifled a sigh. Few understood how close the brothers had been, despite the nine years' difference in age. At twenty-nine, Ricky had possessed a boundless charm which had cloaked the wilful streak he shared with Jason—the same wilful streak that had sent him in the glory of his Guards' captaincy to Waterloo, there to die at Hougoumont. The dispatches had heaped praise on all the fated Guardsmen who had defended the vital fort so valiantly, yet no amount of praise had eased the grief, all the more deep for being so private, that Jason had borne.

For a time the Montgomery clan had held off, aware, as others were not, of the brothers' affection. However, as they were also privy to the understanding that had been forged years before—that Ricky, much less cynical, much less hard than Jason, would take on the responsibility of providing for the next generation, leaving his older brother free to continue his life unfettered by the bonds of matrimony, it was not to be expected that the family's interest in Jason's affairs would remain permanently deflected. Consequently, when Jason had re-emerged, taking up his usual pursuits with a vigour which, Frederick shrewdly suspected, had been fuelled by a need to bury the recent past, his aunts became restive. When their arrogantly errant nephew continued to give no hint of turning his attention to what they perceived as a now pressing duty, they had, collectively, deemed it time to take a hand.

Tipped off by one of Jason's redoubtable aunts, Lady Agatha Colebatch, Frederick had deemed it wise to prod Jason's mind to deal with the matter before his aunts made his hackles rise. It was at his urging that Jason had finally consented to meet with his heir, a cousin many times removed.

The silence was broken by a frustrated snort.

"Damn you, Ricky," Jason grumbled, his gaze on his brother's portrait. "How dare you go to hell in your own way and leave me to face this hell on earth?"

Detecting the resigned undertones in his friend's complaint, Frederick chuckled. "Hell on earth?"

Abruptly straightening and swinging back to his desk, Jason raised his brows. "Can you think of a better description for the sanctified institution of marriage?"

"Oh, I don't know." Frederick waved a hand. "No reason it has to be as bad as all that."

Jason's grey gaze transfixed him. "You being such an expert on the matter?"

"Hardly me—but I should think you could figure as such."

"Me?" Jason looked his amazement.

"Well, all your recent mistresses have been married, haven't they?"

Frederick's air of innocence deceived Jason not one

whit. Nevertheless, his lips twitched and the frown which had marred his strikingly handsome countenance lifted. "Your misogyny defeats you, my friend. The women I bed are prime reasons for my distrust of the venerable bonds of matrimony. Such women are perfect examples of what I should *not* wish for in a wife."

"Precisely," agreed Frederick. "So at least you have that much insight." He looked up to discover Jason regarding him intently, a suspicious glint in his silver-grey eyes.

"Frederick, dear chap, you aren't by any chance possessed of an ulterior motive in this matter, are you? Perchance my aunts have whispered dire threats in your ear?"

To his confusion, Frederick blushed uncomfortably. "Damn you, Jason, get those devilish eyes off me. If you must know, Lady Agatha did speak to me, but you know she's always been inclined to take your side. She merely pointed out that her sisters were already considering candidates and if I wished to avert a major explosion I'd do well to bring the matter to your mind."

Jason grimaced. "Well, consider it done. But having accomplished so much, you can damn well help me through the rest of it. Who the devil am I to marry?"

The question hung in the calm of the library while both men considered the possible answers.

"What about the Taunton chit? She's surely pretty enough to take your fancy."

Jason frowned. "The one with reams of blonde ringlets?" When Frederick nodded, Jason shook his head decisively. "She twitters."

"Hemming's girl then—a fortune there, and word is out that they're hanging out for a title. You'd only have to say the word and she'd be yours."

"She and her three sisters and whining mother to boot? No, I thank you. Think again."

And so it went, on through the ranks of the year's débutantes and their still unwed older sisters.

Eventually, Frederick was close to admitting defeat. Sipping the wine Jason had poured to fortify them through the mind-numbing process, he tried a different tack. "Perhaps," he said, slanting a somewhat peevish glance at his host, "given your highly specific require-ments, we would do better to clarify just what it is you require in a wife and then try to find a suitable candi-date?"

Savouring the excellent Madeira he had recently ac-quired, Jason's eyes narrowed. "What I want in a wife?" he echoed.

For a full minute, silence held sway, broken only by the discreet tick of the ornate clock on the mantelpiece. Slowly, Jason set down his long-stemmed glass, run-ning his fingers down the figured stem in an uncon-scious caress. "My wife," he stated, his voice sure and strong, "must be a virtuous woman, capable of running the Abbey and this house in a manner commensurate with the dignity of the Montgomerys."

Wordlessly, Frederick nodded. Eversleigh Abbey was the Montgomery family seat, a sprawling mansion in Dorset. Running the huge house, and playing hostess at the immense family gatherings occasionally held there, would stretch the talents of the most well-educated miss.

"She would need to be at least presentable—I draw the line at any underbred antidote being the Duchess of Eversleigh."

Reflecting that Jason's aunts, high-sticklers every one, would certainly echo that sentiment, Frederick waited for more.

Jason's gaze had dropped to his long fingers, still moving sensuously up and down the glass stem. "And, naturally, she would have to be prepared to provide me with heirs without undue fuss over the matter." His expression hardened. "Any woman who expects me to make a cake of myself over her will hardly suit."

Frederick had no doubts about that.

After a moment's consideration, Jason quietly added, "Furthermore, she would need to be prepared to remain principally at the Abbey, unless I specifically request her presence here in town."

At that cold declaration, Frederick blinked. "But...do you mean after the Season has ended?"

"No. I mean at all times."

"You mean to incarcerate her in the Abbey? Even while you enjoy yourself in town?" When Jason merely nodded, Frederick felt moved to expostulate. "Really, Jason! A mite draconian, surely?"

Jason smiled, a slow, predatory smile that did not reach his eyes. "You forget, Frederick. I have, as you noted earlier, extensive experience of the bored wives of the *ton*. Whatever else, rest assured my wife will never join their ranks."

"Ah." Faced with such a statement, Frederick had nothing to do but retreat. "So what else do you require in your bride?"

Leaning back in his chair, Jason crossed his ankles and fell to studying the high gloss on his Hessians. "She would have to be well-born—the family would accept nothing less. Luckily, a dowry makes no odds—I doubt I'd notice, after all. Connections, however, are a must."

"Given what you have to offer, that should hardly pose a problem." Frederick drained his glass. "All the *haut ton* with daughters to establish will beat a path to your door once they realize your intent."

"No doubt," Jason returned ascerbically. "That, if you must know, is the vision that spurs me to take your advice and act now—before the hordes descend. The idea of being forced to run the gamut of all the dim-witted debs fills me with horror."

"Well, that's a point you haven't mentioned." When Jason lifted his brows, Frederick clarified. "Dim-witted. You never could bear fools lightly, so you had better add that to your list."

"Lord, yes," Jason sighed, letting his head fall back against the padded leather. "If she's to avoid being strangled the morning after we are wed, my prospective bride would do well to have rather more wit than the common run." After a moment, he mused, "You know, I rather wonder if this paragon—my prospective bride—exists in this world."

Frederick pursed his lips. "Your requirements are a mite stringent, but I'm sure, somewhere, there must be a woman who can fill your position."

"Ah," said Jason, amusement beginning to glimmer in his grey eyes. "Now we come to the difficult part. Where?"

Frederick racked his brain for an answer. "A more mature woman, perhaps? But one with the right background." He caught Jason's eyes and frowned. "Dash it, it's *you* who must wed. Perhaps I should remind you of Miss Ekhart, the young lady your aunt Hardcastle pushed under your nose last time she was in town?"

"Heaven forbid!" Jason schooled his features to a suitably intimidated expression. "Say on, dear Frederick. Where resides my paragon?"

The clock ticked on. Finally, frowning direfully, Frederick flung up a hand. "Hell and the devil! There must be *some* suitable women about?"

Jason met his frustration with bland resignation. "I can safely say I've never found one. That aside, however, I agree that, assuming there is indeed at least one woman who could fill my bill, it behoves me to hunt her out, wherever she may be. The question is, where to start?"

With no real idea, Frederick kept mum.

His gaze abstracted, his mind turning over his problem, Jason's long fingers deserted his empty glass to idly play with a stack of invitations, the more conservative gilt-edged notelets vying with delicate pastel envelopes, a six-inch-high stack, awaiting his attention. Abruptly realising what he had in his hand, Jason straightened in his chair, the better to examine the *ton*'s offerings.

"Morecambes, Lady Hillthorpe's rout." He paused to check the back of one envelope. "Sussex Devenishes. The usual lot." One by one, the invitations dropped from his fingers on to the leather-framed blotter. "D'Arcys, Penbrights. Lady Allington has forgiven me, I see."

Frederick frowned. "What did she have to forgive you for?"

"Don't ask. Minchinghams, Carstairs." Abruptly, Jason halted. "Now this is one I haven't seen in a while—the Lesters." Laying aside the other invitations, he reached for a letter-knife.

"Jack and Harry?"

Unfolding the single sheet of parchment, Jason scanned the lines within and nodded. "Just so. A request for the pleasure, et cetera, et cetera, at a week-long succession of entertainments—for which one can read bacchanal—at Lester Hall."

"I suspect I've got one, too." Frederick uncurled his elegant form from the depths of the armchair. "Thought

I recognised the Lester crest but didn't stop to open it."
Glass in hand, he picked up Jason's glass and crossed to
place both on the sideboard. Turning, he beheld an expression of consideration on His Grace of Eversleigh's
countenance.

Jason's gaze lifted to his face. "Do you plan to
attend?"

Frederick grimaced. "Not exactly my style. That last
time was distinctly too licentious for my taste."

A smile of complete understanding suffused Jason's
features. "You should not let your misogyny spoil your
enjoyment of life, my friend."

Frederick snorted. "Permit me to inform His Grace of
Eversleigh that His Grace enjoys himself far too much."

Jason chuckled. "Perhaps you're right. But they
haven't opened Lester Hall for some years now, have
they? That last effort was at Jack's hunting box."

"Old Lester's been under the weather, so I'd heard."
Frederick dropped into his armchair. "They all thought
his time had come, but Gerald was in Manton's last week
and gave me to understand the old man had pulled clear."

"Hmm. Seems he's sufficiently recovered to have no
objection to his sons opening his house for him." Jason
reread the brief missive, then shrugged. "Doubtful that
I'd find a candidate suitable to take to wife there."

"Highly unlikely." Frederick shuddered and closed
his eyes. "I can still recall the peculiar scent of that
woman in purple who pursued me so doggedly at their
last affair."

Smiling, Jason made to lay aside the note. Instead, his
hand halted halfway to the pile of discarded invitations,
then slowly returned until the missive was once more
before him. Staring at the note, he frowned.

"What is it?"

"The sister." Jason's frown deepened. "There was a sister. Younger than Jack or Harry, but, if I recall aright, older than Gerald."

Frederick frowned, too. "That's right," he eventually conceded. "Haven't sighted her since the last time we were at Lester Hall—which must be all of six years ago. Slip of a thing, if I'm thinking of the right one. Tended to hug the shadows."

Jason's brows rose. "Hardly surprising given the usual tone of entertainments at Lester Hall. I don't believe I've ever met her."

When he made no further remark, Frederick turned to stare at him, eyes widening as he took in Jason's pensive expression. "You aren't thinking...?"

"Why not?" Jason looked up. "Jack Lester's sister might suit me very well."

"Jack and Harry as brothers-in-law? Good God! The Montgomerys will never be the same."

"The Montgomerys are liable to be only too thankful to see me wed regardless." Jason tapped the crisp parchment with a manicured fingernail. "Aside from anything else, at least the Lester men won't expect me to turn myself into a monk if I marry their sister."

Frederick shifted. "Perhaps she's already married."

"Perhaps," Jason conceded. "But somehow I think not. I rather suspect it is she who runs Lester Hall."

"Oh? Why so?"

"Because," Jason said, reaching over to drop the invitation into Frederick's hand, "some woman penned this invitation. Not an older woman, and not a schoolgirl but yet a lady bred. And, as we know, neither Jack, Harry nor Gerald has yet been caught in parson's mousetrap. So what other young lady would reside at Lester Hall?"

Reluctantly, Frederick acknowledged the likely truth of his friend's deduction. "So you plan to go down?"

"I rather think I will," Jason mused. "However," he added, "I intend to consult the oracle before we commit ourselves."

"Oracle?" asked Frederick, then, rather more forcefully. *"We?"*

"The oracle that masquerades as my aunt Agatha," Jason replied. "She's sure to know if the Lester chit is unwed and suitable—she knows damned near everything else in this world." He turned to study Frederick, grey eyes glinting steel. "And as for the 'we', my friend, having thrust my duty upon me, you can hardly deny me your support in this, my greatest travail."

Frederick squirmed. "Dash it, Jason—you hardly need me to hold your hand. You've had more experience in successfully hunting women than any man I know."

"True," declared His Grace of Eversleigh, unperturbed. "But this is different. I've had women aplenty—this time, I want a wife."

"Well, Eversleigh?" Straight as a poker, Lady Agatha Colebatch sat like an empress giving audience from the middle of her chaise. An intimidating turban of deepest purple crowned aristocratic features beset by fashionable boredom, although her beaked nose fairly quivered with curiosity. Extending one hand, she watched with impatience as her nephew strolled languidly forward to take it, bowing gracefully before her. "I assume this visit signifies that you have come to a better understanding of your responsibilities and have decided to seek a bride?"

Jason's brows rose haughtily. Instead of answering the abrupt query, he took advantage of his aunt's waved offer of a seat, elegantly disposing his long limbs in a chair.

Watching this performance through narrowed eyes, Lady Agatha possessed her soul with what patience she could. From experience she knew studying Eversleigh's expression would yield nothing; the strong, patrician features were impassive, his light grey eyes shuttered. He was dressed for a morning about town, his tautly muscled frame displayed to advantage in a coat of Bath superfine, his long legs immaculately clad in ivory inexpressibles which disappeared into the tops of glossy tasselled Hessians.

"As it happens, Aunt, you are right."

Lady Agatha inclined her turbaned head regally. "Have you any particular female in mind?"

"I do." Jason paused to enjoy the ripple of astonishment that passed over his aunt's features. "The lady at present at the top of my list is one of the Lesters, of Lester Hall in Berkshire. However, I'm unsure if she remains unwed."

Dazed, Lady Agatha blinked. "I take it you are referring to Lenore Lester. To my knowledge, she has not married."

When his aunt preserved a stunned silence, Jason prompted, "In your opinion, is Miss Lester suitable as the next Duchess of Eversleigh?"

Unable to resist, Lady Agatha blurted out the question sure to be on every lady's lips once this titbit got about. "What of Lady Hetherington?"

Instantly, she regretted the impulse. The very air about her seemed to freeze as her nephew brought his steely grey gaze to bear.

Politely, Jason raised his brows. "Who?"

Irritated by the very real intimidation she felt, Lady Agatha refused to retreat. "You know very well whom I mean, sir."

For a long moment, Jason held her challenging stare. Quite why his transient liaisons with well-born women evoked such interest in the breasts of righteous females he had never fathomed. However, he felt no real qualms in admitting to what was, after all, now little more than historical fact. Aurelia Hetherington had provided a momentary diversion, a fleeting passion that had rapidly been quenched. "If you must know, I've finished with *la belle* Hetherington."

"Indeed!" Lady Agatha stored that gem in her capacious memory.

"However," Jason added, his tone pointed, "I fail to see what that has to say to Lenore Lester's suitability as my duchess."

Lady Agatha blinked. "Er…quite." Faced with her nephew's penetrating gaze, she rapidly marshalled her facts. "Her breeding, of course, is beyond question. The connection to the Rutlands, let alone the Havershams and Ranelaghs, would make it a most favourable match. Her dowry might leave something to be desired, but I suspect you'd know more of that than I."

Jason nodded. "That, however, is not a major consideration."

"Quite," agreed her ladyship, wondering if, perhaps, Lenore Lester could indeed be a real possibility.

"And the lady herself?"

Lady Agatha spread her hands. "As you must be aware, she manages that great barn of a hall. Lester's sister is there, of course, but Lenore's always been mistress of the house. Lester himself is ageing. Never was an easygoing soul, but Lenore seems to cope very well."

"Why hasn't she married?"

Lady Agatha snorted. "Never been presented, for one thing. She must have been all of twelve when her mother died. Took over the household from then—no time to come to London and dance the nights away…"

Jason's gaze sharpened. "So she's…unused to the amusements of town?"

Reluctantly, Lady Agatha nodded. "Has to be. Stands to reason."

"Hold old is she?"

Lady Agatha pursed her lips. "Twenty-four."

"And she's presentable?"

The question shook Lady Agatha to attention. "But…" she began, then frowned. "Haven't you met her?"

His eyes on hers, Jason shook his head. "But you have, haven't you?"

Under the concerted scrutiny of those perceptive silver eyes, Lady Agatha's eyes glazed as memories of the last time she had met Lenore re-formed in her mind. "Good bone-structure," she began weakly. "Should bear well. Good complexion, fair hair, green eyes, I think. Tallish, slim." Nervous of saying too much, she shrugged and glanced at Jason. "What more do you need to know?"

"Is she possessed of a reasonable understanding?"

"Yes—oh, yes, I'm quite certain about that." Lady Agatha drew a steadying breath and shut her lips.

Jason's sharp eyes had noted his aunt's unease. "Yet you entertain reservations concerning Miss Lester?"

Startled, Lady Agatha grimaced. "Not reservations. But if my opinion is to be of any real value, it would help if I knew why you have cast your eye in her direction."

Briefly, unemotionally, Jason recounted his reasons for marriage, his requirements of a bride. Concluding his recitation, he gave his aunt a moment to marshall her thoughts before saying, "So, dear aunt, we come to the crux. Will she do?"

After a fractional hesitation, Lady Agatha nodded decisively. "I know of no reason why not."

"Good." Jason stood. "And now, if you'll forgive me, I must depart."

"Yes, of course." Lady Agatha promptly held out her hand, too relieved to have escaped further inquisition to risk more questions of her own. She needed time away from her nephew's far-sighted gaze to assess the true significance of his unexpected choice. "Dare say I'll see you at the Marshams' tonight."

Straightening from his bow, Jason allowed his brows to rise. "I think not." Seeing the question in his aunt's eyes, he smiled. "I expect to leave for the Abbey on the morrow. I'll travel directly to Lester Hall from there."

A silent "oh" formed on Lady Agatha's lips.

With a final benevolent nod, Jason strolled from the room.

Lady Agatha watched him go, her fertile brain seething with possibilities. That Jason should marry so cold-bloodedly surprised her not at all; that he should seek to marry Lenore Lester seemed incredible.

"I SAY, Miss Lester. Ready for a jolly week, what?"

Her smile serene, Lenore Lester bestowed her hand on Lord Quentin, a roué of middle age and less than inventive address. Like a general, she stood on the grand staircase in the entrance hall of her home and directed her troops. As her brothers' guests appeared out of the fine June afternoon, bowling up to the door in their phaetons and curricles, she received them with a gracious welcome before passing them on to her minions to guide to their chambers. "Good afternoon, my lord. I hope the weather remains fine. So dampening, to have to cope with drizzle."

Disconcerted, his lordship nodded. "Er...just so."

Lenore turned to offer a welcoming word to Mrs. Cronwell, a blowsy blonde who had arrived immediately behind his lordship, before releasing the pair into her butler's care. "The chambers in the west wing, Smithers."

As the sound of their footsteps and the shush of Mrs. Cronwell's stiff skirts died away, Lenore glanced down at the list in her hand. Although this was the first of her brothers' parties at which she had acted as hostess, she was accustomed to the role, having carried it with aplomb for some five years, ever since her aunt Harriet, her nominal chaperon, had been afflicted by deafness. Admittedly, it was usually her own and her aunt's friends, a most select circle of acquaintances, as refined as they were reliable, that she welcomed to the rambling rooms of Lester Hall. Nevertheless, Lenore foresaw no difficulty in keeping her hands on the reins of her brothers' more boisterous affair. Adjusting her gold-rimmed spectacles, she captured the pencil that hung in an ornate holder from a ribbon looped about her neck and marked off Lord Quentin and Mrs. Cronwell. Most of the guests were known to her, having visited the house before. The majority of those expected had arrived; only five gentlemen had yet to appear.

Lenore looked up, across the length of the black-and-white-tiled hall. The huge oak doors were propped wide to reveal the paved portico before them, steps disappearing to left and right leading down to the gravelled drive.

The clop of approaching hooves was followed by the scrunch of gravel.

Smoothing back a few wisps of gold that had escaped her tight bun, Lenore tweaked out the heavy olive-green-twill pinafore she wore over her high-necked, long-sleeved gown.

A deep male voice rumbled through the open doorway, carried on the light breeze.

Lenore straightened, raising a finger to summon Harris, the senior footman, to her side.

"Oh, Miss Lester! Could you tell us the way to the lake?"

Lenore turned as two beauties, scantily clad in fine muslins, came bustling out of the morning-room at the back of the hall. Lady Harrison and Lady Moffat, young matrons and sisters, had accepted her brothers' invitation, each relying on the other to lend them countenance. "Down that corridor, left through the garden hall. The door to the conservatory should be open. Straight through, down the steps and straight ahead—you can't miss it."

As the ladies smiled their thanks and, whispering avidly, went on their way, Lenore turned towards the front door, murmuring to Harris, "If they don't return in an hour, send someone to check they haven't fallen in." The sound of booted feet purposefully ascending the long stone steps came clearly to her ears.

"Miss Lester!"

Lenore turned as Lord Holyoake and Mr. Peters descended the stairs.

"Can you point us in the direction of the action, m'dear?"

Unperturbed by his lordship's wink, Lenore replied, "My brothers and some of the guests are in the billiard-room, I believe. Timms?"

Instantly, another footman peeled from the ranks hidden by the shadows of the main doors. "If you'll follow me, my lord?"

The sound of the trio's footsteps retreating down the hallway was overridden by the ring of boot heels on the portico flags. With a mental "at last", Lenore lifted her head and composed her features.

Two gentlemen entered the hall.

Poised to greet them, Lenore was struck by the aura of ineffable elegance that clung to the pair. There was little to choose between them, but her attention was drawn to the larger figure, insensibly convinced of his pre-eminence. A many-caped greatcoat of dark grey drab fell in long folds to brush calves clad in mirror-glossed Hessians. His hat was in his hands, revealing a wealth of wavy chestnut locks. The newcomers paused just inside the door as footmen scurried to relieve them of hats, coats and gloves. As she watched, the taller man turned to survey the hall. His gaze scanned the area, then came to rest with unwavering intensity upon her.

With a jolt, Lenore felt a comprehensive glance rake her, from the top of her tight bun to the tips of her serviceable slippers, then slowly, studiously return, coming at last to rest on her face.

Outrage blossomed in her breast, along with a jumble of other, less well-defined emotions.

The man started towards her, his companion falling in beside him. Summoning her wits to battle, Lenore drew herself up, her gaze bordering on the glacial, her expression one of icy civility.

Unheralded, the hall before her erupted into chaos. Within seconds, the black-and-white-tiled expanse had filled with a seething mass of humanity. Her brother Gerald had come in from the garden, a small crowd of bucks and belles in tow. Simultaneously, a bevy of jovial gentlemen, led by her brother Harry, had erupted from the billiard-room, apparently in search of like-minded souls for some complicated game they had in hand. The two groups collided in the hall and immediately emerged into a chattering, laughing, giggling mass.

Lenore looked down upon the sea of heads, impatient to have the perpetrator of that disturbing glance before her. She intended making it quite clear from the outset that she did not appreciate being treated with anything less than her due. The mêlée before her was deafening but she disregarded it, her eyes fixed upon the recent arrival, easy to discern given his height. Despite the press of people, he was making remarkably swift progress towards her. As she watched, he encountered her brother Harry in the throng and stopped to exchange greetings. Then he made some comment and Harry laughed, waving him towards her with some jovial remark. Lenore resisted the urge to inspect her list, determined to give the newcomer no chance to find her cribbing. Her excellent memory was no aid; she had not met this gentleman before.

Reaching the stairs in advance of his companion, he halted before her. Confidently, Lenore allowed her eyes to meet his, pale grey under dark brows. Abruptly, all thought of upbraiding him, however subtly, vanished. The face before her did not belong to a man amenable to feminine castigation. Strong, clean, angular planes, almost harsh in their severity, framed features both hard and dictatorial. Only his eyes, faultless light grey, and the clean sweep of his winged brows saved the whole from the epithet of "austere".

Quelling an odd shiver, Lenore imperiously extended her hand. "Welcome to Lester Hall, sir."

Her fingers were trapped in a warm clasp. To her annoyance, Lenore felt them quiver. As the gentleman bowed gracefully, she scanned his elegant frame. He was clad in a coat of sober brown, his cravat and breeches immaculate ivory, his Hessians gleaming black. He was, however, too tall. Too tall, too large, altogether too overwhelming.

She reached this conclusion in a state bordering on the distracted. Despite standing on the step below her, despite the fact that she was unfashionably tall, she still felt as if she risked a crick in her neck as she endeavoured to meet her disturbing guest eye to eye. For the first time in living memory, maintaining her mask of calm detachment, her shield, honed over the years to deflect any attack, became a major effort.

Blinking aside her momentary fascination, Lenore detected a glimmer of amused understanding in the grey eyes watching her. Her chin went up, her eyes flashed in unmistakable warning, but the gentleman seemed unperturbed.

"I am Eversleigh, Miss Lester. I don't believe we've previously met."

"Unfortunately not, Your Grace," Lenore promptly responded, her tone calculated to depress any pretension, leaving a vague, perfectly accurate suggestion that she was not entirely sure she approved of their meeting now. Eversleigh! She should have guessed. Curtsying, she tried to ignore the reverberations of the duke's deep voice. She could *feel* it, buried in her chest, a curious chord, thrumming distractingly.

Attention riveted by a welcome entirely out of the ordinary, Jason's gaze was intent as he studied the woman before him. She was long past girlhood, but still slender, supple, with the natural grace of a feline. Her features, fine-drawn and delicate in her pale, heart-shaped face, he could not fault. Fine brown brows arched above large, lucent eyes of palest green, edged by a feathering of long brown lashes. A flawless complexion of creamy ivory set off her small straight nose and determinedly pointed chin and the rich promise of her lips. Her eyes met his squarely, her expression of implacable resistance framed by her gilded spectacles.

Unable to resist, Jason smiled, stepping slightly aside to gesture to Frederick. "And this is—"

"Mr. Marshall." If her tormentor was Eversleigh, then his companion's identity was a foregone conclusion. Belatedly realising that she might well be playing with fire, Lenore retrieved her hand from the duke's firm clasp and bestowed it upon Frederick Marshall.

Smiling easily, Frederick bowed. "I do hope you have saved us rooms, Miss Lester. I fear we had not realised what a crowd there would be and made no shift to arrive early."

"No matter, sir. We were expecting you." Lenore returned his smile, confident in her role. As he was the only duke attending, she had allotted the best guest suite to Eversleigh, with the chamber beside for Mr. Marshall. She turned to Harris on the stair behind her. "The grey suite for His Grace, and Mr. Marshall in the blue room." Harris bowed gravely and started up the stairs. Turning back to Frederick Marshall, Leonore added, "No doubt you'll want to acquaint yourself with your quarters. We'll see you both at dinner. Six-thirty in the drawing-room."

With a polite nod and a smile, Frederick Marshall moved up the stairs.

Lenore waited for the large frame on her right to follow, determined not to look up at him until he was safely on his way. The seconds stretched. Eversleigh did not move. An odd nervousness gripped Lenore. Eversleigh stood between her and the crowd in the hall; the sense of being alone with a dangerous companion stole over her.

Having found the novelty of being so lightly dismissed not at all to his taste, Jason allowed the tension between them to wind tight before remarking, in his most equable tone, "I understand, Miss Lester, that you are to be our hostess through this week of dissipation?"

Lenore raised her head, her expression one of remote serenity. "That is correct, Your Grace."

"I do hope you won't be overwhelmed by your duties this week, my dear. I look forward to acquainting myself with what I have obviously overlooked on my earlier visits to your home."

Rapidly calculating that if he had visited before, she must have been eighteen and intent on staying out of his or any other eligible gentleman's sight, Lenore met his gaze with one of limpid innocence. "Indeed, Your Grace? The gardens *are* very fine this year. I dare say you did not get the opportunity to do them justice last time you were here? A stroll about them should certainly prove of interest."

Jason's lips twitched. "Undoubtedly," he replied smoothly, "were you to accompany me."

Trenchantly reminding herself that she was beyond being rattled by rakes, Lenore allowed distant regret to infuse her features. "I'm afraid my duties, as you call them, frequently keep me from my brothers' guests, Your Grace. However, I doubt my absence is noticed—my brothers' entertainments usually prove *remarkably* engrossing."

Jason's eyes glinted; his lips curved. "I can assure you, Miss Lester, that I will certainly notice your absence. Furthermore, I can promise you that the distraction of your brothers' entertainments will be quite insufficient as recompense for the lack of your company. In fact," he mused, one brow rising in open consideration, "I find it hard to imagine what power could deter me from seeking you out, in the circumstances."

His words rang like a challenge, one Lenore was not at all sure she wished to face. But she was in no mood to permit any gentleman—not even one as notorious as Eversleigh—to disrupt her ordered life. Allowing her brows to rise in cool dismissal, she calmly stated, "I greatly fear, Your Grace, that I have never considered myself one of the amenities of Lester Hall. You will have to make shift with what comes more readily to hand."

Unable to suppress a rakish grin at this forthright declaration, Jason brought his considerable charm to bear, softening his smile as he said, "I greatly fear you have misjudged me, Miss Lester." His voice dropped in tone, a soothing rumble. "I would rather class you as one of the attractions of Lester Hall—the sort of attraction that is frequently seen but rarely appreciated."

If it hadn't been for the odd intensity in his curious grey gaze, Lenore might have taken his words as nothing more than an elegant compliment. Instead, she felt shaken to the core. Her heart, for so long safe beneath her pinafore, thudded uncomfortably. With an enormous effort she dragged her eyes from his.

And spied Lord Percy Almsworthy doggedly pressing through the crowd. He fought free and gained the stairs. Lenore could have fallen on his thin chest with relief. "Lord Percy! How delightful to see you again."

"Hello, hello," replied his lordship, trying to sound cheery as he tweaked his wilting collars up around his chin. "Damned crush, what?"

"I'll get a footman to take you to your room immediately." Lenore raised her hand, beckoning two footmen forward. "His Grace was just about to go up," she lied, not daring to glance Eversleigh's way.

"The grey suite, I believe," came a low murmur from her right. To her surprise, Lenore felt long fingers close about her hand. She swung to face him but, before she could do more than blink, His Grace of Eversleigh raised her fingers to his lips and brushed a light kiss across their sensitive tips.

Jason paused to savour the flush of awareness that rose to his hostess's cheeks and the stunned expression that invaded her eyes before reluctantly conceding, "Until later, Miss Lester."

Skittering sensation prickled Lenore's skin. Rocked, she simply stared up at him. To her consternation, a subtle smile twisted his mobile lips before, with a polite nod, he released her hand and, moving past her, ascended the stairs in the footman's wake.

Speechless, Lenore turned to stare at his broad back, wishing she could have thought of some comment to wipe the smug smile from those silver eyes. Still, she reflected as her senses returned, at least he had gone.

Turning back to the hall, she was jolted from her daze by an aggrieved Lord Percy.

"Miss Lester—my room, if you please?"

CHAPTER TWO

"WELL? HOW LONG do you plan to stay, now you've decided Miss Lester will not suit?"

Jason abandoned the view from his windows, his brows lifting in unfeigned surprise. "My dear Frederick, why the rush to so summarily dispense with Miss Lester?"

His expression bland, Frederick strolled forward to sit on the cushioned window seat. "Having known you since seducing the writing master's daughter was your primary aim in life, my imagination does not stretch the distance required to swallow the idea of your marrying a frump. As Lenore Lester is undeniably a frump, I rest my case. So, how soon can we leave without giving offence?"

Taking a seat opposite his friend, Jason looked thoughtful. "Her...er...frumpishness was a mite obvious, don't you think?"

"A matter beyond question," Frederick assured him.

"Even, perhaps, a shade *too* obvious?"

Frederick frowned. "Jason—are you feeling quite the thing?"

Jason's grey eyes gleamed. "I'm exceedingly well and in full possession of my customary faculties. Such being the case, I am, of course, considerably intrigued by Miss Lester."

"But…" Frederick stared. "Dash it—she wore a *pinafore*!"

Jason nodded. "And a gown of heavy cambric, despite the prevailing fashion for muslins. Not just frumpish, but determinedly so. It can hardly have been straightforward to get such unappealing apparel made. All that being so, what I want to know is why."

"Why she's a frump?"

"Why Lenore Lester *wishes* to appear a frump. Not quite a disguise, for she does not go so far as to obliterate reality. However," Jason mused, his gaze resting consideringly on Frederick, "obviously, she has gauged her intended audience well. From her confidence just now, I imagine she has succeeded thus far in convincing those who visit here that she is, indeed, as she appears."

It was all too much for Frederick. "What makes you so sure she is *not* as she appears—a frump?"

Jason smiled, a wolf's smile. He shrugged. "How to explain? An aura? Her carriage?"

"Carriage?" Frederick considered, then waved the point aside. "I've heard my mother lecture m'sisters that carriage makes a lady. In my sisters' cases, it definitely hasn't helped."

Jason gestured dismissively. "Whatever. Miss Lester may dress as she pleases but she cannot deceive me."

His confidence set Frederick frowning. "What about those spectacles?"

"Plain glass."

Frederick stared. "Are you sure?"

"Perfectly." Jason's lips twisted wryly. "Hence, dear Frederick, there is no viable conclusion other than that Lenore Lester is intent on pulling the wool over our collective eyes. *If* you can disregard the impression her appearance invokes, then you would see, as I did—and doubtless Aunt Agatha before me—that beneath the rags lies a jewel. Not a diamond of the first water, I'll grant you, but a jewel none the less. There is no reason Lenore Lester needs must wear her hair in a prim bun, nor, I'll lay any odds, does she need to wear heavy gowns and a pinafore. They are merely distractions."

"But…why?"

"Precisely my question." Determination gleamed in His Grace of Eversleigh's grey eyes. "I greatly fear, Frederick, that you will indeed have to brave the trials and tribulations of a full week of Jack and Harry's 'entertainments'. For we are certainly not leaving before I discover just what Lenore Lester is hiding. And why."

NINETY MINUTES later, the hum of drawing-room conversation filling his ears, Jason studied the gown his hostess had donned for the evening with a certain degree of respect. She had entered quietly and stood, calmly scanning the throng. He waited until she was about to plunge into the mêlée before strolling to her elbow.

"Miss Lester."

Lenore froze, then, slowly, using the time to draw her defences about her, turned to face him. Her mask firmly in place, she held out her hand. "Good evening, Your Grace. I trust you found your rooms adequate?"

"Perfectly, thank you." Straightening from his bow, Jason moved closer, trapping her peridot gaze in his.

The facile words of glib conversation which should have flowed easily from Lenore's socially experienced tongue evaporated. Dimly, she wondered why Eversleigh's silver gaze should have such a mind-numbing effect on her. Then his gaze shifted, swiftly skimming her shoulders before returning to her face. He smiled, slowly. Lenore felt a peculiar tingling warmth suffuse her.

Jason allowed one brow to rise. "Permit me to compliment you on your gown, Miss Lester. I have not previously seen anything quite like it."

"Oh?" Alarm bells rang in Lenore's brain. Impossible not to acknowledge that her novel creation—a silk chemisette, buttoned high at the neck with long buttoned sleeves attached, worn beneath her version of a lustring sack, appropriately named as it fell in copious folds from a gathered yoke above her breasts to where the material was drawn in about her knees before flaring out to conceal her ankles—was in marked contrast to the filmy muslin or silk evening gowns of her contemporaries, cut revealingly low and gathered snugly beneath their breasts the better to display their figures. Indeed, her gown was expressly designed to serve a diametrically opposed purpose. Eversleigh's allusion, thrown at her on the heels of his unnerving smile, confirmed her dread that, unlike the rest of the company, he had failed to fall victim to her particular snare. Disconcerted but determined not to show it, she tilted her chin, her eyes wide and innocent. "I'm afraid I have little time for London fripperies, Your Grace."

A glint of appreciative amusement gleamed in the grey eyes holding hers.

"Strangely enough, it wasn't your *lack* of accoutrement that struck me." Smoothly, Jason drew her hand through his arm. "If I was asked for my opinion, I would have to state that in your case, Miss Lester, my taste would run to less, rather than more."

His tone, his expression, the inflection in his deep voice, all combined to assure Lenore that her worst fears had materialised. What mischievous fate, she wondered distractedly, had decreed that Eversleigh, of all men, should be the one to see beyond her purposely drab façade?

Deciding that retreat was the only way forward, she dropped her gaze. "I fear I must attend my father, Your Grace. If you'll excuse me?"

"I have yet to pay my respects to your father, Miss Lester, and should like to do so. I'll take you to him, if you'll permit it?"

Lenore hesitated, fingers twisting the long chain about her neck from which depended a pair of redundant lorgnettes. There was no real reason to refuse Eversleigh's escort, and she was loath to cry coward so readily. After all, what could he do in the middle of the drawing-room? She looked up, into his eyes. "I believe we will find my father by the fireplace, Your Grace."

She was treated to a charming smile. With intimidating ease, Eversleigh steered her through the noisy crowd to where her father was seated in a Bath chair before the large hearth, one gouty foot propped on a stool before him.

"Papa." Lenore bent to plant a dutiful kiss on her father's lined cheek.

The Honourable Archibald Lester humphed. "'Bout time. Bit late tonight, aren't you? What happened? One of those lightskirts try to tumble Smithers?"

Inured to her father's outrageous remarks, Lenore stooped to tuck in a stray end of the blanket draped over his knees. "Of course not, Papa. I was merely delayed."

Jason had noted how Mr. Lester's restless gaze had fastened on his daughter the instant she had come into view. He watched as the old man's washed-out blue eyes scanned Lenore's face before peering up at him aggressively from under shaggy white brows.

Before her father could bark out some less than gracious query, Lenore stepped in. "Allow me to make known to you His Grace of Eversleigh, Papa."

Mr. Lester's steady gaze did not waver. If anything, it intensified. A sardonic gleam in his eye, Jason bowed gracefully, then accepted the hand the old man held out.

"Haven't seen you in some years, I think," Mr. Lester remarked. "Knew your father well—you're becoming more like him with the years—in all respects, from everything I hear."

Standing beside her father's chair, Lenore studiously kept her eyes blank.

Jason inclined his head. "So I have been informed."

Mr. Lester's head sank. For a moment, he appeared lost in memories. Then he snorted. Lifting his head, he looked out across the crowded room. "Remember being in Paris one year your father was there. Group of us, him included, spent quite a bit of time together. Had a rousing six months—the Parisian *mesdames*—now *there* were women who knew how to heat a man's blood." With a contemptuous wave, he indicated the press of bodies before him. "This lot's got no idea. You—m'boys—don't know what you're missing."

Jason's smile grew harder to suppress. From the corner of his eye, he saw Lenore colour delicately. In his own best interests, he decided to forgo encouraging Mr. Lester to recount his memories in more detail. "Unfortunately, I believe Napoleon's comrades have altered things somewhat since you were last in France, sir."

"Damned upstart!" Mr. Lester ruminated on the emperor's shortcomings for some seconds before observing, "Still—the war's over. Ever think of chancing the Channel to savour the delights of *la bonne vie*, heh?"

At that, Jason smiled. "My tastes, I fear, are distinctly

English, sir." As if to include Lenore in their discussion, he allowed his gaze to rise, capturing her eyes with his before adding with calm deliberation, "Besides, I have a particular project before me which bodes fair to absorbing my complete attention for the foreseeable future."

Despite the quake that inwardly shook her, Lenore kept her gaze steady and her expression serene. Favouring attack as the best form of defence, she countered, "Indeed, Your Grace? And what project is that?"

She had thought to rattle him; although his features remained serious, his expressive eyes warned her she had seriously underestimated him.

"I find myself faced with a conundrum, Miss Lester. A conclusion which, while apparently consistent with the facts, I know to be false."

Mr. Lester snorted. "Sounds just like the musty old theories you so delight in, m'dear. You should give His Grace a hand."

Speechless, Lenore looked up, straight into Eversleigh's gleaming grey eyes.

"An excellent idea." Jason could not resist a small smile of triumph.

To Lenore, the gesture revealed far too many teeth. Eversleigh was dangerous. His reputation painted him in the most definite colours—those of a highly successful rake. "I really don't believe—"

Her careful retreat was cut off by Smithers, announcing in booming accents that dinner was served.

Lenore blinked, then saw a slow smile light Eversleigh's fascinating features. He had scanned the crowd and now stood, watching her expectantly. Reality hit Lenore like a wave. Eversleigh was the senior peer present. As his hostess, it was incumbent upon her to lead the assembled company in to dinner—on his arm. Aware that, at any moment, the restive crowd would work all this out for themselves and turn to see her, dithering, beside her father's chair, Lenore resisted the temptation to close her eyes in frustration. Instead, her serene mask firmly in place, she walked into the wolf's lair. "If you would be so kind as to lend me your arm, Your Grace?"

She was hardly surprised when he promptly obliged. Harris, the footman, arrived to propel her father's chair. Testily the old man waved them on. "Let's get going! I'm hungry."

Yielding to the slightest of pressures, Lenore allowed Eversleigh to lead her towards the door.

Appreciatively viewing the regal tilt of his hostess's golden head as she glided beside him through the waiting throng, her small hand resting lightly on his sleeve, Jason waited until they had reached the relative quiet of the hall before murmuring, "As I was saying, Miss Lester, I have become fascinated by an instance of what I believe might best be described as artful deceit."

Lenore was having none of it. "Artful deceit, Your Grace? To what purpose, pray?"

"As to purpose, I am not at all sure, but I intend to find out, Miss Lester."

Lenore risked an upward glance, insensibly annoyed at the feeling of smallness that engulfed her. She was used to dealing with gentlemen eye to eye; Eversleigh's height gave him an unfair advantage. But she was determined to end his little game. Elevating her chin, she adopted her most superior tone. "Indeed, Your Grace? And just how do you propose to unravel this conundrum of yours, laying all bare?"

Even as the words left her tongue, Lenore closed her eyes, stifling a groan. Where had her wits gone begging? Then her eyes flew open, her gaze flying, in considerable trepidation, to Eversleigh's hard countenance. Any hope that he would not take advantage was wiped from her mind the instant her eyes met his. Silver gleamed in the grey, white fire under water.

"My dear Miss Lester." The tenor of his voice, velvety deep and heavy with meaning, was a warning in itself. "Would it surprise you to learn that I consider myself peculiarly well-qualified to tackle this particular conundrum? As if my prior existence were nothing more than preparation for this challenge?"

The dining-room loomed ahead, a sanctuary filled with polished oak and silver, crystal goblets winking in the light from the chandelier. The sight gave Lenore strength. "I find that extremely difficult to believe, Your Grace. You must be sure to tell me when you have solved your puzzle."

The smile she received in reply made her giddy.

"Believe me, my dear Miss Lester, you'll be the very first to know when I lay my conundrum bare."

By rights, Lenore thought, she should at least be allowed a gasp. Only her determination not to dissolve into a witless heap under Eversleigh's attack allowed her to keep her head high and her composure intact. "Indeed?" she replied, her voice not as strong as she would have liked. As she assumed her chair at the end of the long table, she tried for dismissive boredom. "You intrigue me, Your Grace."

"No, Miss Lester." Jason stood beside her, one long-fingered hand resting lightly on the back of her chair, his eyes effortlessly holding hers. "*You* intrigue *me*."

Others milled about, taking their places along the polished boards. Noise and chatter engulfed the company. Yet Lenore heard all through a distancing mist, conscious only of the intent in the grey eyes holding hers. Then, slowly, Eversleigh inclined his head and released her, taking his seat beside her.

Shaken, Lenore hauled in a quivering breath. Eversleigh was in pride of place on her right; she had purposely installed young Lord Farningham, an eminently safe young gentleman, on her left.

Watching as the company settled and the first course was brought forth, Lenore felt her nerves flicker restlessly. It was Eversleigh and his disturbing propensity to reach through her defences that was the cause of her disquiet. Quite what it was he did to her normally reliable senses she did not know, but clearly she would have to cope with the problem for the next few hours.

To her relief, Mrs. Whitticombe, seated beyond Lord Farningham, monopolised all attention with an anecdote on turtle soup as served by a certain Mr. Weekes.

Taking the opportunity to scan the table, Lenore noted her aunt seated a little way away with Gerald beside her to help. In the middle of the table, Jack and Harry, one one either side, kept the conversation flowing. A good deal of laughter and general hilarity was already in evidence as her brothers and their guests settled in. At the distant head of the table, her father and his old crony, Mr. Pritchard, were deep in discussion. Horses or reminiscences of a more ribald sort, Lenore sagely surmised, her eyes on the two grey heads.

"I have heard, Eversleigh, that there's plenty of grouse down your way this year?"

Lord Farningham's question, uttered in the tones of one well aware of the hazards of approaching one of the lions of the *ton*, jerked Lenore to attentiveness.

But Eversleigh's reply, a mild, "Yes, it'll be a good season, so my gamekeeper assures me. You're in Kent, are you not?" relieved her of anxiety. With every appearance of interest, she listened as Eversleigh discussed game and the keeping of coverts with Lord Farningham.

When the subject ran dry, halfway through the first course as the soup was replaced by turbot in cream sauce with side dishes of mushroom florettes and tongue in port wine, Lenore was ready with a blithe, "Tell me of Eversleigh Abbey, Your Grace. I have heard it is even bigger than the Hall."

The look Eversleigh directed at her was unfathomable but he replied readily enough.

"It is rather large. The original abbey dates to just after the Conquest but my family has made numerous additions over the years. What remains might best be described as a semi-Gothic pile, complete with ruined cloisters."

"No ghost?"

Lenore bit her tongue, steeling herself for his rejoinder. A skeleton or two in the cupboard, perhaps?

Manfully, Jason resisted temptation. Sorrowfully, he shook his head. "Not even a wraith, I'm afraid."

Letting out the breath she had held, Lenore inclined her head and opted for caution in the person of Lord Farningham. Lady Henslaw, seated beside Eversleigh, claimed his attention. As the second course was laid before them, Lord Farningham turned the talk to horses. Mentally, Lenore sat back, pleased to see her father and Aunt Harriet both coping well. Taking a moment to cast her eye over the company, she saw that all was proceeding smoothly. Her staff was experienced; the meal was served and cleared and glasses filled with a minimum of fuss.

She was turning back to the conversation when a commotion in the hall drew all attention. Smithers immediately went out, to return a moment later to hold open the door. Amelia, Lady Wallace, Lenore's cousin, hesitantly entered, her companion, Mrs. Smythe, trailing in her wake.

Jack rose. With a murmured, "Excuse me," Lenore put her napkin aside and went forward.

"Hello, Jack. Lenore." Amelia bestowed her hand on Jack and exchanged an affectionate kiss with Lenore. "I'm sorry to arrive so late but one of our horses went lame." Shielded from the table, Amelia grimaced up at them. "And I had no idea this was one of your 'weeks'."

With a brotherly smile, Jack squeezed her hand. "No matter, m'dear. You're always welcome."

Lenore smiled her agreement. "Don't worry. You can keep me company. I'll put you near Papa until you get your bearings."

"Yes, please," Amelia returned, blonde ringlets bobbing as she exchanged nods with those of the company already known to her.

While Jack played the gallant host, Lenore oversaw insertion of another leaf at the head of the huge table. Once Amelia and Mrs. Smythe were installed, Lenore paused to tell Smithers, "Her ladyship in the rose room, with Mrs. Smythe in the room further down the hall."

Smithers nodded and departed.

Lenore returned to her seat, idly wondering what brought Amelia, now widowed, to Berkshire. Picking up her fork, she glanced up to find Eversleigh, his chair pushed slightly back from the table, his long fingers crooked about the stem of his goblet, watching her, an entirely unreadable expression in his eyes. Lenore frowned in what she hoped was a quelling manner.

Jason's pensive attitude dissolved as he smiled, raising his glass in silent toast. He toyed with the idea of informing his hostess that the ability to remain unflustered in the face of the unexpected was a talent he felt certain his wife should possess. His smile deepened as he wondered what she would answer to that.

After one long look at Eversleigh's peculiarly unnerving smile, Lenore determinedly turned to Lord Farningham, irritatingly aware that, if she allowed herself the liberty, she could easily spend the entire meal staring at the fascinating face beside her.

Reluctantly, mindful of his true aim, Jason devoted himself impartially to Lady Henslaw and the others about for the remainder of the meal.

At the conclusion of the last course, an array of jellies, custards and trifles interspersed with dishes of sweetmeats, Lenore collected Aunt Harriet and led the ladies from the room. As she crossed the front hall, she made a firm resolution that she would not again allow Eversleigh to unsettle her.

"Shameless hussy! That one dresses in pink silk and thinks we can't see through it. A good deal less than she ought to be, mark my words!"

Her aunt's scathing comments, delivered in a highly audible hiss, shook Lenore from her thoughts. She had no difficulty following Harriet's train of thought—Mrs. Cronwell, thankfully some way behind them, was resplendent in lurid pink silk, the low neckline of her clinging gown trimmed with ostrich feathers. Knowing she was safe, Lenore nodded—it was pointless disagreeing. Virtually completely deaf, Harriet could not be brought to believe that her animadversions, perfectly audible to any within a radius of ten feet, were anything more than the merest whispers. Following her erstwhile chaperon across the room, Lenore helped Harriet, grey-haired and stooped, to settle her purple skirts in her favourite chair a little removed from the fireplace.

Seeing her aunt pull her tatting from a bag beside the chair and start to untangle the bobbins, Lenore placed a hand on her arm and slowly stated, "I'll bring you some tea when the trolley arrives."

Harriet nodded and returned to her craft. Lenore left her, hoping she would not become bored and start musing, aloud, on the guests.

Despite the presence of some women she could not in all conscience call friends, Lenore moved easily through the bevy of bright dresses, scattered like jewels about the large room. She had long ago perfected the art of graciously acknowledging those she did not wish to encourage, leaving them a little puzzled by her serene acceptance of their presence. To those who were her social peers she acted the hostess in truth, listening to their gossip, complimenting them on their gowns. It was in gatherings such as this that she learned much of what was transpiring beyond the gates of Lester Hall.

Tonight, however, once she had done her duty and gone the rounds, she gravitated to her cousin's side, intent on learning why Amelia had so unexpectedly arrived.

"It was Rothesay." Amelia made a moue of distaste. "He's been positively hunting me, Lenore."

Standing by the side of the room, out of earshot of the company, Lenore sent Amelia a commiserating glance. "I take it the viscount is to be numbered among those gentlemen who have difficulty in understanding the word *no*?"

Amelia frowned. "It's not so much a matter of his understanding as a sad lack of imagination. I do believe that he simply cannot credit the fact that any lady would refuse him."

Lenore swallowed a snort. At sixteen, Amelia had dutifully acceded to her parents' wishes and married a man forty years her senior. Widowed at the age of twenty-three, left with a respectable jointure and no protector, she was ripe game for the wolves of the *ton*. Determined not to be pressured into another loveless union, Amelia spent her days endeavouring to avoid a union of less respectable state. The gentlemen of the *ton*, however, had yet to accept the fact that the widowed Lady Wallace felt in no pressing need of male protection.

Fleeing London and the importunings of Lord Rothesay, Amelia had come first to her relatives in Berkshire. "I'm sure a few months will be sufficient to cool Rothesay's ardour. I had planned to go to stay with Aunt Mary but she won't be back in Bath before the end of the month." Amelia scanned the crowd, swelling as the gentlemen strolled in, forsaking their port for feminine company.

"As Jack said, you're always welcome here." When Amelia continued to consider the gentlemen as they strolled through the door, Lenore asked, "There is none here who has caused you any bother, is there?"

"No." Amelia shook her head. "I was just checking for any potential problems." Linking arms with Lenore, she smiled up at her. "Don't fret. I'm sure I'll manage to survive Jack and Harry's crowd. They all seem to be well-heeled enough not to need my money and well-mannered enough to accept a dismissal. I must say, though, that I'm surprised to see Eversleigh here."

"Oh?" Conscious of a sharp stab of curiosity, Lenore strolled beside Amelia. "Why so?"

"I had heard," Amelia said, lowering her voice conspiratorially, "that he's decided to marry. I'd have thought he'd be playing host to a collection of the fairest debs and their doting mamas at Eversleigh Abbey, rather than enjoying the delights of one of your brothers' little gatherings."

Aware of a sudden sinking feeling, Lenore resisted the compulsion to turn and look for Eversleigh in the crowd. "I hadn't considered him the marrying sort, somehow."

"Exactly so! The story is that he had no intention of succumbing. His brother was to keep the line going. But he—the brother, I mean—was killed at Waterloo. So now Eversleigh must make the ultimate sacrifice."

Lenore's lips twitched. "I wonder if he considers it in that light?"

"Undoubtedly," Amelia averred. "He's a rake, isn't he? Anyway, from everything I've heard and seen, it's the poor soul he takes to wife who deserves our pity. Eversleigh's a handsome devil and can be utterly charming when the mood takes him. It would be hard work to remain aloof from all that masculine appeal. Unfortunately, His Grace is reputed to be impervious to the softer emotions, one of the old school in that regard. I can't see him falling a victim to Cupid and reforming. His poor wife will probably end in thrall and have her heart broken."

Brows rising, Lenore considered Amelia's prediction. "Charming" was not the word she would have chosen to describe Eversleigh; the power he wielded was far stronger than mere charm. Suppressing an odd shiver, she decided that, all in all, Amelia was right. The future Lady Eversleigh was to be sincerely pitied.

Leaving her cousin with Lady Henslaw, Lenore paused by the side of the room. Under pretext of straightening the upstanding collar of her chemisette, she glanced about, eventually locating Eversleigh conversing with her father, ensconced in his chair by the fireplace. The sight brought a frown to Lenore's eyes. Listening to her father's reminiscences seemed an unlikely joy for a man of Eversleigh's tastes. Still, she was hardly an expert on what a gentleman recently determined on marriage might find entertaining. Shrugging the point aside, she embarked on an ambling progress about the room, providing introductions, ensuring the conversation flowed easily and keeping a watchful eye on some of the more vulnerable ladies. Two such innocents were the Melton sisters, Lady Harrison and Lady Moffat, whom she discovered under determined seige from a trio of gentlemen.

"Good evening, Lord Scoresby." Lenore smiled sweetly at his lordship.

Forced to take her hand, thus relieving Lady Moffat of his far too close attention, his lordship murmured a greeting.

"I hear you have recently set up your town house, Lady Moffat?" Lenore smiled encouragingly at the young matron.

Lady Moffat grabbed her branch like a woman sinking, blithely describing all aspects of her new household. Lenore artfully drew Lady Harrison into the safety of the conversation. Within five minutes she had the satisfaction of seeing both Lord Scoresby and Mr. Marmaluke nod and drift away, vanquished by wallpaper patterns and upholstery designs. But Mr. Buttercombe was only dislodged when Frederick Marshall strolled up.

"I hear the Pantheon bazaar is very useful for all the knick-knacks you ladies enjoy scattering about the place."

Lenore was sure neither young woman noticed the twinkle in Frederick Marshall's eyes, but, seeing the way the sisters responded to his easy address, she was too grateful for his assistance to quibble. He was one of the more easygoing of the gentlemen present and seemed amenable to playing the role of gallant to their ladyships' innocence.

Seeing Smithers pushing the large tea-trolley in, Lenore excused herself and crossed the room to perform her last duty of the evening. Rather than station the trolley by the fireplace, her normal habit, she had Smithers place it between two sets of long windows, presently open to the terrace. With Eversleigh still by her father's chair, the area around the fireplace was likely to prove too hot for her sensibilities.

She had no trouble distributing the teacups, commandeering gentlemen at will. However, she took Harriet's cup herself, not liking to lumber anyone else with the task. One never knew how Harriet would react.

"Thank you, dear," Harriet boomed. Lenore winced and settled the cup on a small table by her aunt's side, confident that by now most of the guests must have realised her aunt's affliction. She turned to leave—and found herself face to face with His Grace of Eversleigh.

"My dear Miss Lester—no teacup?" Jason smiled, pleased that his calculated wait by her father's side had paid the desired dividend.

Lenore told herself she had no reason to quiver like a schoolgirl. "I've already had a cup, Your Grace."

"Excellent. Then, as you've already dispensed enough cups to supply the company, perhaps you'll consent to a stroll about the room?"

The "with me" was said with his eyes. Lenore stared up into their grey depths and wished she could fathom why they were so hypnotic. Perhaps, if she understood their attraction, she would be better able to counter it?

"Just like his father! Forever after lifting some woman's skirts. Not that he'll get any joy from Lenore. Far too knowing, she is." Harriet snorted. "Too knowing for her own good, I sometimes think."

Lenore's cheeks crimsoned with embarrassment. Glancing about, she saw that no one else was close, no one else had heard her aunt's horrendous pronouncements. No one except their primary subject. Drawing a deep breath, she raised her eyes fleetingly to his. "Your Grace, I beg you'll excuse my aunt. She's..." She foundered to an awkward halt.

A rumbling chuckle came from beside her.

"My dear Miss Lester, I'm hardly the type to take offence over such a minor transgression."

Lenore could have wilted with relief.

"However," Jason continued, seizing the opportunity fate had so thoughtfully provided, "I suggest we quit this locality before your esteemed aunt is further stimulated by our presence."

Difficult to counter that argument, Lenore thought, giving conscious effort to maintaining her calm smile as she permitted Eversleigh to place her hand on his sleeve and lead her away from the fireplace. As she fell into step beside him, she saw her aunt's maid Janet and her father's valet Moreton slip into the room. As soon as her father and his sister had finished their tea, it was their invariable custom to retire. Mr. Pritchard would have already gone up. Given what she sensed of the mood of the guests, Lenore felt her own departure would not long be delayed. Catching sight of the Ladies Moffat and Harrison, still under the wing of Frederick Marshall, she decided to drop them a hint.

She attempted to veer in their direction, but her escort prevented her, trapping her hand on his sleeve and raising his brows in mute question.

"I should just like a word with Lady Harrison, Your

Grace." Lenore seasoned her request with a smile and was surprised to see her companion shake his head.

"Not a good idea, I'm afraid."

When she stared blankly at him, Jason explained, "I fear I make Lady Harrison and Lady Moffat somewhat nervous."

Lenore decided she could hardly blame them. Waspishly, she replied, "If you were to suppress your tendency to flirt, my lord, I dare say they would manage."

"Flirt?" Jason turned his gaze full upon her. "My dear Miss Lester, you have that entirely wrong. Gentlemen such as I never flirt. The word suggests a frivolous intent. My intentions, I'll have you know, are always deadly serious."

"Then you are at the wrong house, Your Grace. I have always considered the theme of my brothers' parties to be *entirely* frivolous." Lenore had had enough. If he was going to use her to sharpen his wit upon, then two could play at that game.

"I see," Jason replied, a smile hovering on his lips. He started to stroll again, Lenore perforce gliding beside him. "So you consider this week to have no purpose beyond the frivolous?"

Lenore opened her eyes wide, gesturing at the throng about them. "My lord, you have visited here before."

Jason inclined his head. "Tell me, Miss Lester. Am I right in detecting a note of disdain, even censure, in your attitude to your brothers' parties?"

Catching the quizzical look in his eyes, Lenore chose her words carefully. "I see nothing wrong in my brothers' pursuit of pleasure. They enjoy it and it causes no harm."

"But such pleasures are not for you?"

"The frivolous is hardly my style, Your Grace." Lenore delivered that statement with feeling.

"Have you tried it?"

Lenore blinked.

"With the right companion, even frivolous pastimes can be enjoyable."

Lenore kept her expression blank. "Really? But no doubt you are an expert on the topic, Your Grace?"

Jason laughed lightly, a smile of genuine appreciation curving his lips. "*Touché*, Miss Lester. Even I have my uses."

Oddly warmed by his smile, Lenore found herself smiling back. Before she could do more than register that fact, he was speaking again.

"But tell me, given your antipathy for the frivolous, do you enjoy organising such events as these, or do you suffer it as a duty?"

Try as she might, Lenore could see no hidden trap in that question. Tilting her head, she considered the point. "I rather think I enjoy it," she eventually admitted. "These parties are something of a contrast to the others we have from time to time."

"Yet you take no part in your brothers' entertainments?"

"I fear my pursuits are in a more serious vein."

"My dear Lenore, whatever gave you the idea the pursuit of pleasure was not a serious enterprise?"

Lenore stopped, jerked to awareness by his use of her name. She drew away and he let her, but the fingers of the hand that had rested on hers curled about her hand. "I have not made you a present of my name, Your Grace," she protested, putting as much force into the rebuke as her sudden breathlessness allowed.

Jason raised a laconic brow, his eyes steady on her. "Need we stand on such ceremony, my dear?"

"Definitely," Lenore replied. Eversleigh was too dangerous to encourage.

With an oddly gentle smile, he inclined his head, accepting her verdict. Only then did Lenore look about her. They were no longer in the drawing-room but on the terrace. A darted glance added the shattering information that no one else had yet ventured forth. She was alone, with Eversleigh, with only the sunset for chaperon.

Feeling a curious species of panic stir in her breast, Lenore looked up, but the grey gaze was veiled.

"It seems somewhat odd that you should so willingly organise, yet remain so aloof from the fruits of your labour."

Eversleigh's tone of polite banter recalled her to their conversation. Guardedly, Lenore responded, "The entertainments themselves are not my concern. My brothers organise the frivolity. I...merely provide the opportunity for our guests to enjoy themselves." She looked away, across the rolling lawns, trying to concentrate on her words and deny the distraction assailing her senses. Her hand was still trapped in Eversleigh's; his fingers, long and strong, gently, rhythmically stroked her palm. It was such an innocent caress; she did not like to call attention to what might be no more than absent-minded oversight. He did not appear to be intent on seduction or any similar nefarious endeavour. She strolled with him when he moved to the balustrade and stood, one hand on the stone, her skirts brushing his boots.

About them, the warm glow of twilight fell on a world burgeoning with summer's promise. The sleepy chirp of larks settling in the shrubbery ran a shrill counterpoint to the distant lowing of cattle in the fields. The heady perfume of the honeysuckle growing on the wall below the terrace teased her senses.

Glancing up through her lashes, she saw that Eversleigh's features remained relaxed, hardly open but without the intentness she was learning to be wary of. His gaze scanned the scene before them, then dropped to her face.

"So—you are the chatelaine of Lester Hall, capable and gracious, keeping to your own serious interests despite the lure of fashionable dissipation. Tell me, my dear, have you never felt tempted to…let your hair down?"

Although, as he spoke, his eyes lifted to the neat braids, coiled in a coronet of gold about her head, Lenore knew his question was not about her coiffure. "It's my belief that what you term fashionable dissipation only results in unnecessary difficulties, Your Grace. As I find more delight in intellectual pursuits, I leave frivolous pastimes to those who enjoy them."

"And what particular intellectual pursuits are you engaged in at present?"

Lenore studied him straightly but saw only genuine interest. "I'm undertaking a study of the everyday life of the Assyrians."

"The Assyrians?"

"Yes. It's quite fascinating discovering how they lived, what they ate and so on."

Contemplating the fullness of her lips with a far from intellectual interest, Jason assimilated the information that the lady topping his list of prospective brides considered ancient civilisations of more interest than the present. It was, he decided, an opinion he could not let go unchallenged. "I would not wish to belittle your studies in any way, my dear, but if I might give you a piece of advice, drawn from my extensive experience?"

Warily, half convinced she should refuse to hear him but tempted, none the less, to learn what he was thinking, Lenore nodded her acquiescence.

"Don't you think it might be wise to sample the pleasures that life has to offer before you reject them out of hand?"

For one instant, Lenore nearly succeeded in convincing herself that he could not mean what she thought he did. Then his lids rose; again she found her gaze trapped in silver-grey. Her thoughts scattered, her breathing suspended. A curious lassitude seeped through her limbs, weighting them, holding her prisoner for the warmth that slowly, inexorably rose, a steady tide pouring through her veins from the wellspring where his thumb slowly circled her palm. Dimly, as if it was the only thing that might save her, she struggled to find an answer to his unanswerable question, something—anything—to distract the powerful force she could feel engulfing her. Wide-eyed, she knew she was lost when she saw the grey of his eyes start to shimmer.

With faultless timing Jason drew her nearer. Too experienced to take her into his arms, he relied on the strength of the attraction flaring between them to bring her to him. When her gown brushed his coat he arched one brow gently. When she remained silent, he smiled down into her wide green eyes. "There's a world here and now that you've yet to explore, Lenore. Aren't you curious?"

Held speechless by a timeless fascination, Lenore forced her head to shake.

The lips only inches from hers curved. "Liar."

Against her will, the word fixed her attention on his lips. Lenore swallowed. Her own lips were dry. Quickly, she passed the tip of her tongue over them.

Jason's sudden intake of breath startled Lenore. She felt turbulence shake his large frame, then it was gone. Abruptly, his hands came up to close about her shoulders, setting her back from him.

"The perils of an innocent." His lips twisting wryly, Jason gazed into her confused green eyes. "And you are still an innocent, are you not, sweet Lenore?"

Whether it was his tone or the shattering caress of his thumb across her lower lip that called it forth, Lenore's temper returned with a rush. Clinging to the revitalising emotion, she thrust her chin in the air, her heart thundering in her ears. "Not all women are driven by desire, Your Grace."

She was not prepared for the long, assessing look that earned her. To her fevered imagination, Eversleigh's silver eyes held her pinned, like so much prey, while he decided whether to pounce.

Eventually, one winged brow rose. "Is that a challenge, my dear?"

His voice, softly silky, sounded infinitely dangerous.

Lenore lost her temper entirely. "No, it is not!" she replied, irritated with Eversleigh and his unnerving questions, and with herself, for ever having let him get so far. "I am not here to provide sport for you, my lord. And now, if you'll excuse me, I have other guests to attend."

Without waiting for a reply, Lenore swung on her heel and marched back through the door. Damn Eversleigh! He had thoroughly addled her wits with all his questions. She refused to be a challenge—not for him—not for any man. Stopping by the side of the room to glance over the sea of guests, far more rowdy now than before, Lenore forced herself to breathe deeply. Thrusting the entire unnerving episode from her mind, she looked for

Lady Moffat and Lady Harrison. They were nowhere to be seen. Amelia, likewise, had departed.

Unobtrusively, Lenore made her way to the door, appalled at the extent of her inner turmoil. She would have to avoid Eversleigh.

Which was a pity, for she had enjoyed his company.

CHAPTER THREE

SHE WOULD NOT allow him to take command again. Lenore descended the long staircase at ten the next morning, determined that today would see no repetition of yestereve's foolishness. Beneath the smooth surface of her blue pinafore, worn over a beige morning gown, her heart beat at its accustomed pace. With luck and good management it would continue to do so for the rest of the week.

Years before, she had set her face against marriage, the conventional occupation for women of her station. From all she had seen, matrimony had nothing desirable to offer that she did not already have. She preferred life calm and well-organised; a husband, with the duties and obediences that entailed, let alone the emotional complications, could only disrupt her peace. Hence, she had expended considerable effort in establishing a reputation for eccentricity, while avoiding any gentlemen who might prove a danger to her future. To her select band of acquaintances she was the knowledgeable Miss Lester, sure to be engaged in some esoteric study, a lady of satisfactory wealth and impeccable breeding, fully absorbed with her varied interests, with running her household and her father's estates. And, at twenty-four, beyond the reach of any man.

Or so she had thought. Stopping to shuffle the bright flowers in the vase on the upper landing, Lenore frowned. She had encouraged her brothers to invite their friends to Lester Hall, hoping the activity would cheer her father. He was still recovering from his long illness and, she knew, liked the lively bustle and laughter. She had been confident that, now she was an experienced woman, she stood in no danger from exposure to the gentlemen who would attend.

It had taken Eversleigh less than twelve hours to shake the confidence.

Dusting pollen from her fingers, Lenore straightened, forcing her mind to a more positive bent. She was making too much of the situation; she had nothing to fear. Despite his awesome reputation, no one had ever accused Eversleigh of stepping over the line. He was curious, certainly, given that he had seen past her façade. But, until she had declared her lack of interest in fashionable dalliance, he had not been the least lover-like.

Closing her eyes in momentary frustration, Lenore sighed, then, opening them, stared down the main flight of stairs. She should have known that giving vent to her sentiments would have acted on Eversleigh like a red rag to a bull. No rake could resist such a challenge. Certainly not one who, by all accounts, had half the London *belles* at his feet.

Luckily, the reins were still very much in her grasp. Given that she had insufficient defence against him, the only sane course was to avoid him. Absence was a barrier not even he could surmount.

Below her, the house was quiet. All the ladies would still be abed, too exhausted or too timid to have descended to the parlour for breakfast. The gentlemen, she hoped, would have quitted the house by now. Harry had had a long ride planned to show off his racing colts, stabled at a distant farm.

Determined to adhere to wisdom's dictates, Lenore started down the last of the stairs.

The billiard-room door opened.

"Damn your luck, Jason! One day, I vow, I'll have your measure—then I'll exact retribution for all these defeats."

Recognising her brother Jack's voice, and realising that there was only one Jason among the guests, Lenore froze, wildly contemplating retreat. But it was too late. Strolling forward into the hall, Jack glanced up and saw her.

"Lenore! Just the person. Look here—this black-guard has just taken me for twenty-five guineas and I've no more than five on me. Settle for me, will you, dear sister?"

The request was accompanied by a look of meltingly innocent appeal that Lenore had never been known to resist. She could not do so now, but oh, *how* she wished she could tell her exasperating brother to settle his own debts. At least, those with Eversleigh. With no alternative offering, Lenore descended to the hall. "Yes, of course." Poised, serene, she turned to greet Jack's companion.

Jason took the small hand offered him, noting the nervous flutter of her fingers, like a small bird trapped within his hand. "Good morning, Miss Lester. I trust you slept well?"

"Perfectly, thank you," Lenore lied, retrieving her hand.

"I must off and look at the dogs—Higgs said something about an infection. Papa would have apoplexy if anything serious transpired. I'll meet you at the stables, Eversleigh." With a brisk nod, Jack took himself off.

Viewing her brother's retreating back with uneasy resignation, Lenore murmured, "If you'll come this way, Your Grace?"

Jason inclined his head, falling into step beside her as she led the way down the corridor to a door beyond the billiard-room. It gave on to a small office tucked partly under the stairs. A single window looked out over the lawns behind the house. Ledgers marched, row upon row, along the bookshelves covering one wall. Jason watched as Lenore sat behind the old desk, its surface covered with neat piles of papers and accounts, and drew a key from the small pocket at her waist.

"Is this your domain?"

Lenore looked up. "Yes. I manage the household and the estate."

Propping his shoulders against the window-frame, Jason raised one winged brow. "I've often wondered how Jack and Harry manage. They rarely seem to feel the need to spend time husbanding their acres."

Lenore's lips curved. "As there always seems to be an abundance of entertainments elsewhere to keep them busy and as I find the occupation amusing, we long ago reached an understanding."

"But it can't be straightforward, not being the one in authority?"

Straightening an account book, left open on the blotter before her, Lenore allowed one brow to rise. "I've always been here, and everyone about knows who runs Lester Hall." From behind her spectacles, she viewed the lean length so negligently displayed by the window. Eversleigh dominated her small room, filling it with an aura of masculine energy. At the moment, however, he seemed reassuringly relaxed. Lenore yielded to the promptings of curiosity. "Tell me, Your Grace, do you directly manage your own estates?"

One arrogant brow flew. "Certainly, Miss Lester. That is one responsibility I cannot and would not wish to deny."

"What, then, do you think of these Corn Laws of ours, sir?" Eyes alight, Lenore clasped her hands on the desk and leaned forward eagerly.

Jason paused, studying her face, then replied, "They're not working, Miss Lester."

What followed was a conversation that, for his part, Jason would never have believed possible. But Lenore had the questing nature of a bloodhound once she re-alised he understood first-hand the ramifications of the controversial agricultural laws.

Finally, her thirst for knowledge appeased, she sat back with a sigh. "So you believe they will be repealed?"

"Eventually," Jason admitted, his arms crossed over his chest. "But it will be some time before that's achieved."

Lenore nodded, her mind still busy cataloguing all she had learned. It was a rare blessing to find a gentleman able and willing to discuss such matters with her. Her father had long since lost touch with the outside world; her brothers cared nothing for the political sphere. And there were few gentlemen among her select circle who held estates large enough to comprehend the negative ef-fects of the reactionary laws.

Recalling what had brought her to her office, Lenore shook aside her thoughts and sat up. Pulling out a drawer, she fumbled until she found another key, the pair to the first, still warm in her hand. Rising, she crossed to where a cupboard was set into the bookcase. She inserted one key and unlocked the door, swinging it open to reveal a grey metal safe. The second key unlocked the simple safe. Reaching in, Lenore drew out a small pouch. It was the work of a minute to loosen the strings and shake a handful of golden guineas into her palm. She was busy counting them when a large hand closed over hers, curling her fingers about the coins.

"No. Keep them."

"Oh, no." Lenore shook her head vehemently, too well acquainted with male pride to accept such a boon. "Jack would never forgive me." She looked up, into Eversleigh's grey eyes, one brow rising haughtily when she saw his expression harden.

For a long moment, Eversleigh studied her. "I will not accept any coins from you but I'll undertake to tell Jack the debt was paid in full."

Stubbornly, Lenore shook her head, her lips firming in a mutinous line.

Jason held her steady gaze, his eyes narrowed, his fingers tight about her hand. Then, his lips twisted in a wry smile. "Something else, perhaps," he suggested. His smile deepened. He released her hand but not her eyes. "I will not accept any money in payment of Jack's debt. Instead, Miss Lester, I'll settle for the answer to one question."

Lenore frowned up at him. "What question?"

"Ah, no." Jason stepped back to lean against the bookshelves. He eyed her speculatively. "Not until you agree to settling thus."

Lenore's eyes narrowed. Glancing down at the coins in her hand, she debated the wisdom of making any bargain with a rake. But what could he ask, after all. Twenty-five guineas was no great sum, not in her accounting, yet if she saved it she could put it into her special fund for helping their needier tenants.

"Very well." She dropped the coins back into the pouch and returned it to the safe. Shutting the safe, she locked the cupboard door, all the while reassuring herself that she was the one in charge. Finally, she turned to face Eversleigh. "What is your question, Your Grace?"

Jason smiled. "Why do you persist in hiding your light under a bushel, my dear?"

Lenore blinked. "I beg your pardon?"

The look Eversleigh bent upon her forcibly reminded her of his reputation.

"I asked why you are so assiduous in veiling your attributes from those most likely to appreciate them."

Pressing her hands together, Lenore put her nose in the air. "I have no idea what you mean, Your Grace."

"Let's see if I can explain." Jason straightened, pushing away from the wall. Horrified, Lenore watched, wide-eyed, as two strides brought him to stand directly before her. His hands came up to grasp the bookshelves just beyond each of her shoulders, trapping her between his arms.

Feeling the edges of the bookshelves digging into her spine, Lenore cleared her throat. "I'm convinced you are too much the gentleman to resort to intimidation, Your Grace."

"Believe what you will of me, my dear, but allow me to remove these, before they obscure your very pretty eyes."

Before she could react, Eversleigh had whipped her fogging spectacles from her nose, dropping them on the desk behind him.

Stifling a squeak of sheer outrage, Lenore blinked furiously up at him.

A slow smile was her reward. "A great improvement." For an instant, the silver gaze roamed her face in open appreciation before, with a last unnerving glance at her lips, Jason returned his attention to the matter at hand.

"Permit me to inform you, Miss Lester, that, unlike the majority who have visited here, I am neither blind nor gullible. That being so, I wish to know why you insist on purposely hiding your charms."

In the face of such an attack, there was nothing to do but fight back. "My charms, as you are pleased to call them, are my own, I believe? If it pleases me to keep them hidden, then who has any right to gainsay me?" Lenore felt distinctly pleased with that piece of logic.

"There are many, Miss Lester, who would maintain that a beautiful woman is created for the enjoyment of men. How do you answer the charge of short-changing half the population?"

"*I* am not on this earth to pander to the whims of men, my lord." Head back, eyes flashing, Lenore felt her temper take hold. "Indeed, I've discovered that by avoiding the complications engendered by the male of the species, it is tolerably easy to live a calm and well-ordered life."

Eversleigh's eyes narrowed.

Abruptly realising that she had said too much, Lenore temporised, "That is…"

"No." The single syllable stopped her, drying her stumbling words at source. "I think I see the light."

To her consternation, Eversleigh leaned closer, his narrowed eyes casting a silver net she could not escape. He loomed over her, around her; never in her life had she felt so helpless.

His eyes searched hers. "You don't wish to marry." The words were enunciated slowly, quietly, but were all the more definite for that. "You hide your delights beneath heavy cambric and hope no one will see enough to be interested."

Lenore wished she could shake her head but Eversleigh's compelling gaze prevented prevarication. She summoned a glare. "I see no reason why any man *should* be interested in me, Your Grace."

The reaction to that was not what she had hoped. A slow smile twisted Eversleigh's lips. He shifted, bringing one large hand up to take a large pinch of her clothing, just above the yoke of her gown. Deliberately, he gave the material a brisk twitch, back and forth.

Lenore's shocked gasp filled the room. Her eyes flew wide at the excruciating sensation of her gown shifting over her tightened nipples. Horrified, she batted his hand away.

"Permit me to inform you, Miss Lester, that you have a severely proscribed understanding of the basis of male interest. I suggest you extend your studies before you come to any conclusions."

"As I have *no* intention of marrying, I have *absolutely* no interest in such topics, Your Grace!"

Her declaration focused Eversleigh's attention dramatically. His penetrating gaze bored into her eyes, his expression hardened. Flushed, Lenore held her own, but she could see nothing in the steel of his eyes to give her any clue to his thoughts.

Then, to her considerable relief, he straightened, his hands dropping to his side.

"Miss Lester, has it occurred to you that you have been much indulged?"

Lenore drew breath, determined to keep her chin up. "Indeed, Your Grace. My father and brothers are most supportive."

"They have been slack, Miss Lester." Without warning, he caught her chin on the edge of one large hand, keeping her face turned up to his. The grey eyes once more roamed her features. Lenore could not breathe. His expression was stern, almost forbidding. "Your father and brothers have not done their duty by you. A woman of your intelligence and beauty is wasted outside marriage."

"That is not my opinion, Your Grace."

"I am aware of that, my dear. We shall have to see what can be done to change it."

Paralysed, Lenore stared up at him. Startled conjecture vied with a strange, breathless, senseless yearning, a panoply of thoughts and sensations buffeting her brain. She could think of nothing to say.

The door opened.

"Oh! Excuse me, Miss Lenore, but I've come to do the menus."

Twisting her chin from Eversleigh's grasp, Lenore peeked around him and saw her housekeeper, Mrs. Hobbs, standing uncertainly in the doorway. "Er...yes. Lord Eversleigh and I were just examining the lock of this cupboard. It was stuck." With a warning glance at Eversleigh, Lenore turned towards her desk.

"Ah, well," said Mrs. Hobbs, ambling forward, a large bundle of old menus and receipts clutched to her ample bosom. "I'd better get John to take a look at it, then."

"No, no. It's working now." Lenore cast a desperate glance at Eversleigh, praying he would behave himself and depart.

To her relief, he swept her a graceful bow. "I'm pleased to have been of assistance, my dear. If you have any other difficulties that are within the scope of my poor abilities to cure, pray feel free to call on my talents."

Lenore's eyes narrowed. "Thank you, Your Grace."

Jason smiled, his wolf's smile, and turned to the door. On the threshold, he paused, glancing back to see Lenore close her account book and lay it aside, then draw a pile of menus towards her.

"Miss Lester?"

Lenore looked up. "Yes, Your Grace?"

A long finger pointed at the corner of her desk. "Your spectacles, my dear."

Swallowing a curse, Lenore grabbed the delicate frames and arranged them on her nose, then glanced up, but her tormentor had gone.

"Now. For lunch I'd thought to have…"

Stifling a wholly unexpected sigh, Lenore gave her attention to Mrs. Hobbs.

An hour later, she was staring out of the window, her account book open before her, the ink dry on her nib, when Amelia's head appeared around the door.

"There you are! I'd despaired of finding you."

Lenore returned her cousin's bright smile, laying aside her pen as Amelia crossed the room to subside into the armchair before the desk in a froth of apricot muslin. "I take it last evening passed without incident?"

Amelia waved the question aside. "You were right. They're a perfectly manageable lot. All except Eversleigh. I wouldn't care to have to manage him. But His Grace had taken himself off somewhere. Truth to tell, I retired early myself." She turned to look at Lenore. "I looked for you but couldn't find you anywhere."

Lenore shut her account book with a snap. "I was detained on the terrace."

"Oh? By what?"

"A discussion of the relative merits of present and past civilisations, as I recall."

Amelia grimaced. "One of your dry discussions, I take it?"

Calmly sorting her papers, Lenore did not respond.

"Anyway, you'll be pleased to know I took care of one of your hostessly chores for you."

"Oh?"

"The Melton sisters. They had quite worn down poor Mr. Marshall; I had to rescue him. And that reminds me." Amelia swung about, bright brown eyes dancing. "I've discovered why Eversleigh's here!"

Lenore's hands stilled. "Why?" she asked, hoping Amelia would not detect the breathlessness that had laid siege to her voice.

"Mr. Marshall told me that Eversleigh is dreading the prospect of facing all the matchmaking mamas. I do believe he's here rusticating, recouping his energies before returning to town and facing his fate. He's got *six* aunts, you know."

"Yes, I know," Lenore murmured, her thoughts elsewhere. When Amelia turned an enquiring gaze on her, she added, "They're friends of Harriet's." Lenore cleared her throat. "What sort of woman do you think Eversleigh will marry?"

"A diamond of the first water," Amelia promptly declared. "Whoever of the latest lot fills that description and is suitably connected. It's what's expected, after all. And, for once, Eversleigh seems intent on fulfilling expectations."

Lenore nodded and sank into silence.

After a few moments, her expression pensive, her fingers pleating the ribbons of her gown, Amelia asked, "Tell me, do you know much of Mr. Marshall?"

The question drew Lenore from her own thoughts to gaze in surprise at her friend. "Just how long did it take to rescue him last night?"

Amelia blushed. "Well, I couldn't just leave the poor

man—he was parched for entertainment. Those Melton girls might be very pretty, but *widgeons*, my dear."

Lenore's lips twitched. "I thought you were here to avoid that sort of thing?"

Amelia looked pained. "I came here to avoid being pursued, Lenore. As far as I know, Frederick Marshall has never pursued a woman in his life."

Putting her head on one side, Lenore acknowledged that truth. "I had heard that. Odd, given his association with Eversleigh."

"Yes, but very refreshing." Amelia slanted a glance at Lenore. "Tell me, Lenore, do you still cling to your ideal of a singular existence, without the complications of men?"

Lenore looked down, picking up her papers. "Certainly. It's the only sensible course, given the strictures that rule our lives." She glanced up briefly through her glasses. "I would have thought that you, of all people, would appreciate that."

Amelia sighed, her gaze on the ceiling. "Oh, I know. But, just sometimes, I wonder. If one is not in the marketplace, one cannot buy. And if one is not…" Her brow creased as she sought for words. "If one does not put oneself in the way of love, however will it find you?"

"Love, as you well know, is not for us."

"I know, I know. But don't you sometimes dream?" Abruptly, Amelia swung about in her chair, fixing Lenore with an impish smile. "What happened to those dreams of yours—about being the prisoner of some evil ogre and locked in a tower guarded by a dragon only to be rescued by a tall and fearless knight errant?"

Lenore glanced up from her piles of receipts. "I long since realised that being held prisoner in some musty dungeon was likely to prove quite uncomfortable and that relying on being rescued was a mite risky, given the likelihood of my knight errant's being distracted by a mill, or some such event, and forgetting to turn up."

"Oh, Lenore!" Amelia sat back, pulling a disgusted face. After a moment, she said, "You know, I understand all your arguments, but I've never understood why you're so convinced there's no hope for us."

Lenore paused in her sorting, eyes lifting to the peaceful scene beyond her window as memories of her mother's face, always trying to look so brave, filled her mind's eye. Abruptly, she drew a curtain firmly across the vision. Looking down, she said, "Let's just say that love among the *ton* is a sadly mismanaged affair. It afflicts only one sex, leaving them vulnerable to all sorts of hurts. You only have to listen to the tales of Harriet's friends. How they bear such lives I do not know. I could never do so."

Amelia was frowning. "You mean the…the emotional hurts? The pain of loving and not being loved in return?"

Brusquely, without looking up, Lenore nodded.

"Yes, but…" Amelia's brow was furrowed as she wrestled with her meaning. "If one does not take a chance and give one's love, one cannot expect to receive love in return. Which would be worse—to never risk love and die never having known it, or to take a chance and, just possibly, come away with the prize?"

For a long moment, Lenore gazed at Amelia, a frown deeply etched in her eyes. "I suspect that depends on the odds of winning."

"Which in turn depends on the man one loves."

Silence descended in the small room, both occupants sunk deep in uneasy speculation. Then, in the distance, a gong clanged.

With a deep sigh, Amelia stood and shook out her skirts. She looked up and met Lenore's gaze squarely. "Lunch."

THAT EVENING, Lenore entered the drawing-room, her expression serene, her mind in a quandary. Instantly she was aware of Eversleigh, one of a group of guests on the other side of the room, chatting urbanely. Slipping into her accustomed role, she glided from group to group, playing the gracious hostess with effortless ease. Avoiding the group of which Eversleigh was a part, she came to rest beside Amelia, chatting animatedly with Frederick Marshall, the Melton sisters and two other gentlemen.

"Oh, Miss Lester! I did so enjoy this afternoon!" Lady Moffat, blue eyes bright, positively bubbled with innocent enthusiasm.

"I'm delighted you found so much to entertain you," Lenore replied. Lunch, an *al fresco* affair served beside the lake, had been voted a success by all who had attended. This had excluded the majority of the gentlemen, still busy at Harry's stud. Unfortunately, instead of settling to a quiet afternoon, gossiping or punting on the lake, some of the younger ladies had spied the archery butts, stored in the boat-house. Nothing would do but to stage an impromptu archery contest; Lenore had not had a minute to spare.

"I was just explaining that the dancing this evening was to be entirely informal," Amelia said.

Lenore smiled, feeling infinitely more experienced in the face of the younger ladies' overt eagerness. "Just the house guests. The ball on Friday will be a much larger affair."

"How positively exciting! We'll both look forward to

the event." Lady Harrison exchanged a bright glance with her sister.

Amelia shot a glance of long-suffering at Lenore, severely trying her composure.

The clang of the dinner gong, and Smithers's stentorian "Dinner is served" recalled Lenore to an unresolved dilemma. Would Eversleigh take advantage of country party informality to sit elsewhere at table, leaving her to claim whomever she chose for the seat on her right?

Casting a surreptitious glance across the room, she saw her answer crossing the floor, his stride determined, his eyes on her. Quelling a sudden inner flutter, Lenore raised her head. Eversleigh paused by her side, his grey eyes smiling. With a graceful gesture, he offered her his arm. "Shall we, Miss Lester?"

"Certainly, Your Grace." Lenore placed her fingertips upon his dark sleeve. As they headed for the door, her entire concentration was turned inward, to the task of subduing her skittering nerves and overcoming the odd breathlessness that had seized her.

"Would it help if I promised not to bite?"

The soft words, little more than a whisper in her ear, had Lenore looking upward in surprise. The expression in Eversleigh's eyes, a not ungentle amusement, shook her precarious equanimity even more. It was all she could do to return a haughty look, turning her eyes forward, determined not to give him the satisfaction of knowing how grateful she was for his reassurance.

He was as good as his word, conversing amiably with Mrs. Whitticombe, who had claimed the place on his right, encouraging Lord Farningham to such an extent that, to Lenore's experienced gaze, something close to hero-worship glowed in that young man's eyes. His Grace of Eversleigh could be utterly charming when he chose, but, to Lenore's prickling senses, the powerful predator beneath the veneer, the presence that had made Lord Farningham so hesitant initially, was not asleep. He was merely in a benevolent mood, watching, patient behind his grey eyes.

That evening, the gentlemen quit their port with alacrity, drawn to the drawing-room by the scrape of the violins, bows wielded with enthusiasm by five musicians installed in an alcove. Lenore was constantly on the move, encouraging the more timid of the ladies to join in, ensuring none of the gentlemen hung back. Despite her real liking for the pastime, she rarely danced herself, knowing how awkward most gentlemen found the exercise. She was too tall for even her brothers, only as tall as herself, to partner adequately in any measure beyond the formal quadrilles or cotillions. She was chatting to Mrs. Whitticombe, slightly flushed after a hectic boulanger, when she felt hard fingers close about her elbow.

A *frisson* of awareness informed her of who stood beside her even before she turned to meet his grey eyes.

Bestowing a charming if fleeting smile on Mrs. Whitticombe, Jason turned his gaze upon his hostess. "You're not dancing, Miss Lester. Can I tempt you to honour me with this waltz?"

The invitation was uttered so smoothly that Lenore had smiled her acquiescence before her mind had analysed his words. Reasoning that dancing with Eversleigh, so tall, was too tempting a proposition to have passed up anyway, she allowed him to lead her to the cleared area of the floor.

"Do you encounter much difficulty finding musicians hereabouts?"

Effortlessly he swept her into the midst of the couples swirling under the light of the chandelier. "N-no. Not usually." With an effort, Lenore focused her wayward wits. Dragging in a calming breath, she added, "There are two market towns nearby. Both have musical societies, so we are rarely at a loss."

After a few revolutions, Lenore became reconciled to the sensation of floating. It was, she realised, simply because Eversleigh was so tall and so strong. As she relaxed, the joy of the dance took hold.

Watching her face, Jason had no need of words. "You dance very well, Miss Lester," he eventually said, struck by the fact. She felt as light as thistledown in his arms, an ethereal sprite. The candlelight set gold winking in her hair; even her odd gown seemed part of the magic.

"Thank you, Your Grace." Lenore kept her lids lowered, her eyes fixed on a point beyond his right shoulder, content to let the dance blunt her senses. Even so, she was supremely conscious of the strength in the arm circling her waist, of the firm clasp of his fingers on hers. "Did you enjoy your tour of Harry's little enterprise?"

"Your brother keeps an excellent stud."

"He has told me your own horses are very fine." Glancing up through her lashes, Lenore watched as a small contented smile softened the lines about her partner's mouth. Then the arm around her waist tightened. The area near the door was congested with couples. As Eversleigh drew her more firmly to him before embarking on the tight turn, Lenore forced her mind to the music, letting it soothe her, blocking out the barrage of unnerving reactions assailing her senses. Only thus could she countenance such unlooked-for delight.

She was thoroughly disappointed when the dance came to an end.

Jason's smile was a little crooked as he looked down at her, her hand still clasped in his. "I feel I should return you to your chaperon, my dear, but I'm not sure I dare."

Recalling Harriet's behaviour of the previous evening, Lenore had no hesitation in stating, "I doubt that would be wise, Your Grace. Luckily, I'm far beyond the age of having to bow to such altars."

To her surprise, Eversleigh's gaze became sharper, his expression more hard. "You are in error, Miss Lester. You may not be a débutante but you are a very long way from being on the shelf."

Lenore would have frowned and taken issue, assuming the comment to relate to their morning's discussion, but to her amazement Mr. Peters materialised before her.

"If you would do me the honour, Miss Lester, I believe they're starting up a country dance."

In consternation, Lenore stared at Mr. Peters's bowing form. Eversleigh's invitation had taken her by surprise; she had accepted without thought for the potential ramifications. As Mr. Peters straightened, a hopeful light in his eyes, the full weight of her role settled on Lenore's shoulders. Pinning a smile to her lips, she looked over Mr. Peters's head to where the sets were forming. With determination, she extended her hand. "It would be a pleasure, sir."

A single glance to her left was sufficient to discern the amused glint in Eversleigh's eyes. "If you'll excuse me, Your Grace?"

As she straightened from her curtsy, Eversleigh's gaze was on her face. He smiled; Lenore felt her heart quiver.

Hand over heart, Jason bowed elegantly. "I wish you nothing but pleasure, my dear Miss Lester." His lips curving in appreciation, he watched as, head high, she glided away.

It was some hours later when he ran Frederick

Marshall to earth. To Jason's shrewd gaze, his friend had developed a predilection for Lady Wallace's company.

"Do you plan to remain for the entire week, Your Grace?" Reassured by the presence of Mr. Marshall beside her, Amelia advanced her query, an expression of open innocence on her face.

Dispassionately, Jason studied the fair features turned up to him. Languidly, he raised one brow. "That is my intention." Lifting his gaze to his friend's face, he allowed his expression to relax. "What say you, Frederick? Do you expect to find sufficient here to fix your peripatetic interest?"

Frederick shot him a glare before Amelia turned her questioning face to him. "I see no reason why we should not be tolerably amused for the duration."

"Excellent." Having gained the declaration she sought, Amelia was all smiles. "I'll look forward to your company, sirs. But I really must have a word to Lady Henslaw—if you'll excuse me, Mr. Marshall? Your Grace?" With an artful nod, Amelia left them.

Jason followed her progress towards Lady Henslaw, then turned to see Frederick, similarly engaged. "Let us hope Lady Wallace does not favour purple."

"What?" Frederick turned to him, then glared as his meaning became clear. "Dash it, Jason. It's no such thing. Lady Wallace is merely a means to pass the time—a sensible woman with whom one may have a conversation without being expected to sweep her off her feet."

"Ah." Jason nodded sagely. "I see."

Frederick ignored him. "Speaking of sweeping women off their feet—that waltz you so obviously enjoyed with Miss Lester? Permit me to tell you, not that you don't already know, that it fell just short of indecent."

A subtle smile curved Jason's lips as he stood, looking out over the dancers. "My only defence is the obvious—she enjoyed it, too. She's unquestionably the most graceful woman I've ever partnered."

"Yes, and now the whole company knows it. Do you think she'll thank you for the rest of her evening?"

"That, I had not anticipated." Jason glanced at Frederick, a glint in his eye. "Fear not. I shall come about. Apropos of which, I wanted to ask if you have heard any whispers of my impending fate?"

"I have, as a matter of fact." Frederick continued to study the dancers, his gaze following Lady Wallace's bright curls. "From what I can gather, most who have come direct from town have heard something of your intentions."

Beneath his breath, Jason swore.

Frederick turned, surprise in his eyes. "Does that concern you? It was inevitable, after all."

Grimacing, Jason replied, "I would rather it was not common knowledge but I doubt it'll seriously affect the outcome." Narrowing his eyes, he mused, "However, I will, I suspect, have to expend rather more thought on the correct approach to my problem."

Noting the direction of his friend's gaze, Frederick asked, "I take it you have fixed on Miss Lester?"

"Does that surprise you?" Jason murmured, his attention still on her fair head.

Considering that waltz, and all that it had revealed, Frederick shrugged. "Not entirely. But where lies your problem?"

"The lady has set her mind against marriage."

A paroxysm of coughing had Frederick turning aside. "I beg your pardon?" he asked, as soon as he was able.

Jason's eyes narrowed. "You heard. But if you imagine

I'll pass over the only woman I've ever met who meets my stringent criteria, you and Miss Lester will have to think again."

A MILL IN THE neighbourhood combined with the after-effects of the evening before relieved Lenore of many of her charges for much of the next day. With the gentlemen absent, the ladies were content to rest and recuperate. After officiating at a light luncheon, Lenore found her afternoon loomed blissfully free. She decided to devote the time to her neglected studies.

The library was a haven of peace in the large house. Located in the oldest wing, the stone flag kept the temperature pleasant even in the hottest of weather. Finding the room empty, Lenore threw open the heavy diamond-paned windows, and let the warm breeze, laden with the scents of summer, dance in. Her large desk, set between two windows, faced the door. Dragging in an invigorating breath, Lenore sat down and drew the tome she had been studying towards her. Hands clasped on the leather cover, she paused, eyes fixed, unseeing, on the far wall.

Ten minutes later, with no wish to examine the thoughts that had held her so easily, Lenore determinedly shook them aside. She opened her book. It took fifteen minutes to find her place. Determined to force her mind to her task, Lenore read three paragraphs. Then, she read them again.

With an exasperated sigh, she gave up. Shutting her book with a snap, she pushed back her chair.

She would go and find Amelia, for she was serving no purpose here.

CHAPTER FOUR

BY THE TIME Lenore learned of her brothers' plans for that evening it was too late to circumvent them. She entered the drawing-room, her usual serenity under threat by the thought of what might occur once the assembled company, growing hourly more relaxed, embarked on an impromptu programme of musical events. Her brothers, she was well aware, could draw upon a large stock of ribald ditties; quite how she was to keep them sufficiently in line cast the shadow of a frown on her face.

Eversleigh noticed. When he came to claim her for dinner, Lenore detected the ghost of a smile and a faint questioning lift to his brows.

"I confess to being curious, Miss Lester, as to what fell occurrence has succeeded in marring your calm."

"It is nothing, Your Grace. Pray disregard my megrims."

Jason threw her a glance of haughty superiority. "Permit me to inform you, my dear, that I have no wish whatever to overlook anything that brings a frown to your fair face."

His bombastic tone had the desired effect. Lenore's lips twitched. "If you must know, I am not entirely at ease over my brothers' plans for us to entertain ourselves with musical renderings."

A chuckle greeted her admission. "Confess that it is not our talents that concern you so much as the possible choice of subject and I'll undertake to quell the high spirits of those of the company inclined to excess. Or," he amended, as they came to a halt beside her chair, "at least keep them within the pale."

Frowning openly, Lenore looked into his eyes, remembering her last bargain with him. "I am not sure that you can do so, Your Grace."

"Doubts, Miss Lester?" Jason allowed his brows to rise in mock offence. Then he smiled. "Relax, my dear, and let me handle the matter." When the footman drew out her chair, Lenore sat and settled her skirts, casting a puzzled glance at Eversleigh. As he moved to take his own seat on her right, Jason cocked a brow at her, his smile impossible to deny. "If you want to muzzle licentious behaviour, who better to turn to than a rake?"

Unable to find an acceptable answer, Lenore gave her attention to her soup.

When the company adjourned *en masse* to the music-room, set at the rear of the house, Lenore found Eversleigh by her side. "Invite the Melton sisters to play." Together, they strolled into the large room. "I take it you play the pianoforte yourself?"

"Yes," Lenore replied, wariness echoing in her voice. "But I *don't* sing." Her escort merely smiled his charming smile and escorted her to a seat in the front row. To her surprise, he sat beside her, stretching his long legs before him, giving every evidence of honouring the proceeding with his full attention. Lenore eyed him suspiciously.

His plan turned out to be simplicity itself. At his urging, Lenore invited one after another of the more youthful of the ladies to play or sing. Lady Henslaw, a matron with a distinctly racy reputation, followed Lady Hattersley. Under Eversleigh's gaze, Lady Henslaw preened, then gave a surprisingly pure rendition of an old country air. The applause, led by Eversleigh, left her ladyship with a smile on her face. Mrs. Ellis followed, with a predictably innocent song. She was supplanted by Mrs. Cronwell, who, not to be outdone in maidenly accomplishment, played a stately minuet with real flair.

From the corner of her eye, Lenore saw her brother Harry shift in his seat. Jason saw it too. "Harry next."

Lenore turned to him, consternation in her eyes. "I do not think that would be wise, Your Grace."

Jason dropped his gaze to her face. He smiled, confidence lighting his eyes. "Trust me, Miss Lester."

With a sigh, Lenore turned and summoned Harry. Her brother stood and strolled forward, his walk just short of a swagger. Taking his stance in front of the audience, he drew breath, his eyes scanning the expectant faces before him. Harry blinked. Shifting his stance, he swept the audience again, then, with a slight frown, he waved at Amelia. "Come accompany me, coz."

Without fuss, Amelia went to the piano stool. The song Harry chose was a jaunty shanty, boisterous but in no way ineligible.

To Lenore's relief, her brother appeared gratified by the thunderous applause that crowned his performance.

"Ask Frederick Marshall." Lenore turned at the whispered command. Raising her brows in question, she was treated to a look of bland innocence. "He sings very well," was all the explanation she received.

That proved to be no more than the truth. With Amelia at the keys, Mr. Marshall's light baritone wended its harmonious way through one of the bardic tales, holding the audience enthralled. The tumultuous applause at the end of the piece was entirely spontaneous. The performers exchanged a delighted smile.

"Try Miss Whitticombe next."

Lenore reacted immediately, no longer doubting her mentor's wisdom. Miss Whitticombe held the dubious distinction of being the only unmarried female guest. A plain girl, she had accompanied her mother, a dashing widow. Miss Whitticombe opted for the harp, proving to be more competent than inspired. Nevertheless, her effort was well received.

"Now Jack."

Lenore had to turn in her seat to locate her eldest brother. He stood at the back of the room, shoulders propped against the wall, a look of thinly disguised boredom on his face. Lenore waved to attract his attention. "Jack?" Even from across the room, she saw his eyes narrow as he straightened, then flick from her to Eversleigh and back again.

"No, no, my dear. It's you who should do the honours of the house." A smile Lenore knew boded her no good appeared on her sibling's face. "I suggest a duet. The gentleman beside you will no doubt be happy to join you."

Stunned but far too experienced to show it, Lenore turned to Eversleigh. He met her wide eyes with a charming smile and a graceful gesture to the piano. "Are you game, Miss Lester?"

There was no escape, Lenore saw that instantly. Not sure whose neck she wished to wring, Eversleigh's or Jack's, she allowed Eversleigh to draw her to her feet and escort her to the instrument. A *sotto voce* conference decided the piece, a gentle ballad she felt confident she could manage. Fingers nimble on the keys, Lenore commenced the introduction, distractedly aware of the odd beat of her heart and of Eversleigh standing close behind her.

Afterwards, she could remember little of their performance, but she knew she sang well, her voice lifting easily over Eversleigh's bass. Her contralto was not as well tutored as Amelia's sweet soprano, but, against Eversleigh's powerful voice, it struck the right chord. The final note resonated through the room, their voices in perfect harmony. Clapping burst forth. Eversleigh's fingers closed about her hand. He raised her to stand beside him, his eyes, clear grey, smiling into hers.

"A most memorable moment, my dear. Thank you."

For one long instant, Lenore stared up into his eyes, sure he was going to kiss her fingertips, as he had once before. Instead, his gaze shifted to the watching crowd. Still smiling, he placed her hand on his sleeve.

Deflated, then troubled by the sudden sinking of her spirits, Lenore sighted Smithers with the tea-trolley. She excused herself to Eversleigh, murmuring her thanks for her relief, then forged a determined path through her guests to the relative safety of the teacups. She was grateful to Eversleigh for his assistance, but, in the interests of her own peace of mind, she would be wise to spend much less time in his company.

THE NEXT DAY, Wednesday, dawned bright and clear, with just a touch of mist about the lake. To Lenore's surprise the mild entertainment of the previous evening had engendered a milder attitude among the guests. Everyone seemed more relaxed, ready to trade easy smiles and light conversation in place of the artfully pointed banter and arch looks of the preceding days.

The majority of the ladies had made a pact to attend breakfast in the sunny downstairs parlour. While their appearance initially raised a good many male brows, surprise rapidly faded as the company settled into informal groups about the long board, the ladies, sipping tea and nibbling thin slices of toast, interspersed with the gentlemen, most of whom had made extensive forays among the covered dishes on the sideboard. The talk revolved around possible excursions to fill the afternoon. The gentlemen had already decided on an inspection of the Hall's closer coverts while the morning air was still crisp.

Hovering by the laden side-table, Lenore kept a watchful eye on her charges, ensuring that the younger, less confident ladies encountered no difficulties. Thus far, no contretemps had marred the pleasantry; her hopes were rising that, despite her brothers' inventiveness, the week would pass off more smoothly than she had thought. Assured that all was well, she picked up a plate and helped herself to an assortment of delicacies from beneath the silver domes.

As she was turning away, Amelia came to the sideboard, Frederick Marshall by her side. Her cousin was a picture in a peach-coloured morning gown, her cheeks aglow, her manner slightly flustered. Lenore hesitated, then, with a gracious smile, she nodded her good mornings and left them.

She turned to find a place at the table and was immediately conscious of Eversleigh's grey gaze. He was seated on the opposite side of the table, one long-fingered hand draped over the back of the vacant chair beside him. He was talking to Lord Holyoake but his eyes were on her.

The compulsion to round the table and take the seat she knew would be instantly offered her was strong. With determined calm, Lenore opted to fill the empty place at the foot of the table, smiling at Mrs. Whitticombe and Lady Henslaw on her left, smoothly joining in their conversation. She studiously avoided looking Eversleigh's way but she could feel his gaze, amused, she was sure, rambling openly over the plain brown pinafore she had donned over a long-sleeved white shirt and green cambric skirt.

She told herself she was relieved when he made no move to speak with her. He did, however, catch her eye when she looked up as the gentlemen rose. To her chagrin, she could not wrench her eyes from his smile as he approached and paused by her chair.

"Good morning, Miss Lester." Jason's gaze lifted to include her companions. "Ladies."

With a graceful nod, he acknowledged their ladyships' bright good mornings and Lenore's more subdued greeting before joining the male exodus to the gun-room. Behind him, Lenore frowned at her toast, annoyed that a mere "good morning" should leave her feeling as flustered as Amelia had looked. His Grace of Eversleigh was only being polite.

As the ladies were content to spend the morning ambling about the extensive gardens, gathering their energies for a visit to a nearby folly, the chosen distraction for the afternoon, Lenore took refuge in the library.

The Assyrians, unfortunately, had lost their appeal. She was worrying over her sudden lack of interest in a topic that a week ago had held her enthralled when Amelia came through the door. Her cousin's expression was pensive; with an abstracted smile she came forward to settle with a rustle of skirts on the windowseat close to Lenore's desk. Lenore watched her in silence, swivelling her chair to face her.

Amelia heaved a heavy sigh. "I'm in a fix, Lenore." Frowning, she slanted Lenore a worried glance. "Do you know how to attract a gentleman?"

Lenore's brows flew. "*Attract* a gentleman? I thought your problem was to repel them."

"Precisely," Amelia agreed. "I've experience aplenty in that. Which is probably why I find I haven't the first idea of how to accomplish the other."

"But…why?"

Amelia looked slightly sheepish but, at the same time, quite determined. "It's Mr. Marshall," she confessed. "I've discovered he has no…no *predatory* instincts whatsoever. Oh, Lenore!" Amelia rounded on her cousin, brown eyes alight, her hands clasped before her. "It's so pleasant to be treated as if my wishes were all that mattered. I feel so safe, so *comfortable* with Frederick."

Lenore's eyes widened. "Frederick?"

Amelia waved her hands dismissively. "There's no sense in beating about the bush, Lenore. I want to encourage Frederick to think of me in a more *personal* way. But how does one accomplish such a delicate task without…" Amelia's pert nose wrinkled in distaste. "Well, without giving an impression no true lady would wish to give."

When her cousin looked at her, clearly expecting an answer, Lenore spread her hands helplessly. "I'm the last person to ask such a question, Amelia. I've not the slightest idea how to advise you."

But Amelia was adamant. "Nonsense. You're considered by all to be a most intelligent woman, Lenore. If you would only put your mind to it, I'm sure you'd be able to give me at least a *hint* of how to proceed."

Lenore frowned but dutifully turned her mind to the task. "I suppose," she eventually said, "if you were to encourage him to be with you, by your side as much as possible, he might at least understand that you enjoyed and specifically wished for his company."

"That would certainly be a start." Amelia's gentle features were overlaid by an air of determination. "And the more time I spend talking with him, the more opportunity I'll have to...to nudge his mind in the right direction. But I must make a start immediately or I'll run out of time."

Lenore looked her question.

Amelia cast her a distracted look. "Rothesay." When Lenore showed no sign of enlightenment, Amelia patiently explained, "Frederick is sure to accompany Eversleigh back to London at the end of the week. Given their friendship, it's only to be expected that Frederick will be on hand to support Eversleigh through the mêlée which is bound to engulf him immediately he sets foot in town. After being held at bay for so long, the matchmaking mamas are bound to descend with a vengeance. So, you see, I expect I'll have to return to town rather than go on to Aunt Mary in Bath. But I would rather not risk Rothesay without knowing there was at least some purpose to the exercise."

"And if Mr. Marshall shows interest, you'll risk a confrontation with the viscount?"

Amelia looked out of the window at the sunlight dancing on the smooth surface of the lake. Then she sighed and turned to Lenore, an expression compounded of loneliness and hope on her face. "If Frederick shows any real interest, I believe I'd brave the very fires of hell for a chance of happiness."

The deep yearning in her cousin's voice shocked Lenore. She felt an echo deep inside, a reverberation, like a heavy gong clanging, the pure sound of the truth she was trying to deny. Abruptly rising, she crossed to put her arms about Amelia. She gave her cousin a quick hug. "I wish you luck in your endeavour, my dear."

As she looked down at Amelia's determined face, Lenore felt a host of emotions, hitherto steadfastly suppressed, well up and tumble forth into her consciousness where she could no longer ignore them. The bursting of the dam left her shaken but she pinned an encouraging smile on her lips as Amelia rose.

Slipping her arms about Lenore's slender waist, Amelia returned her hug. "I'm going to put your advice into practice immediately. As Frederick will not pursue me, I shall simply have to pursue him." She headed for the door, pausing at the last to add, "In a perfectly lady-like way, of course."

Lenore laughed, wondering just how much encouragement Frederick Marshall would need. Before she had decided the point, her own thoughts claimed her.

She did not get back to the Assyrians.

LUNCHEON WAS A noisy affair, full of chatter and laughter. Almost all the guests had relaxed, letting down the formal barriers. They congregated by the lake, where the meal was laid out on a long trestle, small tables and checkered rugs scattered over the lush grass by the lake's edge. With Smithers and his cohorts in attendance to supply whatever their hearts desired, the company split into transitory groups, the members moving freely from one to the next. The fare was light, as befitted the scene, a succession of delicacies culminating in the season's first strawberries, served with clotted cream.

"A *tour de force*, my dear. Your strawberries were delicious."

Lenore turned to face Eversleigh, ignoring the odd leap of her pulses as she read the appreciation in his eyes. "Thank you, Your Grace. We have an excellent succession house."

"I'm sure it is excellent, if it falls within your sphere."

Lenore let that pass, merely inclining her head grace-

fully. She moved aside, so that he could join the circle of
which she was a member. He did so, standing by her side
to listen as the other members discussed the projected
trip to the folly.

"Jack said it's quite ancient," Mrs. Whitticombe said.

"And covered with ivy," Lady Henslaw added. "It
sounds positively romantic. Harry said there was an old
story about lovers using it as a trysting place."

Lenore kept her lips firmly shut. Her brothers' imagination had no limits. The old tower had been built as
a lookout in the days of the Civil War. Nothing even
remotely romantic had ever occurred there. The lower
room, the only one large enough to hold more than one
person, had been used as a cow byre until the ivy had
claimed the structure. Still, the views from the vantage
point were excellent; the company would not be disappointed.

"You must have visited this folly many times, Miss
Lester. Are you fired with enthusiasm to see it again?"

Eversleigh's quiet question drew Lenore out of the
circle. Glancing up, she saw something in his grey eyes
that caused her to inwardly quiver. Calmly she looked
away, letting her gaze scan the rest of the company,
before deliberately bringing it once more to his face. "I
fear I would find the excursion somewhat tame, Your
Grace. I think I'll feed the carp in the pond at the centre
of the maze."

She dropped her gaze in a bid to appear unconscious,
but could not resist glancing up through her lashes. Eversleigh's gaze was on her face, his eyes gleaming silver.
As she watched, a slight smile curved his lips. "Undoubtedly a more peaceful place to spend a glorious afternoon."

Her heart skittering, Lenore hung on his next words. To her surprise, Eversleigh looked away.

Following his gaze, Lenore saw Jack approaching, clearly intent on speaking with Eversleigh. Having no desire to meet her eldest brother before he had had time to forget her interference in his plans of the night before, Lenore inclined her head to Eversleigh. With a murmured, "Your Grace," she drifted away.

Jason let her go. The afternoon stretched before them and he had no wish for Jack to divine his interest. Not yet.

"You dog, Jason! What the devil did you mean by assisting Lenore with her little plan last night?"

Jason smiled. "Just to see how you would take it, why else?" His mocking gaze teased Jack. "Besides, your sister was right, if not for the right reasons. Look about you. How relaxed and unthreatened do you think these fair ladies would be feeling today if you and Harry had had your way?"

The comment caused Jack to pause, considering the unfettered gaiety about him.

"You really need to plan your campaigns a little more thoroughly," Jason advised. "Take it from one who knows."

Jack laughed. "Very well. I can hardly argue in the face of your experience. But after last night, I claim the right to another touch at you over the billiard table. Harry'll take this crowd on to the folly. We can have our game, then follow on later."

Jason inclined his head. "An excellent idea."

Ten feet away, ostensibly listening to Lady Hattersley describe the folly on her family's estate, Lenore burned, disappointment, anger and an odd species of shame consuming her. With her usual serene mask firmly in place, she forced herself to wait until Eversleigh's tall figure had disappeared into the house beside Jack before, excusing herself to her guests, she headed for the kitchens. This time, her brother could pay his own debts.

She left the house ten minutes later, a basket of breadcrumbs on her arm. She had considered immersing herself in the Assyrians in an effort to reignite her interest but the day was too glorious to spend indoors and the carp did, in fact, need feeding. Leaving the terrace, she headed for the maze, sited amid a series of informal gardens, designed to lead from one to the other, each with a different feature. The Hall was surrounded by well-tended vistas, with the lake and surrounding lawns before it, the formal parterres and rose garden to one side, the maze with the wilderness and shrubbery on the other. The extensive kitchen gardens and succession houses completed the circle.

As she crossed the first of the trio of gardens leading to the gateway to the maze, Lenore caught a glimpse of peach skirts in one of the interconnecting gardens to the side. A second glance revealed the dark coat of a gentleman hovering protectively. Despite her disgust with her own attempt at encouragement, Lenore sent a wish for success winging her cousin's way before plunging on towards the pool at the centre of the maze.

Once there, she slumped into an untidy heap by the pool's edge, uncaring of her skirts, and settled the basket beside her. As she started flicking crumbs to the ravenous fish, the iniquity of her position engulfed her.

What had possessed her to surrender to the promptings of her unexpected feelings and issue an invitation to Eversleigh? Admittedly he was no threat to her, given that he would be leaving on Saturday morning to return to town and offer for some simpering ninny, diamond of

the first water though she might be. It would undoubtedly be a fitting fate for His Grace. Quite why *she* should
feel disillusioned by the prospect eluded her. Beneath her
self-imposed calm she was honest enough to recognise a
yearning to experience, just once, the thrill other women
felt, the thrill to which they became so disastrously ad-
dicted. She had felt the first glimmerings, the skittering
sensations which prickled along her nerves whenever
Eversleigh was near. Instinctively she had clamped down
on her reactions; now she longed to set them free, just
once, knowing she stood in no danger. Even if she fell
under Eversleigh's spell, he would not seduce her. She
had seen the stern patriarch behind the rake's mask; she
was safe with him.

But was she safe from herself? Would she, too, suc-
cumb to love and leave herself open to the hurt that followed inexorably in its wake? Lenore shifted, frowning
at the fat fish who rose to gobble her crumbs. Perhaps
she should thank Eversleigh, and his liking for billiards,
for denying her the chance of finding out?

Twenty minutes later, Jason headed for the maze, his
mind entirely focused on the woman he was seeking. He
did not delude himself that she had changed her stance
on marriage but, given that she must by now know of his
need to marry, her transparent invitation to spend time
privately with her could only be interpreted as a wish to
discuss the matter. He had hoped to make her question
her views while at the same time reassuring her she had
no reason to fear him; apparently he had succeeded. The
small triumph made his steps more determined.

Her wish to remain unmarried was understandable.
She had been permitted a great deal of independence
and, given her undoubted intelligence, her freedom had
become important to her. He intended reassuring her that

an independent, intelligent woman need not fear marriage to him.

Indeed, with every passing day he became more certain of his choice. Lenore Lester would suit him very well. She fulfilled all his criteria and, if there was a deep inclination that could not readily be accounted for on that basis, he felt no pressing need to examine it. The fact was sufficient.

Once he had dispelled her reservations and reconstructed her vision of matrimony along the lines he had in mind, he had no doubt she would find no further reason to cavil.

Emerging from the twisting hedges of the maze, he found himself on a large square of lawn surrounding a rectangular pond. Edged with blocks of stone, the surface of the pool was carpeted with water lilies. Beside it, he sighted his quarry, idly flicking her fingers to the fish, who rose with ponderous dignity to her bait.

An entirely spontaneous smile curving his lips, he went forward to join her.

Lenore knew he was there when his shadow fell across the pool. Instantly her heart soared, all thoughts of stoic safety forgotten as the knowledge that he had, after all, accepted her invitation reverberated through her. Hurriedly she recalled her scattering senses, determined not to let him see how much he affected her. Calmly, she continued scattering crumbs to the gluttonous carp. "Good afternoon, Your Grace."

Jason stopped beside her. "As I surmised, Miss Lester, this is a most peaceful spot." His eyes rose to the high hedges that surrounded them. Given the absence of most of the party, there was little reason to fear interruption. Had he been intent on seduction, he could not have wished for a better setting.

"Would you care to feed the fish, Your Grace?" Lenore turned to look up at him, holding down the brim of her straw hat to shield her eyes against the glare.

"Not particularly." Jason studied her face, then shifted his gaze to the large spotted fish swimming languidly back and forth before his prospective bride. "They look disgustingly over-indulged."

Head on one side, Lenore studied the fish critically. "You're right. Clearly they need no further sustenance." She was dusting her fingers over the basket when Eversleigh's large hand appeared before her. She glanced up, inwardly grimacing for, with the light behind him, she could not see his face.

For a moment, Jason said nothing, then, "Come. Sit with me in the sunshine." Smoothly he drew her to her feet, inwardly assuring himself that she was too innocent to have understood the reason for his momentary silence. A wrought-iron seat graced one side of the lawn. Picking up her basket, Jason led her across the clipped grass.

Settling her skirts as she sank on to the seat, Lenore quelled an unexpected spurt of disappointment that her attire was not more elegant. It was strange enough that she was indulging her dreams, sitting here alone with Eversleigh. Her senses were already running riot, her awareness rising to unnerving heights. Only her conviction that no danger attended her departure from the strict bounds of conventional behaviour allowed her to sit calmly as he took his seat beside her.

"You will no doubt be pleased to learn that I did not vanquish Jack."

"Indeed? You surprise me, Your Grace." Lenore cast a speculative glance his way.

Jason smiled. "I let him win," he admitted.

"Why?"

"It was faster. He has now taken himself off, thoroughly chuffed, to join the rest of the party." He did not add that Jack had been highly suspicious about his stated intention to spend the afternoon practising over the green baize. "Tell me, my dear, do you have any interest in games of chance?"

"None whatsoever," Lenore replied.

"How many games have you tried?"

Looking up, Lenore was forced to face his scepticism and confess to her ignorance. Not to be outdone, she promptly asked which games he favoured. The list was a long one, especially when he had to explain the features of each.

At the end of it, Lenore looked out over the pool and calmly observed, "With such diverse interests, you must spend much of your time in town at your clubs."

Jason laughed. "I dare say it appears that way. But only in my youth did sitting up all night over the cards hold any temptation." Slanting a glance at her profile, he added, "There are, after all, so many better ways to spend the time."

"Indeed?" The face she turned to him was utterly innocent. "Do you attend the opera, then? Or perhaps the theatre is more to your taste?"

Jason's eyes narrowed. It was on the tip of his tongue to retort that he had, at various times, found elements of interest at both the opera and theatre. Only a firm resolution to remain steadfastly correct in his dealings with his prospective bride kept him from calling her bluff. "I attend both, on occasion."

"Have you seen Keane?" Lenore felt a peculiar thrill at having tempted the wolf and survived.

"Several times. He's an excellent actor provided the part has scope for his talents."

A discussion of the various theatres and the style of plays produced ensued, followed by a ruthlessly pointed examination of that other source of *ton*-ish entertainment, the Prince Regent.

"A keen mind utterly wasted," was Jason's scathing conclusion.

"Particularly given the opportunities he must have had." Considering the facilities available to the Prince Regent. Lenore sighed. "Just being so close to all the bookshops would in itself be a boon to any scholar. I'd dearly love to have Hatchards within reach."

Her pensive comment drew a searching glance from Jason. He had been patiently awaiting the right moment to introduce the topic of marriage, content to spend some time in idle chatter while she overcame her natural hesitancy. Stretching his long legs before him, he crossed his booted ankles, turning slightly so that he could keep her face in view. "Tell me, my dear, if you could design your own Utopia, what would you place within it?"

The unexpected question had Lenore turning to study his face, but she could see nothing beyond encouragement in his eyes. A strange recklessness had her in its grip; she felt no reticence in his presence and marvelled at the fact. It was a heady sort of freedom, knowing she was safe. Head on one side, she considered. "Gardens, certainly. Large gardens, like these." With a wave of her hand, she indicated their surroundings. "So soothing to have a large garden to wander in. Tell me, Your Grace, do you wander your gardens frequently?"

Jason returned her smile. "I rarely need soothing. However," he continued, "the gardens at the Abbey are similar to these, though not, I'm sorry to say, in such perfect state."

"Your wife, no doubt, will remedy that." Lenore shifted her gaze to the pool.

"So I sincerely hope," Jason returned. "So, a garden and the staff to tend it. What else?"

"A house, of course. In the country."

"Naturally. Sufficiently large and appropriately staffed. What of town?"

Lenore grimaced. "I admit that I'm curious to visit London, but the idea of living there does not entice."

"Why not?"

"I hesitate to admit to such an unfashionable attitude but the thought of having to suffer society at large, as would be unavoidable should I take up residence in the capital, dissuades me from doing so."

"I protest you do society a grave injustice, my dear. We're not all fribbles and fops."

"But this is *my* Utopia, remember?"

"Just so. So what else takes your fancy?"

"Well," Lenore temporised, caught up in this strange game, "I enjoy acting as hostess at large gatherings—not much use having a large house and well-trained staff if one does not use them, after all."

"Very true," Jason agreed.

"I also enjoy my work among the folk on the estate. However, if this be Utopia, then I would rather not be in charge of the steward and bailiff."

Jason merely nodded, foreseeing no problem there. The reins of his numerous estates were firmly in his grasp; he needed no help on that front. Remembering her studies, he asked, "What of entertainment? What features most in that sphere?"

"My library. I couldn't live without my books."

"The Abbey has an extensive library. My father was

an invalid for some time and took delight in restocking it to the hilt."

"Really?"

It was plain to the meanest intelligence that, of all the subjects they had touched upon, this was the one nearest her heart. Jason looked down into her green eyes and smiled. "There's a huge range of classics as well as many newer volumes."

"Have you had it catalogued?"

"Unfortunately not. My father died before he was able to attend to the matter."

The realisation that she would never see his library dimmed Lenore's excitement. "You should have it done," she told him, looking forward once more.

When she remained silent, Jason prompted, "You haven't mentioned people in this Utopia of yours—a husband and children to make your house a home?"

The question shook Lenore. From any other man she would have imagined the query to stem from mere supposition. But Eversleigh knew her mind on that subject. "I see no reason to complicate my life with a husband, Your Grace."

"You're an intelligent woman, Lenore. If a man were able to offer you all your heart desires, would you still not allow a husband into your life?"

Slowly, her heart thudding uncomfortably, Lenore turned to face him. A strange fear had seized her throat, making it difficult to breathe. "Why do you ask, Your Grace?" He was still sitting at his ease beside her, his large frame relaxed, one arm stretched along the back of the wrought-iron seat. But the expression in his grey eyes, the unshakeable, implacable determination of a hunter, sent an unnerving combination of fear and yearning spiralling through her.

"I should have thought that was obvious, my dear." Jason held her gaze. "You have, no doubt, heard rumours that I intended to wed?"

"I never listen to gossip, Your Grace," Lenore said, frantic to deny the scarifying possibility that, moment by moment, gained greater substance.

Exasperation glowed briefly in Jason's eyes. "Just so that you may be assured on the subject, the rumours are correct."

"Everyone's expecting you to marry a débutante—a diamond of the first water." Lenore rushed the words out despite the breathlessness that assailed her. Her mind was reeling in sheer fright at the vision forming with dreadful clarity in her brain.

A supercilious expression infused Jason's features. "Do I strike you as the sort of man who would marry a witless widgeon?"

Lenore forced herself to look at him with some vestige of her customary composure. "No. But I expect not all diamonds of the first water are widgeons, Your Grace." Pressing her hands tightly together in her lap, she desperately sought for a way to hijack the conversation. But her wits had seized, frozen into immobility by what she could see inexorably approaching.

Jason inclined his head. "That's as may be, but I've seen too much of overt beauty not to know its real value." Deliberately, he let his gaze skim her figure as she sat rigidly erect, on the edge of the seat. His voice deepened. "As I said before, you have a very limited understanding of what excites a gentleman's interest, Lenore."

He sensed rather than saw her quiver. Swiftly he moved from that topic. "You have told me what you desire from life, what you consider important. I'm willing and able to provide all that you've named, in return for your hand in marriage."

"And all that that entails." Inwardly aghast, her face registering blank dismay, Lenore pronounced the words as a sentence.

Jason frowned, his gaze fixed on her face. "It entails nothing beyond what you might expect. As we both know, you do not find my company insupportable." He hesitated, then added more gently, "I believe we will deal very well together, Lenore."

Giddiness seized Lenore. His version of her fate was clearly stated in the grey eyes so ruthlessly holding hers. Realisation of the danger she faced, and of how far she had already travelled down the road she had promised herself never to tread, swamped her. Her face drained of all colour. "No," she said, and felt herself start to shake. "I cannot marry you, Your Grace."

"Why?" Jason uttered the question quietly but compellingly. His eyes narrowed. "And why invite me here if not to discuss that very subject?"

Desperate, Lenore retorted, "I did not invite you here."

The long look she received in reply shook her to the core.

Quietly, Jason said, "I suggest, my dear, you take a different tack."

Dragging in a shaky breath, Lenore stated, "Your Grace, I'm greatly honoured that you should consider me as your bride. However, I'm convinced I am unsuited to marriage."

"Why?"

The question had lost nothing of its force in being repeated. Lenore took refuge in remoteness. "That, I fear, is none of your business."

"I'm afraid, my dear, that I disagree." Jason heard his

voice gaining in strength, in merciless incisiveness. "In the circumstances, I feel I deserve more than inclination as an excuse. We're both intelligent adults. Despite your aloofness from it, you understand our world as well as I."

Temper, belatedly, came to Lenore's rescue, lending her the strength to defy him. How *dared* he insist she accede to a loveless marriage simply because it was the way of the world? Her green gaze hardened, gold glints appearing in the clear depths. Her lips firmed into a stubborn line. "Permit me to inform you, Your Grace, that you are undoubtedly the most conceited, arrogant, *overbearing* male it has ever been my misfortune to meet." The combination of panic and fury was distinctly unsettling yet Lenore knew no other emotion would serve her now. Imperiously, she rose to her feet, drawing herself up, daring, even now, to meet his silver gaze. "I do not wish to marry. That, for most gentlemen, would be reason enough. Regardless of your thoughts upon the matter, I do not need to explain myself to you."

Jason shifted, his shoulders coming away from the back of the seat, his ankles uncrossing.

Abruptly, Lenore's fury deserted her. Eyes wide, she dropped her defiant stance, taking a rapid step back, panic well to the fore. Her gaze was still locked with his. Nothing she saw in the silver-grey encouraged any belief that she had won her point. With a desperate effort, she dragged in enough breath to say, "If you'll excuse me, Your Grace, I've many important tasks to which I must attend."

Snatching up her basket, she ignominiously fled.

Exasperated, his own eyes narrowed with annoyance, Jason let her go, scowling at the gap in the hedges through which she disappeared. He was, he hoped, too wise to press her now. She could have a few hours to think things through, to tame her wilful ways and acknowledge the appropriateness of his offer. If she didn't, he would do it for her.

To his eyes, the matter was plain. There was, he was now sure, no rational motive behind her wish to remain unwed. Instead, it appeared that his bride-to-be had been allowed to go her independent way for too long. Independence was all very well but in a woman, in their world, there were limits. She had reached them and now looked set on overstepping them. She needed a strong hand to guide her back to acceptable paths. And, as her father and brothers had proved too weak to carry out that charge, it clearly fell to him to accomplish the task.

Abruptly standing, his expression hard and unyielding, Jason stalked back towards the house.

If he was going to dance to society's tune, it would damned well be with Lenore Lester in his arms.

CHAPTER FIVE

No one, Lenore was determined, would know that anything was amiss. She entered the drawing-room that evening, a serene smile on her lips, her calm and gracious façade firmly in place. Beneath that mask, dread anticipation walked her nerves. A quick glance about the room confirmed the signal of her senses: Eversleigh was not there. A flicker of relief fed a hope that, perhaps, he had already taken his leave. Lenore squashed the thought. Eversleigh had not accepted her refusal. He would come at her again, nothing was more certain.

Laughing and chatting with the guests occupied no more than half her mind. The rest was a seething cauldron, feeding her tensions, tying her stomach in knots. In the end it was almost a relief to see him enter, just ahead of Smithers. His eyes scanned the room, fixing on her. Lenore stopped breathing. Calmly, he crossed the room, pausing by her side, elegantly offering his arm with a bland, "Miss Lester."

With a cool nod, Lenore placed her hand on his sleeve, subduing by main force the tremor in her fingers. She kept her head high but her lids lowered, unwilling to risk his gaze. As they started for the door, she glanced briefly at his face. No expression lightened his harsh features; the granite planes of cheek and brow gave no hint of any emotion. Nevertheless, that single glance assured her that His Grace of Eversleigh was dangerously intent.

A shiver of apprehension ran through her. She suppressed it, steeling herself for the ordeal she was sure dinner would prove to be.

Beside her, Jason felt the tremor that ran through her. Consciously he tightened his grip on his temper, tried further than it had been in years by the woman gliding elegantly by his side. Despite her peculiar gowns, this evening's a creation in dun-coloured silk, she possessed the power to sway his senses simply by walking beside him. His inclination was to engage her in the most pointedly difficult conversation of her life. He resisted the temptation, knowing she was on edge. His forbearance, entirely out of character, amazed him but he shied away from examining his motives. Time enough for that once he had got her agreement to wed.

Throughout the first course, Lenore was both subdued and unusually nervous as she waited for the axe to fall. Eversleigh, seated on her right, was too large a figure to ignore. But when, in the general conversation, he allowed a comment on marriage to pass untouched, she risked a puzzled glance at him. His eyes met hers. His face was still impassive; Lenore inwardly quaked. Then he asked her a question. Hesitantly, aware of the ears about them, she forced herself to answer. Before she knew what was happening, they were having a conversation of sorts, he asking innocuous questions, she responding. The exchange was stilted, Lenore could not conquer her trepidation, but, to the company at large, all appeared normal.

Lenore led the way from the drawing-room, grateful for the respite even if it was temporary. Eversleigh, for whatever reason, had held off throughout dinner. She held no illusions that he would allow the entire evening to lapse without speaking to her again. Luckily, the consensus had called for a repeat of the dancing held earlier in the week. Thanks to Eversleigh, she would be too busy to spare more than a dance for him. And she had her own plans for surviving that ordeal.

The gentlemen wasted no time over their port. They joined the ladies just as the musicians started up. As Lenore had foreseen, she was promptly solicited for the first dance, this time by Lord Percy.

"Must congratulate you, Miss Lester," his lordship stated, barely able to turn his chin past his collars and the folds of his enormous cravat. "This week's been a great success. A formidable success, yes, indeed!"

Lenore murmured an acknowledgement, her senses focused on Eversleigh. He had entered at the rear of the gentlemen, accompanying Harry. As Harry moved away to claim a partner, Eversleigh paused by the side of the room, scanning the dancers.

Abruptly, Lenore gave her attention to her partner, plastering a bright smile on her lips. "Did you enjoy the folly, my lord?"

"Oh, yes!" gushed Lord Percy. "Such dramatic views. Do you paint landscapes, Miss Lester? Very partial to a sensitive landscape, y'know."

"I'm afraid watercolours are not my forte, my lord."

"But you *sing*, Miss Lester. I was quite moved by your piece with Eversleigh t'other night. Utterly captivating, y'know. I was really much affected."

Lord Percy moved on to describe other duets he had been privileged to hear. Lenore allowed him to ramble on, an attentive expression on her face, her mind elsewhere.

To her surprise, Jack claimed her for the next dance, a country reel which, Lenore recalled, he himself had taught her.

"Well, Lennie? How goes things, m'dear? Everything as calm and peaceful as I told you it would be?"

Lenore returned his smile. "I'll admit that there've been no real difficulties, but I would not go so far as to credit either Harry or you with having made any contribution to my peace."

Jack waved his hand airily. "You mean Tuesday evening. A miscalculation, my dear. Eversleigh set me straight."

"Eversleigh?"

"Mmm. Devilish knowing, is Eversleigh. Well, he was right." A wave indicated the crowd about them. "Had better sport today than we've had all week."

Understanding that the activity her brother was referring to had nothing to do with competitive games, Lenore was not clear on the connection to Eversleigh but decided to leave well enough alone. "Do you see much of Eversleigh in town?"

"Some." Jack twirled her about. "Top of the trees, is His Grace. Spars with the Gentleman himself, is a darling of Manton's, an out-and-outer of the highest degree."

"Oh?"

"Gracious, Lennie. You may hide in the country but you ain't blind, m'dear. You've been sitting next to the man for five days."

"Well, yes," Lenore admitted. "But such things are not entirely obvious, you know." Nevertheless, her memory promptly conjured up the sensation of Eversleigh's arm about her when they had waltzed, of the strength of the muscles beneath his sleeve. She had noticed, certainly, but, used to the vigorous males of her family, she had found nothing remarkable in the fact. Eversleigh was simply slightly taller, his shoulders slightly broader, his chest slightly wider, his muscles slightly harder, his strength that much more compelling.

"But it's not just that, you know." Jack seemed to have taken a notion to widen her knowledge. "Eversleigh's got something of a reputation—not just over women, although there's that, of course. Well—" Jack gestured as they turned with the music. "He's a past master there. But he's a lot more powerful than that. Has connections all over, involved in all sorts of schemes and he's as rich as Croesus to boot." He paused to cast an affectionate glance her way. "He doesn't have to call on his sister to pay his debts."

Lenore returned his smile. "Does he have a sister?"

Jack shook his head. "Nor brother either, not now. Ricky, his younger brother, was killed at Waterloo." He shot her a glance. "Wouldn't mention it if I was you."

"Of course not."

"Anyway, that's the reason he has to marry. Wouldn't mention that to him, either."

"I can assure you that marriage is the very last topic I would mention to His Grace."

"Good. Mind you, it'll be like the passing of an era— Montgomery marrying. He's been a...well, an idol of sorts to us all."

"He's not that much older than you."

Jack shrugged. "A few years. But it's all that experience, you know." He slanted her a rakish grin. "Dashed if I know how he's fitted it all in."

Lenore let that pass as the dance separated them. When she joined hands with Jack again, he was deep in cogitation.

"All in train for Friday night, then? No problems looming on the horizon?"

The vision of Eversleigh, somewhere in the crowd

about them, waiting to pounce, came forcibly to Lenore's mind. But any thoughts of seeking her brothers' or father's aid in dismissing Eversleigh had died with Jack's eulogy. Eversleigh was exactly the sort of gentleman her family would wish her to wed. And no one in all of Christendom would understand her refusal of his suit. He was wealthy, powerful and devastatingly handsome. They would think she had run mad.

"Everything's organised. The whole neighbourhood's accepted, so there'll be quite a crush."

"Excellent." Jack whirled her to a stop, bowing elegantly before her. He winked as he straightened, raising her from her curtsy. "And now I'll leave you to your own devices, m'dear. As the effective host, I'm much in demand."

Laughing, Lenore waved him away, but his words rang in her ears. Her own devices. She would have to deal with Eversleigh herself, quickly and decisively.

The opportunity to do so materialised almost instantly. The strains of a waltz drifted over the heads of the dancers. Lord Farningham appeared out of the crowd. Seeing the question in his eyes, Lenore inwardly sighed and smiled encouragingly. He had almost reached her when hard fingers curled possessively about her elbow.

"Our dance, I believe, Miss Lester."

Lenore cast one glance up at Eversleigh's hard face and knew it would be pointless to argue. Besides, this meeting between them had to come. The relative privacy of a waltz, surrounded by other guests, was a safe venue. Summoning an apologetic smile, she held out her hand to Lord Farningham. "I had forgot. Perhaps the next waltz, my lord?"

"Yes, of course." Blushing slightly, Lord Farningham bowed.

Without further speech, Eversleigh led her to the floor, drawing her into his arms as if she was already his. Determined to remain in control, Lenore ignored it, locking her mind against the sensations teasing her senses. "I'm glad to have this opportunity to speak with you, Your Grace, for there is something I wish to say."

"Oh?" Jason looked down at her, his expression forbidding. "What is that?"

Fixing her gaze on the space beyond his right shoulder, Lenore shut her ears to his warning and produced her rehearsed speech. "I am, as I said, sincerely honoured by your proposal. I think, however, that you have not yet accepted my refusal. I wish to make plain to you that my decision in this matter is unalterable, irrevocable. In short, there is nothing you could say or do that would convince me to marry. I would like to point out that this aversion of mine is not personal in nature. I simply do not feel inclined to marriage and, as you must be aware, there is no reason at all for me to wed."

"You are wrong, Miss Lester."

The strength in those words shook Lenore. She blinked, then recovered to ask haughtily, "Which part of my reasoning is at fault, Your Grace?"

"*All* of it."

The conviction in his tone brought Lenore's eyes to his. A will infinitely stronger than hers blazed in the grey depths.

"For a start," Jason said, his accents clipped and definite, "you're not honoured by my proposal in the least, you're scared of it. You know damn well I've not accepted your refusal. There are more reasons than you know why we should wed. And as to there being nothing on this earth that could change your mind, don't tempt me, Miss Lester."

The threat was clear but Lenore was past caring. With a toss of her head she transferred her gaze into space. "I've given you my answer with as much reason as I can, Your Grace. If you chose to ignore it, that is none of my affair. However, I'm sure you can understand that I do not wish to discuss the matter further."

Lenore felt the arm about her tighten, drawing her closer to his hard frame. Valiantly, she disregarded the hammering of her heart, keeping her head high and her expression untroubled.

"I'm very much afraid, Miss Lester, that I'm not as easily persuaded as other men. You have had your say; now it's my turn."

His hand was burning her back through the thick silk of her gown. But Lenore managed to infuse her features with an air of supreme indifference as she countered, her voice steady, her gaze tinged with boredom, "And *I'm* very much afraid, Your Grace, that if you mention the word 'marriage', or any of its synonyms, I—shall—scream." The last three words were delivered with emphasis; Lenore allowed her mask to momentarily slip to reinforce them with a glare. Then, smoothly, she looked away, confident he would not call her bluff in the crowded drawing-room.

A long silence followed her threat. When Jason broke it, his voice was even, perfectly controlled. "Very well, Miss Lester. I shall have to use other means to demonstrate your errors. However, do remember this was your idea."

Apprehension flooded Lenore.

"Perhaps I should start with the fantasies I have of your hair, loose and flowing in waves about you? Of course, in my dreams, you wear nothing else. Your hair is like silk, is it not? I dream of running my fingers through it, draping it over your charms."

Lenore's eyes flew wide. A blush rose to her cheeks. She did not dare look at him.

His face calm and impassive, Jason drew her still closer, so that his thighs brushed hers with every step. "And then there's your eyes. Lucent pools of green, like the hazy green in the summer distance. I dream of how they'll glow when I make love to you, Lenore, of how they'll darken with passion…"

Lenore tried to shut her ears but nothing kept out the tenor of his voice, reverberating through her body. Despite all her efforts, her mind heard his words, his slow, sensual descriptions of her body, of how he would make love to her. His arm about her waist kept her upright, effortlessly whirling her through the turns, the sensation of his thighs against hers emphasising his words.

Inwardly Lenore burned, anger at his strategy melting in the fire his words evoked. Her skin was alive, nerves flickering with anticipation. A self she did not know stretched and purred, luxuriating in the shocking glow of his visions. And still the descriptions rolled on, his voice dropping to a deep caress as explicit as his fantasies.

It was the longest waltz Lenore had ever danced.

When it came to an end and he released her, she felt like sinking to the floor but pride kept her knees functioning. She forced herself to draw breath and turn to him, extending her hand. With a superhuman effort she kept her face as impassive as his. "Thank you, Your Grace, for a most informative dance. I'm sure you'll understand if I decline any further invitations."

With the slightest of curtsies, Lenore headed straight for the tea-trolley, making a timely entrance under

Smithers's direction. Her hands shook as she dispensed
the cups. Twice she had to stop and drag in a calming
breath. Once the chore was completed, she cast a quick
glance about. Her father and Harriet were in their servants' care; she had no wish to approach any member
of her family in case they sensed her agitation. Amelia
would have been a reassuring refuge, but, when she located her cousin's fair curls, she saw Frederick Marshall
beside her.

Determined not to give Eversleigh the satisfaction of
seeing her run under fire, Lenore settled on Mrs. Whitticombe, joining that lady's circle and remaining there
for the rest of the evening.

From the opposite side of the room, Jason watched
her, his face impassive, a frown in his eyes.

"Miss Lester is in the library, Your Grace. Tucked away
in the old wing, it is."

"Thank you, Moggs." Jason did not turn from the view
beyond his chamber windows yet his mind was not filled
with the shifting green of the canopies nor the rolling
hills in the distance. As it had been for the past forty-
eight hours, his mind was consumed with thoughts of
Lenore Lester.

Moggs, his valet, moved quietly about the room, as
self-effacing as ever. Moggs was a creature of silence,
capable of so merging with the background that most
overlooked his existence. His ability to garner the most
surprising information had stood his master in good
stead. Jason had frequently used his talents when in pursuit of the numerous mistresses who littered his past. He
had, however, felt reluctant to set Moggs on Lenore's
trail. But his prospective bride had left him no choice.

It was Friday, the last day of the house party. The afternoon sun was already slanting across the treetops. If he did not gain Lenore's agreement today, certain difficulties would arise. Returning to town without a firm understanding did not appeal, any more than did facing the matchmaking mamas and his aunts with their favourites in tow. But to stay at Lester Hall and continue his strange wooing would mean taking at least Jack into his confidence. That, he was reluctant to do, not least for fear that familial pressure might be brought to bear on Lenore. He was no coxcomb but it was impossible not to acknowledge how society viewed the position of his duchess. And while he had castigated Lenore's family as having been less than effective in their duty towards her, he did not imagine they were fools. They would urge Lenore to accept; he was not prepared to wager on the outcome.

The day before, Thursday, had tried his temper to the limit. He rarely felt moved by the emotion but Lenore prodded it effortlessly. Despite his extensive experience, she had succeeded in avoiding him throughout the long day. He had spent the hours in a fruitless endeavour to come up with her, learning in the process that Lester Hall was extremely large, its grounds more so. He had stumbled on numerous couples in his wanderings, Frederick and Lady Wallace included. That discovery had made him pause, but only for a moment. It was Lenore he wished to find, but he had not found her.

She had entered the drawing-room, serene as ever, and had remained coolly aloof throughout dinner. Hampered by the eyes about them, knowing no one had yet seen anything odd in his attentions to his hostess, he had yielded to the promptings of caution and kept a rein on his tongue. But his plans for her evening had been dashed. When he returned to the drawing-room with the rest of the gentlemen it was to find she had flown. She had pleaded a headache and left her cousin to tend the teacups.

That had been the last straw. He had spent the evening here, in his chamber, examining the reasons for his overwhelming desire to marry her and her alone. They were sound. Aside from satisfying all his needs, he was convinced that marriage to him would be, very definitely, in her best interests too. He had carefully studied the matter from every angle. There was a cloud over her future which she was refusing to see. The idea of leaving her to her fate as an unwed spinster in a household run by her brother's wife was not one he viewed with any favour. What joy would she have then, stripped of the position she presently held, no longer the driving force in the family, the central cog about which they all turned? He was determined to make her face that fact. And allow him to rescue her from her fate.

He had told her she was wasted outside marriage—he had meant every word. She was born to rule a large household, just as he had been born to head a large family. She had the makings of a matriarch, a strength to match his own. And while he was not proud of his behaviour on the dance-floor, the exercise had confirmed his rake's assessment that she was as attracted to him as he was to her. If he had come to Lester Hall with her seduction in mind, he had no doubt he would have attained his goal by now.

Slowly, Jason stood and stretched his long limbs, conscious of the tension rippling beneath his control, determined, today, to keep it suppressed. Her very vulnerability on that front, the quivering response of her slender frame every time he touched her, rendered any further approach by that route ineligible. Not until they were wed. Desire was all very well but it was no acceptable reason for marriage.

She was in the library, alone. He intended to talk with her frankly, show her what her future held in unequivocal terms. She was, first and last, an intelligent woman.

Settling his cuffs, Jason headed for the door and the library in the old wing.

When he reached the library the door was ajar. Quietly, he entered and saw her, standing by the open window, her arms wrapped about her, deep in thought. He considered the door, deciding to close it, the latch making no sound as he eased it home. Then, silently, he crossed the room, pausing before the desk beyond which she stood.

It was pleasant inside the library, the stone flags warmed by the sunshine. She had discarded her pinafore; it lay neatly folded on a nearby chair. A fine silk blouse moulded to her curves; the embroidered waistband of her brown velvet skirt encircled her tiny waist while the skirts fell in soft folds to the floor. Jason studied her face. Her expression was pensive, her fingers picking restlessly at the material of her sleeves. It occurred to him that she was an inherently calm woman—and he had seriously disrupted her peace. An urge to close the space between them and wrap her in his arms, to assure her that he had no thought beyond ensuring her future free of care, rose up, so strong he had to close his eyes to will away the impulse. Opening them, he shifted, as restless as she. The ring on his right hand struck the desk.

Lenore turned with a gasp, her eyes widening as they confirmed the belated warning of her senses. Instinctively, she moved to place the desk between them, struggling to summon her habitual mask to conceal her recent thoughts. They, alone, had left her weak. "Are you interested in a book to pass the time, Your Grace?" To her relief, her voice was steady.

Jason studied her, then shook his head. "I'm interested in you, Lenore. You and nothing else." Slowly, he moved to come around the desk.

Instantly, Lenore drifted in the opposite direction. "My lord, your pursuit of me is senseless." Ignoring the erratic beating of her heart and the dizzying acceleration of her pulse, she glanced at the door. It was too far away. Her fingertips tracing the edge of the desk, she rounded the end, her eyes lifting to his face. The calm implacability she saw there sent a *frisson* of apprehension through her. "There must be countless women who would welcome the chance to be the next Duchess of Eversleigh."

"Scores." Jason advanced without pause.

"Then why pick me?" Lenore threw the comment over her shoulder as she hastened past the front of the desk.

"For a host of excellent reasons," Jason ground out. "Which I'm perfectly willing to share with you, if only you'll stand still! For God's sake, Lenore! *Stop!*"

Passing the back of the desk for the second time, Lenore did, swinging to face him. In a single lithe movement, Jason vaulted the desk, landing in front of her. With a stifled shriek, Lenore put up her hands to push him away. Jason caught them in his, taking a single step to swing her back against the desk. Deliberately, he placed her hands, palms flat, on the desk behind her, trapping them under his, leaving her leaning backward while he leaned over her.

It had been his firm intention to discuss the reasons for their marriage with his infuriating bride-to-be, calmly, logically. Instead, as he looked down at her, all logic went winging from his head.

Lenore stared up at the stern face above hers, coherent thought suspended. Her senses were in turmoil. Bare minutes before she had been deep in dangerous dreams, demonstrating to her rational mind just why Eversleigh was such a threat to her. Now that threat had materialised, in the flesh. A frightening anticipation streaked through her. Eyes wide, she shivered.

The silk of her blouse rose and fell with every agitated breath she took.

The sight held Jason transfixed. He had been fighting his inclination for days—he had no reserves left to fight hers as well. Slowly, almost dreading what he would see, he lifted his gaze. To the slim column of her throat, and the pulse that beat wildly at its base. To her full lips, parted slightly. To her eyes, wide, peridot-green, filled with a potent blend of virginal hesitancy and raw desire.

Lenore sensed the struggle he waged but was powerless to help. The tension in the muscles of the arms brushing hers, in his thighs where they pressed hard against hers, told a clear tale. Held by a fascination older than time, she could do nothing to aid her own release. In that instant she did not know if she wished to escape. Instead, she watched, mesmerised, as the eyes holding hers changed from grey to silver, then to a shade that shimmered.

With a strangled groan Jason gave up the unequal fight. And lowered his lips to hers.

It was not a gentle kiss, but in her innocence, Lenore didn't care, held in thrall by the turbulent passion behind it. Her wits, already half seduced by her own dangerous imaginings, were swept away by the reality. Untutored, she sought to appease the hard demand of his lips, her lips instinctively softening, then parting under his.

Any vague idea Jason had possessed of a single, short, salutory kiss—to appease his demons and to demonstrate unequivocally the unwisdom of her looking at him with desire in her eyes—disappeared, drowned beneath the tide of passion her unexpected invitation evoked. He took instant advantage, slanting his lips over hers, confidently taking possession of her soft mouth with a slow, plundering relentlessness that shook him as much as it shook her.

Lenore shuddered, her senses reeling. She felt his hands leave hers, his arms lifting to enclose her, drawing her against him. His strength surrounded her, seducing her more completely than his kiss. Free, her hands lifted, hovering uncertainly before settling on his shoulders. She felt the muscles beneath his coat shift restlessly at her touch. Immediately she splayed her fingers, gripping hard, amazed and then enthralled by the response she drew forth, the tension that wound suddenly tighter, tautening the muscles of his large frame. Hesitantly, she kissed him back, thrilled to feel his soaring response, startled to find a similar reaction coursing her veins.

The sensation was addictive. Her senses, so long reliably content, revelled in the magic they wove. Like pagans, they swirled to the rhythm and demanded more. Wantonly she leaned into his embrace, delighting when his arms tightened, crushing her breasts against the hard wall of his chest. Cast into a realm beyond reality, Lenore had no defence against the power that engulfed her, no reason to fight the tide. Instead, blinded to the tenets of wisdom, her upbringing and society's mores, she followed where her senses led, freely responding, meeting every demand he made of her and wanting more.

Which was considerably more encouragement than Jason's frayed control could resist. He shifted his hold, one hand dropping to the small of her back, drawing her hips against his. Lenore shivered in his arms, her body

pressing against his in flagrant invitation. The last ves-
tiges of Jason's once vaunted control cindered. He felt
her fingers tangle in the soft hair at his nape. Slowly, he
eased her back, bringing one hand up to cup her breast.

Shivery pleasure cascaded down Lenore's spine; heat
swelled her breasts. She responded immediately, her
kisses more urgent, her mind, her body eager to experience more. Infuriatingly slow and patient, Jason's long
fingers caressed her, drawing forth a gamut of sensations she had never felt before. As her nipples tightened
to painful little buds, Lenore felt a curious heat unfurl
deep inside. Entranced, she made no demur when Jason's
fingers slid down the row of pearly buttons closing her
blouse. It felt deliciously right when he brushed aside the
fine material, searching for the ribbons of her chemise.
A gentle tug and the bows were undone. If she had not
been kissing him, she would have caught her breath. As
it was, she felt her senses slide over some invisible precipice as her silk chemise slithered to her waist. The cool
caress of the air on her naked breasts was dispelled by
his fiery touch.

Desire streaked through Lenore. She gasped and broke
free of their kiss. Her head fell back, her lids fell as pure
sensation raced along her nerves. Time and place were
no more—her whole being was alive in a world of sen-
suous pleasure. As Jason leaned nearer, she shifted her
hands from his shoulders to thread her fingers through
his rich chestnut hair, fascinated by the silky texture and
the thick, tumbling locks.

Jason drew a ragged breath, struggling to retrieve his
will from the web she had lured it into. But her allure was
too strong for even him to break. He could no more stop
breathing than deny his fingers the right to caress the
creamy mounds bared to his sight. The feel of her satiny

skin seared his fingertips, burning itself into his memories. She was even more beautiful than he had imagined, her breasts a perfect fit for his large hands, their peaks pink crests, puckered with passion. Passion he had aroused. The realisation shook him, but her soft murmur as his fingers gently teased, knowingly tantalised, was like a siren's song, dispelling reservations, dispelling all thought. Even as he lowered his head, part of him marveled at that fact.

Trapped in a world of sensual delight, Lenore revelled in all she could feel. His subtle caresses sent her senses spinning. Then his hands left her; one tactile sensation was replaced with another. She gasped, then whimpered with desire as his lips caressed her, his tongue gently rasping one tightly budded nipple. Lenore's fingers tightened convulsively, tangling in his hair as wave after wave of desire crashed through her.

As she felt her bones melt under the onslaught, she was conscious of only one thought. She didn't want him to stop.

Enthralled in desire, neither heard the approaching footsteps nor the click as the latch lifted.

"Here we are! The library. Knew it had to be somewhere. Plenty of books—" Lord Percy came to an abrupt halt as his gaze came to rest, goggling, on the pair behind the desk.

At Lord Percy's first word, Jason disengaged, pulling Lenore to him, crushing her protectively against his chest. As he took in the stunned looks on the faces of the three ladies crowding behind Lord Percy—Mrs. Whitticombe, her daughter and Lady Henslaw—he knew that nothing would erase the image they must have beheld as the door had swung open.

Prevented from seeing what had befallen, her cheek

pressed against Eversleigh's coat, his heart thundering in her ear, Lenore struggled to recall her wits from the deep haze still engulfing them.

To everyone's surprise, it was Lord Percy who rescued them all. Abruptly turning, he threw out his arms, flapping to usher the ladies out. "Go and see the succession houses. I'm told they're very fine."

Without a single backward glance, he herded the ladies into the corridor and firmly shut the door.

The sound of the latch dropping home, a cold clang, jolted Lenore back to reality. Slowly, she eased herself from Eversleigh's embrace, aware of a sense of loss as she left its comfort. She steeled herself against it, dragging in breath after breath. Her mind raced, picking up the threads, trying to weave them into a cohesive picture as her fingers automatically fumbled with the buttons of her blouse. Suddenly, she felt very cold.

Wrapping her arms about her, she stepped back, blinking as she fought to regain her composure. Slowly, she brought her head up to stare at Eversleigh's face. The angular planes seemed softer, but she couldn't be sure. He was breathing rapidly. She saw him blink, as if he, too, was as affected as she. But that couldn't be so.

"You tricked me." She made the statement coldly, a deliberate indictment.

Jason blinked again, a frown gathering. Collecting his wits was proving a strain. Not only did he have to shackle his desire, now rampant, and assimilate the shock of their discovery, together with its attendant ramifications, but he had yet to succeed in convincing himself that what had occurred was real. Too much of it seemed like a dream. Never before had any woman undermined his control as Lenore had so effortlessly done. Dazed, he scrambled to catch up with her thoughts.

Unaware of his difficulties, Lenore drifted around the desk, pacing back and forth before it, her features hardening, her entire body stiffening as all that had occurred crystallised in her brain. "I wouldn't agree to marry you, so you arranged *this*!" Her voice gained in force. *"This farce!"* Gesturing dramatically, she flung a glance loaded with scorn at the man standing still and silent behind the desk. "When I would not agree willingly, you sought to trap me into marriage. Tell me, Your Grace," she asked with awful disdain, contempt filling her eyes, "did Lord Percy make his entrance too soon? How far were you prepared to go in compromising my honour to gain your ends?" To her horror, her voice broke as a damning self-pity rose beneath her fury.

Abruptly, Lenore swung to face her nemesis over the desk. Head high, she looked him straight in the eye. "You, Your Grace, are undoubtedly the most *despicable* rogue it has ever been my misfortune to meet! Regardless of *what* might transpire, regardless of what whispers and scandal you call down upon me, I will *not* marry you!"

Her denunciation ended on a high, quavering note.

Her fury was nothing to his. With a superhuman effort, Jason forced himself to stand, silent, expressionless, and let her words hit him. His face felt like marble—cold and hard.

When he said nothing, made no attempt to defend himself against her wild accusations, Lenore's composure crumbled. Catching her breath on a hysterical sob, she turned blindly for the door and fled, her heart twisting painfully with every step.

In a feat bordering on the miraculous, Jason succeeded in forcing himself to remain still and silent behind the desk. Inside, his rage, a cold and deadly flame, seared him. As the danger peaked, every muscle in his body clenching in the effort to contain the explosive emotion, he forced himself to recall that Lenore had been upset, hysterical, not in command of herself.

The rationalisation did not ease the sting of her words. Gradually, the danger passed, leaving mere anger in its wake. Even so, Jason refused to give in to the impulse to go after her; he had sufficient knowledge of his own temperament to know that if he found her, her dignity would not survive intact. Instead, dragging in a deep breath, he focused his mind on what needed to be done, first to remove the threat to her reputation, secondly to secure her hand in marriage.

For one fact was now written in stone. Lenore Lester was his. He would not leave Lester Hall without her promise to marry him.

Not after that kiss.

His eyes grey coals, his expression like stone, His Grace of Eversleigh stalked from the room.

CHAPTER SIX

AT FIVE-THIRTY, despite the dull throbbing in her temples and the sickening disillusion that had her in its grip, Lenore entered the drawing-room prepared to greet her father's guests. In honour of the ball, she had allowed her maid to dress her hair high, with large soft curls falling in drifts about her ears and throat. Her lustring sack of magenta silk glowed richly, cream lace filling in the expanse from its square neckline to the base of her throat, her long sleeves fashioned from the same material. She hoped the gown would underline her status; tonight she had every intention of courting the title of ape-leader.

Jack was waiting for her, strikingly handsome in a dark blue coat over ivory inexpressibles. He winked at her. "Ready to greet the hordes?"

"Hardly hordes," Lenore replied absent-mindedly. "If you recall, we agreed to invite only six couples to join us for dinner. The rest won't arrive until eight."

Jack threw her a sharp look, then offered, "Took a gander at the ballroom. Doing us proud, Lennie."

Taking his arm, Lenore summoned a smile. Leading him towards the main doors where they would take up their stance, she tried to deflect the concern she saw in his blue eyes. It was prompted, she knew, by the harried expression she was only just managing to conceal. "I'm sure everything will turn out splendidly, just as long as you and Harry toe the line. The staff have worked like slaves and the guests have thrown themselves into the spirit of things with abandon. There's been such demand for the crimping tongs, the maids are well nigh dead on their feet."

Jack laughed. To Lenore's relief, he said no more.

A bare two hours had elapsed since her dramatic meeting with Eversleigh; she had yet to regain her calm. She had fled the library to immediately fall victim to her hostessly chores. Mrs. Hobbs had caught her in the front hall. After she had given her blessing to the substitution of pheasant pie for the roasted grouse, Smithers had come up, wanting her opinion on the positioning of the heavy épergné in the centre of the table. Next, it had been Harris with a request for guidance in the matter of how many footmen should be stationed in the supper-room. A succession of similar questions and difficulties had kept her from the sanctuary of her room, from giving way to temper and tears in equal measure.

Whenever she thought of what had happened, her emotions threatened to overwhelm her. Knowing she could not afford to be distracted, not tonight, with so many eyes to see, she pushed the jumble of outrage, guilt and hurt betrayal to the back of her mind. With a smile firmly in place, her serenity to the fore, she stood beside her brother and prepared to greet their neighbours.

As the first of the house guests drifted into the room, chatting easily, Lenore heard the clang of the front door-bell. She turned to Jack. "Papa isn't down yet."

Jack grimaced. "Doubt that he'll show, not till later." When Lenore gazed at him, bewildered, he said, "Never one for doing the pretty, you know that."

Lenore sighed. Retrieving her smile, she turned as Smithers announced Major and Mrs. Holthorpe. Their other neighbours arrived in good time, the ladies making the most of this opportunity to brush shoulders with their London sisters and catch up on both fashion and the latest *on-dits*. Conversation buzzed, punctuated by gay laughter. When the time to announce dinner was at hand and her father had yet to appear, Lenore cast a questioning glance at Harriet. Her aunt shrugged. Wondering if perhaps her father had been taken ill, Lenore started for the door.

She had cleared the crush of the guests and was but a few yards from the double doors when they swung inwards, propelled by two footmen. Her father entered, Harris pushing his chair. Beside it walked Eversleigh.

Lenore froze, presentiment dropping like a cold cloak about her shoulders.

"Friends!" Archibald Lester, wreathed in smiles, waved a lordly hand at his guests. He saw Lenore, too distant for her face to be properly in focus, and his smile grew brighter still. As the guests, as a body, turned to face him, he continued, his old voice carrying easily over the last shreds of dying conversations. "It's a pleasure to welcome you to Lester Hall. Doubly so for I've an announcement to make!"

Jason, standing alongside, his gaze fixed unwaveringly on Lenore, stiffened. He turned to Archibald Lester, only to hear his host declaim, "I have today given my blessing to a union between my daughter, Lenore, and Jason Montgomery, Duke of Eversleigh."

A buzz of excited comment rolled through the room. Archibald Lester beamed with pride and gratification.

All expression leaching from her face, Lenore stood as if turned to stone.

Two strides brought Jason to her side. His face lit by a charming smile, his eyes filled with concern, he caught her icy fingers in his and smoothly raised them to his lips. "Don't faint." He searched her large eyes, wide and empty, for a glimmer of consciousness.

The warmth of his lips on her fingers tugged Lenore back to reality. Dazed and utterly undone, she blinked up at him. "I never faint," she murmured, her mind completely overwhelmed.

Jason bit his lip and glanced over her head; they had mere seconds before the hordes descended. "Smile, Lenore." His voice held the unmistakable if muted tones of command. "You are *not* going to break down and embarrass yourself and your family."

Vaguely, Lenore's eyes rose to his, slowly focusing as his words sank in. He was right. Whatever he had done, however hurt she might feel, now was no time for hysterics.

To Jason's relief she straightened slightly, a little of her rigidity falling away. A smile, a travesty of her usual calm confidence, appeared on her lips. But panic shadowed her eyes.

"You can weather this, Lenore. Trust me." His whispered words were loaded with reassurance. Placing her hand on his sleeve and covering it with his, he turned her to meet their well-wishers. "I won't leave you."

He didn't. Strangely, it seemed to Lenore that his support was the only thing that kept her functioning throughout that interminable evening. She should have been too furious to accept his help, to trust him, yet she knew instinctively that he would not fail her. It seemed the most natural thing in the world to lean on his strength.

Luckily, Amelia reached her first, throwing her arms about her and hugging her with joy. As her cousin disengaged, casting a puzzled glance at her weak smile, Lenore dragged and bullied and goaded her wits into action, forcing her features to her bidding. The muscles of her face relaxed into a gay if brittle smile. She got no chance to thank Amelia, nor to respond to her, "Good luck!" as the other guests pressed forward, none wishing to appear backward in congratulating the next Duchess of Eversleigh. She responded as best she could to their felicitations, thankful for Eversleigh's presence, a solid prop to sanity by her side. He kept his fingers entwined with hers, imparting calm strength even as his ready tongue deflected the more ribald comments.

Dinner was delayed. When Smithers eventually interrupted the chorus, Eversleigh drew her free of the throng, leading her in advance of them all as was his right. As usual, he sat beside her, an unnerving but unshakeable protection against any untoward questions. But by that time Lenore had herself in hand. Clamping an iron lid over the turmoil within allowed her to respond to both conversation and organisational queries with something approaching her usual calm grace. As long as she did not allow herself to think of what had occurred, she could cope.

Her father had ordered champagne to be served. As she took an invigorating sip of the bubbly liquid, Lenore caught Eversleigh's eye. To the casual observer his expression was exactly what one would expect—gratified, proud, confident in his triumph. As she studied the concern, the real worry etched in the grey eyes, Lenore wondered if only she could see past his mask. Allowing her lids to fall, she glanced away. Seconds later, she was startled to feel the gentle touch of his fingers on hers, then shocked when her fingers automatically returned the brief caress.

Firmly resettling the iron lid over her treacherous emotions, Lenore threw herself into the conversation.

They rose from the table just before eight, the gentlemen escorting the ladies into the huge ballroom. With long windows and high ceiling, it filled the entire ground floor of one wing. "Oohs" and "aahs" came from all sides as the guests took in the massed spring blooms and the first of the summer roses, tumbling in profusion from every available site. Draped in garlands from the musicians gallery, looped around every pillar, frothing from vases and urns, the flowers scented the warm air and lifted spirits to new heights.

The receiving line was a trial Lenore could have done without. Even though the rest of their neighbours were prompt, there was time enough in between arrivals for her seething emotions to slip loose. One minute she felt like murdering the man beside her, the next, when the touch of his fingers on hers eased her away from disaster, her heart swelled, with reluctant gratitude for his unwavering support, and with something else that she dared not name.

With every passing minute, the turmoil of her thoughts, the tangle of her emotions, intensified. And all she could do was smile and nod and allow her father, in his chair beside her, to introduce Eversleigh as her betrothed.

In her confusion, she did not hear the musicians start up. It was Eversleigh who drew her attention to the fact, smiling down at her father as he settled her hand on his sleeve. "I suspect we should open the ball, sir, if you'll release your daughter to me."

"She's all yours, m'boy." Archibald Lester beamed and waved them to the floor.

Reflecting that her father was definitely to be classed with old dogs—beyond changing—Lenore allowed herself to be led to the edge of the huge area of polished parquetry revealed as the guests drew back.

Smoothly, Jason drew her into his arms, feeling the effortless glide as she matched her steps to his. They waltzed as if they were made for each other, their bodies, his so large, hers slender and tall, natural complements in line and grace.

Lenore let the bright colours of the ladies' gowns whirl into an unfocused blur as they precessed, revolution after smooth revolution, down the long room.

"Your ball has all the hallmarks of success, my dear."

Allowing her gaze to shift to his face, Lenore studied his expression before remarking, her own expression calmly serene, "Particularly after my father's little announcement."

Jason's lips momentarily firmed into a line before he forced them to relax back into a smile. "An unfortunate misunderstanding." He held her gaze, his own steady and intent. "We must talk, Lenore, but not here. Not now."

"Certainly not now," Lenore agreed, feeling her control waver. A misunderstanding? Was it not as she had thought? Abruptly, she looked away, over his shoulder, relieved to see others taking to the floor in their wake.

"Later, then. But talk we must. Don't try to escape me this time." Jason saw her slight nod and was content. Prey to a host of conflicting emotions, the only one he felt sure of was anger. Anger that his wooing of her had gone so disastrously wrong. Anger that such a simple task as offering for a wife had somehow laid siege to his life. But he knew what needed to be done, to reassure her, to smooth away the confused hurt that lingered in her large eyes.

But fate had decreed he would get no chance that night. By the time the last carriage had rolled down the drive and the last of the houseguests had struggled wearily upstairs, his betrothed was dead on her feet. From the foot of the stairs, he watched as, turning from the main doors, she suffered a hug from each of her eldest brothers and a smacking kiss from Gerald. Lenore received their approbations with a smile that struggled to lift the corners of her lips.

"G'night."

Jason nodded as Harry, stifling a yawn, passed on his way upstairs. With a sleepy smile, Gerald followed.

With Lenore on his arm, Jack approached. "Time for a game before you leave us tomorrow, o, prospective brother-in-law?"

Jason held Jack's gaze for an instant, then inclined his head. "I'll catch up with you in the morning."

"Right-ho! Sleep well." With a rakish salute, Jack left, making no demur when Lenore lingered.

Absent-mindedly, Lenore rubbed a hand across her brow, trying to ease the ache behind. "Now, Your Grace. Perhaps the library—"

"No. You're exhausted. There's nothing that needs saying that won't survive the night."

Numbly, Lenore blinked up at him. "But I thought you said—"

"Go to bed, Lenore. I'll see you tomorrow. Time enough then to sort matters out." When she continued to look blankly at him, Jason reached for her elbow. Gently but purposefully, he urged her up the stairs.

In the end, Lenore went readily, too tired and too grateful to argue further.

She said not a word as they traversed the long corridors. In the dim light, Jason studied her face. She looked so fatigued, so unutterably fragile, now she had laid aside her social mask. When they reached her door, he set it ajar. Taking her hand in his, he raised it to his lips, brushing a gentle kiss across her fingertips. "Sleep, Lenore. And don't worry. We'll talk tomorrow." With a wry smile, he bowed her over the threshold.

She entered, then paused, casting a puzzled glance back at him. Slowly, she closed the door.

"You'd best be stirring, Miss Lenore. 'Tis past eleven."

Groaning, Lenore burrowed her face deeper into her soft pillow, hiding from the light that rushed in as her maid, Gladys, thrust the bedcurtains aside.

Gladys, a motherly soul, eyed her charge shrewdly. "And there's a note here from that duke."

"Eversleigh?" Lenore turned her head so rapidly her cap fell off. "Where?"

With a knowing nod, Gladys handed over a folded sheet of parchment. "Said you were to have it once you were awake."

Ignoring her cap, Lenore took the note, settling back on her pillows, the folded parchment between her hands as Gladys bustled about the room, shaking out Lenore's evening gown, exclaiming at the way it had been carelessly tossed on a chair.

Lenore eyed the inscription on the front of the note. "Miss Lester" stared back at her in bold black letters.

Despite her conviction that she would fall instantly asleep the moment her head touched the pillow, rest had been a long time coming. As soon as she had settled in the dark, safe and secure in her feather bed, the cauldron of her emotions, simmering all evening, had boiled over. For a while she had let them seethe, shedding frustrated, fearful tears, drawing comfort from the release. Then she had tried to decide where she stood.

One point was clear. The rage that had overpowered

her in the library had been misplaced. Recalling her accusations, she squirmed. Eversleigh had deserved none
of them. She would have to apologise, an act that would
further weaken her position in the necessary negotiations
for her release from their unexpected betrothal.

That was as far as she had got in her musings, despite
another hour or two's fruitless cogitation. Eversleigh's
real concern and care for her, not just that evening, but
demonstrated in so many ways now she looked back on
their short association, undermined the image she had
tried to erect of him, the ruthless tyrant perfectly ready
to ride roughshod over her feelings. She had no firm
idea of what had transpired between His Grace and her
father—until she had the facts in her hands, she would be
wise to reserve judgement. And, despite all the shocking
revelations of the day before, she still did not know *why*
His Grace of Eversleigh was so set on marrying her.

All of which left her in a very uncertain state.

Lenore grimaced, then unfolded the note.

"I'll wait for you in the library," was all he had written.

Her lips twisting in self-mockery, Lenore laid the note
aside, along with a childish wish to remain safely in bed,
pretending the day before had been nothing more than
a bad dream. Downstairs and all about the house, the
guests would be preparing to leave. She should be present, lending her aid in a thousand different ways. Today,
however, she felt not the slightest qualm in leaving her
brothers to their own resources. Her staff were well-
trained; her presence was not essential.

With a deep sigh, Lenore sat up. "No," she said, shaking her head at the grey gown Gladys held up. "There's
a primrose muslin in there somewhere. See if you can
find it—I believe its time has come."

The muslin proved to be more gold than yellow, its scooped neckline perfectly decent although the soft material draped about Lenore's slim figure in a way far removed from her stiff cambrics and pinafores. Harriet had ordered it up from London two years before in a vain attempt to interest Lenore in fashion. Staring at her reflection, Lenore decided it would do. She had coiled her braided hair about her head; to her eyes, her slender neck, now fully revealed, was too long.

Giving herself no time to change her mind, and her gown, she descended to the library.

He did not hear her enter. Seated in the chair before her desk, he had the text she had been studying, a history of the Assyrians, in his hand. Afflicted by a sudden breathlessness, Lenore paused, seizing the rare moment to study him. The planes of his face seemed less angular, his expression less forbidding. There was still a great deal of strength, in his face, in the long body relaxed in the chair, but, to her, now, the impact was more reassuring than threatening, more desirable than dangerous. Slowly, Lenore drew nearer, conscious of her deep fascination. A lingering shadow of the delight she had felt when last in this room touched her.

Jason heard her and turned. His gaze met hers, keenly perceptive, searching for signs of her mood. "Good morning, my dear."

Carefully gliding past the desk, Lenore nodded. "Your Grace."

For a moment, realisation of what she was wearing held Jason still. Then, shutting the book and laying it aside, he stood.

"I must apologise, Your Grace, for my outburst yesterday." Lenore hurried into the speech, desperate to clear that particular hurdle. Rather than take the seat behind the desk, she stopped beside the window, her gaze on the garden, holding herself erect, head high as she recalled her embarrassing behaviour. "I realise my accusations were unfounded and entirely out of order." She inclined her head in Eversleigh's direction, too tense to look directly at him. "I pray you will excuse me."

"I believe you were somewhat overwhelmed at the time," came the smooth reply.

Lenore looked around to find he had come to stand on the other side of the window, negligently propping one shoulder against the frame, his grey eyes oddly gentle as they studied her.

The blush that rose to her cheeks was another irritation. Biting her tongue on the unwise retort that her mind had instantly supplied, she forced her voice to an even tone to say, "At the time, I was not thinking with my customary clarity."

Jason's lips curved. "Granted." His voice retained its even, reassuring tone as he added, "Apropos of that event, you'll be relieved to know that neither Lord Percy nor any of the three ladies can recall anything of it. In fact," he mused, "it's doubtful that they recall having been anywhere near this room."

Lenore blinked. She returned his unwavering scrutiny for a full minute before remarking, "One of the benefits of being born to the purple?"

Jason's smile reached his eyes. "One of the *few* benefits of being born to rule."

A puzzled frown settled over Lenore's brows. "But why?" she eventually asked, curiosity overcoming reserve. "Surely their…interruption strengthened your hand?"

She glanced up to meet a stern, not to say forbidding, frown.

"My dear Lenore, if you imagine I'd allow any breath of scandal to touch my future wife's name—worse, would permit the slightest suggestion that I offered for her to rectify some slight to her honour—you are greatly mistaken."

She had to have imagined it, for he had not altered his stance, yet Lenore was certain he had somehow grown larger, taller, infinitely more intimidating. She felt her eyes grow round. "Oh."

"However," Jason said, letting his sudden tension seep away. He looked down, examining the signet on his right hand. "If we are on the subject of apologies, you have my very humblest, Lenore, for the shock you were subjected to last night. It was not my intention that any announcement be made. I had merely asked your father for permission to pay my address to you in form." He looked up as he spoke, capturing her eyes with his, willing her to understand. "I think, somehow, he misunderstood."

The sincerity in his tone, in the grey of his eyes, the look which was, she suspected, as close to beseeching as he would ever get, shook Lenore. Breathless all over again, she swung her gaze away, out of the window, to the weeping cherry gracing the lawn. "He does that, I'm afraid. He hears only the words he wishes to hear and disregards the rest."

That was the truth. Her father was the worst sort of manipulator—had been for years. But it was the revelation that Eversleigh had not sought to conspire with her sire behind her back that shook Lenore to her very soul. Unfortunately, having her reading of his character thus confirmed did not make the task before her any easier. Drawing a determined breath, she hurried on. "However, even though we might agree that neither of us is to blame for the predicament we now find ourselves in, there is still that very predicament to be faced."

"Which predicament is that?"

Lenore turned to face him only to find his expression improbably bland. Her eyes narrowed. "To all intents and purposes, Your Grace, we are betrothed. Everyone who attended last night believes that to be so."

Jason merely nodded, watching her closely.

Her worries flooding back, Lenore drew herself up, pressing her hands tightly together, crushing the front of her skirt. "My lord, I would ask you to release me from this…this unforeseen contract."

Jason's stern expression returned; Lenore's heart quavered.

"That, my dear, would be very difficult to do."

"But you *could* do it—we could say we were mistaken."

Jason's winged brows rose. "But I'm not mistaken." Lenore allowed her exasperation at that arrogant statement to show. Jason disregarded it, straightening away from the window-frame. "Even if I were prepared to allow you to waste your life here—"

"I am *not* wasting my life!"

"With old civilisations?" A contemptuous wave indicated her desk. "You have a life to live, Lenore. You must live it in the present, not the past."

"I have plenty to occupy my present, Your Grace."

"Jason. And if you're referring to your position as chatelaine of Lester Hall," Jason said, advancing to stand in front of her, "how long do you think that will last once Jack weds?"

Her face told him all. Lenore stared up at him, her expression utterly blank. "Jack…" She blinked, struggling to bring the idea more firmly into focus.

"It comes to us all." The statement held more than a hint of irony. When Lenore remained silent, Jason added more gently. "You cannot expect to remain in your position of eminence here, my dear."

It was a major effort to wrench her mind about to view her life from a different perspective, but, once she had done so, Lenore felt utterly defeated. She had concentrated for so long on getting her present established as she wished, she had overlooked the future. And her brothers, of course, had never encouraged anyone to think of their marrying.

"If you'll consider the matter, my dear, I think you'll see that marriage to me will assure you of the position, the status, you deserve."

Jason studied her face, then continued, his words softly seductive. "I need you far more than the Lesters, Lenore." A little staggered by how truthful he was being, he quickly added, "Besides the Abbey, which, God knows, is large enough to house a brigade and frequently does, there's the London houses, as well as minor estates in Leicestershire, Northumberland and Cornwall."

Her gaze abstracted, a frown tangling her brows, Lenore shifted restlessly, casting a troubled glance up at him. "I can understand why your aunts wish you to wed, Your Grace."

"Jason." Jason paused, then carefully played his trump card. "Besides, you wouldn't want to destroy your father's peace of mind." Instantly, he knew he had struck true. Lenore looked up, her expression revealing her suspicions. Relentlessly, Jason pressed his advantage home, his eyes, deadly serious, holding hers. "My offer lifted a great weight from his shoulders. He has worried about you, and your future, for years. From what he let fall, our betrothal will greatly ease your aunt's mind, too. Apparently, she's felt responsible for your state, imagining herself to have failed in imbuing you with suitable sentiments."

"No!" Lenore was appalled. Vehemently, she shook her head. "I decided what I wanted to do. It was no fault of theirs."

"That may be so, but you cannot deny their concern for your welfare."

"But…" Raising a hand to brush back a wisp of hair, Lenore felt the web of her situation closing about her. Distractedly she looked up, into the calm of Eversleigh's eyes.

Moved by an emotion she was not at all pleased to have to acknowledge, invoked by the helpless look in her eyes, Jason, with the greatest reluctance, chanced his all on one last throw. "My dear, if you can give me one sane, rational reason why we should not wed, I'll do what I can to dissolve our betrothal."

Lenore's mind jumped at the offer, even if her emotions lagged behind. Her eyes brightened, only to dim as the truth of her position sank in. She stared up into his eyes, confirming that the offer was indeed genuine, that he was giving her an opportunity to save her heart.

She couldn't take it.

No lady or gentleman of her class would consider her fear of being hurt, of giving and receiving nothing in return, her very fear of loving, to be a sane and rational reason, not in any circumstances. And how could she dash her father's joy? For she had seen it clearly, had not needed Eversleigh to tell her how proud and relieved her parent had been. There was, as she had feared in the dark of last night, no escape.

Swallowing, Lenore allowed the past to slip away, jettisoning her image of her future and, knowing there was no alternative, she allowed his image to fill the void. Dropping her gaze, she stared at her linked hands. "I have no reason to advance, Your Grace."

She missed the sudden easing of tension in Jason's shoulders as he let out the breath he had been holding. "Jason," he corrected softly. Her reluctance, he knew, stemmed from some peculiar female fear. He would lay it to rest—once she was his.

Lenore looked up, then, slowly, inclined her head, letting her lashes fall. "Jason."

For a moment, all was still. No sound broke the silence bar the cooing of doves from beneath the window and the shrill call of starlings in the cherry tree. Lenore felt the odd tension that held them. Nervous of where it might lead, she shook her shoulders and straightened, raising her head to look out of the window once more. "Given that it seems we are to wed, Your Grace—Jason," she amended, "I would like to know what you expect of me—precisely why you have determined that I am to be the next Duchess of Eversleigh."

Jason frowned. "I'm certain you'll fulfil the demands of that role admirably, my dear."

"Be that as it may, I should like to know precisely what duties you believe that role to encompass." Lenore kept her gaze on the cherry tree, knowing without looking that he was wearing his forbidding expression.

Jason eyed her profile. He did not like her question but relief at her acceptance of his suit prompted him to answer. Having considered the matter so frequently in recent days, his reasons for marriage were crystal-clear in his mind. He omitted his first stipulation. After their interlude of the previous afternoon, he needed no further confirmation of her state. Only a virgin could have responded so...so... Abruptly, he hauled his mind away from that track. "As a wife, I need a woman of breeding who can act as my hostess, someone with the requisite talents and experience to run a large household and to officiate at both formal and large family gatherings." Jason forced himself to step back, leaning against the window-frame, folding his arms against temptation. "I do not need a giddy miss, more intent on her own enjoyment than solicitous of her guests' welfare. You, on the other hand, have impeccable credentials in that area."

Lenore inclined her head. "What sort of entertainments do you generally hold at the Abbey?"

Jason told her, watching her reactions, elaborating freely when he saw she was inclined to interest. After outlining the huge family gatherings held at Christmas and occasionally in summer, and the numerous estate and country events held in the house or grounds, he described the Abbey in more detail, the number of guest-chambers and reception-rooms, the current levels of staffing, as far as he remembered them. Lenore asked questions, which he answered as best he could, eventually admitting, "The Abbey has been without a chatelaine for more than ten years. You'll find much that needs your attention."

Lenore eyed him straightly. "And I'll have a free hand in all household matters?"

A charming smile answered her. "I'll leave all such affairs in your capable hands. My steward, Hemmings, and my secretary, Compton, will assist you as you desire. The management of estate business, however, will remain in my hands."

Graciously, Lenore inclined her head. "I have no wish to interfere in such areas. Tell me, do you have any schemes for assisting your labourers, your tenants and their families?"

Jason shook his head. "As I said, you'll find much to

keep you occupied. Without a lady of the house to over-see such enterprises, they tend to be put aside."

"But I'd have your support to institute such measures as I felt were justified?"

"Provided they met with my approval."

Lenore studied him, then decided the caveat was acceptable. Nodding, she broached the subject on which she expected less success. "Will you expect me to spend much time in London?"

Despite her even tone, Jason detected her unease. He remembered their discussion in the maze; she did not expect to enjoy life in London. The fact should have cemented his triumph. Instead, to his surprise, he heard himself say, "I usually spend all of the Season and the Little Season in town. While I would not wish you to remain at Eversleigh House if I was not in residence, I'd urge you to experience life in the capital before you turn your back on it." He saw her eyes cloud and hastened to add, "However, if, after you've tried them, you find the balls and parties not to your taste, I'll raise no demur to your remaining principally at the Abbey, provided you agree to journey to London should I require your presence." He made the concession with reluctance, hoping very much that she would find sufficient interest in the hurly-burly of *ton*-ish entertainments to keep her by his side.

His offer was a great deal more than Lenore had expected. "So—I'm to be your hostess, and take responsibility for the management of your houses. And if I find London unamusing, I may retire to the country." All in all, the position was not without attraction. For one of her skills, the challenge of rejuvenating Eversleigh Abbey was a potent lure.

Jason nodded. "There is, of course, the matter of the succession."

Lenore switched her gaze away from his, suddenly finding the cherry tree utterly captivating. "I comprehend that you require an heir, Your Grace."

"Jason. And it's *heirs*." Lenore shot him a nervous glance. "Plural," Jason added, just to set the matter straight. "As things stand, if I were to die without issue, the title and all my estates would devolve to a distant cousin. The main line has certainly been sufficiently fecund but, unfortunately, the majority of children have been female. I'm the only duke since the first to have had a brother. At present, the next male in line is many times removed and has had no training in either estate management, in the involved politics of a large and wealthy family nor, I'm sad to say, even in how to comport himself with sufficient dignity to carry the role." He paused, sensing that she was listening intently despite her refusal to look at him. "Consequently, I'm keen to ensure the title remains with my branch of the family."

Not knowing what else to do, Lenore nodded. "I understand." Her voice sounded strained, the relief of moments before clouded by realisation of the other side of the coin. She held severe reservations over her ability to deal with Eversleigh on a personal level without falling in love with him. Yesterday had been an eye-opening experience on more than one front. But she had no choice but to take a chance—to risk falling victim to the vulnerability that afflicted her sex. She would try very hard to keep her distance, but...

"And those are the reasons which prompt you to marry me?" The question was out before she could stop it. Lenore bit her lip and waited.

Jason hesitated, then, his lips firming against an un-nerving impulse to say more, he nodded. "Yes."

What had she expected? Lenore suppressed the small, sharp pang of disappointment that twisted through her. At least he had dealt openly with her; now she knew where she stood.

Clearing her throat, she focused her mind on more concrete problems. "Do you have any strong preference for when we should wed, Your—Jason?"

Greatly relieved to hear that question on her lips, Jason answered without reservation. "As soon as possible, which means in four weeks."

"Four weeks!" Lenore deserted the cherry tree to round on him. "We can't possibly be married in four weeks."

One winged brow rose. "Why not?"

Aghast, Lenore stared at him. She had imagined she would have months to come to terms with her new situation. Four weeks was not nearly long enough to strengthen her defences. "Because…because…" Abruptly, she took refuge in anger. "Because you *cannot* simply decide such matters and expect me to meekly agree."

Jason frowned. "'Meek' is not a word I would use in conjunction with your fair self, my dear. If you would come down out of the boughs for long enough to examine my circumstances, you would see why any delay is to be avoided."

Puzzled, Lenore looked her question.

Rapidly, Jason formulated an answer, rejecting out of hand any idea of telling her the truth. "As you know, the notion that I intend to wed is currently circulating among the *ton*. If I return to London without our immi-nent wedding as protection, I'm likely to be mobbed by matchmaking mamas, seeking to convince me to change my mind and marry their witless daughters instead."

The vision of hordes of matrons, plumes aquiver, lying in wait to pound on him made Lenore's lips twitch. Jason saw it and pounced on her instead.

"It's no laughing matter, I assure you. I was hounded for years when I was younger; you wouldn't believe some of the stratagems the harpies employed."

Lenore arched one brow sceptically. "Why am I so convinced you would survive even their latest manoeuvres unscathed?"

Jason threw her a warning look. "Anyway, at our respective ages, no one will think marrying in four weeks the least odd."

Lenore had her doubts but held her tongue. If marrying Eversleigh was to be her fate, and as he was so set on it, she might as well face it in four weeks as four months. Perhaps, with less time, she would not get so nervous over those duties she had not before performed.

"Your father has agreed," Jason continued, watching her more carefully. "We'll be married in Salisbury Cathedral. One of my father's cousins is the present bishop— my family have a long association with the bishopric. Jack and I will handle the arrangements. Harry and Gerald will travel with your aunt and father to Salisbury."

Struck dumb, Lenore simply stared.

After an instant's hesitation, Jason embarked on his plans for her. "We assumed you'd wish to use the time to refurbish your wardrobe. Jack has agreed to stay back until Tuesday. He'll escort you to town then. As your aunt cannot act as chaperon, my aunt, Lady Agatha Colebatch, will perform that duty. I believe you're acquainted with her?"

Stunned, overwhelmed, Lenore nodded. "She's one of Aunt Harriet's oldest friends."

"Good. I don't think she's in town at present. It may take me a day or two to track her down. She'll know which modiste to take you to. As I've persuaded your father to allow me to foot the bill, you may order what you please."

Lenore blinked. "But...but that's not..."

Jason waved one hand dismissively. "Your father and Jack have agreed."

Beyond amazed, Lenore stared up at him. "Tell me, do you always organise people's lives for them?"

Cool superiority met her gaze. "When they need organising and I wish to achieve some goal, yes." Jason watched as she swallowed that piece of arrogance, hoping he had distracted her sufficiently from the question of who was financially responsible for her trousseau. He had had to argue long and hard to wring that concession from the Lester men; only their inability to give him an assurance that Lenore would not appear in London in pinafores had forced them to accede to his odd request.

Unconvinced that he was not engaged in some sleight of hand but unable to see any motive beyond his obvious wish to get their marriage over and done with, an unsurprising reaction given that he had been driven to the altar as it were, Lenore sighed. Slanting him a glance from beneath her lashes, she saw he was waiting for some sign of her capitulation. Inwardly grimacing, she raised her head. "As we have agreed to marry, and as you clearly wish it so, I'll agree to marry you in four weeks, Your Grace."

Jason flashed her a brilliant smile. Lenore felt a slight blush rise to her cheeks. Seeing it, Jason's smile deepened. He straightened and moved closer.

Abruptly, Lenore decided that four weeks were four weeks; she should take advantage of what time was left to her. "And now, if you'll excuse me, Your Grace, I have many tasks awaiting my attention." She bobbed a slight curtsy, rising as he took her hand. He raised it to his lips; she steeled herself to feel his kiss on her fingertips. It came, a tantalisingly light caress. Immediately overpowered by a shaft of pure desire, as, turning her hand, he pressed a far more intimate kiss into her palm.

Lenore's knees shook. She drew herself up, saying the first words that came to her tongue. "I sincerely hope, Your Grace, that you will not regret choosing me as your bride."

Jason's grey gaze sharpened. "Regret? Never, Lenore."

The reverberations of his vow echoed within her as, with a slight nod, Lenore turned and walked to the door.

Jason stood and watched her go, shackling the urge to call her back to reassure her that *she* would never regret marrying *him*.

CHAPTER SEVEN

TUESDAY DAWNED and, as His Grace of Eversleigh had decreed, Lenore, with Jack lounging beside her, headed for London in the Lester carriage. Eversleigh himself had taken his leave of her after luncheon on Saturday; he had promised to meet her at Lady Agatha Colebatch's house in Green Street.

Amelia had left Lester Hall the previous day, also bound for London. Her cousin had been bubbling with plans; Lenore hoped that Frederick Marshall brought her the happiness she deserved. Amelia had been as stunned as she at the news of her betrothal but, unlike herself, had seen nothing to quibble about. Instead, Amelia had enacted the part of rapturous joy for her, praising Eversleigh to such an extent that Lenore had been forced to avoid her for some hours, in case her sharp tongue punctuated the balloon of Amelia's illusions.

She herself had spent the hours since Eversleigh's departure in a state of unaccustomed inertia. While marriage to Eversleigh had seemed a most concrete proposition when he had been standing beside her, once he had gone she had considerable difficulty believing in her fate. In control of her life for so long, she felt adrift, rudderless. Even slightly lost.

With a determined effort, Lenore shifted her gaze to take in the streets of London. They had entered the capital some time before; Green Street could not be far off.

Noise had been her first impression of the seat of the fashionable, an unending cacophony of calls and cries of vendors and street urchins, stridently vying against the constant rumble of carriage-wheels on the cobbles and the brisk clop of hooves. The lilting music of buskers threaded a magical note through the din. Beyond the carriage window, people bustled past on the pavements, hurrying home as twilight approached. In less than the distance of a field, she was sure she had seen more people than she had in her entire life before. Eventually the meaner dwellings gave way to neat brick houses, crammed cheek-by-jowl along the busy road. Then these, too, fell behind, replaced first by larger town houses, handsome with their brightly lit windows, and then by mansions set back from the road.

Their trip had been uneventful, beyond confirming Eversleigh's insight into her family's affairs. Out of the blue, Jack had asked for her help, once she was established as Eversleigh's duchess, in the matter of finding him a bride.

"The old man's been looking so much better since receiving Eversleigh's offer for you, I'll end feeling guilty if I don't." When she had looked her puzzlement, he had explained, "You've been one of his concerns; I've been the other. Now Eversleigh's bitten the bullet, I suppose I should think about getting leg-shackled. Put the *pater*'s mind at rest, y'know."

Leaning her head against the squabs, Lenore quelled a resigned sigh. She was, however reluctantly, going forward into the only life open to her. It was up to her to make of it what she could. Swaying as the carriage lumbered around a corner into a quiet street lined with tall town houses, she allowed herself to wonder, fleetingly, just how much might be possible if she put her heart into her marriage.

The carriage slowed, then rocked to a halt before an elegant town house, two rows of handsome windows visible above the pavement with dormers set in under the roof. As Lenore looked out, the doors were thrown wide. Light spilled forth, illuminating the shallow steps.

Jack descended first, then handed her from the coach. Within minutes, they were being ushered into the drawing-room by her ladyship's intimidating butler.

"Lenore, dear child! Welcome to London." Pushing aside the small buhl table on which she had been idly playing cards, Lady Agatha rose majestically, her haughty features relaxing in sincere welcome.

Lenore glided forward, intending to curtsy before her hostess, but Agatha would have none of it, catching her hands and drawing her into a scented embrace. "Nonsense, my dear. We need not stand on ceremony, you and I." Her gimlet gaze fastened on Jack, watching his sister's reception with an indulgent smile. He caught her ladyship's eye and immediately made his bow.

"I have to thank you, Lester, for bringing your sister to me. Eversleigh said to make his apologies—he had to visit the Abbey on urgent business, something to do with the settlements. Your sister and I will be spending the evening very quietly; Lenore needs to look her best tomorrow. Dare say you'd prefer to dine at your club?"

Hiding a grin at this masterly dismissal, Jack inclined his head. "Indeed, yes, ma'am, if all's well here?"

Lady Agatha nodded imperiously. "You may be content that it is." She held out a hand, watching critically as Jack bowed over it. "You may look in on your sister some time, but I warn you, we'll be busy tomorrow."

Jack nodded. With a brotherly wink for Lenore, he departed.

As the door closed behind him, Agatha waved Lenore to sit beside her on the chaise. "Hope you don't mind, my dear, but men, brothers especially, are devilish in the way sometimes."

Entirely in the dark, Lenore found herself nodding.

Agatha was studying Lenore's gown, a frown in her obsidian eyes. "By the by," she said absent-mindedly. "Eversleigh also intends to drop in on Henry on the way back from the Abbey, just to make sure all's well."

Lenore looked blank. Agatha noticed and explained. "My cousin, the Bishop of Salisbury. He'll be officiating, of course." Relinquishing Lenore's old-fashioned travelling dress to view the far more attractive future, her ladyship sighed. "It'll be the event of the year, of course. We haven't had an Eversleigh wedding for an age, quite literally. The entire town will turn out, mark my words."

Struggling to view the event with something of her hostess's enthusiasm, Lenore felt her confidence waver. But her ladyship was full of revelations. Swivelling to face Lenore, she said, "Can't tell you how pleased we all are, my sisters and I, that you agreed to take Eversleigh on. Didn't think you would, quite frankly."

Faced with the candid query in her ladyship's dark eyes, Lenore blushed slightly as she struggled to find words to explain how her betrothal had come about. "I'm afraid matters became rather tangled. As it transpired, I didn't have a great deal of choice in the matter."

She stopped, halted by her ladyship's disgusted snort.

"Great heavens, Lenore! This really won't do. Don't tell me *you*, of all women, have allowed my arrogant nephew to ride roughshod over you *already*?" Incredulity infused her ladyship's patrician features with an almost comic quality.

Lenore bit her lip and tried to explain. "It wasn't so much that—he did not force me to agree. But it seemed, the way things had fallen out, that there really was no alternative."

With a dramatic gesture, Lady Agatha fell back against the cushions. "Don't tell me—I see it all. I hesitate to disillusion you, my dear, but that's precisely why Eversleigh is so peculiarly successful in getting his own way. Things always fall out so that *his* way seems the *only* way. It's a most trying habit. We're all counting on you to break him of it."

Somewhat startled, Lenore quickly disclaimed. "I greatly fear, Lady Agatha, that I'm unlikely to wield sufficient influence with His Grace to effect any such transformation."

"Nonsense!" Lady Agatha viewed her sternly but not unkindly. "And you may call me Agatha. Eversleigh does, except when he's being difficult. But as for your not being in a position to influence Eversleigh, my dear, I rather suspect you have not entirely comprehended the position you will fill."

"We have discussed the matter," Lenore began diffidently. "Within the bounds of my duties, I see little prospect for a…a closer interaction of the sort needed to…to—"

"*Just* as I suspected!" Agatha reclined more comfortably and prepared to set her charge straight. "Regardless of whatever…" she waved a hand airily "*functional* duties my nephew consented to discuss, you may be sure he did not choose you as his duchess, above all others, purely on the basis of your ability to carry out said duties. Jason may be a pragmatist when it comes to matrimony, but I'm convinced he would never offer for a woman he could not deal with on a personal level."

"I believe we will deal very well together, Lenore..." Eversleigh's words echoed in Lenore's mind. Was this what he had meant?

"By personal," Lady Agatha continued, "I do not mean the sort of association a gentleman may form with, for instance, one of the fashionable impures. That, I need hardly tell you, is something quite different." She waved the indelicate subject aside. "No. The sort of relationship a man like Eversleigh will expect to share with his wife is one based on mutual respect and trust. If that is there, and I for one am sure it must be, then you need not fear, my dear. Eversleigh will listen to your arguments, your opinions. If, that is, you choose to tell him."

The prospect her ladyship's words conjured up held Lenore silent.

"That, of course, is why we hoped you'd accept his suit. Jason needs a duchess with character, and the ability to make herself heard, to act as a balancing force. To make him more human, if you take my meaning."

Lenore was not entirely sure that she did, but the opening of the door brought a halt to her ladyship's discourse.

"Yes, Higgson?" Lady Agatha waited while her butler ponderously bowed.

"You wished to be reminded that dinner would be served early, my lady," Higgson stated, his voice as heavy as his movements. "Miss Lester's maid is waiting in her room."

"Thank you, Higgson." Agatha turned to Lenore. "Eversleigh mentioned that your maid at Lester Hall would not be accompanying you to town and suggested I find a suitable girl. Trencher is my sister Attlebridge's dresser's niece. I'm sure she'll know the ropes. But if she's not to your liking, you have only to say and we'll find another."

Lenore blinked. "Thank you. I'm sure she'll prove suitable." Inwardly, she wondered how far Eversleigh's organisational powers extended.

But, ten minutes later, having been sent upstairs with orders to rest and recuperate before dinner, Lenore found herself thankful her fiancé had had the forethought to solicit his aunt's assistance. Trencher was a treasure. Of about Lenore's age, she was small and deft in her movements, severely garbed in dark brown as befitted her station, her pale face intent under a neat cap. She had unpacked Lenore's trunk, laying her brushes out upon the polished surface of the elegant dressing-table and had ordered a hot bath.

"I hope you'll excuse the liberty, miss, but I thought as how you'd be bone-jarred, having travelled all day."

Lenore sighed and smiled her approval. She was, in fact, feeling distinctly jolted, but was uncertain as to how much of the effect could be ascribed to her father's well-sprung coach.

After a soothing soak, Trencher urged her to lie down on the luxuriously soft bed. "I'll be sure to wake you in plenty of time to get dressed for dinner."

Perfectly certain Trencher would not fail her, Lenore surrendered to what was, for her, a most unusual luxury. It was not, she told herself, as she climbed up on to the feather mattress, that she was tired. Rather, she could use a period of quiet reflection the better to analyse Agatha's view of her marriage. Despite these intentions, she fell deeply asleep the instant her head touched the pillow.

When Trencher woke her an hour later, her maid had no comment to offer on her outmoded gowns. Lenore had packed only the most acceptable and had left her pinafores and her spectacles behind. Her days of concealment, she felt quite sure, were past. Viewing her reflection in the long cheval glass, she grimaced.

Trencher noticed. "It'll only be for tonight, miss. Her ladyship said as how Lafarge'd be sure to be able to make something up straight away for a customer like you. And there's no company tonight, just you and her ladyship, so you've no need to blush."

After blinking several times, Lenore decided not to reveal her ignorance by questioning Trencher. She reserved her questions for Agatha, waiting until they were comfortably seated about one end of the dining table, with only Higgson hovering nearby.

"Who, exactly, is Lafarge?"

"Ah! Trencher mentioned her, did she?" Agatha looked up from her soup. "Quite the most exclusive modiste in London, my dear. She's agreed to do your wardrobe, which, let me tell you, would be a boon to any lady. A positive genius with gowns of all types. We're expected at her salon at ten tomorrow."

"That's why I have to look my best?"

Recalled to her soup, Agatha nodded, adding, "The most important person you'll ever have to convince of your beauty."

Soup spoon suspended, Lenore stared. "But I'm no beauty."

Dismissively, Agatha waved the point aside. "Used the wrong word—attractiveness, style, call it what you will. That certain something that some women have that makes them stand out in a crowd. That's what Lafarge will be looking for. She's agreed to consider taking you on as a client, but she could change her mind."

Appalled, Lenore considered this unexpected hurdle.

She had rather thought that, as the customer, she would choose her supplier. Obviously, in the case of fashionable modistes, this was not the case.

"Don't concern yourself over the matter," Agatha said, pushing her plate away. "No reason she won't see something interesting in you."

Lenore had no answer to that.

"I'd thought to take this opportunity to fill you in about Eversleigh and the family. Once it's known you're here, we'll be inundated with invitations—unlikely we'll get much chance of quiet nights."

Lenore noted the satisfied glint in her ladyship's dark eyes. Her hostess was clearly looking forward to being the cynosure of all attention.

"I take it you're aware of Ricky's death?"

Lenore frowned. "Eversleigh's brother?" When Agatha nodded, she said, "Jack told me he was killed at Waterloo."

"Hougoumont," Agatha supplied. "Gloriously tragic. Typical of Ricky, really."

When her hostess did not immediately continue, Lenore hesitantly asked, "What I wasn't clear about was why Jack thought that was the reason Eversleigh had to wed."

"Now that," said Agatha, helping herself to a dish of mussels in white wine, "is a typical piece of Eversleigh organisation." She glanced shrewdly at Lenore before adding, "Always felt you were one young woman I did not need to beat about the bush with, so I'll tell you simply. Eversleigh never intended to marry. Something of a cold fish, Jason, not given to the warmer emotions. At least," she amended, considering her point, "that's what he thinks. Deeply cynical and all that. He and Ricky had a...a pact, so that Ricky was to be the one to marry and his son would ultimately inherit the title."

"And Waterloo dashed that plan?"

"Indeed, yes." Agatha nodded portentously. "And rather more besides." She paused pensively, then shook herself and looked at Lenore. "Jason and Ricky were very close, so Hougoumont smashed more than Jason's plans for a fancy-free future. Even I would not care to mention Hougoumont in Jason's hearing."

"I understand." Lenore stared unseeing at the slice of turbot on her plate.

"Mind you," Agatha continued, waving her fork to dispel the sudden gloom, "I'm beginning to wonder if that wasn't an example of the Almighty moving in strange ways."

Lenore looked up. "How so?"

"Well, I dare say Ricky would have made an acceptable duke—he was trained to it, as was Jason. And the family would have accepted his sons to succeed him." Pushing a mussel about on her plate, Agatha grimaced. "It's just that we would all prefer Eversleigh—that is, Jason—to be succeeded by his own son. Particularly, if *you* were there to ensure said son did not take after his father in absolutely all respects." Agatha waved her knife at Lenore. "Jason's plan was well enough, but he was always one to assume others could perform any task as well as he. But Ricky could never have been as decisive as Jason—no, nor as commanding. He simply wasn't as powerful, as unshakeably strong. And, when it comes to ruling a very large family, and very large estates, it's precisely that quality which makes all the difference."

Lenore raised her brows to indicate her interest but made no other reply. As she had hoped, Agatha rambled on, giving her a sketchy outline of the family estates together with an abbreviated history of the Montgomerys, refreshing her memory of Eversleigh's aunts and their numerous offspring. By the time Agatha waved her upstairs for an early night, Lenore's head was spinning with the effort to store all the information her hostess had let fall.

She rose early the next morning, still attuned to country hours. Trencher was there, bubbling with suppressed excitement at the thought of her mistress's visit to Lafarge's famous salon. As she allowed herself to be gowned in the gold muslin, the most acceptable dress she possessed, Lenore viewed her maid's affliction with a lenient eye, aware that no such emotion had yet touched her. Breakfast was served on a tray in her room, as was Agatha's habit. Afterwards, Lenore strolled in the small gardens behind the house, waiting for her hostess, trying to quell the trepidatious flutter of her nerves and the strange yearning for Eversleigh's large figure to appear, to lend her strength for the coming ordeal—her first crucial step into his fashionable world.

AGATHA'S CARRIAGE pulled up outside a plain door wedged between two shops on Bruton Street. Above the door hung a simple sign—"Mme Lafarge, Modiste".

Handed down from the carriage, Agatha shook out her skirts and eyed the door shrewdly. "Lafarge only makes for a select few. Hideously expensive, so I've heard."

Joining her hostess on the pavement, Lenore turned to stare. "Isn't she your dressmaker?"

"Heavens, no! I might be well-to-do but I'm not *that* rich." Agatha straightened her straight back and headed for the door. "No—Eversleigh arranged it."

Of course. Lenore's lips tightened momentarily. She

permitted herself a frown, then shrugged and followed her mentor up the steep stairs beyond the plain door.

Madame Lafarge was waiting in the large salon on the first floor. The room was elegantly furnished, gilt chairs upholstered in satin damask set in a tight circle facing outwards from the centre of the floor. Mirrors were discreetly placed around the walls, interspersed with wall hangings in a soothing shade of pale green. Madame herself proved to be a small, severely neat, black-haired Frenchwoman who stared unblinkingly at Lenore throughout the introductions.

These completed, she reached for Lenore's hand. "Walk for me, Miss Lester," she commanded in heavily accented English, drawing Lenore clear of the chairs. "To the windows and back."

Lenore blinked, but when Agatha nodded, complied, hesitantly at first, then with more confidence as she returned to where Madame waited.

"*Eh bien.* I see now what *monsieur le duc* means." Stepping close, Madame peered up into Lenore's eyes. "Yes—greens and golds, with nothing pink, white or pale blue. *M'moiselle* is twenty-four, yes?"

Dumbly, Lenore nodded.

"*Très bien.* We do not, then, need to be cramped in our choice." The little modiste's face relaxed into a smile of approval. Her eyes narrowed as she walked slowly around Lenore before nodding decisively. "A *merveille*— we will do very well, I am thinking."

Taking this to mean Madame had found that elusive something in her, Lenore felt some of her tension evaporate.

Abruptly, Madame clapped her hands. To Lenore's surprise, a young girl put her head around one of the wall hangings. A torrent of orders delivered in staccato French greeted her. With a mute nod, the girl disappeared. A bare minute later, the wall hanging was pushed aside to admit a procession of six girls, each carrying a semi-completed outfit.

Under Madame's supervision, Lenore tried on the garments. Madame fitted them expertly, extolling the virtues of each and the use to which she expected each to be put, gesticulating freely to embellish her words. The ground was littered with pins but her advice could not be faulted. Agatha sat regally on one of the chairs, actively interested in all that went on.

It was not until she was trying on the third outfit, a delicate amber morning gown, that the truth dawned on Lenore. She was unusually tall and slender yet the dresses needed only marginal adjustments. Her head came up; she stiffened.

"Be still, *m'moiselle*," hissed Madame Lafarge from behind her.

Lenore obeyed but immediately asked, "For whom were these dresses made, Madame?"

Lafarge peered around to stare up at her face. "Why—for you, Miss Lester."

Lenore returned her stare, recalling that Madame had not even bothered to take her measurements. "But... how?"

Lafarge's black eyes blinked up at her. "*Monsieur le duc* gave me an..." Her hands came up to describe her meaning. "An understanding of your comportment and your *taille*, you understand? From that, I was able to fashion these. As you see, his memory was not greatly at fault."

A shiver travelled Lenore's spine but she was unsure of the emotion behind it. Agatha had been right— Eversleigh was far too used to organising all as he wished. The idea that her wardrobe would bear the imprint of his hand, rather than hers, was far too much for her to swallow.

Parading before the glass and admiring the way the long amber skirts swirled about her, Lenore made up her mind. "I should like to see these other gowns you've made up."

Besides the three gowns she had already tried on, a green muslin walking dress, a teal carriage dress and the amber creation, Lafarge had made up three evening gowns. Trying on the first of these, Lenore felt a definite qualm. Studying her reflection, the way the fine silk clung to her body, emphasising her height, her slimness and the soft swell of her breasts, she wondered if she would ever have the courage to actually wear the gown. The neckline was cut low, barely avoiding the indecorous. Aside from the tiny puffed sleeves, her arms were entirely bare; she could already feel gooseflesh prickling her skin. The other two gowns were in similar vein.

"You wish to view the rest as well?"

Turning, Lenore stared at Lafarge. "Madame, what, exactly, has His Grace ordered?"

Lafarge spread her hands. "A wardrobe of the very finest—all the materials to be the very best as suited to your station. Dresses, gowns, coats, cloaks, nightgowns, petticoats, chemises, peignoirs." Lafarge ticked the items off on her fingers, then spread them wide. "Everything, *m'moiselle*, that you might need."

Even Agatha looked stunned.

Lenore had had enough. "Have any of these items been made up?"

Sensing that her hopes for the soon-to-be duchess were teetering on some invisible precipice, Lafarge hurriedly summoned her girls with all the items thus far created on His Grace of Eversleigh's orders.

Lenore ran her fingers over the delicate materials. As she held up a chemise, a peculiar thrill went through her. The garment was all but transparent.

Watching her client closely, Lafarge murmured, "All was created at *monsieur le duc*'s express orders, *m'moiselle.*"

Lenore believed her but did not understand. Eversleigh had ordered a wardrobe that tantalised—for her. She frowned, laying aside the chemise to pick up a peignoir with a matching nightgown. As the long folds unravelled, her breathing seized. Slowly, deliberately, she turned so that Agatha was granted a full view of the gown. "Surely this is not what other women of the *ton* wear?"

Agatha's face was a study. Not knowing whether to be scandalised or delighted, she grimaced. "Well—yes and no. But if Eversleigh's ordered them, best take 'em." When Lenore hesitated, she added, "You can argue the point with him later."

When I'm wearing them? Lenore quelled another distracting shiver.

"They are not, perhaps, what I would create for all my young ladies, but, if you will permit the liberty, *m'moiselle*, few of my young ladies could appear to advantage in these. And," Lafarge added, a little hesitantly, "*monsieur le duc* was very definite—he was very clear what he wished to see on you, *m'moiselle.*"

Lenore had gathered as much but was still unclear as to his motives. Leaving such imponderables aside, she wondered what to do. As Agatha had noted, Eversleigh's organisational habits left very little room for manoeuvre. More than half the items were at least partly made up;

Lafarge must have had her workrooms operating around the clock. Idly fingering a delicate silk chemise, Lenore made her decision. "Madame, did His Grace give permission for me to add to this collection?"

Lafarge brightened perceptibly. "But yes." She spread her hands. "Anything you wished for you were to have, provided it was in a suitable style."

The caveat did not surprise her. Lenore nodded. "Very well. In that case, I wish to double the order."

"Comment?" Lafarge's eyes grew round.

"For every article His Grace ordered, I wish to order another," Lenore explained. "In a different style, in a different colour and in a different material."

Agatha burst out laughing. "Oh, *well done*, my dear," she gasped, once she had caught her breath. "An entirely fitting reaction. I had wondered how you would manage it, but that, at least, should set him back on his heels."

"Quite," Lenore agreed, pleased to have Agatha's support. "I could hardly be so insensitive as to not appreciate his gift, but neither will I be dictated to in the matter of my own wardrobe."

"Bravo!" Clapping her hands, Agatha raised them to Lenore in salute. "Heavens! But this will take an age. Are you free, Madame?"

"I am entirely at your service, my lady." Shaking her head at the incomprehensible ways of the English, Madame summoned her assistants. Far be it from her to complain.

The following hours were filled with lists, pattern cards and fabrics. As she argued the rival merits of bronzed sarcenet over topaz silk, and cherry trim over magenta, Lenore felt some of Trencher's excitement trip her. Agatha encouraged her to air her views. In the end, Lafarge paused to say, "You 'ave natural taste, *m'moiselle*. Strive to retain it and you will never be anything but elegant."

Lenore beamed like a schoolgirl. The appellation "elegant" was precisely what she was aiming for. It seemed only fitting if she was to be Eversleigh's bride.

At last, having duplicated the long list approved by His Grace, they paused to refresh themselves with tiny cups of tea and thinly sliced cucumber sandwiches.

Suddenly, Lafarge set her cup aside. "*Tiens!* Fool that I am—I forgot the bridal gown."

She clapped her hands, issued a stream of orders and the repast was cleared. The curtains at the back of the shop parted to permit her senior assistant to enter, reverently carrying a gown of stiff ivory silk covered in tiny seed pearls.

Lenore simply stared.

"That's Georgiana's wedding gown—or part of it, if m'memory serves." Agatha looked at Lafarge.

The modiste nodded. "*Monsieur le duc*'s mama? *Mais oui*. He asked for the gown to be re-made in a modern style. It is exquisite, no?"

All Lenore could do was nod, eyes fixed on the scintillating gown. As she climbed into it, she shivered. The gown was unexpectedly heavy. Lafarge had exercised her own refined taste in its design; the high neckline with its upstanding collar and long tightly fitting sleeves met with Lenore's immediate approval. The long skirts fell from just below her breasts straight to the floor, the long line imparting a regal elegance most suitable for a ducal bride.

Once the gown had been adjusted and removed, Lafarge hesitantly brought forward a silk confection. "And this, *monsieur le duc* ordered for your wedding-night."

Resigned, Lenore shook out the shimmering folds and

held them up. Agatha stifled a chuckle. "I dare say," was all the comment offered. She handed the scandalously sheer, tantalisingly cut nightgown and matching peignoir back to Lafarge. "I expect you had better send them with the rest."

It was after two when they descended once more to the carriage. The first of the gowns, three day dresses and one evening gown ordered by Eversleigh, would be delivered that evening, along with some chemises and petticoats. As she followed Agatha into the carriage, Lenore heaved an unexpectedly satisfied sigh.

Agatha heard it and chuckled. "Not as boring as you expected, my dear?"

Lenore inclined her head. "I have to admit I was not bored in the least."

"Who knows," Agatha said, settling herself back on the seat. "You might even come to enjoy town pleasures. Within reason, of course."

"Perhaps," Lenore replied, unwilling to argue that point.

"Tell me," Agatha said. "Those gowns you ordered—not in the usual style but not in your usual style, either. Don't tell me Eversleigh has succeeded where your aunt, myself and my sisters all failed?"

A subtle smile played on Lenore's lips. "My previous style was dictated by circumstances. Situated as I was, going about the estates alone, with my brothers bringing their friends to stay, it seemed more practical to wear gowns that concealed rather than revealed, dampened rather than excited. As you know, I did not look for marriage."

Head on one side, Agatha studied her charge. "So you don't mind Eversleigh's choices?"

"I wouldn't go quite so far as *some* of the styles he favours, but..." Lenore shrugged. "I see no reason, now I'm to be wed, to hide my light under a bushel any longer."

Agatha chuckled. "And you wouldn't get any bouquets from my nephew for attempting to do so."

Lenore smiled and wondered how long it would be before Eversleigh came to see her.

HE CAUGHT UP with her the next day. On her way to convey a shank of embroidery silk left in the upstairs parlour to Agatha in the morning-room, Lenore was half-way down the stairs before she heard the rumble of Eversleigh's deep tones below. After a fractional hesitation, she continued her calm descent.

Jason turned as she gained the hall tiles, his grey gaze sweeping from her hair, neatly braided and coiled, over her modish amber morning gown with its delicate fluted chemisette, to the tips of her old-fashioned slippers peeking from beneath the dress's scalloped hem. Seeing his gaze become fixed, Lenore had no difficulty divining his thoughts. She went forward with her usual confident air, her hand outstretched. "Good morning, Your Grace. I trust I see you well?"

With a slight, questioning lift to his brows, Jason took her hand and, without preamble, raised it to his lips. "I apologise for not being here to greet you. Business took me to Dorset and thence to Salisbury, as I hope Agatha explained."

Quelling the now familiar sensation that streaked through her at his unconventional caress, Lenore retrieved her hand. "Lady Agatha has been most kind." Turning to lead him to the morning-room, she added, "You will, no doubt, be happy to know that yesterday she and I visited a certain Madame Lafarge, who is, even now, endeavouring to create a wardrobe fit for the Duchess of Eversleigh. We plan to visit the shoemakers, glovers and milliners tomorrow. Tell me, my lord, do you have any particular makers you wish to recommend?"

The airily polite question was more than enough to put Jason on his guard. "I'm sure Agatha will know who is best," he murmured.

Agatha was delighted to see him, promptly informing him of a ball to be given by her sister, Lady Attlebridge, the following evening. "Mary's agreed to use the event to puff off your engagement. A select dinner beforehand, so you'd best be here by seven. My carriage or yours?"

Jason frowned. "I've sent the main Eversleigh carriages to be refitted, so it had better be yours, I imagine."

Lenore noted his slight constraint and, after years of tripping over her brothers' secrets, wondered if he had intended the refit as a surprise for her.

"I had thought to take Miss Lester for a drive in the Park." Jason smoothly turned to Lenore. "That is, if you'd like to take the air?"

There was, in fact, little Lenore would have liked better. Buoyed by the bracing effect of Agatha's encouragement, she was determined to make a start gaining experience dealing with her husband-to-be while she still had his aunt behind her. "You're most kind, Your Grace. If you'll wait while I get my pelisse?"

Jason merely nodded, sure she would not keep his horses waiting.

Making an elegant exit from the morning-room, Lenore hurried upstairs. The day was unseasonably cool; she was eager to try out the new cherry-red pelisse delivered from Lafarage's this morning. It was an item Eversleigh had ordered; she was determined to give him no warning of her other purchases prior to Lady Attlebridge's ball. Ringing for Trencher, she tidied her hair, fastening it with extra pins given she as yet had no suitable bonnet; she refused to have it cut nor yet to wear a scarf. Shrugging into the pelisse and buttoning it up, Lenore turned this way and that before her cheval glass, admiring the soft merino wool edged with simple ribbon and trimmed at collar and cuffs with grey squirrel fur. The pastel amber of her gown did not clash with the deep cherry. Then she noticed her slippers.

Grimacing, Lenore turned to Trencher. "My brown half-boots and gloves. They'll have to do until I can get something to match. Perhaps tomorrow?"

Descending the stairs busy with the last buttons on her gloves, Lenore did not see Eversleigh at their foot.

"Commendably prompt, my dear."

Lenore looked up, straight into his grey eyes and found them warm with appreciation. She smiled but did not deceive herself that he had not noticed her gloves and boots.

"That shade of red suits you to admiration," Jason murmured as, taking her hand, he led her to the door.

Lenore bit back her impulsive rejoinder, to the effect that it was hardly surprising if his taste found favour in his eyes. Letting her lashes fall, she replied, "It's not a colour I have previously had a chance to wear. I must admit I rather favour it."

The gleam of pride in his eyes as he lifted her to the box seat of his curricle filled her with a curious elation.

The drive to the Park was accomplished swiftly, the traffic in the more fashionable quarters having markedly decreased. It was the first of July and many of the *ton* had already quit the capital. Nevertheless, there were more than enough of the élite left to nod and whisper as

His Grace of Eversleigh swept past in his curricle, an elegant lady beside him.

Lenore revelled in the speed of the carriage, bowling along at a clipping pace. She had been driven in curricles before, but never on such smooth surfaces. Jason's matched greys were, she suspected, Welsh thoroughbreds; the carriage, sleek and perfectly sprung, was no great load for them. Above their heads, the sun struggled to pierce the clouds; the breeze, redolent with the scents of summer, whipped her cheeks.

Bethinking herself of the one item she should make a point of mentioning, Lenore leant closer to Eversleigh. "I must thank you for my bridal gown, my lord. It's truly lovely."

Briefly, Jason glanced down at her. "It was my mother's. My parents' marriage was, by all accounts, a highly successful one. It seemed a fitting omen to re-use my mother's gown."

Not quite sure how to take his words, Lenore made no reply, keeping her gaze on the passing trees and the occupants of the carriages about them.

Noting the sensation their appearance was causing, Jason sought to clarify the matter. "The announcement of our betrothal will appear in the *Gazette* the day after tomorrow, after the announcement at my aunt's ball." He glanced down at the fair face beside him, refreshingly open, her complexion aglow. He smiled wryly. "I had to make sure all my major connections, such as my uncle Henry, heard of it first from me, else there'd have been hell to pay."

Lenore returned his glance with a grin. "I can imagine. Your family is very large, is it not?"

"Very! If you were to ask how many could claim kinship I would not be able to tell you. The Montgomerys, I fear, are a somewhat robust breed. While the direct line has dwindled due to accident, the collateral lines continue to increase unabated."

"Will they all be attending our wedding?" Lenore asked, struck by the possibility.

"A large number of them," Jason replied, his attention on his horses. Only when he had successfully negotiated the turn and had the leisure to glance again at Lenore did he perceive her worried frown. "You won't have to converse with them all."

"But, as your wife, I should at least know their names," she countered. "*And* their associations. Great heavens—and you've left me only three weeks to learn them all."

Belatedly perceiving his error, and foreseeing hours spent in recounting his family connections—a topic that had always bored him witless—Jason groaned. "Lenore—believe me. You don't need to know."

Fixing him with a steady gaze, Lenore enunciated carefully, "*You* might be able to wander through a reception ostensibly given by you without a qualm despite not knowing everyone's name. *I* cannot."

Jason glared at her. "Great gods, woman! You'll never get them all straight."

"Am I right in supposing you wish us to marry in three weeks?"

Jason scowled. "We *are* marrying in three weeks."

"Very well," Lenore continued, her tone perfectly even. "In that case, I suggest you lend me your assistance in coming to grips with your relatives. And your friends among the *ton*. Some I know; others I don't. I'll need some assistance in defining those you wish me to acknowledge, and those you do not."

Her careful words reminded Jason that she did,

indeed, know some of his "friends" he would not wish her to encourage. And there were yet others who might claim friendship who he would not wish her to countenance.

Considering the task ahead of her, Lenore frowned. "We'll have to prepare a guest-list. Perhaps I could use that?"

Jason felt a sudden chill. "Actually," he replied, "the guest-list has already been prepared."

Silence greeted this pronouncement. While he rehearsed his defence—there was only three weeks, after all—he was well aware that, regardless, she had good cause to feel annoyed. More than annoyed.

"Oh?"

The lack of ire in the query brought his head around. But nothing he could see in her mild green gaze gave any indication of aggravation. Which was impossible. The fact that she was shutting him out, hiding her feelings, and that he could not penetrate her mask if she so wished, rocked him. Abruptly, he focused on his horses. "Your father started the list, Jack and your aunt made some additions and I dictated the whole to my secretary."

Again, a painful minute passed unbroken. "Perhaps you would be good enough to ask your secretary— Compton, is it not?—to furnish me with a copy of this list?"

"I'll call to take you for a drive tomorrow afternoon. I'll bring you a copy and we can discuss it during the drive." Jason heard his clipped accents, quite different from his habitual drawl, and knew his temper was showing. Not that he had any right to feel angry with her, but she threw him entirely with her cool and utterly assumed calm. She had every right to enact him a scene and demand an apology for what was, he knew, high-handed behaviour of the most arrogant sort. Instead, she was behaving as if his transgression did not matter—why that fact should so shake his equilibrium he was at a loss to understand.

Keeping her gaze on the carriages they passed, a serene smile on her lips, Lenore gave mute thanks for her years of training in the subtle art of polite dissimulation. The Park, she was certain, was not the place to indulge in heated discussions. Not that she had any intention of discussing her fiancé's error with him later. He would only use logic and reason to make his actions seem perfectly reasonable, a fact she would never concede. Besides, there were other ways of making her point. His irritated tone had already provided a modicum of balm for her abraded pride. Guilt, she recalled, had always turned her brothers into bears. The thought cheered her immensely.

"Perhaps we could make a start with members of the *ton*. Who is that lady in the green bonnet up ahead?"

Determined not to let another awkward silence develop, Lenore continued to quiz her betrothed on personages sighted until, after half an hour, he turned his horses for Green Street once more.

CHAPTER EIGHT

As the Colebatch carriage rumbled down Park Lane, Lenore clutched at the edge of her velvet evening cloak, her expression serene, her stomach a hard knot of apprehension. Her silk gown was entirely concealed by the dark green cloak, one Eversleigh, sitting opposite her, had ordered. Although the evening was fine, there was just enough chill in the air to excuse her need for warmth; she had been cloaked and waiting when he had arrived to escort them to Attlebridge House.

Beside her, Agatha was in high gig, resplendent in midnight-blue bombazine with a peacock feather adorning her black turban. Her patrician features were animated, her black eyes alert. It was plain she expected to enjoy the evening immensely. Lenore swallowed, easing the nervous flutter in her throat, and risked a glance at Eversleigh. Superb in severe black, his ivory cravat a work of art, her fiancé was the epitome of the elegant man about town. His heavy signet glittered on his right hand; a single gold fob hung from the pocket of his embossed silk waistcoat.

His features were in shadow but, when they passed a street-lamp, Lenore found his grey eyes steady on hers. Her breath caught in her throat. He smiled, gently, reassuringly. Lenore returned the smile and, looking away, wondered whether she was that transparent.

In an effort to distract herself from the coming ordeal,

she reviewed the list of those Montgomerys she was shortly to meet. Thanks to Agatha, she had the immediate family committed to memory. Given that she was already acquainted with Eversleigh's aunts, she felt few qualms about the social hurdles facing her tonight. It was an entirely different hurdle, one she had erected herself, that had her nerves in unanticipated disarray.

True to his word, Eversleigh had arrived to drive her in the Park that afternoon armed with a copy of all three hundred names on their guestlist. She had spared a thought for the unfortunate Compton, required to produce the copy in less than twenty-four hours. At Agatha's suggestion she had restricted her queries to those of his friends included on the list, leaving the family connections to be later clarified by Agatha. Any awkwardness that might have existed had been ameliorated by her shy thanks tendered for the present he had sent her that morning.

That had been extremely disconcerting. She had returned with Agatha from a most successful expedition— bonnets, gloves, slippers and boots had consumed most of their morning, leaving her with little opportunity to dwell on the iniquitous behaviour of her fiancé—to discover a package addressed to herself, left in Higgson's care. Removing the wrappings, she had discovered a pair of soft kid half-boots in precisely the same shade of cherry-red as her new pelisse, together with a pair of matching pigskin gloves. Accompanying these had been a chip bonnet with long cherry ribbons. There had been no card.

Agatha had crowed.

Any doubts she had harboured over who had sent her such a gift had been laid to rest when she had tried on the boots in her chamber, exclaiming over their perfect fit.

Trencher had giggled, then admitted that a person named Moggs, known to be in Eversleigh's employ, had materialised in the kitchens the previous afternoon, asking for her shoe size.

The episode had left her shaken. The idea that Eversleigh had turned London upside down—or, more likely, kept some poor cobbler up half the night—just to make this peace with her was distinctly unnerving. His abrupt dismissal of her thanks, as if his effort meant nothing at all, almost as if he did not wish to acknowledge it, had been even more odd.

Throughout their drive, she had kept her eyes glued to his secretary's scrawl and bombarded him with questions. Despite a certain reluctance, she had wrung from him enough answers to satisfy.

The bright lights of Piccadilly swung into view. Lenore quelled a shiver of expectation, drawing her cloak closer.

Ten minutes later, they pulled up outside Attlebridge House in Berkeley Square. Jason descended then turned to assist first his aunt, then his fiancée to the pavement. As Lenore stepped down from the carriage, her cloak parted slightly, affording his sharp eyes a glimpse of silver-green. His lips twitched. Inwardly he sent up a prayer that Lafarge had adhered to her usual standards. After his gaffe over the guest-list, he did not feel sufficiently secure to object even had Lenore donned a pinafore.

Trapping her hand on his sleeve, he detected the tremor in her fingers. Capturing her wide gaze, he smiled encouragingly, trying to banish the lingering memory of the feelings that had swamped him in the Park the day before. The feelings that had sent him home in a savage mood, to give Moggs a most peculiar set of orders. Typically, Moggs had achieved the desired result quietly and efficiently. Yet the fact that he had felt such a compelling urge to prove to his wife-to-be that he was not an ogre was disturbing. She was an intelligent woman—there should be no need to go to such lengths.

As he waited beside her for his aunt's door to swing open, he recalled Lenore's thanks, tendered with a smile of rare sweetness. He had been decidedly brusque, thrown off-balance by the sudden thought that, while he had frequently showered diamonds on his mistresses, he wooed his bride with boots.

And then they were inside the hall, and the moment of revelation was upon them.

Gripped by sudden shyness, Lenore allowed Jason to remove the velvet cloak from her shoulders. Trying for an air of sophisticated confidence, she twitched her skirts straight, then, her head high, fixed her eyes on Agatha's face.

Warm approval shone in Agatha's black eyes. "You look absolutely *splendid*, my dear." Her peacock feather bobbed with her nod. "Doesn't she, Eversleigh?" This last was uttered pointedly in an attempt to prod her nephew to speech. Agatha glared at him but his eyes were fixed on Lenore.

Lenore knew it. The silence from beside her was complete, but she could feel his gaze roving over her shoulders, bared by the wide neckline of her gown, then moving down, over her breasts, outlined by the high waist, then down, down the long length of her filmy skirts, cut narrow to emphasise her height and slenderness. A slow blush rose to her cheeks. In desperation, she tweaked the delicate cuffs of the long, fitted sleeves over her wrists.

Becoming aware of how long he had stood, gawking like a schoolboy, Jason tried to speak, but had to pause

and clear his throat before he could do so. "You look…
exquisite, my dear."

At the deep, strangely raspy words, Lenore glanced
up, into his eyes—and was content. Then he smiled and
she felt a quiver ripple from the top of her head all the
way to her toes.

"Shall we go in?" Smoothly, Jason offered her his
arm, unable, for the life of him, to take his eyes from
her. The silver-green silk clung and slid over her curves
as she moved to his side. The gown was more concealing than any he had ordered yet, oddly, it was far more
alluring to have such promise so tantalisingly withheld.

Success, Lenore found, was a heady potion. As she
placed her fingertips on his silk sleeve her entire body
tingled with the thrill of conquest, of having brought the
silver light to his eyes. The sensation left her breathless.
Side by side, both so tall, she a graceful counterpoint to
his strength, they strolled into the large drawing-room.

All conversation halted.

Wide-eyed stares rained upon them; the entire company followed their stately progress to Lady Attlebridge,
an imposing figure standing before the fireplace. There
was not a shred of doubt who the focus of interest was
that night.

And so it proved. To Lenore's abiding relief, Eversleigh remained firmly entrenched by her side, resisting
any number of attempts, some subtle, others less so, to
either distract him, or displace him. When her memory
failed, he prompted or, as happened more frequently,
when her memory was blank, because neither he nor
Agatha had recalled certain of his connections, he duly
filled her in, his charming smile warming her all the
while.

From his sudden stiffness when they hove near, she

deduced his aunts were his greatest concern, an observation she found particularly interesting. When the fact that she knew them finally registered as they were leaving Lady Eckington, the most redoubtable and unpredictable of the six, he murmured, "They know you, don't they?"

Lenore opened her eyes wide. "I thought you knew," she murmured, turning to smile as one of his cousins passed by. "They often visit Lester Hall. They're all friends of Harriet's. I've known most of your aunts since I was—oh, twelve or so."

Jason raised his brows, surprised yet cynical as realisation dawned. Given the favour of his formidable aunts, Lenore would have no need of his support in establishing her social position. Which was a relief. Nevertheless, his voice held a disgruntled note when he said, "I had thought to have to protect you from them. The next time they come calling with me in their sights, I'll know who to hide behind."

Lenore's eyes widened but she laughed the comment aside. "Never mind that—just tell me who the lady in the atrocious purple turban is. She's been trying to attract our attention for ages. On the sofa by the wall."

Obediently, Jason slowly turned. "That, dear Lenore, is Cousin Hetty. Come. I'll introduce you."

And so it went on. The dinner proved no greater ordeal than the drawing-room; by the end of it, Lenore felt entirely at home among the Montgomerys. An official announcement of their engagement was made at the end of the meal, and their healths drunk in the finest champagne before the company moved to the ballroom, keen to meet the incoming guests and spread the news.

Lenore glided through the throng on Jason's arm, smiling and nodding, her head in a whirl. She was thankful the long windows to the terrace were open, allowing a gentle breeze to cool the heated room. Despite the time of year, Lady Attlebridge's rooms were full. Bodies hemmed her in, the colours of coats and gowns blending like an artist's palette. As she clung to Jason's arm, grateful for the reassuring pressure of his fingers on hers, her responses to the introductions and congratulations became automatic.

Then the musicians struck up.

"Come, my dear."

As if he had been waiting for the signal, Eversleigh drew her away from the crowd, into the area miraculously clearing in the middle of the floor. As she felt his arm go around her, Lenore remembered. The waltz— their engagement waltz. "Ah," she said, relaxing into his arms. "I'd forgotten about this."

"Had you?" Jason raised one arrogant brow. "I hadn't."

He watched her eyes cloud with delicious confusion.

Lenore blinked, the only way to break free of his spell. Fixing her gaze in convenient space, she prayed he could not hear her thudding heart. "Tell me, my lord. Is Lord Alvanley an accomplished dancer?"

"Accomplished enough," Jason returned, quelling his grin. "But Alvanley's claim to fame is his wits, rather than his grace. Furthermore, given he's half a head shorter than you, I would not, if I was you, favour him with a waltz." He considered the matter gravely. "A cotillion, perhaps. Or a quandrille."

Lenore's eyes narrowed, but, before she could formulate another distracting question, Jason took charge.

"But enough of my friends, my dear—and *more* than enough of my relatives," he added, frowning when she opened her lips. "I would much rather hear about you."

"Me?" The words came out in a higher register and without the languid dismissiveness Lenore had intended, owing to the fact that Jason had drawn her closer as they approached the end of the floor. His hand burned through the fine silk of her gown, his thighs brushing hers as they whirled through the turn. When they straightened to precess back up the room, he did not relax his hold. Luckily, other couples were crowding on to the floor, obscuring everyone's view.

"You," Jason confirmed. "I sincerely hope you cancelled the gowns I ordered from Lafarge." Lenore looked up, eyes wide. Jason smiled. "Your style is uniquely yours, my dear. I like it far better than any other."

More flattered than she would have believed possible, Lenore stared up at him. "Actually, my lord—"

"Jason."

Lenore felt her fingers tighten around his. She forced them to relax. "Jason, the gowns you had ordered were perfectly appropriate. It's merely that, at least until I get used to such styles, I fear I would find wearing the more revealing gowns unsettling. No doubt I'll get used to such things in time."

"Lenore, I would prefer you to dress as you wish. Your own style is much more becoming and infinitely more appropriate than the current mood. I would be happy to see you always garbed in gowns such as you are wearing tonight."

"Oh." Lenore looked deep into his eyes but could see nothing beyond an unnerving sincerity. She drew a deep breath. "In that case, my—Jason, I suspect I should warn you to expect a very large bill from Madame Lafarge."

A smile of considerable charm lit Jason's face. He chuckled. "I see. What did you do—double the order?"

Eyes on his, Lenore nodded.

For a moment, he could not take it in. Then, the trepidation in her wide eyes, her suspended breathing, registered, confirming the reality. For the first time in a very long while, Jason was at a loss, sheer incredulity obstructing coherent thought. In the end, his sense of humour won through. His lips lifted in an irrepressible grin, breaking into a smile as he saw her confusion grow. Drawing her slightly closer, he sighed. "You will, no doubt, be relieved to know that settling with Lafarge will not greatly dent my fortune. However," Jason continued, his eyes holding hers, "next time you wish to upbraid me for my high-handed ways, do you think, my dear, that you could simply lose your temper? I find your methods of making me sorry rather novel, to say the least." Not to mention effective, but he was not so far lost to all caution as to say such words aloud.

"I…ah…" Lenore did not know what to say. His grey eyes, gently quizzing her, were far too perceptive to risk any white lie. As the fact that he was disposed to view her actions in an understanding, even conciliatory way sank in, she summoned enough strength to tilt her chin at him. "If you would refrain from acting high-handedly in the first place, my lord, I would not need to exercise my temper in any way whatever. Which would be greatly to be desired, for I find it extremely wearying."

Delighted by her haughty response, Jason could not resist asking, his voice low, "And if I refrained from all high-handed behaviour? Would you be suitably grateful, Lenore?"

Her heartbeat filling her ears as his eyes caressed her face, Lenore struggled to keep her feet on the ground. Her bones felt weak, a sensation that had afflicted her once before. Too concerned with keeping her senses under control, she made no effort to answer him.

The confusion in her eyes was answer enough for Jason.

The music stopped. Reluctantly, he freed her, tucking her hand into his arm, a subtle smile curving his lips.

Released from his gaze, Lenore dragged in a steadying breath.

"Great heavens! Lenore!" Spun about, Lenore felt her hand caught, then she was slowly twirled about. Jack came into view, studying her avidly. Coming to a halt in time to see him shoot a glance loaded with masculine meaning at her fiancé, Lenore tugged to get her brother's attention.

"How is Papa?"

Jack blinked, as if struggling to take her meaning. "Papa? Oh, he's fine. Couldn't be better. And his health will improve no end when he gets a look at you. What happened to your pinafores?"

"I left them at home," Lenore stated with awful deliberation. "Along with my spectacles," she added before he could ask. "Come and dance with me. I need the practice."

Leaving Jason with the mildest of nods, she led the way to the floor.

While circling the floor with Jack, she prised his news from him. He had returned to Lester Hall on Wednesday, to set her father's mind at rest that all was well with her. Apparently all was likewise well at Lester Hall, although Harriet and her father both missed her. However, the arrangements for them to attend her wedding were well in hand; the prospect was the cause of considerable excitement in the household.

"God knows! Some of the servants have asked permission to make the journey, so you might catch sight of some familiar faces in the crowd outside the church."

Lenore was touched, but, already, Lester Hall and its

affairs were fading in her mind, overlaid by the more pressing demands of her new role.

Harry came up as Jack led her from the floor. After making comments sufficiently similar to Jack's to earn a stern warning from Lenore, he, too, commandeered her for a dance. At the end of it, however, he insisted on returning her to her fiancé's side, revealing that he had been so instructed by his future brother-in-law and was not about to queer his pitch in that direction.

Lenore did not quite know what to make of that but she was too relieved to be once more in Jason's protective presence to protest.

He was talking to Frederick Marshall when she joined him. Lenore could not miss the stunned look on Frederick's face when he saw her.

"My dear Miss Lester." Coming to himself with a start, Frederick bowed gallantly over Lenore's hand. Straightening, he blinked. "Er…" Appalled by the words that had leapt to his tongue, Frederick struggled to find suitable replacements.

Reading his friend's mind with ease, Jason helpfully explained, "She left her pinafores at Lester Hall."

Bending a glance both haughty and innocent upon him, Lenore asked, "I do hope, Your Grace, that you're not missing them? Perhaps I should send for them, if it would please you?"

Jason was too old a hand to be rolled up so easily. His lips curved appreciatively, his grey eyes gleamed. "I'd be only too pleased to discuss what you might do to please me, my dear. Naturally, I'm delighted that you seek to make my pleasure your paramount concern."

Any possibility that his speech was uttered in innocence was rendered ineligible by the expression in his eyes. Caught in his web once more, Lenore turned hot, then cold, then hot once more. With an effort, she dragged her gaze from his, glancing at Frederick but with little hope of rescue.

She had, however, underestimated Frederick. More used to Jason's ways than she, he sent his friend a stern glance before enquiring, "Have you weathered the Montgomery clan, then? They're somewhat daunting, are they not?"

Lenore grasped the unexpected lifeline, applying herself to a discussion of her fiancé's huge family, thereby, she later realised, punishing him most effectively.

It was not long afterwards that Agatha caught up with them. "If you want my opinion, we should leave now. Best not to give them time to grow too accustomed — keeps their interest up, y'know?"

Jason, his eyes flicking over Lenore's radiant face and seeing the increasing weariness behind her polished mask, inclined his head. "I bow to your greater experience of such matters, dear aunt."

The carriage was summoned; they took their leave of their hostess, Lenore and Agatha receiving an invitation to take tea the following Tuesday.

Ensconced in the carriage, wrapped up in her cloak once more, Lenore sighed as the flambeau lighting the Attlebridge House steps fell behind, her evening's hurdles successfully overcome.

Seated opposite, Jason watched the shadows wreath her face. He smiled. "Well, my dear. Was the ordeal as bad as you had feared?"

Lenore straightened. "Why, no, my lord." She turned to face him fully, rearranging the folds of her cloak. Remembering his requirements of a bride, she added, "I don't believe I will find any real difficulty in either attending or hosting such entertainments."

Jason inclined his head, a frown gathering in his eyes.

"Lady Mulhouse invited us to her rout next week." Lenore turned to Agatha. "And Mrs. Scotridge asked us to tea."

Agatha heaved a contented sigh. "Ah, me! I'd almost forgotten what it's like to be in the eye of the storm. Despite the fact that it's the tag-end of the Season, I dare say life will be hectic for the next few weeks."

Eyes narrowing, Jason watched his aunt stifle a yawn. If nothing else had been achieved at his aunt Attlebridge's ball, the occasion had demonstrated that in her new incarnation Lenore held a potent attraction for the prowling males of the *ton*. No less than five fascinated acquaintances had stopped by his side to remark on her beauty. Placing an elbow on the carriage windowsill, Jason leant his chin on his fist and stared, unseeing, at the passing façades.

After some moments, he shifted his gaze to the object of his thoughts, sitting serene and content only feet away, her face intermittently lit by the street-lamps as she watched the houses slip past. The wheels rang on the cobblestones as he pondered his problem, his gaze fixed, unwaveringly, on the face of his bride-to-be.

As the carriage slowed for the turn into Green Street, Jason stirred. "If tomorrow is fine, perhaps you'd care to drive to Merton with me? My great-aunt Elmira lives there; she's an invalid and will be unable to attend our wedding but she's an avid gossip and will be livid not to have met you."

He ignored Agatha's stunned stare, his attention on Lenore.

Lenore brightened, her spirits lifting at the thought of a drive in the country. Fresh country air was something she was already missing, although she had no intentions of admitting to such weakness. "I'd be delighted to accompany you, my lord." She smiled, feeling as if the final cachet had been added to her evening. "I would not have it thought that we were in any way backward with our attentions to your family."

"You need have no fear of that," Jason returned somewhat ascerbically. "My family, as you will learn, would never permit it."

As the carriage slowed before his aunt's house, Jason allowed himself a small, self-deprecatory smile. The course he had just set his feet upon was not one he would, of his own volition, have followed. However, given that his peace for the rest of his life might depend on the outcome, three weeks of his time seemed a small price to pay.

For Lenore, the weeks following the announcement of their betrothal passed in a constant whirl. Visits were crammed between engagements of every conceivable sort—balls, parties, routs, drums. The obligatory appearance at Almack's was accomplished; she was greatly disappointed by the bare rooms and the refreshments she had no hesitation in stigmatising as meagre. Also wedged between *ton*-ish dissipations was a reunion with Amelia; her cousin agreed to act as matron of honour and was duly introduced to Lafarge to be fitted for her gown. Lenore had two fittings of her wedding gown and the severely cut maroon velvet carriage dress she would wear on her departure from the wedding breakfast, all squeezed into her last hectic week. The only periods of calm in her disordered world were those she spent with Eversleigh.

She had initially been surprised to find him assiduous in his attendance upon her, dutifully escorting his aunt and herself to every evening engagement, frequently taking her driving in the Park, arranging an evening at the theatre to see Keane, always by her side whenever the occasion permitted. He also organised outings which took her out of the bustle of the *ton*, for which she was more grateful than she felt it wise to reveal. They drove in Richmond Park and visited numerous beauty spots. He took her for a tour around London in his curricle, pointing out the sights the guide-books acclaimed, walking with her in St Paul's and along the leafy avenues by the river.

When, however, unnerved by her response to his continuing thoughtfulness, to the sense of protection she felt when he was by her side, she had hesitantly commented to Agatha on the unexpectedness of his constancy, her mentor had dismissed the point with an airy wave. "Hardly surprising. Never a fool, Jason."

The cryptic comment did nothing to ease Lenore's inner wariness; as the days passed, it grew, along with a suspicion that her fears of marriage were well on the way to being realised.

And then, before she had time to come to grips with her affliction, her wedding eve was upon her.

IT WAS PRECISELY three weeks after Lady Attlebridge's ball. In the dim light of a crescent moon, Jason strolled the balcony of the Bishop of Salisbury's palace, looking back over the days of his betrothal, very thankful they were about to end. He would be glad to leave behind the unexpected uncertainty which had prompted him to keep Lenore close, spending as much time with her as propriety allowed. The endeavour had stretched his talents to the full. He had even sent Moggs out for a guide-book.

His admiration for his betrothed had increased dra-

matically. He was reasonably sure she did not enjoy life
in London—she had been right in predicting her dislike.
Her transparent enjoyment of the days they had spent
out of the capital or in pursuits outside the *ton* had con-
trasted with her considered appreciation of their evenings' entertainments. However, not even his sharp eyes
had detected the slightest crack in the smoothly serene
façade she showed to the world. Her performance had
been faultless. The subtle change when, alone with him,
she laid aside her social mask, was one he had learned
to savour.

Smiling, Jason looked up at the stars, diamonds scattered in the black velvet sky. He owed Agatha a debt, not
least for refraining from comment on his unfashionable
predilection for his fiancée's company. Needless to say,
Frederick thought he had run daft.

The end of the balcony rose out of the dark. Jason
leaned on the railing and breathed deeply. Away to the
left, beyond the glow of the town's street-lamps, he could
see the pinpricks of light that marked Ashby Lodge, the
home of his cousin Cyril. The Lester Hall household had
been quartered here; Lenore had returned to spend the
last night before her wedding under the same roof as her
father.

Tomorrow, they would wed amid the pomp and ceremony traditional in his family. The town was crammed
with members of the *ton* who, as Agatha had predicted,
had returned from all corners of the land to attend. The
wedding breakfast would be held here, under Henry's
auspices, after which he and Lenore would depart for
the Abbey.

Straightening, his lips curving, Jason considered
the future, conscious of nothing more than keen anticipation. No sense of mourning for his hedonistic free-

dom, no last-minute hesitations. Casting one last look across the treetops to where his betrothed was no doubt sound asleep in a high-necked, long-sleeved nightgown, quite unlike the one she would wear tomorrow night, he grinned and turned back towards the house.

He was well satisfied with the way things had fallen out. Not just as he had hoped but rather more than he had expected.

REPLETE, lulled into a pleasant daze by the steady rocking of the coach, Lenore reviewed her wedding with sleepy content. The event had been remarkable if for no other reason than that she had had no hand in organising it. Her opinions, certainly, had been solicited—by Agatha, by Jack and even by Eversleigh, the latter with a pointed care which had set her lips twitching. Agatha and the reliable Compton, a neat, very serious man of middle age who hid his capabilities behind gold-rimmed glasses, had borne the brunt of the task; from beginning to end, all she had to do was follow instructions—a novel and oddly agreeable experience. She had been free to enjoy her wedding, to savour to the full the fluttering nerves that had assailed her as she had walked down the aisle, her hand on Jack's sleeve. Muted whispers over her gown had rippled through the congregation, bringing a thin frown to the Bishop's face. She had hardly noticed, her attention commanded by her husband-to-be, standing tall and straight before the steps. Frederick Marshall had stood beside him, a happy coincidence given Amelia's role. When Jack gave her hand into Eversleigh's care, her fingers had shaken; his hand had closed firmly over hers, stilling the movement, steadying her nerves. From that moment on, all had flowed smoothly.

Happily content, Lenore yawned. The only action she

had been responsible for that day was the careful aim she had taken when she had paused on the steps of the carriage, surrounded by well-wishers, and thrown her bouquet. If she had not caught it, the large posy of rosebuds and hothouse blooms would have hit Amelia in the face. The memory of Amelia blushing delightfully with Frederick Marshall by her side, his dark head bent as he congratulated her, brought a satisfied smile to Lenore's face.

As the carriage rolled on, the regular beat of the hooves of the four chestnuts drawing it caught her attention. Both horses and carriage were a wedding gift from her husband. She slanted a glance at him, seated beside her on the pale green leather, his long legs stretched out, his hands folded over his waist, his chin sunk in his cravat, his eyes shut. Lenore grinned. Allowing her gaze to roam the carriage, noting the bright brass fittings and velvet cushions and hangings, she recalled the looks of envy it had elicited from the belles of the *ton*. Few could boast husbands who thought of such extravagant gifts; diamonds were easy, individualised carriages and horses required rather more thought. Casting an affectionate glance at her sleeping spouse, Lenore smiled.

Turning her gaze once more to the scenery flashing past, she wondered how long it would be before they reached the Abbey. Already the sun was starting to slip from its zenith.

"You should try to get some sleep." Jason, far from sleep himself, opened his eyes. "We're still hours from the Abbey."

"Oh?" Lenore swung to face him. "Will it be dark when we get there?"

"Close. But I told Horton to stop at the top of the drive—from there, you can see the house clearly. There should be light enough to view it."

Lenore mouthed an, "Oh," noting that her husband's eyes were once more shut. His words focused her mind on the evening, a subject she had thus far avoided. She considered the likely schedule, too nervous to ask for confirmation. She would have to meet the servants, and have a quick look about the main rooms before supervising her unpacking. After that would come dinner. Determined not to let her imagination undermine her confidence, Lenore firmly stopped her thoughts at that point. Eversleigh—Jason—was probably right. A nap would not go amiss. Settling into her corner, warm in her sleek velvet carriage dress, she closed her eyes. Gradually, the excitement of the day fell away. Lulled by the gentle swaying of the carriage, she slept.

She half awoke when a particularly deep rut sent her sliding into Jason. His arms closed about her, stopping her fall. Instead of releasing her, he shifted her, pulling her into a more comfortable position against him, her head on his shoulder. Sleep-fogged, Lenore saw no reason to protest. His body provided a firm cushion against which she could rest, his arms about her ensured her safety. Lenore drifted back into slumber, entirely content in her husband's arms.

Jason was far less satisfied with her position, wondering what form of temporary insanity had prompted him to draw her so close. But he could not bring himself to push her away. She shifted in her sleep, snuggling her cheek into his shoulder, one small hand slipping beneath his coat to rest against the fine linen covering his chest. Jason closed his eyes, willing away his reaction. After a long moment, he squinted down at her, shaking his head in resignation. Then, settling his chin on her coiled braids, he closed his eyes and, fully awake, indulged his dreams.

He shook her gently awake as the carriage rocked to a halt just beyond the main gates of his principal estate. "The light's fading but I think we're in time."

Blinking, Lenore followed as he descended from the carriage, turning to hand her down. Directly before them, the sun was dying in a cloud of bright purple and rose, sinking behind the opposite rim of the valley. Below, gentle slopes surrounded enormous gardens, laid out about a massive pile of stone—Eversleigh Abbey. Stepping to the lip of the bank, Lenore recalled her husband had described his home as Gothic. Towering turrets stood at the four points of the main building, smaller ones marked the ends of the wings. A dome rose from somewhere behind the main entrance, itself an arched and heavily ornamented structure. The broad sweep of the façade faced the drive, the wings at right angles to the main building, enclosed more gardens. Cast in grey stone, Eversleigh Abbey dominated its landscape yet seemed curiously a part of it, as if the stone had grown roots. Her home, Lenore thought, and felt a shivery surge of excitement grip her.

"There used to be a fourth side to the courtyard, of course," Jason said from beside her. "There are cloisters around the inner side of the east and west wings."

"From when it was a monastery?"

He nodded.

"Where is the library housed?"

Jason raised his brows.

Ignoring his supercilious expression, Lenore pointedly lifted one brow and waited.

With a reluctant smile, Jason capitulated. "The main building, west corner." He pointed to two huge arched windows set into the façade. "There are more windows on the west."

As they watched, lights started to appear in the house. Two large lamps were carried out and set in brackets to light the front steps.

"Come. They'll be waiting. We should go down."

Jason took her arm and Lenore turned, consumed by an almost childish eagerness to see her new home.

By the time the carriage pulled up on the broad sweep of gravel before the front steps, twilight had taken hold. Handed down from the carriage, Lenore looked up at the massive oak doors and the soaring stone arch above them. She peered about, trying to discern the features of the gardens before the house.

"They won't disappear during the night," Jason commented drily.

Accepting that truth, Lenore allowed him to lead her up the steps. Long before they had reached them, the doors were swung wide. The hall within was ablaze with light. A chandelier depending from the huge central beams threw light into every corner. Tiled in grey and white, the large rectangular room was filled with a small crowd of people. The butler, at the head of the assembled company, bowed majestically.

"Welcome, Your Grace." Then he bowed again. "Your Grace."

For a moment, Lenore wondered why he had repeated himself. Then she realised and blushed. Jason, an understanding smile on his face, led her forward.

"Allow me to present you to your staff, my dear. This is Morgan, who has been with us forever. His father was butler before him. And this is Mrs. Potts."

Lenore smiled and nodded, acknowledging the greetings of each servant as Morgan and the reassuringly cheerful Mrs. Potts conducted her down the line. Behind her, she heard Jason issuing quiet orders to his valet, the one named Moggs. He had been with Jason at Salisbury but had come down ahead of them with Trencher and the luggage. The introductions seemed interminable; Lenore juggled names and occupations, resolving to ask for a list at the earliest opportunity. At the end of the line, Jason took her hand, dismissing the gathering with a nod.

Glancing down at her, his expression resigned, he lifted an enquiring brow. "I suppose I had better show you the library before you set out to discover it yourself and get lost."

Lenore smiled sweetly, gracefully taking his proffered arm as he turned towards an archway. By the time they reached the library door, she was grateful for his fore-thought. Many of the main rooms were interconnecting; the way far from direct. If left to herself, she would certainly have got lost.

The library was enormous; the small fire burning in the hearth did nothing to dispel its cavernous shadows. Jason strolled forward and lit a branch of candles. Then he took her hand and led her on a circuit of the room, holding the candlestick high to light their way.

"There must be thousands and thousands of books here." Lenore's hushed whisper drifted into the stillness.

"Very likely," Jason replied. "I've no idea of the number—I thought I'd leave that to you."

"Are they in any order?"

"Only vaguely. My father always seemed to simply know where things were, rather than work to any plan."

Forming her own plans to bring order to what appeared one step away from chaos, Lenore let her eyes roam upwards, to where rows of books seemed to disappear into shadows. Staring up, she realised the ceiling was a very long way away and the wall did not seem to meet it. "Is there a gallery up there?"

Jason glanced upwards. "Yes. It goes all the way around." He turned her about and pointed to where a set of wooden stairs led up. "Those lead to it."

Turning about, eyes wide, Lenore realised the gallery ran along above the windows, too. It would be a perfect place to have her desk.

Viewing the total absorption that had laid hold of his wife, Jason, his fingers locked about hers, recrossed the long room. Placing the candlestick down on the table by the fireplace, he snuffed the three candles with the silver snuffer that lay beside the tinderbox.

Only as the light died did Lenore return her attention to him. With a satisfied smile, Jason turned for the door. "You can see the rest of the house tomorrow." He opened the door and ushered her into the corridor. "I've given orders for you to be served supper in your room. Your maid should be waiting upstairs."

"Yes, of course." Quelling her skittering pulse, Lenore glided beside him, a host of impetuous and far too revealing questions hovering on her lips. She was perfectly certain he would have made plans for the evening—she was not at all certain if knowing them would help her.

At the top of the grand staircase, Jason turned her to her right. "Your apartments are along here." He stopped at a polished oak door and opened it, standing back for her to precede him. Lenore went through, into her bedroom.

It was all in greens and golds, soft colours blending and contrasting with the ivory wallpaper. The furniture was of polished oak, gleaming in the light from the candles scattered in candelabra and sconces throughout the room. All the knobs she could see were brass, including those at the corners of the huge tester bed. Drapes of pale green gauze depended in scallops from the frame above the bed; the counterpane was of silk in the identical shade of green. Velvet of a darker green curtained the windows while the stools and chairs were upholstered in amber velvet.

Slowly, Lenore turned, eyes round as she drank in the subtle elegance, her lips parting in wordless approval. Her gaze met her husband's. Jason lifted his brows in mute question.

"It's *lovely*!"

Pleased, more by the delight in her eyes than by her words, Jason smiled. Placing an iron shackle over his inclinations, he shut the corridor door behind him and strolled to a door on the left. "I'll leave you to get settled. The bell-pull's by the mantelpiece." He paused, his hand on the doorknob, his gaze, beyond his control, roving over her. "Until later, Lenore."

With a nod, he went through the door, shutting it firmly behind him.

Slightly breathless, Lenore eyed the door. Presumably, it led to his chamber. She swallowed, her mouth suddenly dry. At least she would not have to endure a formal dinner, facing him over the length of a long polished board with doting servants hovering on their every word. But would that have put off his unnerving "later" for longer?

With a determined wriggle of her shoulders, Lenore shook aside her silly trepidations. She was hardly a missish deb, fresh from the schoolroom.

Crossing to the mantelpiece, she examined the delicately embroidered bell-pull. Then, with a determined tug, she rang for Trencher.

CHAPTER NINE

"YOU'D BEST COME OUT now, miss—I mean, Y'r Grace, or you'll go all crinkly."

Lazily, Lenore opened her eyes, squinting through the steam still rising off her bathwater. "In a moment." Closing her eyes, she tried to recapture her dozy, care-free mood but Trencher's words had been well chosen. With a resigned sigh, Lenore sat up.

Trencher hurried to tip the extra bucket, left to keep warm by the fire, over her as she stood, water coursing down her ivory limbs. Rinsed, she stepped from the large tub. Once she was dry, Lenore shrugged on the soft silk robe Trencher held out and headed through the door to her bedchamber. Trencher went to the bell-pull, sum-moning the menservants to empty the bath, then hurried through after her, shutting the connecting door firmly.

Relaxed, Lenore sat before her dressing-table to brush free the long strands of her hair, washed and towelled dry earlier. As she worked through the tangles, she watched Trencher, reflected in the mirror, laying out an ivory silk nightgown and peignoir on the bed. *Ivory* silk? Lenore turned. "Not that one, Trencher."

Trencher cast her an anxious glance. "But Y'r Grace, *His* Grace asked that you wear it tonight."

With an exasperated grimace, Lenore ceased her brushing. What now? Rebel and cause an embarrassing and potentially difficult scene? Or capitulate—just this once? The thought of trying to explain to Eversleigh why she had chosen not to humour him decided the matter.

"Very well." Lenore resumed her brushing, relegating her choice of nightwear to the realms of the unimportant.

Relieved, Trencher hurried to help her with her hair. When the tresses were gleaming like polished gold, sleek and silky on her shoulders, Lenore stood and allowed Trencher to help her into the nightgown. With a distinctly jaundiced eye, she viewed the result in her glass. In Roman fashion, the gown featured a deeply plunging neckline, the two sides of the bodice meeting at the point below her breasts where the raised waistline was gathered in by a silken tie. Sleeveless, with its skirts falling to the floor, the nightgown was otherwise unremarkable. Until she moved. Then, the side slits, from high on her thighs all the way to the floor, became apparent. Studying the effect, Lenore shook her head.

Silently, she held out her hand for the peignoir. Of the flimsiest silk gauze, it hid nothing; rather, seen through its shimmering veil, her long, bare limbs took on an even more alluring quality.

Catching sight of Trencher's awed face in the mirror, Lenore reflected that, at least for her maid, the evening was living up to expectations. "Leave me now." As an afterthought, she added, as nonchalantly as she could, "I'll ring for you when I need you in the morning."

Watching the door shut behind Trencher, Lenore shook her shoulders to dispel the panic hovering, waiting to pounce, if only she would let it into her mind.

Dinner, a deliciously delicate meal, had been served to her in the adjoining sitting-room; all that remained now was to wait. Trying not to think, she dispensed with the peignoir and climbed into bed, feeling the soft mattress settle under her, the silk sheets whispering against her skin. A long shiver shook her from her shoulders to her heels. After considering the possibilities, she plumped up the pillows and settled against them, a wary eye on the door to her husband's room. In an effort to distract her mind, she dutifully studied all the pieces of furniture she could see from her perch, mentally cataloguing them, then went about the room again, doing the same with the ornaments. Finally, her eyes fastening on the clock on the mantelpiece, she realised she had no idea when "later" was.

And if she sat here for much longer, wondering, she would be a nervous wreck by the time her husband came in. With a disgusted grimace for her inner quaking, Lenore reached for the book on her bedside table.

There was nothing there.

Frustrated, she glanced about. Other items from the trunk which should have carried her current reading had also yet to appear. With a groan, Lenore fell back on her pillows. Condemned to wait in steadily growing nervousness for her husband.

Abruptly, she sat up. An instant later, she was out of bed, grimacing as she hauled on her totally inadequate peignoir. Looking around, she spotted the high-heeled slippers that went with the outfit, placed side by side just under the bed. Lenore looked hard at the heels, then left them where they were.

Easing open her door, she strained her ears but heard nothing. Fervently hoping all the servants were safely behind the green baize door, she tiptoed down the corridor and slowly descended the stairs. Feeling very like a wraith in her filmy garments, Lenore slipped along the corridors and through the unlighted rooms, heading unerringly for the library. Gaining the large room, she closed the door carefully behind her.

The fire had gone out but the curtains had not been drawn, allowing the moonlight to spill in through the large square-paned windows. It was no great feat to kindle a match and light the branch of candles left on the table by the fireplace. Feeling her tension ebb as she looked about her, Lenore started towards the nearest bookcase.

She had only meant to spend a moment selecting a suitable volume, but, as the wavering light of the candle revealed find after exciting find, Lenore ignored her freezing feet and the chill that had started to penetrate her thin gown. The thrill of discovery lured her from shelf to shelf. She was leaving one bookcase to pass to the next, when she walked straight into a large body.

Lenore screamed and recoiled, raising the candlestick high.

Simultaneously, Jason reached for the candlestick. As he took it from her slack grasp, hot wax fell on his hand. Swallowing a yelp, he swore beneath his breath. Glaring at his wife, he transferred the candles to his other hand but before he could tend to the wax, cooling rapidly, Lenore had caught his hand between hers and was brushing the wax away.

"What a silly thing to do!" She examined the small burn, then licked her finger and applied it to the spot. "I wouldn't have burnt the books."

"It wasn't the books I was worried about."

Jason's tone jerked Lenore back to reality with a stomach-seizing thump. "Oh." Carefully, she glanced up through her lashes. Her husband's handsome face bore an expression of unflinching determination. Which was far from reassuring, especially when coupled with the silver gleam in his eyes.

Assuming that realisation of her shortcomings had

tied her tongue, Jason hauled back on the reins of his temper. "Would you mind explaining, madam wife, just what you're about?"

"I was looking for a book," Lenore replied warily.

"Why?"

"Well…I usually read before I go to sleep. Trencher has yet to unpack my books so I thought I might borrow one from here." As she tendered her perfectly reasonable explanation, Lenore noticed her husband was fully dressed, a handkerchief knotted about his throat as if he was going riding. Perhaps later was a great deal later. "But don't let me disturb you," she said, a touch of haughtiness creeping into her tone as she wrestled with unexpected disappointment. "I'm sure I can find my way back to my room."

Jason shut his eyes. After a long moment, he opened them, fixed his errant wife with a steely stare and enunciated slowly, "First, as of today, all these books are yours—you don't need to 'borrow' them. Second, you won't need any bedtime reading—not for the foreseeable future. Third, you have *already* disturbed me—*greatly*! And as for my letting you find your way back to your room alone—when pigs fly, my dear."

Stunned, Lenore stared at him.

Reaching out, Jason wrapped his fingers about her wrist. Without more ado he headed for the door, dragging her along behind him. He had entered her room to find her gone. Vanished. Without trace. In the worst panic of his life, he had thrown on his clothes and rushed downstairs, straight out of the morning-room windows heading for the stables, convinced for some reason that she had bolted. In the heat of the moment, he had wondered if insisting she wear that outrageous nightgown had been one arrogant step too many. But, traversing the terrace that ran along the front of the house, he had passed the library windows. And seen the wavering candlelight flitting from bookshelf to bookshelf.

Pausing to thump the candlestick down on a table and snuff the candles with licked fingers, Jason realised he could hear the ring of his boot-heels on the flags but no sound at all from Lenore. Puzzled, he glanced down at her feet. "Where the devil are your slippers?"

His irritated tone penetrated Lenore's shocked daze. Her chin rose. "I did not wish to attract the attention of the servants, my lord."

"Jason. And why the hell not? They're *your* servants."

Lenore abandoned her attitude of superiority to glare at him. "I would not feel *the least* comfortable being sighted by the staff in my present state of dress."

Jason glared back. "Your present dress was not designed to be worn in a library." Her comment, however, focused his attention on what he had been trying not to notice—how very alluring his wife looked in diaphanous silk backlit by moonlight.

"Jason!" Lenore squealed as she felt herself hoisted into his arms. "My lord!" she hissed, as he strode purposefully towards the door. He paid no attention. "For God's sake, Jason, put me down. What if the servants see us?"

"What if they do? I married you this morning, if you recall."

He kicked the half-open door wide and strode through. Lenore clung to him, her arms about his neck. It was distinctly unnerving to be carried along so effortlessly.

As Jason passed the front door, he sent a silent prayer of thanks heavenwards. If he had not sighted the candleflame in the library, he would have roused the whole household to look for his wandering bride. The commiserating looks from his footmen would have driven him insane.

She was driving him insane.

Sensing that she had teased his temper to a degree where conciliation might prove wise, Lenore remained silent as she was carried up the stairs. But at the top, Jason turned to the left.

"My lord—er—Jason. My room—it's the other way." Assuming he had simply forgotten, she pointed out this fact without undue fuss.

"I know."

Panic clutched her stomach. "Where are you taking me?" With bated breath, she awaited his answer.

Jason stopped and juggled her to open a door. "I rather thought I'd have you in my bed tonight."

His conversational tone did not convince Lenore that his phrasing was anything other than intentional. But it was too late for panic. The door of his room clicked shut behind them.

And before her loomed the largest four-poster bed she had ever seen.

Jason strode across the thick carpet and, standing her briefly on her feet by the bed, divested her of her peignoir before depositing her on the silken coverlet.

Lenore made no sound—her throat had seized. She watched as Jason stalked to the other side of the bed, whipping off his neckerchief and flinging it aside. As he sat down on the bed to pull off his boots, curiosity got the better of trepidation. "Aren't you going out?"

His second boot hit the floor. Jason turned and stared at her for a moment, then stood and pulled his shirt from his breeches. "I'm not dressed like this for visiting the neighbours. These are my wife-hunting clothes."

The truth dawned on Lenore. She choked, panic and

embarrassment laying siege to her tongue. She watched as he peeled off his shirt, dropping it on the floor. Her eyes stretched wide; her heart started to thud. When his hands fell to his waistband, she decided she had seen enough.

Hearing rustling, Jason glanced up to discover his twenty-four-year-old bride had disappeared beneath the bedclothes. "For God's sake, Lenore! You've got three brothers."

"You are not my brother," came distinctly from the lump in the bed.

Jason's sense of humour, sternly suppressed for the past ten minutes, very nearly got the better of him. Quickly, he finished undressing and slid into the bed beside her. She was wrapped in the coverlet, facing the other way. Propped on one elbow behind her, he considered his options.

Frozen, Lenore wondered, with what little mind was left to her, what he would do.

He pinched her bottom.

"Ow!" Incensed, she rounded on him.

And found herself in his arms. Panic flared, only to be submerged by an even more frightening anticipation as he drew her closer. Lenore strove to distract them both. "That hurt!" She tried to glare but, finding his eyes coming closer and closer, she had difficulty focusing.

"Perhaps I should soothe it with a kiss?" Jason murmured, his lips curving as they gently touched hers.

Lenore froze, her wide-eyed stare telling him more clearly than words how scandalous she found his suggestion.

Jason raised a brow. "No?" He sighed dramatically, then bent to feather another kiss across her lips. "Perhaps later."

Later? Regardless of his prowess, Lenore did not think so. She tried to shake her head to deny it all—her feelings, his words, the excitement she could feel rising inside her—but one of his hands framed her jaw. He surged up, leaning over her. Then his lips settled firmly on hers.

Lenore's lids fluttered shut, all thought suspended.

She had not known quite what to expect—more of the magic she had felt in the Lester Hall library, certainly—but was there anything that could surpass that for sheer delight?

In the long moments of her wedding-night, she learned that, indeed, there was.

To Jason, those same long moments were the culmination of an unusually long courtship—he had never waited for a woman so long. Nor, to his secret amazement, had he ever wanted a woman so much. Introducing his wife to the pleasures of the flesh was a prize he had promised himself, a prize he had actively sought, a prize he had every intention of savouring. To the full. He did not rush her, seeking instead her active participation at every stage along the course he had charted—the longest route he could find to fulfilment. When he slipped her night-gown from her, dropping it over the side of the bed, he was conscious of a sense of wonder, of awe, that all he saw was now his—not conquered but given—a prize beyond price.

She moved sensuously on the sheets, as if savouring the feel of the silk against her smooth skin. He reached his hands into her hair, spreading his fingers and drawing them free, letting the long tresses fall like spun gold across the pillows.

From under heavy lids, Lenore studied his face, recognising the desire and need etched in his shimmering eyes.

The realisation fed the flame that burned steadily inside her. She arched lightly, pressing her breast to his wandering hand. He smiled and bent his head. Pleasure streaked through her, leaving her gasping. She heard him chuckle. Lacing her fingers into his hair, she tugged gently, until he looked up, then drew his lips to hers.

He taught her the ways of kissing, how to meet him halfway. He taught her to feel no shame in her wild response to his most explicit caress. His hands were like a conjuror's, roaming her fevered skin, seeking out each secret spot and stroking it to life. His kisses reassured and excited, beckoning her forever onwards, down the path of her desire. She clung to him, seduced by the feel of hard muscle shifting beneath her small hands. And when, after what seemed like an eternity of travelling through a landscape of pleasure, he joined with her to climb the last passionate heights, she learned what it was to soar freer than air, to blaze brighter than the sun before, consumed in the starburst of heightened pleasure, she became selfless, only aware of his heartbeat and hers, mingled, the essence of life.

Slowly, like a vessel refilling, her overloaded senses returned. Sated, sleepy, she returned his soft kisses, barely aware of his murmured praises. When he drew her against him, Lenore smiled to herself, an unconscious self-satisfied smile, then settled, fulfilled and content, by his side.

A CREAK WOKE Lenore. Puzzled, she blinked and tried to sit up, only to find a heavy weight across her waist. Struggling around, she gasped as her eyes met her husband's sleepy grey gaze—and she remembered, simultaneously, where she was, who she was with, how she came to be there and what had happened. A strangled sound, half surprise, half embarrassment, escaped her.

"Hush!"

One large hand came to cradle her head, gently pressing her back to the pillows.

"Moggs—get out."

For an instant, stunned silence greeted this order. Then Lenore heard the bedroom door click quietly shut.

Jason caught his wife's gaze, and tried to keep his lips straight as he explained. "You'll have to excuse Moggs. Doubtless he thought I was alone."

"Oh." That was all Lenore could manage. She did not have her nightgown on. And he did not have a nightshirt on either.

The effect of her discovery was written in her large eyes, palest peridot, bright and clear. Jason read the message, his lips curved in anticipation.

Some vague idea that this was not how things should be—that she should, by rights, have been in her own bed and he in his by dawn—drifted into Lenore's mind. And then out, as his lips claimed hers and the memory of the night's shared pleasures drew her into the sweet vortex again.

It was hours before she rang for Trencher.

THE WEEKS that followed were an idyllic time for Lenore, a period lifted from her deepest dreams—those she had never acknowledged. Her days were filled with laughter and happy enterprise as Jason introduced her to his home. He was never far from her side as the summer days followed each other, sunshine and fair weather mirroring their interaction. The nights brought pleasures of a different sort, an enthralling web of sensation that wrapped them together with its silken strands. And through it all, like a swelling tide, ran a deepening, burgeoning realisation of what she had sensed was possible, what she had feared. But, in that halcyon time, it seemed that no dark cloud could intrude.

AS HE SAT UP and swung his legs over the edge of his wife's bed, Jason aimed a playful smack at her bottom, naked beneath the silk sheet.

"Ow!" Lenore turned to frown direfully at him, rubbing her abused posterior. As he stood and drew on his grey silk robe, her expression turned sulky. Her lips pouted, but her eyes teased. "Didn't I please you, my lord?"

His grey eyes soft as he gazed down at her, Jason laughed. Catching her hand, he leaned over her to raise it to his lips. "You always please me, Lenore, as you very well know. Stop fishing for compliments."

Lenore's smile was dazzling.

Jason ducked his head and planted a kiss on her offended rump. When she merely giggled, he raised a brow at her. "In fact, your progress in your study of certain of the wifely virtues can only be described as remarkable."

Serenely content, Lenore turned to lie back on her pillows. "I had heard you were a very experienced teacher, Your Grace."

Jason's brows rose, his expression coolly superior, but Lenore detected the twinkle in his eyes. "I will admit that in certain disciplines I have been labelled a master. However, natural aptitude and overt enthusiasm are beyond my poor powers to call forth." Cinching the tie of his robe, he swept her an elegant bow. "Those talents, my dear, are entirely your own." With a rakish smile and one last lingering look, Jason strolled across the room towards his chamber. The long windows were open; a summer breeze played with the fine curtains. Outside, a bright day beckoned, yet he had to exert all his will-power to leave his wife's bed.

Turning back at the door, he watched as she stretched languorously, like a sleek cat, sated and satisfied. They had been married more than a month yet her allure had not faded. He found her daily more fascinating, more tempting, their mutual passion more fulfilling. Which was not at all what he had expected.

"You have to admit, my dear, that this marriage of convenience has, in fact, been highly convenient for us both." With a slight smile, which did not succeed in disguising the frown lurking in his eyes, Jason turned and left the room.

Lenore returned his light smile with one of her own, yet, when he had gone, her expression slowly sobered. A puzzled frown knitted her brows.

Clouds found the sun. Suddenly chilled, Lenore pulled the coverlet up around her shoulders. Had he intended his last comment as a warning that she should not let herself forget the basis of their marriage?

With a snort, she turned on her side to stare mood-ily at her nightdress, draped crazily over a chair where it had fallen the evening before. She was in no danger of forgetting their marriage—any part of it. She knew only too well that this was her time in paradise—that soon, this phase would end and he would leave to pursue his life as he had before. She had known how it would be from the start, when they had discussed his reason for marriage in the library at Lester Hall. Her role as he saw it was engraved in stone in her mind, but she had deter-mined to focus on the present, to enjoy each moment as it came and lay up a store of memories, so that when the time came to bid him goodbye, she would be able to do it with dignity.

Grumpily, Lenore pushed aside the coverlet and, shrugging on her robe, rang for Trencher.

THE FIRST HINTS of gold had appeared in the green of the Home Wood on the day Jason and Lenore left its shady precincts to canter in companionable silence across the meadows to the forested ridge beyond.

Holding his grey hunter to a sedate pace, Jason slanted a protective glance at Lenore, beside him on a dainty roan mare. In the last weeks, she had ridden over much of the estate, accompanying him whenever he rode out, eager to learn all she could of the Abbey's holdings. Yet she was a far from intrepid horsewoman, recently admitting, when he had twitted her over her liking for the slowest mount in his stables, that she preferred to drive herself in a gig. His eyes opened, he had, from then on, taken the gig whenever possible. When he had tentatively suggested he buy her a phaeton and pair, she had laughed at him, breathlessly disclaiming all wish to travel faster than the pace of a single, well-paced beast. Jason's lips twitched. His wife, he had finally realised, liked to play safe. She did not take risks; she was happy as she was, content with who she was, and sought no additional thrills. She liked calmness, orderliness—a certain peace.

It had taken him weeks to realise that he had seriously disrupted her peace by uprooting her from Lester Hall. Ever after, he had sought to make it up to her, never entirely sure if he was succeeding, for there was still a side of her that remained hidden, elusive, a part of her he had yet to touch, to claim, to make his own.

The thought brought a frown to his eyes.

As they neared a hedge, Jason drew on his reins, turn-

ing his horse's head. "This way," he called and Lenore
followed. He led her through a gate, then down a narrow
lane, turning aside on to a bridle path cutting deep into
the forest slope.

Slightly nervous, as ever, atop a horse, Lenore kept
her placid mare's nose as close as she dared to Jason's
gelding's rump. Jason had explained that the lookout he
wished to take her to could not be reached by a carriage.
She hoped the view would be worth the journey.

As they wended their way upwards, between the boles
of tall trees, the smell of damp earth and the tang of
crushed greenery rose from beneath their horses' hooves.
And then they were in the open once more.

Lenore gasped and reined in. Before her, the Eversleigh valley lay unfurled, a patchwork of fields dotted
with cottages, the Abbey planted like a grey sentinel
in their midst. "How beautiful!" she breathed, her eyes
feasting on the panorama.

Jason dismounted and came to lift her down. While he
tethered the horses, Lenore looked her fill, then glanced
about. The lookout was no more than a natural clearing
on the side of the hill. A broad expanse of sun-warmed
grass, protected from the winds by the trees about, provided a perfect picnic spot. A small stream bubbled and
gurgled through rocks to one side, spreading to form a
small pool before tumbling over the lip to disappear on
its journey downhill.

It was too late in the day for a picnic, but Lenore saw
no reason not to avail herself of the amenities. She sat
down, then, feeling the sun strike through her riding
jacket, took it off, folding it neatly before laying it down
and stretching full-length, her head on the velvet pillow.

With a smile, Jason came up and stretched out beside
her, propped on one elbow, a speculative light in his eyes.

Lenore saw it. She struggled up on her elbows and squinted into the distance. "Having brought me here, my lord, you may now proceed to tell me what I am looking at."

Jason laughed and obliged. For the next twenty minutes, prompted by her questions, he described the layout of his tenant farms and gave her a potted history of the families who held them.

When her questions ran out, they lapsed into silence, perfectly content, the afternoon golden about them.

Dulled by his deep satisfaction in the moment, Jason's faculties slowly turned to focus on his contentment—at how odd it was that he should feel so very much at peace, as if he had gained his life's ambition and was now content to lie here, beside his wife, and revel in life's small pleasures.

His gaze dropped to Lenore, lying prone beside him, her eyes shut, a peaceful smile gently curving her lips.

Desire shook him—desire and so much more. A wealth and breadth of feeling for which he was entirely unprepared rose up and engulfed him.

Abruptly, Jason looked away, across the valley, only to have his gaze fall on the Abbey. In the past six weeks Lenore had somehow become a part of it, synonymous in his mind with his home. She was its chatelaine, in spirit as well as fact.

Allowing his mind to lose itself in aspects of his wife he found less confounding, to let the suffocating sensation that had overcome him dissipate, he dwelt on her success in taking up the reins of his household. Not that he had expected anything less. Her confidence in that sphere stemmed from experience and all in his employ had been quick to recognise that fact. He had held aloof, but had watched avidly. His wife had a natural flair for command, for organisation—the entire staff had fallen under her spell, Moggs included. He would not, in future, need to concern himself with matters within her jurisdiction.

Which meant that there was no real reason he could not return to town. September was here, the *ton* would be filtering back to the capital in preparation for the Little Season. The total apathy that filled him at the thought of the social whirl, his milieu for the past decade and more, unnerved him. Why had he changed?

"Penny for your thoughts?"

Startled, Jason glanced down to find Lenore smiling up at him. He blinked, erasing all telltale expression. He shook his head. "They wouldn't interest you."

He would have recalled the words, and his brusque tone, but it was too late. A frown crossed Lenore's brow. Her eyes leached of expression.

"I apologise for having intruded, Your Grace."

Abruptly, Lenore scrambled to her feet, all pleasure in the afternoon shattered. Briskly, she set about brushing down her skirts, shaking out her jacket before shrugging into it and buttoning it up.

Languidly, endeavouring to hide his irritation, Jason rose to his feet. Damn her questions—how could he explain his thoughts when he did not understand them himself? When they might be too dangerous to put into words? They had made an arranged marriage—he had no right to expect more. And no assurance he could get more, even should he make the demand.

What already lay between them was more than he had hoped for—he had no wish to risk it.

Assuming the faintly bored air he used to deflect the curiosity of other women, he turned the matter aside with a superior, "My dear Lenore, it is not the fashion for married couples to live in each other's pockets."

Lenore bit her tongue against the temptation to reply. She went to where her mare was peacefully cropping grass and busied herself untying her reins. Inwardly berating herself for being so foolish as to let his rejoinder bother her—for it was no more than the truth and she knew it—she silently vowed that, henceforth, she would not again fall into error, would never again forget that theirs was an arranged marriage and nothing more. From now on, she would keep her distance, as he, apparently, intended to keep his.

Jason lifted her to her saddle, then swung up to his own. Turning the grey's head back down the track, he led the way down, distracted and abstracted. Through the turmoil of his thoughts one fact stood out, immutable and unchanging. He had stated, clearly and decisively, his reasons for marrying. Lenore had accepted him on that basis, agreeing to leave her sanctuary and brave what he now recognised had been a challenging world. She was succeeding on all fronts—he could ask no more of her than that.

But if he could have his heart's desire—ask and be granted all that he wished—what then?

The grey jibbed.

His expression stony, Jason brought his horse under control and gave his attention to the ride home.

IN THE DAYS that followed, Lenore made a concerted attempt to establish a daily routine that excused her from her husband's side. Telling herself it was no more than what she would need when he was no longer in residence, she organised her day so it was full to overflowing, leaving no time for rides or picnics, or for any moping. And if her household chores were insufficient to fill her time, there was always the library. She had yet to complete a list of the types of books present, let alone consider how best to arrange them.

For his part, Jason endeavoured to respect her transparent wish for her own life, her own interests. How could he not? This was undoubtedly how their lives should be lived, he with his concerns, she with hers. There was no necessity, given the relationship they shared, for any closer communication. He knew it.

Yet, deep down, he didn't like it. At first, he told himself his odd affliction would pass, that it was merely a temporary derangement of his senses, a reaction, perhaps, to taking a wife at his advanced age and so much against his inclination. But, when he found himself propped against the wall of the corridor in the west wing, gazing moodily at the library door, dismissing his present inclinations became that much harder. Fate, he finally decided, was playing games with him.

The surrounding families had not been backward in welcoming Lenore to their circle. She dutifully played hostess to the expected visits; subsequently she and Jason were invited to the parties and dinners at which their neighbours amused themselves. They had dined with the Newingtons, and were descending the long flight of stone steps before Newington Hall, their hosts waiting on the porch above to wave them on their way, when fate sent Lady Newington's fox terrier, escaping from the confines of the house, to nip at the carriage horses' legs.

Chaos ensued.

Both horses reared, then plunged, tangling the traces. The footman, who had been holding the carriage door, swore and dashed after the dog, trying to shoo it from under the frightened horses' hooves.

"Wait here!" Jason left Lenore on the bottom step and ran to the horses' heads. Horton, caught by surprise, was struggling with the reins, trying to calm his charges to no avail. Another minute and one or both of the prize chestnuts Jason had bought to pull his wife's carriage would have a leg over the traces.

Lenore watched as Jason caught the offside horse's harness just above the bit, calming and soothing the panicking beast. But Horton could still not control the wheeler; the horse reared again, dragging on the traces. Lenore heard Lord Newington puffing his way down the steps and waited no longer. She ran to the wheeler, catching its head as she had seen Jason do, crooning soothing nothings to the snorting animal.

Prodded by the footman, the dog scooted from under the carriage and made for the shrubbery.

Slowly, peace returned to the scene before Newington Hall. The horses, sensing the departure of the devil that had attacked them, calmed, still snorting and shifting restlessly but no longer in danger of doing themselves injury.

With a sigh of relief, Lenore let the huge head slip from her grasp. She glanced at her husband—and realised her relief was premature. His lips were a thin line; his grey eyes glinted steel. He was furious and only just succeeding in keeping his tongue between his teeth.

A cold vice closed about her heart. Lenore turned away as Lord Newington reached her.

"I say, Lady Eversleigh! Damned courageous and all that—but dangerous, m'dear—want to watch out for such beasts, y'know."

"Precisely my thoughts," Jason said through clenched teeth. "Perhaps, my dear, you should sit down in the carriage. We'd best be on our way."

Allowing him to hand her into the carriage, Lenore held her tongue as Jason took his leave of Lord Newington and climbed in after her. Outside, the light had almost gone; in the shadowy carriage, she could not make out his expression.

He waited until they gained the main road before saying, "It's my fervent hope, my dear Lenore—nay, my *express wish*—that in future, when I give you a direct order, you will obey it."

Shaken by the violence of his feelings, Jason did not mute his scathing accents. He turned his head and saw that, far from appearing contrite, Lenore's head was up, her chin tilted at a far from conciliatory angle.

"If that is the case, my lord," Lenore replied, "I suggest you endeavour to instil your orders with more sense. You know perfectly well the wheeler would have broken a fetlock, if not worse, had I not calmed him." That her husband should so repay her aid hurt more than she would have believed possible. But she was not going to let him see that she cared. "Lord Newington would never have reached him in time, and even then, I doubt his lordship would have had the strength to do the job. I did—and all ended well. I do not in the least understand why you're so piqued. Surely not simply because I disobeyed you?"

Her sarcastic tone proved too much for Jason's temper. "God grant me patience," he appealed. "Has it not occurred to you, my dear, that I might, conceivably, be concerned for your welfare? That I might, just possibly, feel responsible for your safety?"

Lenore's wide stare told him more clearly than words that such a notion had never entered her head. She was appalled by the idea. In her experience, people who felt responsible for one's safety invariably ended by trying to proscribe one's existence. The possibility that her husband harboured such feelings, in a proprietorial way, was alarming. "But why should you?" she continued. "We might be married but I can hardly allow that to be sufficient cause to permit you to dictate my actions in such circumstances."

"If your actions weren't so damned foolhardy, I dare say I shouldn't wish to dictate them at all!"

Lenore's temper soared to dizzying heights. Putting her nose in the air, she stated, "I fail to see, my lord, why you should so greatly exercise your sensibilities over my poor self. Given the businesslike nature of our relationship, I really don't see that you need feel *responsible* for me. If I take hurt as a result of my own actions, I do not believe that reflects on you. I consider my life my own concern."

"Until you provide me with heirs you may forget that particular consideration."

Deprived by his chilly words of any of her own, Lenore sat rigid on the carriage seat and uncharacteristically wished her life were over. She felt bereft, struck numb with despair. His tone, cold and hard and utterly uncompromising, confirmed beyond doubt how he saw their union. His only interest in her revolved about whether she could fulfil her role as his wife—giving him the heirs he sought was one part of the contract—a part she had yet to fulfil. Lenore blinked back the moisture welling in her eyes. She had wondered why he had dallied for so long instead of returning to his usual haunts in London. Now she knew. And once she had delivered on that part of her promise, his interest in her would evaporate—his statement implied as much—how much more clearly did she need to have it said?

He had married her for his reasons, there was nothing more to their marriage than that.

Her spine rigid with the effort of preserving her composure, Lenore was grateful for the enclosing dark. Hidden in its shadows, she pushed the hurt deep, reminding herself of the household, the position, the library she had gained through marrying Jason Montgomery.

The carriage was nearing the boundary of his estates before the red haze of temper lifted sufficiently for Jason to realise just what he had said. Appalled, by the fact that she could so overset his reason as well as by his apparent insensitivity, he rapidly cast about for some means to mend his fences. But what could he say?

His fury had been invoked by shock—but he could hardly confess to that. The fact she would do what she deemed right regardless of any danger to herself horrified him. How could he possibly feel confident leaving her if that was the way she might behave, even when he was there to order her otherwise? He had thought her liking for non-hazardous pursuits would have saved him any angst—obviously not so. Lenore preferred playing safe, but if that was not possible, she would do what was necessary. Unfortunately, she was clearly not prepared to take his ridiculous sensitivity into account in so doing.

Even more unfortunately, he felt prohibited from making said sensitivity plain, aware he had limited grounds for feeling so. Worse, she would doubtless see it as an imposition on her rightful freedoms. He had no wish to reward her exemplary efforts to fill the role of the Duchess of Eversleigh by placing what she would see as unwarranted constraints on her behaviour.

But he had to say something. The silence in the carriage had become darker than the night outside.

"Lenore…" For the first time in his entire career,

Jason was lost for words. He could not explain what he felt—he did not know himself.

As it transpired, Lenore was not ready for explanations, her struggle not to cry consumed too much of her mind. She put a hand to her temple. "I'm afraid I have a headache. If you do not mind, I would rather we did not talk, Your Grace."

Stiffly, Jason inclined his head in acceptance of her request. Resettling his head against the squabs, he wondered why her headache should hurt him so much.

Lenore managed to hold her head high as Jason handed her down from the carriage before the Abbey. She trod up the steps, her hand on his sleeve, but when they reached the hall, she murmured, "My headache, my lord—I believe I'll retire immediately."

Jason merely bowed, apparently indifferent, and let her go.

For the first time since coming to the Abbey, Lenore slept alone.

CHAPTER TEN

How COULD she have overlooked it? Appalled, Lenore stared at the pages of her diary, her mind numb, her fingers trembling.

She had woken early, but had lain, listless in her bed, for hours. Finally rising and ringing for Trencher, she had dressed for the day but had shied from facing her husband over the breakfast-table. Instead, she had sat at the little escritoire by the wall near one window and opened her diary to record the events of the previous evening— depressing though they were.

No words had come. No light comments to record her swelling misery. In an effort to ease her gloom, she had flipped back through the recent pages, filled with glowing happiness and an unstated hope she now knew to be forlorn.

It was then it had struck her.

They had been married in late July. It was now mid-September. August had been a blissful month, totally unmarred by the usual occurrence. For one who had been regularly afflicted ever since she was thirteen, the conclusion was inescapable.

She was pregnant.

With child.

Very possibly bearing Jason's heir.

For one very long moment, she considered not telling him. But that was impossible. Much as she might wish to prolong the time he spent with her—surely last night had simply been his reaction to her supposed indisposition?—she doubted she could keep the news from him and still keep her self-respect. He was waiting for this to occur before he returned to London. He was only doing what his family wished in that respect; the need for an heir was obvious, even she understood that. The requirement had been the principal element in his reason for marrying.

And now she had met it.

Staring, unseeing, at the pale pages inscribed with her flowing script, Lenore called on all her inner strength. She must tell him—and then show a brave face when he took his leave of her. That would be the hardest part. For it had happened much as she had predicted: she had fallen in love with him—when, exactly, she did not know, but weeks ago, certainly. Deeply, totally, irrevocably in love.

And she had known it for weeks, but had tried not to acknowledge it, knowing this day would dawn. Now it had, and she had to carry on, do what she had to and pretend it didn't hurt.

With her usual calm Lenore closed her diary and pushed it into the desk drawer. Then she stood and smoothed down the skirt of her green muslin morning gown before heading for the door. She had to find her husband and tell him the glad tidings—before she broke down and cried.

But Jason was not at the breakfast-table; when applied to, Morgan informed her he thought his master had gone riding.

There was nothing to do but retreat to the library and try not to think of the black cloud hanging over her.

In the end, Lenore did not set eyes on her husband

until dinnertime. Arriving in the drawing-room just ahead of Morgan, he looked so severely handsome that she had to blink rapidly to clear her vision. She accepted his arm into the smaller dining parlour where they sat at either end of the table with space for six between. The presence of the servants made private conversation impossible. Jason seemed abstracted; after casting about and coming up with no subject for inconsequential chatter, Lenore followed his lead and kept silent.

But when it came time for her to leave him to his port, her confidence faltered. What if he did not join her in the drawing-room? Twisting the fingers of one hand in the other, she stood as Morgan pulled back her chair. "My lord," she began hesitantly. "There is something I must discuss with you, if you would be so good as to spare me a few minutes."

Jerked from his thoughts, Jason looked up, frowning as his sharp eyes detected her distress. "Yes, of course, my dear. I'll join you in a moment." God—had it come to this, that his wife needs must make an appointment to see him?

As the door closed behind her, Jason drained his wine and waved aside the decanter a footman proffered. "Leave me."

Alone with his thoughts, he grimaced. What the devil had happened between them? He had spent all day in a fruitless endeavour to define just what had changed— was it him or her or had they both altered in just a month? With a despondent sigh, he pushed back his chair and stood, stretching, trying to shake the tension from his shoulders.

Whatever had happened, he could not concentrate on anything other than the fact that his wife was worried about something. Useless to try to focus on his problem until he had straightened hers out.

Lenore had only just settled in her favourite chair by the hearth when Jason came through the door. She immediately sat up, clasping her hands tightly in her lap. He smiled reassuringly, coming forward to take the chair opposite, stretching out his long legs and crossing his booted ankles.

"Well, madam wife, you perceive me all ears. What has occurred to put you in such serious vein?" In an effort to lighten her mood, Jason tried for a bantering note. "Let me guess—you've discovered that many of the books in the library are fake? No? Don't tell me—you've conceived of a wish to redecorate in the romantic style and want my permission to drape the front hall in yards of pink silk?"

When his ridiculous *badinage* raised not a glimmer of response, Jason became seriously alarmed. He straightened in his chair, his expression sober. "Lenore, what is it?"

"I..." Lenore looked at him helplessly. "I'm pregnant." Despite her best intentions, she could not make the fact sound like anything other than the catastrophic occurrence she felt it was.

As it transpired, Jason did not notice, too bowled over by her news. A streak of pure elation seared through him, followed by a jumbled medley of pride, joy and truly humble thanks to a fate that had given him all this. As the first flush of reaction faded, he realised he was grinning inanely. Then his eyes sought Lenore's only to find that her head was bowed, her gaze on her interlaced fingers, twisting in her lap. "My dear, you've made me the happiest man alive."

Lenore looked up, startled by the sincerity ringing in

his tone. "Oh…I mean, yes. That is…" Lenore faltered to a stop, nonplussed. She could hardly tell him it was not entirely her doing—he would laugh at her. Instead, she took a deep breath and, holding her serene mask firmly in place, forced herself to take the next step. "In the circumstances, I expect you'll be returning to London shortly, will you not?"

She had intended to keep her gaze level with his, but could not prevent it falling. Consequently she did not see the frown that passed through Jason's eyes, or the way his jaw clenched as his moment of joy was abruptly curtailed.

For a moment, Jason thought he had not heard her aright. Then his world came crashing down about his ears. She wanted him to leave. He had played his part in fulfilling the expectations of their marriage; he was free to depart. As if from a distance, he heard himself say, "Yes, I rather suppose I will."

An inane response. He did not want to leave but what else was he do do? Stay and make a fool of himself over a wife who did not want him?

He cleared his throat. "There are a few things I should attend to but I expect I'll head back in a day or so."

It was an effort to draw breath but, now the moment was upon her, Lenore found the strength to carry through her charade. Looking up, into his grey eyes, she smiled. "I was wondering, my lord, if you could get me some books from Hatchards? There are one or two studies on cataloguing I would like to consult before I make a start on the library. If you could send them down to me as soon as possible I'd be extremely grateful."

It was not her gratitude he wanted. But, if that was all she was offering, so be it. Stunned, confused, Jason studied her, his expression bleak. "I'd be happy to do so.

If you'll give me your list, I'll have my secretary arrange for the matter to be attended to immediately when I reach town."

She managed to keep her mask from slipping even though the thought that her request would be handled by his secretary slipped under her guard and hurt dreadfully. Lenore inclined her head, her smile still in place. "Thank you, my lord. I'll write it down immediately, if you'll excuse me. I would not wish to have you delay for it."

Defeated, Jason stood as she rose. With a regal nod, she passed by him, gliding gracefully to the door.

Lenore paused with her hand on the knob. "Goodnight, my lord."

"Goodnight, madam wife."

His tone was cold, distant, very far from the warmth they had once shared. Stifling her sigh for what she knew she could never have, Lenore closed the door behind her.

Jason slumped back into his chair, covering his eyes with one hand, the other clenching into a fist on his knee. For a long time, he sat motionless, his mind aimlessly scanning the recent past, forming and discarding possible futures. Eventually, he sighed deeply and sat up, running his hands over his face. What to do?

Hours later, he climbed the stairs with no answer to hand. Undressing and donning his robe, he automatically headed for Lenore's room but pulled up short, eyeing the door. She was pregnant—and had all but declared she expected him to leave, his duty done. That was certainly not his inclination but unless he was prepared to stake a claim to something more—to declare his wish that their marriage should be more than the cold-blooded arrangement he had originally sought—did he have the right to demand more of her? If he went in, would she welcome him to her bed? Or simply accommodate him rather than make a scene?

With a smothered groan, Jason turned away from the door, drifting to the window to stare out at the dark. Lenore had left him with a decision to make and make it he must. What did he really want—of marriage, of life, of Lenore?

He had thought he had known, that his habits were set, yet she had changed him, changed him so much he could not recognise himself. And no longer had any confidence that he knew where he was headed or what was best for him. After thirty-eight years of unmitigated hedonism he felt like a dithering fool, unable to shake free of his confusion and take a firm step forward. His uncertainty paralysed him, destroying his usual decisiveness, making him vacillate when his temperament called for action. The tangled web of his emotions was tearing him apart.

Perhaps he should leave. Lenore clearly did not want him, regardless of whatever he might want of her. He had wanted a bride who would fulfil his reasons for marriage—he had got what he had asked for; he could not complain.

But he could minimise the pain he now felt. There was nothing to prevent him taking her up on her offer to release him from waiting on her here in the country. In London, there would be plenty of women eager to warm his bed—there always had been and, if he knew anything of women, his marriage would only whet their appetites.

Glancing down at the shadows on the floor, Jason thought of the scene when he told her he was leaving. What would she do? Smile brightly and scurry off to get her list of books?

With a smothered curse, he shrugged off his robe and climbed into his bed. He would leave tomorrow morning. Early. Without her wretched list. She could send it on. At least, that way he would not have to endure her smiles as she waved him goodbye.

VACUOUS CHATTER engulfed Jason the instant he set foot in Lady Beauchamp's salon. After two nights in less elevated circles, he was back in the bosom of the *ton*. Wandering aimlessly through the crowd, nodding to acquaintances sighted through the crush, he wondered, not for the first time in the past three days, just what he was doing here. He had arrived at Eversleigh House to find a stack of invitations waiting on the desk in his library; this was the third night of stale air and loud voices he had endured in his search for… His expression hardening, Jason forced himself to continue with the thought, the one he had grown adept at avoiding. He was searching for relief from his fascination with his wife.

He knew no other word for it, the emotion he felt for Lenore. The poets had another, but he was not comfortable with that. Frustrated fascination seemed damning enough to have to admit to.

"Ho! Jason!"

Jason turned to see Frederick pushing through the bodies towards him. They shook hands, Frederick thumping his shoulder.

"Where've you been? Looked to see you long before this."

"The Abbey," Jason replied shortly.

"Oh." Frederick glanced more carefully at him, then looked about. "Where's Lenore?"

Having expected this question, Jason had no difficulty keeping his expression untroubled. "She remained at the Abbey."

"Oh?" Frederick looked worried. After some hesitation, he asked diffidently, "Nothing amiss, I take it?"

Jason opened his eyes wide. "She *prefers* the country, remember?"

"Well, yes, but newly wed and all that, y'know. Thought she'd have come up with you this once."

"She didn't," Jason replied curtly, feeling his mask slip. Abruptly, he asked, "What's all this I've been hearing about Castlereagh?"

After ten minutes' intense speculation on the latest political scandal, Jason left his friend to move among the brightly clad, exotically scented matrons who had for years provided him with the opportunity for scandal of a different sort. Not that any of his affairs, conducted as they always had been with discretion, had ever been the subject of a duel, nor even much more than speculation. While casting his eye over the field, he met Agatha.

"There you are, Eversleigh. 'Bout time, too." Agatha fixed her nephew with a shrewd eye. "So you've finally managed to drag yourself away from the amenities of the Abbey, have you?"

To his chagrin, Jason flushed and could find nothing to say.

Agatha chuckled. "Where's Lenore? I haven't sighted her yet."

As his aunt glanced about, trying, from her far from sufficient height, to see about her, Jason stated bluntly, "She's not here."

"Oh?" Agatha's eyes gleamed. "Not *indisposed*, is she?"

The prospect of having his wife's condition broadcast to the *ton* stared Jason in the face. His expression hardened. "She stayed at the Abbey."

"Oh." Agatha's face showed clear evidence of her bewilderment. "But…" She frowned, then added, "Dare say you're both old enough to know your own minds, but it would really be much better if Lenore was to come to town now, to be presented as your duchess. Plenty of time later to stay in the country. Best, I would have thought, to get the part of the business she dislikes over with now. Doesn't pay to disappoint the expectations of the *ton*, y'know."

With that sage advice, and looking rather more troubled than she had before she had met him, Agatha nodded and moved on.

Jason returned her nod absent-mindedly, his brain busy with her words. Agatha had her finger firmly upon the shifting pulse of *ton* approbation; no one knew this world better than she. Although he had not previously considered her point, it did not take much thought to suspect her advice was sound. Perhaps he should convey her thoughts to Lenore?

"Eversleigh! It does my heart good to see you back among us, Your Grace."

With a slightly sceptical lift to his brows, Jason turned to bow over the hand of Lady Ormsby, a spectacular beauty whom he had long suspected of having designs on him. Only a few subtle sentences were needed to confirm that fact. Her ladyship gave him to understand that, now that he had provided himself with the additional safety of a wife, a further piece of camouflage for any illicit affair, she felt that nothing now stood in the way of their pursuing a more intimate relationship.

Nothing, Jason mused, his temper stirring at her ladyship's dismissive reference to his wife, beyond his own lack of interest. In days past, he would very likely have accepted Lady Ormsby's invitation. Now, looking into her hard blue eyes, he could not understand what had ever attracted him to her like. They had no softness, no womanly gentleness, none of the spontaneous sensuality he had found in Lenore. The idea of compromising his now much higher standards, of accepting such unattractive liaisons in lieu of his conjugal rights, appalled him. It was not possible.

Extricating himself from Lady Ormsby's clutches without causing undue offence required a not inconsiderable degree of talent. Finally quitting her ladyship's side, leaving her disappointed but not slighted, Jason ruefully reflected that this was the third night he had had need of that particular art. The undeniable conclusion from his three days of distraction was becoming increasingly hard to avoid.

He missed Lenore. During the day, he prowled about town, finding no joy in the pursuits that had filled his life for years. Yesterday, when her brief letter enclosing her list had arrived, he had pounced on it. Compton had not even seen it—*he* had gone to Hatchards and bought her books for her, adding two he thought she might like to the pile before having it wrapped and sent down to the Abbey. For the rest of the day he had wandered about, eschewing his clubs for the fresher air of the parks, his mind filled with imaginings of how his wife was filling her day.

As for his nights, they were lonely and miserable. When it came down to it, he had spent much of his life alone, but now he felt more alone than ever before, cold, as if his arms longed for her warmth.

"Eversleigh! Good God, man, look where you're going! You've trodden on my flounce."

Abruptly called to order, Jason hurriedly removed his foot from his aunt Eckington's purple flounce and nodded in greeting. "My pardon, Aunt."

"So I should hope." Lady Eckington fixed her basilisk stare, known to have reduced Hussars to meekness, upon him. "Where's your wife? Haven't seen her yet but that's hardly surprising in this crush."

There was nothing like familial pressure, Jason decided, to force one to acknowledge the error of one's ways. He smiled at his aunt, knowing his imperviousness to her intimidation always annoyed her. "She remained at the Abbey for a few days more—I came up to ensure everything was as it should be at Eversleigh House. I plan to go down tomorrow and bring her back with me."

"Excellent!" Lady Eckington's ostrich feathers bobbed. "A very wise move. She'll no doubt wish to establish herself in society while the leniency extended to a newly-wed wife is still hers."

Jason stored that one up for Lenore, should she prove difficult.

"Must say," her ladyship declared, her gaze fixed on Jason's face, "I'm glad to see you taking your responsibilities seriously, Jason. A workable marriage can make all the difference, y'know. And Lenore's an exceptional choice—getting your marriage on a solid foundation would be well worth your effort."

With a nod, Lady Eckington bustled away. Jason watched her go, a smile on his lips, for once in total agreement with his father's eldest sister.

HAVING MADE his decision, for good or ill, Jason wasted no time. Leaving London the next day, he spent the night at Salisbury, arriving at the Abbey in the early afternoon. Leaving his groom to drive his curricle to the stables, he strode up the steps to where the front doors were propped wide. As he crossed the threshold, his eyes not yet adjusted to the dimmer light, his ears were assailed by a shriek.

"Damnation, Morgan! Oh! It's you, Your Grace. Begging your pardon, m'lord, but we weren't expecting you."

Blinking, Jason saw Mrs. Potts heave herself up from her knees. Glancing about, he met the accusing stares of a gaggle of maids, all on their knees scrubbing the hall tiles. Two scrambled up to mop up the pool of water he had sent across the floor when he had kicked one of their buckets.

"Her Grace decided 'twas time to have a clean-up in here," said Mrs. Potts, drying her hands on her apron as she came forward. "Quite right, too."

"I dare say," Jason replied. "Where is your mistress?"

"In the library, Y'r Grace."

Where else? "Don't disturb yourself, Mrs. Potts. I'll go to her there."

"Yes, Y'r Grace. Er...will you be staying, m'lord?"

Jason halted, frowning. "How long I remain depends on Her Grace. However, we'll both be leaving for town in a few days, at most."

Mrs. Potts beamed. "Yes, of course, Your Grace."

With a benevolent nod, Jason turned and headed for the library. The instant he stepped through the doors, he saw Lenore had made a start on her cataloguing. There were piles of books everywhere, emptied from the shelves and balanced one upon the other in stacks as high as his shoulders. Closing the door gently behind him, he glanced about but could not see her. Carefully he wended his way through the stacks, stepping softly.

Up in the gallery, Lenore was seated on a cushion on the floor, staring out of the large windows before her, a book on the medicinal properties of herbs open in her lap. She had not turned a page for nearly an hour.

Despite her efforts to hold back her dismal thoughts, they persisted in trapping her whenever she allowed her mind a moment's respite from the activities she had organised. The first four days following Jason's departure had passed in a dull haze, her mind never really winning free of the aching loneliness that had gripped her on reading his brief note, stating that he had altered his plans and had left early that morning, bidding her a distant adieu until he returned. Yesterday, she had declared "Enough!" and made a determined effort to get her new life back on track. She had her position, her own household to run—it was time she commenced running it again. She had a library to catalogue—she had started in with a vengeance. She had a child, growing within her, and that was what, all too often today, had seduced her mind from the task at hand.

She had not previously given a child much thought— how would a new small person fit into her life? Would a child, their child, ease the empty ache she now felt in that part of her heart that Jason had claimed as his, had filled and now left void? Somehow, she could not quite believe that it would. But she had all that she had been promised—and her memories. She had no cause for complaint.

With a deep sigh, she looked down at the book in her lap, trying to remember why she had been studying it.

"I might have guessed."

Lenore looked up, straight into her husband's grey eyes, and only just managed to keep her joy from bursting forth. He stood a few feet away, one shoulder propped against the window-frame, horrendously handsome, his driving cloak with all its capes hanging from his broad shoulders to his calves. For a moment, her senses swayed, urging her to fly to his arms. With an effort, she shackled them, forcing herself to calm. Serenity intact, she smiled. "Good afternoon, my lord. We did not look to see you return so soon. Is anything wrong?"

Faced with a far calmer reception that he had hoped for, Jason did not return her smile. Her attitude dashed his unacknowledged hopes, making it plain that she had not missed him as he had missed her, that she was perfectly content cataloguing her damned library. "My aunts asked after you," he offered in explanation. "They believe you should come up to town and make your social début as my wife now rather than later. They were quite adamant on the matter and, having considered their arguments, I suspect they're right."

While listening to this cool recitation of his eminently sensible reasons for returning, Lenore shut the book in her lap and placed it aside. Taking the hand he offered, she rose and brushed down her skirts. "So you wish me to go back to town with you?"

To Jason, her reluctance was obvious. Slamming a door on his emotions to protect them from further hurt, he inclined his head coolly. "I believe it'll be best for you to appear in town at least for the Little Season."

Casting a last, resigned glance at her piles of musty tomes, Lenore allowed him to tuck her hand in his arm and lead her from her sanctuary. The idea of going to town with him—to have to watch from the sidelines as he enjoyed himself in the company of other women, all more attractive to a man of his tastes than she could ever be—filled her with dread. Her feelings, only just soothed after the trauma of his leaving, would be raked raw anew. How could she face it?

She would have to face it, her inner voice noted. He was not asking for anything outrageous; in fact, he was probably doing the right thing in insisting she go to

London. If Agatha and the rest of his aunts thought she should, then they were probably right. And she could never explain why she was so very reluctant to leave the secure peace of the Abbey—not to anyone.

Leading her from the library, Jason felt a perverse pleasure in dragging her from her books. Immediately he acknowledged the feeling, he was appalled. What was this fascination of his reducing him to?

As it transpired, having accepted the inevitable, Lenore had too much to do to brood on the fact. On her discovering that her husband intended to dally no longer than was necessary for her to get herself organised, her hours were filled with giving orders—for the household in her absence, to Trencher over which gowns she wanted packed. They departed after luncheon the next day.

As the carriage rattled over the cobbles, Lenore put her head back on the squabs and sent up an urgent prayer for deliverance. She could not endure much more swaying. She had never before been so afflicted and suspected the cause was not far to seek. This was what happened to women with child, or so she had read.

The long journey had been uneventful enough. The first stage to Salisbury had not been that long; she had coped quite well, the carriage rattling along at a good pace over the uncrowded roads. They had spent the night with Jason's uncle, taking to the road after breakfast. Breakfast had been a mistake. Luckily, Jason had spent much of the day on horseback. He had decided to take his favourite hunter to town, presumably, Lenore supposed, so that in November he could travel on direct to his hunting box in Leicestershire while she returned to the Abbey. He had elected to ride, allowing Trencher to travel in the carriage with her, leaving space for the groom beside the coachman on the box. Trencher, she had discovered, was a fount of wisdom on childbearing.

"Three of m'sisters have had six of 'em, my lady. Don't you fret. This'll only last a little while. Best try to get your mind off your stomach—think of something nice."

Lenore thought of Jason, and the hours they had shared in her bed at the Abbey. Which had led to her present predicament, which in turn led her thoughts back to the nausea that threatened to overwhelm her.

By the time Jason had displaced Trencher on the outskirts of the capital, she had felt a lot better. As her husband had been unfailingly kind in a highly distant fashion, Lenore was reluctant to attract his somewhat unnerving attention; she had said nothing of her indisposition.

But the slow, rocking progress through the crowded streets of the capital had sorely tried her fortitude.

"We're here." Beside her, Jason sat up. As the carriage rocked to a final halt, he reached for the door. Alighting, he turned to hand her down. Lenore quit the coach with alacrity. As she walked up the steps by her husband's side, she heaved a sigh of relief to have her feet on solid ground.

Jason heard her sigh but interpreted it quite differently.

Lenore had visited Eversleigh House but briefly in the weeks before their marriage, her only concern then to determine if she wished any of the chambers other than her own to be redecorated. She hadn't. The current vogue for white and gilt had never found favour with her; the solid polished oak with which Jason had filled his house, the deep greens and reds and blues of the upholstery, were much more to her taste. There had been nothing to change; Jason had claimed as his prerogative the redecoration of her rooms. It was, therefore, with a sense of expectation that she allowed him to lead her up the stairs at the conclusion of the traditional servants' welcome in the hall.

"These are your rooms." Jason set the door wide and stood back, his eyes going to her face, keen, despite the continuing hurt that ate at his confidence, to see if she liked what he had had done.

Slowly, Lenore entered, eyes drawn immediately to the bed. Of pale polished oak, it was wide but not overly high, the mattress sunk into the base. High above its centre, a gold ball hung, suspended from where she could not tell. From it depended a tent of green silk, pegged out to the four corners of the bed where four slim columns of turned wood ran upwards to support it. It was an elegant bed of unusual design, the floral carvings that marked the headboard repeated on the footboard. Silks and satins in a melding of pale greens covered the expanse. It looked remarkably comfortable.

Turning, Lenore saw that all the furniture—the large dressing-table, an escritoire, two cheval glasses and three huge wardrobes—as well as a selection of occasional tables, sidetables, chairs and stools scattered about the large room, were all in the same fine wood upholstered in greens and soft golds.

Letting out a long sigh of pure appreciation, Lenore glanced about, locating her husband by the dressing-table. Meeting his watchful gaze, she smiled, utterly unaffected, her mask put aside. "It's absolutely lovely, my lord. Just what I would have wished for."

Her words, she was pleased to note, brought a slight smile to her husband's lips. He had, she had noticed, been rather sombre of late.

"I'd hoped for your approval. And I hope you approve of these, too."

Drawing nearer, Lenore saw that his hand rested on a large, flattish velvet case.

"I had these made up for you," Jason said, lifting the lid of the case. "Using some of the stones in the older pieces of the family collection. The diamonds are in the safe downstairs—I'll show them to you later. But I thought these are probably more your style at present."

Lenore did not answer. Eyes wide, she stared at the range of necklaces, earrings, pendants, rings and brooches revealed within the case. Winking in the last of the afternoon sunlight, emeralds and topazes, pearls and peridots glimmered and shone against the black satin lining. Slowly, Lenore sank on to the stool before the dressing-table, her fingers stealing to the jewels. Her jewels. She had never had much in the way of jewellery—her mother's pearls had come to her, but the rest of the family collection was in keeping for Jack's wife.

As her fingers caressed a delicate peridot and pearl necklace, she glanced up, blinking rapidly, at her husband. She wanted to thank him, but "Oh, Jason," was all she could say, and even then her voice quavered.

Luckily, he seemed to understand, for he smiled, much more his old teasing self, and reached for the necklace.

"Here, try it on."

He fastened the catch at the nape of her neck. Lenore stood and stepped away from the table, the better to view her reflection in the mirror above it. Jason stepped back but remained behind her, watching over her shoulder as she fingered the delicate pearl drops.

Finally, drawing in a shattered breath, Lenore smiled mistily at him in the mirror. "These are truly exquisite, my lord. I don't know how to thank you."

His eyes dropped to her throat, as if studying the necklace. From behind, his fingers came, first to trace the strand as it encircled her neck, then to caress her sensitive nape. "No thanks are required, my dear. You're my wife, after all."

His words were light; not so the expression in his eyes. As his head lowered, his object clearly to place a kiss on her throat, Lenore panicked.

Turning, she blurted out the first thing that came into her head. "Regardless of that fact, my lord, these are the most wonderful gifts I've ever been given. I do thank you, most sincerely."

She could not bear to look into his eyes. The silence stretched, then was broken when he said, "I'm overjoyed that they meet with your approval, my dear."

His tone was distant again, miles away.

"I'll leave you now. No doubt you'd like to rest." Feeling as if someone had landed a direct hit to his stomach, Jason forced himself to stroll to the door. His hand on the knob, he paused. "My aunt Eckington is giving a ball tonight. If you're not too tired, I suspect it would be wise for us to attend."

"Yes, of course," Lenore agreed, desperate to make amends for her rebuff. "I'm sure I'll be perfectly recovered by then." Shyly, trying to read his expression across the slowly darkening room, she added, "I'll take great delight in wearing some of your gifts tonight, Jason."

"I'll look forward to seeing them on you," he replied, coldly formal. With a polite nod, he left the room.

Appalled, Lenore sank on to the stool before her dressing-table, one hand pressed to her lips. She knew perfectly well why she had shied away from that kiss— one kiss was all it would take for him to have her in his arms—and, once that happened, there would be only one

end to their embrace. Not that she feared the outcome—
oh, no. That, she longed for with all her being. But his
leaving her at the Abbey had forced her to acknowledge
the depth of her feelings, the totally consuming, all-en-
compassing love she felt for him.

And she was no longer sure she could keep it secret,
certainly not if he surprised her as he had just then. She
had no desire to forbid him her bed; she had thought he
would come to her at night, when she could keep up her
guard, endure her love in silence, protected from his too-
perceptive gaze by the dark.

For it would never do to let him know she loved him—
not as she did. It would embarrass her and probably him,
too, although he would never let her see it. He would be
kind and gentle and as caring as could be, but he would
not love her.

That had never been one of his reasons for marriage.

CHAPTER ELEVEN

LATER THAT EVENING, Jason, his emotions under the severest control, propped the wall of his aunt's ballroom and watched as his duchess made her bow to polite society. His aunt Eckington's ball was the perfect venue; his senior paternal aunt commanded an awesome position in the *ton*. With Lady Eckington and her sister's support, Lenore's success was assured.

Not that his wife needed any help. She looked superb, all traces of tiredness vanished, her gleaming hair coiled about her head, her ivory shoulders bare. She had worn a pearl and emerald necklace, one he had given her, with her stunning deep green gown. The matching bracelets, worn high on her forearms, caught and diffracted the light. She looked gorgeous; he could not tear his eyes from her.

At the very hub of all attention, Lenore suffered an interminable round of introductions conducted by her hostess, ably seconded by Agatha. They ensured she met all the senior hostesses—to her considerable surprise, all these august matrons seemed only too pleased to exchange words and invitations with her. Then she realised that, as the Duchess of Eversleigh, she herself was now of their group; they were only seeking to establish social connection with the latest member of the highest echelon in the *ton*.

The realisation gave her courage to endure the smiles

and nods and arch questions. The danger in admitting to her condition was obvious. Once Jason's aunts learned she was carrying the heir, for so they would see it, they would hem her about, fuss and fume over her—they would drive her mad. So she blithely turned aside all their delicately probing questions. Her years of experience stood her in good stead; her new awareness of her station allowed her the liberty of distance, if she chose to assume it. Two hours of intense activity saw her feet firmly on the road to social success.

"Phew!" Agatha threw her a heartening glance. "You've done well, my dear. I know it's all a bit trying, especially as you don't look to be in town much. But having the position counts, when all's said and done. It would do you no good to ignore it."

Lenore acknowledged her mentor's words with a smile, inwardly wondering where Jason was. She still felt horrendously guilty over her afternoon's gaucherie. Try as she might, she had not been able to mend her fences, for he had given her no opportunity to do so. In fact, he had been so distant, she had barely found a chance to smile at him, let alone thank him as she ought for his thoughtful gifts. And if he continued as he was, she doubted she would get a chance.

Perhaps that was as well. When he came to her tonight, she would apologise and make him laugh, then thank him as he had wished her to do this afternoon.

"Lady Eversleigh, my dear. A pleasure to see you in town."

Lenore turned to find Lord Selkirk, a friend of Harry's, by her side. She held out her hand. "Good evening, my lord. Are you here for the duration or merely until the next meeting at Newmarket?"

"Dash it, m'dear. I'm not such a tipster as all that."

"Lenore, dear. How's life with His Grace of Eversleigh?"

Absorbed with turning aside such jocular queries, before she knew it Lenore was surrounded by a small court of acquaintances, friends of her brothers and some of the young ladies she had met in the weeks before her wedding. There was no escape from their chatter. Lenore smiled serenely and bore up under the strain, determined none would be able to say that the Duchess of Eversleigh was not up to snuff.

But she was wilting. In the heat of the ballroom, with the press of bodies all about her, the air close and increasingly stale, she started to feel her senses slide and wondered, in desperation, if she could break free. The conversation about her became a droning buzz in her ears.

"There you are, my dear."

Jason's strong voice hauled her back to reality an instant before faintness took hold. Lenore looked up at him with relief in her wide eyes and a small, tight smile on her lips.

Jason understood. He had crossed the room as soon as he had realised how long she had been standing at the centre of her circle. While no gathering, no matter how large, held the slightest power to overwhelm him, he knew she felt differently. He took her hand in a comforting clasp and, with the briefest of nods to her court, led her to the dance-floor.

Lenore came back to life to find herself held in her husband's arms, slowly circling the room in a waltz. She blinked rapidly. "Th-thank you, my lord. I…didn't feel at all the thing, just then. The lack of air, I expect."

"No doubt." Jason glanced down at her. "We'll leave after this dance."

Lenore was too grateful to take umbrage at his edict.

When she found herself seated beside him in the carriage, she wondered whether now would be a propitious time to thank him for her jewels. She tried to discover some way of introducing the topic, racking her tired brain to yield some innocuous phrase. Unconsciously, she leaned her head against his shoulder. Two minutes later, she was sound asleep.

Realising as much, Jason kept silent. Deep in consideration of his latest discovery on the fascinating topic of his wife, he was thankful she was not awake to further confound him. He had quite enough to deal with with this latest revelation. Standing in his aunt's ballroom, watching his wife smile and laugh at other men's sallies, seeing her attention focused on them, however innocently, he had been racked by a powerful emotion he could only describe as jealousy. He *was* jealous—of the entire *ton*, for the women who claimed her friendship were also included in his sights.

Relaxing back against the leather, he drew a deep breath. After a moment's hesitation he stretched a protective arm about his sleeping wife, settling her safe against his side. A strong surge of emotion rocked him, but he was getting used to the effect she had on his system and no longer felt surprise at such happenings. This, he knew, was how he wanted things between them, her alone with him, comfortable and secure.

Which was why he had no intention of boasting of her condition. A word to his aunt Eckington as they were leaving had reassured him Lenore had not mentioned the fact. That did not surprise him; his wife was intelligent enough to guess how his aunts would behave once the news was out. His reasons for keeping mum were rather more serious. From his vantage point by the wall, he had seen a number of gentlemen eye his wife speculatively. None had dared approach her; the wolves of the *ton* had a tried and true approach to succulent young matrons who appeared within their orbit—he should know; he had perfected the art. They would not approach a young wife until she was known to be bearing her husband's child. With this point established, most husbands could be relied on to become complacent, keeping to their clubs, leaving their front door unattended. Once it became known Lenore was pregnant, she would become fair game—most tempting game, if he had read the looks on his peers' faces aright. Although he had no intention of ever becoming a complacent husband, he would much rather his wife was not exposed to the lures of the *ton*'s greatest lovers.

He glanced down at her face, what he could see of it, and felt his features relax. She had done well, his duchess. She had appeared exactly as he would have wished, gracious, with just a touch of hauteur in her manner to keep the unintroduced at bay. She would do well in the *ton*—she would succeed there as she had in all the other endeavours she had taken on in marrying him.

When the carriage stopped outside their door, and she did not wake, he carried her inside, soothing her confused murmur when she woke in the light of the hall. To his surprise, she blinked up at him, then smiled and, clasping her arms more tightly about his neck, placed her cheek on his shoulder and allowed him to carry her upstairs.

As he did so, he noted that she did not feel any heavier. It seemed strange that she was carrying his child, that it was growing apace within her, yet there was nothing in her slender figure to attest to the fact. Just as well. With any luck, the Little Season would be over before their news became too obvious to hide.

She was asleep again by the time he reached her room. Trencher, hurrying along the corridor, was taken aback to find her in his arms. At his nod, she opened Lenore's bedchamber door, hanging back as he strode to the bed and gently laid his wife down.

Jason stood by the bed, drinking in the flawless symmetry of his wife's features. Slowly, he let his gaze travel down, over the gentle swell of her breasts, along the slender lines of her body and the long, smooth curves of her thighs. There was nothing he wished for more than to be able to stay here, with her, for the rest of the night. But after this afternoon, he no longer had the confidence to press his claims.

He had thought the desire that had burned between them would never die, even if it had nothing more concrete beneath to support it. After this afternoon, he was not even sure of that. Her rejection, unconsidered though it had been, had been all the more damning for that. He had surprised her and she had reacted automatically— there was no surer measure of a woman's true feelings, he knew that well. Lenore was willing to be his wife— but she had never agreed to be more than that.

He was aware of Trencher, hovering by the door. He beckoned her forward. "Try not to wake her," he whispered. "And let her sleep in the morning."

With that injunction, he headed for his room before his baser instincts could rebel and change his mind.

THE NEXT MORNING, Lenore awoke, stretched, and immediately knew she was alone. Surprised, she swung around—and wished she hadn't. Not only did the smooth pillow beside her bear testimony to the fact that she had not made her peace with her husband as intended, her head was now swimming.

"Oh, dear," she murmured weakly, putting a hand to her brow. It felt slightly clammy.

It was still clammy half an hour later, but by then, she felt slightly better, well enough to stand somewhat shakily and cross to the bell-pull.

"Oh, Y'r Grace! Looks like it's got to you good and proper."

Trencher came bustling up to where Lenore had collapsed in a chair. Chafing her hands, the maid eyed her with concern.

"Now don't you go getting up. I'll just duck downstairs and get some weak tea."

Lenore opened her eyes in alarm.

Trencher saw her horrified look and smiled reassuringly. "Take my word for it—me mam says it works every time."

Ten minutes later, fortified with sweet weak tea, Lenore did, indeed, feel more like herself. "Is that going to happen every morning?"

"For a while, at least. Some, it goes most of the way."

Closing her eyes, Lenore shuddered. Did Jason know, she wondered, what she was going to have to go through to provide him with his heir? She hoped so—in fact, if he didn't, she would make sure she told him.

No, she wouldn't. What could he do about it? She couldn't run from town the day after making her curtsy as the Duchess of Eversleigh—what would all the ladies who had invited her to tea think? If she admitted to this weakness, Jason would feel honour-bound to send her back to the country. He had been so generous—she could not contemplate letting him down. Particularly after yesterday afternoon.

Eyes still closed, Lenore heaved a weary sigh. She had yet to settle her accounts from yesterday afternoon.

Recalling the incident, she frowned. Ever since she had told him of her pregnancy, Jason had not come to her bed. She had explained his absence first on the grounds that he had clearly made the decision to leave early the next morning and had decided not to disturb her, and later, when he had returned to the Abbey but not to her bed, because they were travelling the next day. At Salisbury they had been given separate rooms, of course. But, if he had wished to exercise his conjugal rights, why had he not come to her last night, or at the very least, this morning? Clearly, he had not thought her too tired yesterday afternoon.

Rubbing her fingers across her brow, Lenore admitted to her mind a series of facts she had been staunchly ignoring for the past week. Jason had not been the least reluctant to leave her at the Abbey. He had only come to fetch her to town at the behest of his aunts. Yesterday afternoon had merely been an opportune moment. There was no evidence that he bore any deep-seated wish to maintain a close relationship with her now the business of his heir had been satisfactorily set in train. In short, his interest in her had waned.

Why had she thought otherwise?

Because she loved him and had entertained hopes beyond the possible.

Drawing a shuddering breath, Lenore forced her eyes open. "Perhaps, Trencher, I should lie down again—just for a while." *Until I can face the day,* she thought, as Trencher helped her to her bed.

Downstairs, in the sunny breakfast parlour, Jason studied the remnants of his substantial breakfast with a jaundiced eye. The fact that his wife had decided to adopt the habit of most fashionable women and stay in bed until noon, and thus would not be joining him, had finally sunk in.

"No, Smythe. No more coffee." Waving his butler away, Jason rose and, picking up the *Gazette*, headed for the library.

Once there, he prowled the room before settling, reluctantly, in the chair behind the desk. He frowned at the correspondence Compton had neatly stacked by the blotter. With a frustrated sigh, Jason swung his chair about and stared out of the long windows. He could not go on like this.

He had gone down to the Abbey with high hopes, only to have them dashed. What had he expected? He had given Lenore not the slightest indication that his interest went any deeper than the conventional affection a gentleman was supposed to feel for his wife, in the ill-judged expectation that his affliction would pass. It had only grown stronger, until now it consumed his every waking hour, leaving him bad-tempered and generally confused. Leaning his elbows on the arms of the chair, he steepled his fingers and rested his chin on his thumbs. As the long-case clock in the corner ticked on, his grim expression slowly lightened. Eventually, taking his hands from his face, Jason allowed his lips to relax in a small, self-deprecatory smile.

He would have to see the Little Season out; impossible to achieve anything in town—not with every man and his dog, let alone the gossip-mongers, watching. The fact that His Grace of Eversleigh was stalking his wife would make the most sensational *on-dit*. Once they were back, alone at the Abbey, he could lay siege to her sensibilities in earnest, rekindle the embers of passion that had burned so brightly and make her want him as much as he wanted her. Until then, all he needed to do was make sure she came to no harm and that no harm, in the form of the wolves of the *ton*, came to her.

With a decisive nod, Jason turned back to his desk. After a moment's consideration he drew a sheet of paper towards him. Dipping his pen in the inkstand, he wrote a short note to Compton, instructing him to deal with affairs as he thought best until further notice as his employer had weightier matters on his mind. Leaving the note in a conspicuous spot, Jason rose and, feeling as if he was seeing daylight for the first time in weeks, strolled out.

"Pass me that pot, Trencher."

With a sigh, Lenore held out her hand for the small pot of rouge she had sent Trencher to buy that morning. She had never used the cosmetic before but there was no denying she needed it now. Her cheeks were pallid, her eyes too large.

Hesitantly, Trencher handed her the small jar. "Are you sure, Y'r Grace? You've got such lovely skin—seems a shame, somehow."

"It'll be an even greater shame if Lady Albemarle and her guests see me like this." With a grimace, Lenore opened the pot and picking up a haresfoot, dipped it in. Carefully, she brushed the fine red powder across her cheekbones, trying to make the addition as inconspicuous as possible.

It was the end of her first week in London as the Duchess of Eversleigh. She had been fêted and, to her dismay, positively fawned upon by some of the more select of the *ton*'s hostesses. Being Jason's wife, she had realised, made her something of a drawcard, a fact which had left her at the centre of attention for far longer than she liked. Thus far, she had coped.

But her morning sickness was tightening its grip. Not only was she unable to rise much before noon, a fact camouflaged, luckily, by fashionable habit, but in the last two days she had started feeling nauseated in mid-afternoon. Today she had tried not eating at luncheon, taken at Lady Harrison's small town house with a gaggle of other young ladies, and had nearly shamed herself by fainting in the park. How to overcome her increasing problems without absenting herself from a full schedule of visits was a quandary she had yet to solve. But if her illness became any worse, she would have to do something.

Studying the effects of her ministrations, Lenore laid the rouge pot aside and stood. "My gown, please."

Trencher hurried over with a gown of silver spider gauze. Once encased in the scintillating folds, Lenore paraded before her cheval glass. It was her fervent hope that her undeniably elegant body would deflect notice from her less than healthy countenance.

Spreading the shimmering skirts wide, she wondered if Jason would be present tonight. She was due to leave shortly for Lady Albemarle's rout, taking Agatha up in her carriage. Like most husbands, Jason did not accompany her on her engagements, not unless they were invited together for a dinner or some special occasion. However, he knew which functions she attended; he might or might not look in on them. Thus far, he had been at every ball and party she had, a fact which had brought her mixed joy.

Mentally shying from the joy her husband brought her, she focused on the far more serious question of whether he would notice her rouge. His eyes were sharp—if he noticed, would he guess her reasons for using it? Deciding there was no point in trying to predict His Grace of Eversleigh's actions if he did, Lenore let her fingers trail over the delicate peridot and diamond necklace, one of Jason's gifts, that she had clasped about her neck. She could never wear any of the pieces without feeling a pang of guilt that she had not, yet, had a chance to thank him as she would wish.

Shaking aside her dismal thoughts, she waved to Trencher. "That small silver fan—and the matching reticule, I think." While Trencher rummaged for the required articles, Lenore fell to considering her social schedule. As yet, she had formed no firm friendships, although there were many who sought her out. Occasionally she ran across Amelia, but her cousin was still consumed by her pursuit of Frederick Marshall; Lenore did not feel comfortable in distracting her attention. Nevertheless, the weeks ahead were rapidly filling with engagements; she herself was hosting a tea party for a select group of ladies next Tuesday.

Every noon she would leave Eversleigh House for some *ton*-ish affair—a luncheon of one description or another. That was invariably followed by an afternoon tea, or a drive in the Park in company with ladies of her circle. At some time after five o'clock she would return home to change for dinner. She and Jason had yet to share a meal over the long table in the dining-room; they had dined, together or separately, elsewhere every day since she had arrived. The dinners would lead to balls or parties—impossible not to attend at least two every night.

She was heartily sick of it all. But she was determined to see the Little Season out, establishing the position of the Duchess of Eversleigh. She owed it to Jason and she had no intention of failing him in however small a degree.

Accepting her fan and reticule from Trencher, along with her long silver gloves, Lenore disposed these articles appropriately, then stood for Trencher to swing her black velvet evening cloak over her shoulders.

"You look just lovely, my lady."

Bestowing a sceptical look upon her helpful maid, Lenore, head high, swept out of her room and down the stairs to do battle with her particular dragon—the *ton*.

The Albemarles' ball was indistinguishable from the others, all equal, in Lenore's opinion, in their forgettability. She danced with those gentlemen she considered suitable, thankful that the unsuitable had thus far kept their distance. In dispensing with her pinafores, she had expected rather more problems from that direction and could only be grateful if her position as Jason's wife precluded their active interest. And, as had happened for the past seven nights, her husband also attended Lady Albemarle's function. She sighted him through the throng, speaking with the very attractive Lady Hidgeworth and some other gentleman. Her ladyship had placed her hand on His Grace of Eversleigh's black sleeve.

He saw her and bowed slightly. Lenore nodded politely in return, then wished she had not when he detached himself from Lady Hidgeworth's somewhat possessive conversation and strolled, all languid elegance, across the ballroom towards her.

Surrounded by a small coterie of five ladies and three gentlemen, Lenore pretended not to notice her approaching danger. Her heart thumped uncomfortably. Would he notice her rouge?

"Well met, my dear."

At his smoothly drawled comment, Lenore had no

option than to turn to him, extending her hand and praying the light of the chandeliers would not reveal her secret. "My lord, I confess I'm surprised to find you here."

Lenore hoped the comment would keep his mind on the company and not on her.

Jason smiled down at her, his mind engrossed with its habitual subject. "Are you, my dear? But how so, when there are so many attractions among Lady Albemarle's guests?"

Lenore blinked. He could not mean her, so presumably he meant Lady Hidgeworth and her like.

Straightening from his bow, Jason kept her hand in his, drawing nearer as his eyes scanned her face. She was looking peaked. And was that rouge on her cheeks? Lowering his voice, he murmured, "Are you quite well, my dear. You look rather tired."

"Do I?" Lenore opened her eyes wide. "I assure you, my lord, I'm thoroughly enjoying myself. Perhaps the wind in the Park has dried my complexion slightly? I must get Trencher to look out some Denmark lotion. Heaven forbid I develop any wrinkles!"

Wondering who it was she was impersonating with such a fatuous response, Lenore kept her expression politely impassive and waited, her breath caught in her throat, to see if she had succeeded in deflecting her husband's dangerous interest.

"Heaven forbid, indeed," Jason murmured, all softness leaching from his expression. There were times when his wife retreated behind a subtle screen beyond which he could not reach. It galled him that such a reserve could exist, that she could keep her thoughts and emotions from him if she so wished. That was something he was determined to change, just as soon as he got her back to the

Abbey. "As you are so well entertained, madam, I will leave you to your friends."

With a smile which did not reach his eyes, he bowed and moved away. Turning back to her friends, Lenore felt her heart sink, as if a weight had been attached and let fall as he left.

Contrary to his intimation, Jason went only as far as the nearest wall, where a convenient palm afforded him some respite from the attention of the loose ladies of the *ton*. To his considerable annoyance, they, plural and singular, seemed of the fixed opinion that if he was in London, he was available. Their invitations would have made a whore blush. As he appeared unable to convince them of the error in their assumption, he had been forced to fall back upon a gentleman's last defence—he now ignored them, heartily wishing that they would return the compliment.

His gaze fixed broodingly on his wife's fair head, Jason reviewed the current state of play. He was not at all convinced by his wife's airy reassurance—or was his secret hope that she would soon tire of the bright lights of town and wish of her own accord to return to the Abbey colouring his assessment? If it had been any other woman, he would find no inconsistency with her professed enjoyment— she was surrounded by many, potential friends as well as the inevitable toad-eaters, all vying to excite her interest. She was a social hit on anyone's scale; if she wished, she need never have a moment's peace in her life again. None of which sat well with his knowledge of Lenore—his Lenore—the one who preferred gigs to riding and the company of musty tomes to that of the swells. She, he was quite sure, would not be enjoying herself in Lady Albemarle's ballroom.

Letting his gaze roam the long room, he automatically

noted the position of the more dangerous rakes. None had yet braved his wife's circle. Most would have noted his presence at her evening entertainments and drawn the conclusion he wished them to draw.

Jason's lips twitched, then firmed into a severe line as the prospect of Lenore's having an interest in another gentleman swam across his consciousness. Reluctantly, watching her laugh at some sally, he considered the possibility. It did not seem at all likely; there were none of the subtle signs of hyper-awareness he was adept at reading present in her manner—only when he hove in sight did she become skittish. Yet he had to acknowledge the unnerving fact that, if she was harbouring any illicit passion, he might not know of it, given that as yet impenetrable reserve she could deploy to conceal her innermost feelings.

As Lenore accepted the arm of gangly Lord Carstairs and allowed him to lead her to the dance floor, Jason grimaced and, straightening, moved away from his protective palm. Convention made it difficult for him to dance frequently with his wife—not when she was so sought after by others.

Lenore's movements in the evenings were easy enough to follow, given he was prepared to brave any chance observer noting his peculiar pastime. The evenings, however, were not the time of greatest threat. Her afternoons were filled with a succession of entertainments, some for ladies only, but there were others at which the town beaux took care to appear. And where husbands, by and large, were considered *de trop*.

A problem, but not nearly so immediate as Lady Dallinghurst, bearing down on him from the right.

"Jason! I vow it's an age since I've had a chance to speak with you alone, my lord."

"In case it's escaped your notice, Althea, we're surrounded by at least three hundred other human beings."

Lady Dallinghurst made so bold as to put her hand on his sleeve. "And since when has that ever stopped you, Your Grace?"

Jason looked down, into her pretty pink and white face and felt pity for the absent Lord Dallinghurst. Althea Dallinghurst was a Dresden doll who played the game hard and fast. Lifting his brows, his expression nothing if not supercilious, Jason asked, "Dallinghurst in town?"

Lady Dallinghurst's eyes gleamed. Her hold on his arm tightened.

"No. And he won't be back for a month!" She looked up at him, clearly expecting a proposition of the most explicit nature.

"Pity. There's a horse I'd like to see him about. Tell him I'm interested when you see him next, will you, my dear."

With a polite nod, Jason moved into the crowd, leaving a very stunned lady behind him. It was, he decided, time to suggest to his wife that they leave and travel on to Lady Holborn's affair, the next on her never-ending list, before he was provoked into making a wrong move and some slighted madam, with intuition fuelled by fury, guessed just how highly unfashionable was his interest in his wife.

THE NEXT AFTERNOON brought near-disaster for Lenore. She had opted to attend Lady Hartington's luncheon, an *al fresco* affair in the extensive gardens of Hartington House. Because of the distance from town, the luncheon continued all afternoon, with the guests enjoying the amenities of the gardens. To Lenore, it was a welcome relief from the stuffy salons of the capital. All went well, until Lady Morecambe and Mrs. Athelbury, with both of whom Lenore was on good terms, became possessed of the idea of punting on the lake.

"Do come with us, Lenore. Lord Falkirk has offered to pole us about."

Seeing nothing against the venture, Lenore agreed. Together with her friends, she crossed the wide lawn to where a punt was drawn up at the water's edge. Young Lord Falkirk had already assumed his place in the stern, the long pole gripped firmly between his hands. "A quick trip to the fountain and back, ladies?"

They laughingly agreed. In the middle of the shallow lake, an island of stones was crowned by a fountain which fed a small waterfall, the whole, in reality, a disguise for the small waterwheel concealed in the rocks which caused ripples on the otherwise glassy surface of the protected lake.

Mr. Hemminghurst followed them down and gallantly assisted them to board, handing them in with a flourish. Smothering their giggles, they took their seats on the punt's narrow crossboards. There was only just room enough for all three.

"Off we go, then!" With a sturdy heave, Lord Falkirk poled off.

Almost immediately, Lenore had second thoughts. By the time they were halfway to the rocks, she could feel each rolling wave created by the waterwheel as it passed under the punt. Her stomach started to move in synchrony. As they neared the rocks, she pressed a hand to her lips. The nape of her neck was warm and growing warmer—a very bad sign.

"Isn't it delightful!" Lady Morecambe leaned out to pull the boat closer to the island, rocking the boat dreadfully.

Lenore shut her eyes tight, then quickly opened them again. "Yes, quite," she managed, before setting her teeth again. An ominous chill was spreading over the back of her shoulders.

Luckily, the other three occupants of the punt were more interested in the cunning way the waterfall had been created to hide the wheel assembly than in the odd hue she was sure her skin had assumed. Breathing deeply, Lenore told herself that they would head back now, that the rocking would get less with every yard they came closer to the shore. If she could just hold on, she would see this through, without giving her secret away. Agatha, she remembered, was in the crowd on the lawn, and Lady Attlebridge, too. Along with half the female members of the *ton*. This was the last place on earth to fall victim to her affliction.

After declaiming with what Lenore felt to be quite unnecessary long-windedness on the mechanism that drove the wheel, Lord Falkirk turned the punt around. Gradually, Lenore felt her glazed vision improve. The bank, and salvation, were only a few yards away. She blinked, then frowned, as her sight now revealed many of the other guests lining the edge of the lake, laughing and waving at them.

Naturally, Lady Morecambe and Mrs. Athelbury waved back. Perforce, Lenore had to join in, struggling to fix a smile on her lips. But with the increased movement, added to by Mrs. Athelbury leaning out of the punt to flick water at those on the shore, the punt was rocking quite hideously again.

Lenore felt the blood drain from her face. Any minute… She closed her eyes, very close to defeat.

"There we are!"

With a grand gesture, Lord Falkirk ran the punt aground.

Letting out the breath she had been holding in a shuddering sigh, Lenore waited patiently for the other two ladies to clamber out, drawing most of the gathering crowd's attention, before allowing Lord Falkirk to assist her to shore.

Once on *terra firma*, the young man looked at her in concern. "I say, are you all right, Lady Eversleigh? You look dev'lish pale."

Summoning a smile, Lenore plastered it on her lips. "Just a touch of the sun, I suspect, my lord. I think I'll sit down in the shade for a minute. If you'll excuse me?"

Leaving his lordship casting puzzled glances at the light clouds covering the sun, Lenore headed for a wooden seat placed under a willow. The drooping branches of the willow gave her a modicum of privacy in which she could risk hunting in her reticule for the smelling salts Harriet had given her years before. She had never thought to use them, but, sighting the little bottle among the trinkets on her dressing-table, she had added it to the contents of her reticule the week before. Sending a thank-you prayer Harriet's way, Lenore took a cautious sniff then leaned back and closed her eyes.

To her relief, the crowd had moved on in the opposite direction to view the sunken garden. She was left in peace under the willow, a reprieve of which she took full advantage. Only when she was sure she could stand and walk without tempting disaster did she emerge and, finding the first of the guests departing, rejoined the crowd only to say her farewells.

Returning directly home in the swaying carriage, she only just managed to gain her chamber before the inevitable overcame her.

Trencher, tipped off by Smythe, came rushing up to assist her. Finally, with wet cloths laid over her brow, Lenore lay, weak and exhausted, stretched out on her bed. It was nearly five o'clock. Soon, she would have to get up and commence the long process of dressing for the evening.

"You'll feel lots better after a bath, my lady," said Trencher, echoing Lenore's thoughts. "But rest awhile now. I'll call you when 'tis time."

Lenore did not even try to nod. Total immobility seemed the only defence against this particular illness. She drifted into a light doze but all too soon she heard the sounds of her bath being readied in the small bathing chamber next door. The splashing of the water as it poured into the tub pulled her mind back to full consciousness.

This afternoon's near catastrophe could not be repeated—not if she wished to preserve her secret. Luckily, she had devised a plan. A plan that would, she fervently hoped, achieve her twin aims of concealing her indisposition while keeping the Duchess of Eversleigh circulating among the *haut ton*. A plan so simple, she was confident none would detect her sleight of hand.

With a deep sigh, Lenore removed the cloth from her forehead and slowly, gingerly, sat up. The room swayed gently before settling into its proper place. She grimaced. It was definitely time to put her plan into action.

CHAPTER TWELVE

WITH A PERFECTLY genuine smile on her lips, Lenore whirled down the long ballroom of Haddon House, laughing up at Lord Alvanley as that jovial peer partnered her in a vigorous country dance. It was a week since Lady Hartington's luncheon and, Lenore reflected, her plan had worked wonders.

She laughed at Lord Alvanley's opinion of Lady Mott's latest coiffure, her confidence waxing strong. She had become adept at this charade, projecting the image of blissful enjoyment expected of a new peeress. She could rattle along with the best of them, prattling on about nothing of more serious consequence than their latest bonnets or exclaiming over the monkey Lady Whatsit had got from her latest lover. A charade of the superficial, while beneath her rouge her cheeks were still pale and her mind longed for quieter surrounds and more meaningful pastimes.

But she was determined to preserve her disguise until the Little Season ended and she could retire with honour to Dorset. It was the least she could do to repay her husband's generosity.

"An excellent measure, m'dear," his lordship said as they came to a swirling stop. "Tell me, do you plan to open up that mansion of your lord's down in Dorset?"

While she waxed lyrical about the Abbey and her future plans for its use, Lenore became aware of an odd tingling at her nape, a sensation she associated with her husband's attention. Was he here? She had not seen him that day and was depressingly conscious of an urge to turn about and search the brightly dressed crowd for a glimpse of his elegant form.

Suppressing her highly unfashionable impulse, she nevertheless could not resist turning slightly, scanning the crowd while ostensibly discussing the most acceptable composition of house parties with his lordship.

From the corner of her eye she detected a movement, a black coat detaching itself from the brightly hued background. He *was* here—and was coming to speak with her. Desperately trying to dampen the excitement that swelled in her breast, Lenore realised Lord Alvanley was looking at her, an expectant expression on his good-natured face.

"Er...I do believe you're right, my lord," Lenore hazarded. She heaved an inward sigh when his lordship all but preened.

Then he glanced up. "Here—Eversleigh! I've just had a capital notion—your wife thinks it so, too."

"Oh?" Jason strolled up, favouring Lenore with a nod and an appraising stare. He shook hands with the viscount. "Just what are you hatching, my friend?"

"Just a little party, don't y'know. A convivial gathering—just the old crew, none of these hangers-on. At the Abbey, old man! Just what your lady wife needs to set her in full trim. We were thinking of just after Christmas—what d'you think?"

One look at Lenore's face, at the way her eyes widened before she blinked, bringing her features under control, was enough to tell Jason the truth. "I think," he replied, taking possession of one of her hands before she could commence wringing it and give herself away entirely, "that you have cast a glib spell over my susceptible wife." Jason calmly switched his smile from his friend to Lenore. "However, we'll certainly consider your 'capital notion', will we not, my dear?"

"Yes, of course." Lenore felt a slight blush warm her cheeks. Glancing up, she met her husband's grey gaze, warm and reassuring, and felt her heart tremble. Abruptly, she conjured a smile and trained it upon Lord Alvanley as he bowed before her.

"Farewell, my dear Duchess," his lordship said, wagging a playful finger her way. "But a last warning. Don't let your reprobate of a husband monopolise your time—not at all the thing, not at all."

With a roguish smile, his lordship departed, merging into the crowd.

Jason quelled an impulse to grimace at his back. Monopolise his wife's time? If only he could. He glanced down; when Lenore persisted in studying his shoes, he calmly raised the hand he was still holding to his lips. She immediately looked up. As his lips caressed the back of her fingers, he felt them tremble. Her eyes, firmly trapped in his gaze, widened. "I'm glad I caught you, my dear. You've been cutting such a swathe through the ballrooms I feared I might not catch you up."

Struggling to keep her voice matter-of-fact, Lenore let her lashes hide her eyes. "Have you been looking for me, my lord?"

"After a fashion." Realising that to remain stationary with his wife was to invite interruption, Jason tucked her hand into the crook of his elbow and steered her towards the side of the room. "I wondered if you might care to ride with me in the Park one morning. My hunters need exercise. I keep a number of mounts suitable for you here in town—you don't need to fear to trust them. Given that you seem to have hit your straps with *ton*-ish entertainments, I thought you might like to savour yet another of London's pleasures."

The elation Lenore had felt on hearing he had been looking for her, and that for the express purpose of requesting her company, sagged dramatically. She could not—dared not—accept. No matter how much her heart longed to do so, her stomach would never permit it. Unconsciously, her fingers tightened on his sleeve. "I…that is…" Desperately, she sought for some acceptable white lie. She could not even get out of bed in the mornings, not at the time he rode. But she had not told him of her indisposition—after all her hard work to avoid doing so, to avoid any possibility of his feeling compelled to urge her to return to the Abbey before she had become established socially, she felt deeply reluctant to do so now. In desperation, she fell back on the fashionable excuse. "I'm afraid, my lord, that I would find it extremely difficult to meet with you at that hour."

That was the literal truth, even though she knew he would interpret it in an altogether erroneous way. She was hardly surprised to feel his instant withdrawal, although none watching them would have seen anything amiss.

"I see—no need to say more." Jason tried very hard not to feel rejected. He forced himself to smile down at her. "You're bent on taking the *ton* by storm, my dear, making up for your years of absence with a vengeance." Entirely against his will, his smile took on a wistful air. "Don't burn the candle at both ends, Lenore. It never does work."

For one heart-stopping moment Lenore stared up into his eyes, wondering what it was she had glimpsed there.

Simultaneously, both she and Jason became aware of

another, hovering before them. She turned and beheld Lord Falkirk, he of the punt, eyeing her, and her husband, uneasily. Having gained their attention, he grew even more nervous.

"The cotillion," he said, as if stating the obvious. When they both continued to stare uncomprehendingly, he blurted out, "My dance, y'know, Lady Eversleigh."

"Oh…yes, of course." With an effort, Lenore gathered her wandering wits. She turned, with the greatest reluctance, to her husband. "If you'll excuse me, my lord?"

"Of course." With consummate grace, Jason bowed over her hand. As she disappeared in the direction of the dance-floor, her hand on Lord Falkirk's arm, he had to fight an almost overwhelming urge to remove her forthwith from this ballroom, London and the *ton* and take her back to the Abbey with all speed. His inexperienced wife had certainly overcome her dislike of *ton*-ish entertainments. In fact, he would not wager a groat she had not changed her opinion entirely on such pastimes. Her enjoyment of the balls and parties seemed all too genuine.

As he settled his cuffs and looked about for the refreshment-room, Jason admitted that he did not wish that last to be so. An unnerving fear that he was losing his wife—the Lenore he had married, the Lenore he now wanted beyond all reason—had started to prey on his mind.

He was turning aside to hunt up a footman when his sleeve was twitched.

"Good evening, Your Grace. Tell me, are you finding this singularly pretentious ball as boring as I am?"

Closing his eyes, Jason prayed for patience. Where were they coming from? It was as if the bored wives of the *ton* had declared open season—on him. Smoothly turning to bow over Eugenia, Lady Hamilton's hand, he allowed his brows to rise. "Do you find this boring, Eugenia?" As if seeing the thronging guests for the first time, Jason lifted his quizzing glass, rarely if ever used except in instances such as this, and scanned the multitude. "Dear me. I believe you may well be right." The glass swung about to focus on Lady Hamilton. For a pregnant instant, Jason viewed her through it, as if examining the pale blonde curls clustered about her sharp face and the voluptuous curves daringly revealed for all to see, before letting the weapon fall. "There do seem to be an enormous number of boring people present. I fear I've been so engrossed in conversation I had failed to remark the fact."

"You were talking to your *wife*!" Lady Hamilton snapped.

Jason's grey eyes, cold and hard, swung down to impale her. "Precisely." He let a measured period elapse, to make sure that barb struck home, before, with the slightest of polite nods, he said, "If you'll excuse me, Eugenia, I'm thirsty."

From her position in the cotillion Lenore saw him turn away and let out the breath she had been holding. They were shameless, every last one. Even had she not come to London with a very accurate idea of her husband's past history, the blatant advances made to him by certain of the so-called ladies of the *ton* would have made all clear to a novice. And she was no novice. She knew all too well what they were offering—it was a wonder he had not yet taken any of them up on their invitations.

As she obediently twirled through the next figure, the idea that he had, but she did not know of it, arose to torment her. In an effort to hold back the tide of sheer misery that welled at the thought, Lenore forced her mind to another puzzling point. What did that odd look mean, the softer light she had seen, quite clearly, just for a moment, in his eyes?

"Lady Eversleigh!"

Just in time, Lenore avoided a collision. Whispering her apologies to Lord Falkirk, she sternly warned herself to keep her mind on the business at hand. That her husband felt some degree of affection for her was no great discovery—witness his many kindnesses. The gentle expression in his eyes owed its existence to that— and nothing more. And his words of concern might just as well stem from an entirely proprietorial interest in her health—and that of his heir. No need to puzzle any longer—there was no mystery there.

She would have to stop her silly yearnings—they could only cause her grief.

"Thank you, my lord." Lenore rose from her final curtsy and gifted Lord Falkirk with a brilliant smile. "Perhaps you could escort me to Lady Agatha?" she suggested. "I think she's near the door."

Perfectly willing to be seen with one of the brightest lights in the *ton* on his arm, Lord Falkirk readily agreed.

Fixing a suitable smile on her lips, Lenore glided graciously by her escort's side, sternly reminding herself of her purpose. She could not simply go home—the night was yet young. But at least she could gain a respite by Agatha's side, before she threw herself once more into the fray—the hurly-burly of being the Duchess of Eversleigh.

It was a difficult task, constantly to perform as if her whole existence revolved about the glib conversations, the innuendo and cynical laughter, the glittering carousel of the *ton* at play. Particularly when her eyes kept straying out over the pomaded heads, searching for elegantly waving chestnut locks atop a tall frame. Now and again, he hove into view, always in the distance. Lenore struggled to shackle her jealousy for those unsighted women who stood before him, warmed by his slow smile.

"I vow and declare, my dear, it's all becoming far too heated—this argument between Lennox and Croxforth. And all over a horse, would you believe it?"

Nodding her head at Lady Morecambe's assessment, Lenore tried to keep from yawning. She had left Agatha to join her little clique—Lady Morecambe and Mrs. Athelbury, Mr. Merryweather, Lord Selkirk and Mr. Lawton. Miss Dalney, on the arm of Lord Moresby, had just come up. On the outskirts of this inner group, Lord Rodley, Mr. Hemminghurst, Lord Jerry Penshaw and a few other younger gentlemen hung, hopeful of gaining recognition but unsure how to most acceptably make their presence felt. Within the protective confines of her little circle, Lenore knew she would meet no challenge to her equanimity. "Perhaps they should simply sell the poor animal and halve the proceeds?"

Barely listening to the laughs this produced, Lenore allowed her mind to slide away. Having contributed her mite to keep the conversation flowing, she was woolgathering, her gaze idly scanning the crowd, when her husband again hove into view—but this time much nearer, approaching rapidly and, quite possibly, with intent.

Immediately, Lenore brightened, consciously infusing enthusiasm into her expression, a smile of dazzling brilliance on her lips. "Will you be attending Lady Halifax's drum tomorrow, my lord?" With a show of eagerness, she quizzed Lord Moresby. From the corner of her eye, she saw her husband's progress slow. "I've heard that her gatherings are always a sad crush."

"Indeed, yes," his lordship replied.

"I heard," said Miss Dalney, leaning forward to speak across his lordship, "that at her last ball, part of the balustrade on her stairs was dislodged by the crowd trying to ascend."

Lenore looked suitably impressed, mentally making a note to put Lady Halifax's affair at the bottom of her list. Lady Morecambe made a comment and Lenore took the chance to cast a surreptitious glance her husband's way. To her relief, he was deep in conversation with Lord Carnaby and seemed no longer interested in her.

In thinking so, she was wrong. While trading information on horseflesh with Lord Carnaby, another amateur of equine bloodlines, a large part of Jason's mind was absorbed in noting how scintillating his wife appeared. She was bright-eyed, radiant. She needed no help in braving the world of the *ton*—she had it at her pretty feet.

"I'll let you know if I hear any more about that bay of Salisbury's." With a nod, Lord Carnaby moved on, leaving Jason to his musings.

They weren't pleasant. A niggle of an entirely unexpected sort had inserted itself into his brain. Was Lenore's effervescent charm, the bloom in her cheeks, the wide starry gaze merely brought on by enjoyment of the *ton*'s offerings? Or was there more to it than that? Could it be that some gentleman, perhaps, was responsible for the transformation in his wife?

Suppressing a low growl, Jason shook off his unsettling thoughts and headed for the card-room. He could not believe Lenore had found a lover—would not believe it. Not Lenore—his Lenore.

Yet such things happened. Every day. None knew that better than he.

Once inside the card-room, Jason halted, dragging in a

deep breath. Seeing a footman passing with a loaded tray, he took a glass of brandy. Taking a soothing draught, he calmed himself with the reflection that he was letting his jaundiced view of *ton*-ish wives colour his expectations. As far as his wife was concerned, there was no evidence to support such a notion.

Was there?

ONCE SOWN, the seed would simply not die, no matter how hard he struggled to kill it. Five days later, Jason stood, moodily staring out of the windows of his library and, defeated, considered how to put paid to his suspicions. That such thoughts were unworthy—of himself, of Lenore— he was only too well aware. But he was also aware of the dreams—nay, nightmares—that had come to haunt him.

Despite his very real inclination, he had not returned to his wife's bed. The knowledge that she evinced no real interest in him was depressing; the idea she might yield him his rights out of duty was simply appalling. Sinking into the chair behind his desk, Jason grimaced. Impossible not to admit to a certain measure of cowardice, yet what rake of his extensive experience would not, in the circumstances, feel reticent? Never in his life had a woman turned him down; he had never had to ask for a woman's favours. That the first woman to find him resistible should be his own wife was undoubtedly fate's revenge. Demanding his dues was beyond him, a course entirely repugnant. Once they were alone at the Abbey, he would work on her susceptibilities, draw her to him once again, heal the breach that had somehow developed between them. And rekindle the embers that still smouldered into a roaring blaze from which something more permanent than mere passion would emerge.

Until then, he would have to contain his desire and

concentrate instead on retaining his sanity. The first step was to convince himself that his ridiculous suspicions were just that. Leaning back in his chair, Jason focused his mind on his task—how to discover with whom his wife spent her time.

Her evenings were accounted for. Despite her full schedule, she had shown no inclination to deviate from the list Compton left on his desk every morning; no danger there. Her luncheon engagements were rather more hazy, yet, from experience, he knew that was not a favoured time for seduction. Empty stomachs had a way of interfering with carnal appetites. Afternoons, on the other hand, were prime time.

And Lenore's afternoons were veiled in secrecy—at least, from him.

Frowning, Jason reluctantly discarded the obvious solution. He could not set Moggs on her trail, no matter how obsessed he became. Regardless of the truth behind her smiles, regardless of his fears, it would be unforgivable to allow any of his staff to get so much as a whiff of his suspicions.

The steady drum of his fingers on the blotter was interrupted by the click of the door latch.

"Are you receiving?" With a confident air, Frederick entered.

Jason threw him an abstracted smile and waved him to a chair. "What brings you here?"

Subsiding into the chair, Frederick stared at him. "It's Thursday, remember?"

When Jason continued to look blank, Frederick sighed. "Dashed if I know what's got into you these days. You're promised to Hillthorpe and yours truly this afternoon for a round at Manton's."

"Ah, yes." Jason shifted in his chair. "I've been somewhat absorbed with another matter—our engagement momentarily slipped my mind." He flashed Frederick a charming though far from contrite smile and pushed his chair back from the desk. "But I'm only too willing to accommodate you now you've jogged my memory."

"Humph!" As Jason stood and came around the desk, Frederick struggled up out of the comforting depths of the armchair. "Perhaps I should mention your wandering wits to your duchess—saw her just now at Lady Chessington's."

Jason halted in his progress to the door. "Oh?"

"Yes. Luncheon. She was there, along with the usual crowd. Exhausting. Don't know how they all do it. Think Lenore went on to Mrs. Applegate's after that. Gave it a miss, myself."

"An undoubtedly wise move." Jason nodded absentmindedly as his route to salvation clarified in his brain. As Frederick drew level, he clapped him on the shoulder. "How's Lady Wallace?"

"Amelia? Er…" Trapped, Frederick threw him an irritated glance. At sight of Jason's wide eyes, he scowled. "Damn it, Jason. It's nothing like what you're thinking."

Abruptly assuming his patriarchal persona, Jason raised his brows. "I certainly hope not. I might remind you that Lady Wallace is now a connection."

Frederick looked struck. "So she is. Forgot that."

"Well, I haven't. So I'll take it amiss if you're merely trifling with the lady's affections, dear chap."

Frederick narrowed his eyes. "Jason…" he said warningly.

But Jason only laughed. His interest in the day miraculously restored, he waved Frederick through the door. "Come on. Let's find Hillthorpe. Suddenly, I'm in the mood to take the pips out of the aces."

IT SHOULD, in fact, be child's play to track his wife's movements through the *ton*. Buoyed with confidence, Jason strolled through the crowd at Lady Cheswell's rout, his smile at the ready, his manner easy and urbane, his eyes searching for Mrs. Applegate.

After allowing Frederick to win their round at Manton's, the least he could do to repay his friend for his help, all unconscious though it had been, he had made a brief foray to the Park. From the high perch of his racing phaeton, scanning the fashionable crowds had been simple enough. Lenore had not been there. Presumably, she had spent the afternoon at the Applegates' or some similar function. He was quite sure Mrs. Applegate would be able to confirm his duchess's movements; Lenore had become such a hit, few missed her presence and most, even Frederick, took note of whither she was bound.

The crowd before him shifted, revealing his quarry resplendent in bronzed bombazine. She did not even wait for him to reach her before exclaiming, "Your Grace! What a pleasant surprise."

Suppressing his natural response to such gushing sentiment, Jason kept his most unintimidating smile firmly in place. Taking Mrs. Applegate's chubby fingers in his, he bowed politely. "My dear Mrs. Applegate." Straightening, he considered her with affected surprise. "I confess to being amazed to see you, ma'am. I'd heard your tea this afternoon was positively exhausting."

Flushing with pleasure, Mrs. Applegate fanned her cheeks. "Very kind in you to say so, Your Grace. I'm only sorry Lady Eversleigh was otherwise engaged. Lady Thorpe and Mrs. Carlisle were particularly anxious to make her acquaintance. Perhaps you might drop a word in her ear, my lord? I hold an 'at home' every second week and would be most pleased to have her attend."

"Yes, of course." A sudden chill enveloped Jason's heart. He glanced about. "If you'll pardon me, ma'am, I've just sighted someone I must catch."

With an elegant bow, he detached himself from Mrs. Applegate's clinging toils and headed into the crowd. Not the Park, not Mrs. Applegate's. So where had Lenore spent her afternoon?

Seeing the dark head of Lady Morecambe pass before him, he swung into her wake. When she paused by a group of ladies to allow another to pass before her, Jason stopped by her side. "Good evening, Lady Morecambe."

Theresa Morecambe jumped and swung about. "Oh, Your Grace! You gave me quite a start."

Looking down into her blue eyes and seeing the relief therein, Jason drew his own conclusions. But he was only interested in discovering *his* wife's afternoon pastimes. Bowing briefly over Lady Morecambe's hand, he fixed her with a cool and somewhat stern gaze. "I believe you spend a great deal of time with my wife, Lady Morecambe?"

There was nothing in the tenor of his words to cause offence, but he was not the least surprised to see Theresa Morecambe's eyes widen. With a visible effort, she pulled herself together, then airily shrugged. "Now and then. But we're not forever in each other's pockets, Your Grace. You must not be thinking so." Under his relentless gaze, Lady Morecambe's defences wavered. She rushed on, "In fact, this afternoon I attended Mrs. Marshall's drum. Lady Eversleigh was otherwise engaged—I assume she attended Mrs. Dwyer's musical afternoon—a most rewarding and, er…enlightening experience, I'm sure."

Struggling to keep his lips straight, Jason nodded. "I dare say." With the curtest of bows, he let Lady Morecambe flee. He gave a minute to consideration of which of his peers was the guilty party in her case, before hauling his mind back to his own unknown. Where had Lenore gone?

The next half-hour went in a vain search for Mrs. Dwyer. Forced to the conclusion that that particular young matron had not featured on Lady Cheswell's list, Jason stood stock-still by the side of the ballroom, a black cloud of suspicion drawing ever nearer.

"Good God, Eversleigh! Stop standing there like a rock. There's a chair behind you, if you haven't noticed. I need it—and you're in the way."

Blinking, moving aside automatically, Jason found himself facing his father's youngest sister. "You have my heartfelt apologies, Agatha." Smoothly, he helped her to the chair.

Settling herself in a cloud of deep purple draperies, Agatha humphed. "No sense trying any of your flummery on me, m'lad."

Jason's lips twitched but he held his tongue.

Looking up at him, Agatha's black eyes narrowed. "But what are you doing here, propping the wall? Watching your wife hard at work?" With a nod, she indicated the set Lenore had joined on the dance floor. "Exhausting, ain't it?"

"Exceptionally." Try as he might, Jason could not keep his disapproval from colouring his tone. "I find it hard to believe she is not, now, enjoying what she once professed to abhor."

Agatha chuckled. "Well, if she's convinced you, she needn't fear any other finding her out."

Knowing his aunt harboured a definite soft spot for Lenore, Jason let that remark pass unchallenged.

"Still, at least she escaped Lady Fairford's effort today. I don't know how some of these people find their way into the *ton*, believe me I don't. The most shabby entertainment—nipcheese from beginning to end. I went on to Henrietta Dwyer's—timed it well; the singing was over but I didn't see Lenore there. No doubt she went to Lady Argyle's 'at home'. If I'd had any sense, I would have gone there to start with."

Feeling very much like a drowning man making one last desperate attempt to grab hold of a buoy, Jason made his excuses to his aunt and set out on Lady Argyle's trail.

In the centre of the crowd thronging Lady Cheswell's dance-floor, Lenore smiled and chatted, no longer afraid that her mask would slip but rather less sure about her temper. The sheer banality of the exercise was taking its toll; she was bored and rapidly losing patience. "Naturally, my lord," she replied to Lord Selkirk, "I would not favour pink ribbons on such an outfit. I suspect Mr. Millthorpe would only find they tangled in his fobs. He seems to have quite an array, don't you think?" A gale of laughter greeted this purely accurate observation. Lenore converted her grimace to a look of puzzled consideration as she studied the extravagant dandy holding court but paces away. As Mr. Millthorpe seemed to count such attention no more than his due, she did not feel she was committing any social solecism in so doing. Was this all they thought of—silk ribbons and bows?

Behind the solid façade of the Duchess of Eversleigh, Lenore inwardly sighed, hoping that she possessed the fortitude to carry her through the next weeks. Agatha, Lady Eckington and company were all agreed that she should not host any major entertainment until next

Season. Which meant that all she had to do was continue to appear at the balls and parties, smiling and dancing, a devotee of all things frivolous. The dreary prospect was enough to make her feel ill. Thankfully, her resistance to indisposition had improved dramatically, at least in the evenings; as long as she adhered to her plan, she was confident her health would see the Season out. It was her temperament that was strained; she had never before had to suffer fools gladly.

"My dear Duchess! Allow me to compliment you on your gown, my dear."

Mentally girding her loins, Lenore turned to exchange polite nods with Lady Hartwell. "How do you do, Lady Hartwell. Madame Lafarge will be delighted to know you approve of her style. Are you enjoying your evening?"

A little taken aback by this forthright response, Lady Hartwell rallied. "Why, yes, my dear. Such a sad crush, is it not? But I wanted to make sure you had received my note about my little gathering tomorrow. Dare I hope you'll be able to attend?"

With the ease born of frequent repetition, Lenore smiled at Lady Hartwell, just the right combination of regret and reluctance in her eyes. "Indeed I got your note, but I regret I'm promised elsewhere for the afternoon. Perhaps next time?"

Fleetingly laying her hand on her ladyship's gloved arm, as if appealing for her understanding, Lenore was not surprised to see resigned acceptance overlay her ladyship's annoyance. She had her routine perfected to an art.

After promising to attend her soirée later in the month, Lenore parted from her ladyship, returning once more to the safety of her own circle. Lady Hartwell's invitation was the sixth she had refused for the following afternoon. The number of ladies desirous of her company over tea would have made Harriet cackle.

Nodding to Lady Argyle as she passed her in the crowd, Lenore banished her boredom, casting herself once more into the fray—the chattering, glimmering, clamouring world of the *ton*.

For her, the time to leave could not come soon enough.

When, at last, the evening was done and she was handed into her carriage by her husband, she merely smiled sleepily at him, then subsided into silence, grateful for the darkness that cloaked her tiredness from his perceptive gaze. It was comforting, the way he was always there to escort her home. At times like this, when her willpower had been sapped by the demands of the ball and her resistance was low, she found it impossible not to admit, to that inner self who knew all her secrets, that she could not imagine any other gentleman giving her the same sense of security, of being protected against all harm. The vibrant strength of him as he sat beside her, his thigh brushing her silken skirts, came clearly to her senses.

Abruptly, blinking back her tears of frustration, Lenore turned to stare out of the carriage window, into the gloom. She had had her taste of paradise; she should be content with her memories—they were more than many others had to warm them.

Beside her, Jason sat, chilled to the marrow, a man condemned. As the carriage ambled over the cobbles towards Eversleigh House, he watched the façades slip past, his hand fisted so tightly his knuckles ached. Long before it had been time to quit Lady Cheswell's ballroom, he had exhausted all avenues of salvation. Lenore had not been at Lady Argyle's; there had been no other entertainments held that afternoon at which a lady of her station would have appeared.

Which left one vital question unanswered, a suffocating cloud of uncertainty pressing down blackly upon him, making it difficult to breathe and even harder to think.

Where *was* Lenore spending her afternoons—*and with whom*?

CHAPTER THIRTEEN

IN THE DAYS that followed, Jason verified beyond all possible doubt that his wife was absenting herself from the *ton*'s afternoon entertainments. His mood vacillated between cold cynicism and the blackest despair. One minute he had convinced himself that he did not need to know who she was dallying with, the next he was overcome by a primitive urge to find the gentleman responsible and flay him to within an inch of his life. In his more rational moments he wondered how it had all come about, why he had been unwise enough to let such a black fate befall him.

It was Agatha who brought the matter to a head.

Pacing restlessly before the fire in his library, the October morning grey beyond the long windows, Jason read for the twelfth time his aunt's missive. Quite why Agatha had nominated eleven o'clock for a meeting when she rarely rose before noon was a mystery. Likewise, he felt there was some significance in the fact that she had elected to call on him, rather than summoning him to attend her. Unfortunately he could not fathom what it was. Nevertheless, there could be no doubt that she was coming to tell him what he was not at all sure he wished to hear. Presumably Agatha had discovered what he had not—with whom Lenore was trysting.

The sound of the front doorbell halted him in his tracks. Lifting his head, he heard his aunt's tones, unusually muted, in the hall. Squaring his shoulders, Jason braced himself to hear the unwelcome truth.

Smythe held the door open as Agatha swept in.

"Good morning, Aunt." Smoothly, Jason went forward and gave her his arm to the chaise.

"Glad you found the time to see me, Eversleigh." Agatha subsided on to the chaise, settling her heavy green carriage dress and placing her muff beside her. As the door clicked shut behind Smythe, she raised a worried face to Jason, standing by the fireplace, one arm braced against the mantelpiece. "It's about Lenore. Don't know what your plans are, but you should take her back to the Abbey immediately."

Despite the fact that he had expected as much, hearing it said brought the misery that much nearer. His heart a solid lump of cold stone in his chest, Jason steeled himself to learn which sprig had stolen Lenore from him.

All Agatha saw was the hardening of the planes of his face. Already austere, his features took on an intimidating cast. Agatha allowed her own stubbornness to show, wagging a stern finger at him. "Oh, her little deception has been quite clever and entirely successful thus far, I'll grant you, but she won't get away with it forever."

Jason could bear it no longer. "For God's sake, Agatha, cut line. Who the devil *is* the bounder?" He ground the question out, then swung on his heel, restlessly pacing the hearth rug. "That's *all* I want to know. I'll call him out, of course." The last was said with a certain measure of relief, even relish. At last he could do something, strike out at someone, to relieve his frustration and bitter disappointment.

Agatha stared at him as if he had run mad. "Have you lost your wits? If you're to blame any man, it would have to be yourself. And how can you call yourself out, pray tell?"

Jason halted, total bewilderment replacing his look of predatory rage.

Agatha waved him to a chair. "For God's sake, do sit down and stop towering over me. Remind me of your father when you behave like that."

Too taken aback to protest, Jason did as he was bid.

"I'm merely here to bring to your notice the fact that Lenore is not well." Agatha fixed her nephew with a penetrating stare. "*If* she's breeding, she should be back at the Abbey. You know perfectly well she does not enjoy life here in town. It's my belief the air's not good for her, either. And the strain of supporting her new position, on top of all else, is proving too much."

"Nonsense." Jason had regained his composure. Obviously, his aunt was not as *au fait* with his wife's doings as he had thought. "She's enjoying herself hugely—throwing herself into the fray with the best of them." His tone was dismissive, laced with contempt.

Agatha's brows rose to astronomical heights. "Nonsense, is it? And just how much do you know of your wife's life, sir? It might interest you to know that, when I did not see her at any of the afternoon engagements over the past week, I became suspicious. When she did not appear at Mrs. Athelbury's tea, I stopped by here yesterday at four. And what did I find?"

Transfixed, Jason waited, every muscle tensed. *Here*? In his house?

Agatha's eyes narrowed. "I'd wager my best bonnet she was laid down upon her bed, fast asleep. *That's* why she looks so much better in the evening than she does at luncheon. Spends her afternoons recouping so no one will see how worn down she is. Doesn't sound like enjoyment to me."

Jason's brain was reeling. "Did you see her?"

"Oh, yes." Agatha sat back. "Those fools of yours woke her before I knew what they were about. Half green, she was—so you needn't tell me I'm not right. She's breeding, is she not?"

Absent-mindedly, Jason nodded. Lenore was not playing him false—had never done so—had never even thought of it.

When her nephew remained silent, absorbed with his thoughts, Agatha humphed. "What the devil is going on between you two? You're head over ears in love with each other, which anyone with eyes in their heads can see, and you're both playing fast and loose—for all the world as if you're trying to convince yourselves, and the *ton*, that isn't so." Agatha paused to draw breath. Seeing the stunned expression on her nephew's face, she rushed on, determined to have her say. "Well—it's not working, so you might as well make the best of it and take off for the country!" She glared belligerently at Jason.

Jason stared back. The idea that the entire *ton* was privy to what he had hitherto believed a deep personal secret left him staggered. Foundering in a morass of relief, consternation and uncertainty, he voiced the first thought that entered his head. "Lenore doesn't love me. We did not marry for love."

"*You* may not have—who said you had?" Agatha opened her eyes wide. "I remember your reasons for marriage quite clearly—you needn't repeat them. But what do you imagine that's got to do with it?" When Jason made no response but, instead, looked set to slide back into melancholy absorption, she added, "And as for Lenore's not loving you—you know nothing about the matter. Well—we all know what rakes are like—and let's face it, dear boy, you're one of the leaders of the pack. Never do know anything of love. Blind, you know. Rakes always are, even when it hits them in the face."

Jason recovered enough to bestow a warning glance.

Agatha was unimpressed. "You aren't going to try to tell me that you don't love her, are you?"

Jason coloured.

"Ah ha! And I'm just as right about Lenore—you'll see. Or you would, if you'd only *do* something about it."

"That, my dear aunt, I think I can safely promise." Feeling that he had allowed his aunt to lead the conversation long enough, Jason straightened in his chair. Agatha frowned, as if recalling some caveat to her deductions.

Glancing up, Agatha found her nephew's grey gaze fixed on her face. "Tell me," she said, narrowing her eyes. "Did you, by any foolish chance, tell Lenore why you wanted to wed her—your 'reasons for marriage'?"

"Of course, I did."

"Merciful heavens!" Agatha declared in disgust. "By all the gods, Jason, I'd have thought you could do better than that. An approach, no better than the veriest whipster."

Jason stiffened.

"Positively useless!" Agatha continued. "No wonder Lenore has been so set on this charade of hers—with no cost counted. She thinks to please you, to give you want you said you wanted—a marriage of convenience—no!—a marriage of *reason*." Her tone scathing, her expression no less so, Agatha gathered her muff and fixed her errant nephew with a stern glare. "Well, Eversleigh! A nice mull you've made of it. Your wife's been endangering her health and that of your heir just to give you the satisfaction of knowing your duchess is accepted by all the best people. I just hope you're satisfied." Imperiously, Agatha rose. "I suggest, now that I've shown you the error of your ways, you take immediate steps to rectify the situation."

Her message delivered, in a most satisfying way, for she had rarely had the pleasure of seeing her intimidating nephew so vulnerable, Agatha bestowed a curt nod upon him and left him to his task. Feeling justifiably pleased with her morning's work, she swept out.

Left to mull over her words, Jason was unsure whether he stood on his head or his heels. Luckily, the numbing sensation did not last, blown away by sheer relief and heady elation. Lenore was still his. Feeling oddly humble, he silently vowed he would take nothing for granted with respect to his wife henceforth. Dragging in what seemed like his first truly relaxed breath in a week, he stood and strode determinedly to the door.

It was time and past he had a long talk with his wife.

Upstairs, Lenore had just staggered from her bed. Unaware of any impending danger, she was engaged in her customary occupation on first rising—contemplating the roses about the rim of the basin left in readiness on a side-table. She had long ago ceased to fight the nausea that engulfed her as soon as she came upright and took two steps. It was a thing to be endured. So she clung to her bowl and shut reality from her mind, waiting for the attack to pass.

Feeling her legs weaken and her knees tremble, she grasped the bowl more firmly and sank to the carpeted floor. In acute misery, she tried to think of other things as spasm after spasm shook her.

The click of the door-latch penetrated her blanket about her senses. Trencher, no doubt, with her washing water. Lenore remained silent on the floor. She had no secrets from Trencher.

His hand on the door knob, Jason surveyed his wife's room. He had knocked gently but had heard no response. Puzzled, his glance swept the rumpled bed, the drawn curtains. Perhaps she was in the small chamber beyond? Frowning, he took a step into the room and closed the door behind him.

Turning, his vision adjusting to the dimmer light, he looked across to the door that led into Lenore's bathing chamber. And saw her bare feet and the hem of her nightgown on the floor beyond the bed.

"Lenore!"

His exclamation shook Lenore firmly into reality. She lifted her head, barely able to believe her senses. But the heavy footsteps approaching the bed did not belong to Trencher.

"Go away!" The effort to imbue her words with a reasonable amount of purpose brought on another bout of retching.

Jason reached her, his expression grim. "I'm here and I'm staying." Appalled to see her so pale and weak, he sank on to the floor beside her, drawing the long strands of her hair back from her face, letting her slump against him as the paroxysm passed.

Lenore longed to argue but his presence was more comforting than she would have believed possible. His warmth struck through her thin gown, easing her tensed muscles. His hands about her shoulders imparted a strength of which she was sorely in need.

For the next few minutes, Jason said nothing, concentrating on supporting his wife, his hands moving gently, soothingly, over her shoulders and back.

Then the door opened and Trencher came hurrying in.

Seeing him, she came to an abrupt halt, only just managing not to slosh the water in the ewer she carried on to the floor.

One look at her face was enough to tell Jason that his wife's maid was well aware of his ignorance of Lenore's indisposition. His eyes narrowed.

Recovering, Trencher came hurrying forward to place the ewer on the washstand. "Oh, Your Grace! Here, I'll take care of her."

"No. *You* can get her a glass of water and a damp towel. *I'll* take care of her."

Even through the dimness shrouding her senses, Lenore heard the determination that rang in his tongue. Despite her present circumstances, despite everything, she felt a ripple of pure happiness that he should be so adamant in his desire to help her, in claiming his right to do so. He was only being kind but she was in dire need of his kindness.

When Trencher returned with the glass and towel, Jason coaxed Lenore to drink, then, ignoring her weak protests, gently washed her face, cradling her in his arms. Handing the towel to the hovering maid, Jason raised a brow at his wife. "Better?"

Suddenly shy, Lenore nodded. Jason's arms slipped from her as he stood. Before she could even sit up, he bent and lifted her into his arms. Lenore clutched at his lapel, her eyes meeting Trencher's awed gaze.

Jason strode around the bed and deposited his wife on her pillows. Anticipating Trencher, he transfixed her with a steely glance and fluffed Lenore's pillows himself, before settling her back on them and tucking the eiderdown about her.

Seeing the maid gather the towel and basin and head

for the door, Jason said, his tone coldly commanding, "Your mistress will ring when she has need of you."

Eyes wide, Trencher bobbed a curtsy and withdrew, pulling the door shut behind her.

Making a mental note to have a word—several words, in fact—with his wife's maid, and his valet, on the subject of leaving him in ignorance of such vital matters as his wife's health, Jason turned his attention to Lenore. Smoothly taking her hand in his, he sat on the edge of the bed.

From beneath her lashes Lenore looked up at him, not at all certain of what would come next. Yet the unconscious movement of his thumb over her knuckles erased any trepidation.

His expression non-committal, Jason looked down at her. "How long has this been going on, Lenore?"

The concern in his voice tied Lenore's tongue. She looked down, picking at the lace edge of the eiderdown with her free hand while considering how much it would be wise to admit. She wished with all her heart to confess all and return to the Abbey, but the Season was not yet ended.

When she did not immediately reply, Jason's brows rose. "Since you arrived in town?"

Looking up, Lenore jettisoned all thoughts of prevarication. "Virtually," she admitted, her voice low.

Jason sighed and looked down, his fingers interlacing with hers. "My dear, I wish—very much—that you had told me. I'm not a monster." His fist closed about her hand, then relaxed slightly. Mindful of Agatha's words that Lenore had only followed her odd course to achieve what she believed he desired of her, he added, "There's nothing I can do to relieve you of your present susceptibility but I would not wish you to tire yourself further on my account."

"Oh, but I'm perfectly… At least, later…" Eyes wide, Lenore leapt in to avert any decree. But when her eyes met his, and she saw the comprehension and perception therein, she faltered to a stop.

One of her husband's brows had risen sceptically.

"Perfectly all right later in the day? *Well*, even? Perhaps I should warn you, my dear, that I do not take kindly to having the wool pulled over my eyes."

Under his stern grey gaze, Lenore shifted uneasily but the affection in his tone, in his expression, gave her the strength to reply, "But truly, Jason, I *can* manage. I would not wish the *ton* to think your wife was incapable of carrying her position with credit."

"The *ton* may think what they please. However, in this instance, I think you're making too much of their inconstancy and too little of their sense. You've succeeded as my duchess far better than I'd hoped, Lenore. None of those who matter will hold your desertion of their balls against you, certainly not when they learn the cause." Entirely unconsciously, Jason's gaze skimmed possessively over his wife's body. When his eyes returned to her face, he saw she was blushing delicately. He smiled, squeezing her hand gently before raising it to his lips. "Who knows?" he murmured, his eyes quizzing her. "They might even be jealous."

Lenore blushed even more. Wishing she possessed the will to retrieve her fingers, for it was exceedingly hard to think with his lips on her skin, she felt obliged to argue for the conservative course, the course she did not wish to follow in the least. "The Season will be over in a few weeks, my lord. It will be time enough to return to the Abbey then."

Jason shook his head. "We're leaving for the Abbey tomorrow morning, Lenore. At least—" He broke off, regarding her ruefully. "As early as you can manage it."

They were the words Lenore had both feared and longed to hear. Yet she could not let them pass without challenge. "But—"

"No buts." Jason's voice was firm. "You may tell me your engagements and I'll have Compton cancel them."

"But—"

"You'll stay safely in bed until it's time for luncheon. I'll send someone up with a tray—better still, I'll bring it myself." Jason rose. "We can remain here all day, or, if you wish, I could take you for a stroll in the square. Tonight, I fear you'll have to continue to bear with my unfashionable company, for I do not plan to go out. We'll have dinner together and then you must rest." At the end of this recitation, his gaze dropped to Lenore's face. "Do you have any more buts, madam wife?"

Not sure whether she wished to glare or laugh, Lenore compromised. "I fear there's an impediment to your plans you've overlooked, my lord."

Abruptly eschewing his arrogant stance, Jason asked, "Don't you wish to spend your day with your husband? Or is it that you do not wish, in your heart, to return home to the Abbey with me?"

Lenore's heart turned over. What her heart wished, she was convinced she could never have. But she was a little bemused by Jason in vulnerable vein and was at a loss to know how to word her reply.

Sensing her predicament, Jason smiled, raising the hand he still held to clasp it more securely between his. "Forgive my levity, my dear. What is it I've overlooked?"

A little relieved, but not entirely at ease for the soft light that glowed in his grey eyes made her heart stand

still, Lenore ventured, "I'm not…entirely sanguine as
to how I shall manage in a carriage all the way to the
Abbey."

"We'll travel slowly. No need to rush. We'll only go
as far each day as you can manage." Jason scanned Lenore's face, noting the circles under her large eyes, the
absence of her usual sparkling glance and the frown,
born of strain, that haunted her pale green gaze. She
had pushed herself hard to fulfil his wishes. "No more
arguments, Lenore. I'm taking you back to the country
tomorrow." With a smile to soften the absolute nature of
that decree, Jason laid her hand down on the quilt. "Rest
now, my dear. I'll wake you for lunch."

Feeling as if, somewhat against her will, a considerable weight had been lifted from her shoulders, Lenore
watched him leave. He had not said what had brought
him to her room at such an hour but whatever it had been,
the outcome had never been in doubt. She had known all
along that Jason was not the sort of inconsiderate husband who would take no interest in his wife's health,
even had she not been carrying his child. Given that his
concern was real, albeit the sort of emotion a gentleman
felt for one in his care, his determination to take her back
to the Abbey was not to be wondered at. What she was
far less sure about was whether he planned to remain
there with her. And whether he had asked, or was thinking of inviting, others to join them in Dorset.

With a deep sigh, Lenore closed her eyes, luxuriating in the knowledge that she did not have to get up, get
dressed and attend some luncheon party, pandering to
the constant demands of her position.

As sleep hovered near, ready to claim her, she realised
she did not know which she feared more—if Jason stayed
at the Abbey, alone, in her company, would she be able

to maintain the inner mask she wore constantly, the one that hid her love from his sight? Yet, if he invited guests to join them and the ladies, as so many ladies did, made a play for him, would she be able to hide the jealousy that, to her surprise, had started eating at her soul?

Dismissing the answer as one of life's imponderables, Lenore slipped wearily over the threshold of sleep, into that realm where dreams were the only reality.

THEY REACHED the Abbey on the morning of the third day. As she emerged from the carriage and felt the flags of the steps firm beneath her feet, Lenore sighed deeply, relief and appreciation clear in her eyes as they met her husband's. She turned to greet Morgan, then sighting Mrs. Potts at the top of the steps, she waved before placing her hand on Jason's sleeve.

"Dare I suspect you are pleased to be home, madam?"

At his soft drawl, Lenore cast him a teasing glance. "Indeed, my lord. I have not forgotten I have yet to get far in my cataloguing of your library."

"Ah, yes." Jason returned her smile, no longer perturbed by her abiding delight in musty tomes.

At the top of the steps, Mrs. Potts sank into a deep curtsy. "Delighted to welcome you home, Your Grace, ma'am."

"I'm delighted to be back, Mrs. Potts."

"I should mention, Mrs. Potts," Jason cut in smoothly, "that Her Grace is in dire need of chicken broth. I believe that's what my mother swore by during her confinements?"

Mrs. Potts's face lit up. "Dear me, yes! Wonderful for picking a lady up when the babe gets you down. Now just you come along, my lady. We'll get you to bed straight away and I'll bring you a bowl. You must be quite worn down with all that gadding about in London."

Swept up by the irresistible force of Mrs. Potts fired with a zeal to tend to the well-being of the next generation, Lenore was parted from her husband. When she managed to get a look at him, on her way up the stairs, Mrs. Potts directly behind her, she saw a smugly satisfied smile on his face. Lenore shot him a speaking glance, which dissolved against her will, into a misty and grateful smile, before surrendering to her fate.

Indeed, she had need to recoup. The journey had been painfully slow. Jason had ordered that the carriage, the most well-equipped money could buy, should be driven at a spanking pace. That way, he had explained, the springs and speed took the worst out of the bumps. Even so, they had not been able to cover more than twenty miles without halt. Sunk in the luxury of her tub, filled to the brim with blissfully warm, scented water, Lenore closed her eyes and recalled her husband's unfailing support. He had grown adept at gauging how long she could last, and organising their stops so that she could wander on his arm through delightful little villages, or stroll on a green. Their night-time stops had been at the best inns where her comfort had been assured. Always the best parlour and the biggest bedroom. Her only complaint was that she had spent the nights alone in the big beds, but she had accepted that philosphically. She had his company and his affection—she had no right to expect more.

The day passed swiftly. After the promised chicken broth, Lenore dozed for a few hours. Refreshed, she dressed and descended to the parlour. After an hour reacquainting herself with her household, her husband found her. At his suggestion, they strolled on the sun-warmed terrace. It had been weeks since Lenore had been conscious of the sun on her face; it seemed appropriate that it should shine on her return to her home.

Later, she poured tea for them both. The time flew as they entertained each other with wickedly accurate reflections on the *ton*'s notables. Then it was time for dinner, taken as had been their habit earlier in the year, in the smaller dining salon.

When the covers were finally drawn, Lenore sighed, deeply content, very glad Jason had insisted on bringing her home. When he raised a brow at her, she said as much, adding, "I already feel very much better."

As she realised her motive in stating that fact, Lenore blushed. Abruptly, she took another sip of wine, hoping the candlelight would hide her reaction. Yet was it wrong for a wife to invite her husband's attentions. Right or wrong, acceptable or not, she just wished she had more of an idea of how to go about it.

Despite her hopes, the candlelight was in no way dim enough to hide her blush from Jason's sight. Her words, and her reaction, sent his hopes soaring. But still he moved cautiously. "We'll have to ensure we do nothing to overtire you."

Her senses at full stretch, Lenore detected the subtle undertones in his deep voice. Hesitantly, she answered, "I don't think anything I do here could overtire me."

Ignoring the clamour of his desire, Jason smiled encouragingly, his eyes holding hers across the length of the table. "Perhaps you should retire early? There's no reason to stay up. I expect I'll come up soon myself."

Finding her lips suddenly dry, Lenore had to pass the tip of her tongue over them before replying, her voice slightly husky, "Perhaps I should."

A footman came to assist her to her feet. Jason stood, then, when she had gone, with one, last, lingering look, he subsided once more into his chair, waving aside the port, indicating instead the brandy decanter. Did she know what she did to him when she looked at him like that? What she would do to any man with the unspoken appeal in her large eyes? Suppressing a shudder of pure desire, Jason took a very large sip of his brandy.

Later, fortified by a large dose of the best brandy in his cellars, Jason eyed the plain panels of the door in front of him. Drawing a breath of purest satisfaction, he turned the handle and crossed the threshold.

From the depths of her feather mattress, Lenore heard him enter and could not quite believe it. Was she asleep already and dreaming? But no. The large male body, warm and hard, that slid into the bed beside her was no dream.

With a sound halfway between a cry and a sigh, Lenore turned to welcome him, only to find herself in his arms. They closed possessively, passionately, about her.

Much later, his wife warm and fast asleep beside him, Jason heaved a contented sigh.

Agatha, bless her heart, had been right.

CHAPTER FOURTEEN

IT WAS PAST NINE the next morning and Jason was deep in yesterday's *Gazette* when the door to the breakfast parlour opened. Assuming it to be one of Morgan's minions come to consult with the butler over some household matter, Jason did not look up. Not until Morgan's voice floated over the top of the pages.

"Perhaps I should clear this all away, Your Grace, and fetch you a fresh pot of tea? And perhaps some toast?"

Jason emerged from behind his newspaper in time to see Lenore subside into the chair Morgan held, a grateful look on her face.

"Thank you, Morgan. Just one slice of toast, I think."

Folding the paper and setting it aside, Jason waited until Morgan and the footman departed, burdened with the remnants of his substantial breakfast, before fixing his wife with a concerned frown. "Should you be up and about so early?"

Lenore smiled, albeit a trifle weakly. "I feel a great deal better this morning." Belatedly realising how that might sound, she rushed on, "Mrs. Potts advised against languishing in bed unless I need to sleep."

"Really?" One of Jason's brows had risen. "I fear I must take exception to such strictures. There are other reasons for languishing in bed, which I hope to have you frequently consider."

Blushing furiously, Lenore shot him a glance she

hoped was sternly reproving. Luckily, Morgan appeared with her tea and toast and put an end to such risqué banter.

As she sipped the weak tea, Lenore tried to appear unconscious of the steady regard of her husband's grey eyes. He seemed content to watch her, as if time was of no importance. In the end, she asked, "Do you have much business to attend to down here?"

Jason shook his head. "The harvests are virtually all in. There's not much to be done until early next year." He watched as Lenore nibbled at her toast then grimaced and pushed the plate aside. She was still very pale. "Compton comes down from London every now and then, when there's any business that needs my attention." Remembering that his wife was well acquainted with the workings of country estates, and that she liked going about, seeing work progress, he ventured, "There are some cottages being rethatched in the village. Perhaps, later this morning, we could ride over and take a look at the result? Or would you rather go in the gig?"

Consulting her stomach took no more than a minute. Reluctantly, Lenore shook her head. "I don't think I could. I may be well enough to come downstairs, but I would rather not chance a carriage today. And as for riding, it's perhaps a good thing that I'm not a devotee of the exercise."

She looked up to see a frown on her husband's handsome countenance.

Jason caught her eye. "Is that why you refused my invitations to go riding in town? Because you were too ill?"

Lenore nodded. "The very idea of galloping over the greensward, in the Park, no less, was enough to make me blanch." Laying aside her napkin, she stood.

Recalling the hurt he had felt when she had declined his offer, Jason, rising, too, fixed her with a stern look. "Might I request, madam, that in future, you refrain from keeping secrets from your husband?"

At his mock severity, Lenore chuckled. "Indeed, my lord, I dare say you're right. It would certainly make life much easier." She took the arm he offered and they strolled into the hall. "However," she said, glancing up at him through her lashes, "you must admit you had no real wish to be seen riding in the Park with me. Your aunts told me you never escort ladies on their rides."

"My aunts are infallible on many points. However, while I would not wish to shatter your faith in their perspicacity, I fear predicting my behaviour isn't one of their strengths." Jason glanced down to capture his wife's wide green gaze. "In this case, for instance, while they're perfectly correct in noting that I've never seen any point in accompanying females on their jaunts in the Park, I consider accompanying my *wife* on such excursions a pleasure not to be missed."

Lenore wondered whether the odd weakness she felt was due to her indisposition or to the glow in his grey eyes. Whatever, she wished she had learned to control her blushes, for he was entirely too adept at calling them forth. She no longer had any defence, not when he chose to communicate on that intimate level she shared with no one else.

Raising her hand to his lips, Jason smiled, pleased to see the colour in her cheeks. "I must go and look at those cottages. I'll hunt you up when I return."

With that promise, he left Lenore in the hall and strode to the front door.

When the heavy door had shut behind him, Lenore shivered deliciously. Wriggling her shoulders the better to throw off his lingering spell, she strolled into the morning-room. Jason's behaviour throughout this morning, both before and after he had left her bed, led to only one conclusion. He intended to reinstate their relationship, exactly as it had been in the month following their wedding.

Sinking on to the chaise before the blazing fire, Lenore folded her arms across the carved back and gazed out at the mist shrouding the hilltops. Contented anticipation thrummed, a steady beat in her blood. Things had changed since August. Then, she had been on a voyage of discovery; this time she knew what was possible, knew what she truly wished of life. Coming back to the Abbey and resuming their relationship felt like returning to a well-loved and much desired place, a home. An acknowledgement that they had shared, and could still share, something that they both now valued.

It was more than she had expected of her marriage— a great deal more.

The only cloud on her horizon was how long it would last—how long Jason would be content with her and country life. Her green eyes darkening, she considered her prospects. The peace of country living had never been his milieu. Her mental pictures had always positioned him against a backdrop of *ton*-ish pursuits. If nothing else, her time in London had convinced her she could never bear more than a few weeks of such distraction; her mind was not attuned to it.

Biting her lips, Lenore frowned. Could his warning that not even his aunts could predict his tastes be a subtle hint, conscious or not, that they were changing? He had denied any plans to invite acquaintances to join them, now or later. Likewise, he had given her to understand that he expected to remain at the Abbey, alone, with her, for the foreseeable future.

With a deep sigh, she stretched her arms, then let herself fall back against the cushions on the chaise. Inside, she was a mass of quivering uncertainty. Despite her determination not to pander to her secret yearnings, hope, a wavering flame, had flared within her. She had his affection and his desire; she wanted his love. That their sojourn here alone would allow that elusive emotion a chance to grow was the kernel of her hope. Unfortunately there seemed little she could do to aid the process.

Her fate remained in the hands of the gods—and those of His Grace of Eversleigh.

"THAT ONE GOES OVER there." Lenore pointed at a stack of leather-bound tomes, precariously balanced near the window.

"How the devil can you tell?" Jason muttered as he lugged an eight-inch-thick, gold-embossed red-calf bound volume to the pile, one of thirty dotted about the library.

Without looking up from the book open in her lap, Lenore explained, "Your father had all of Plutarch's works covered in that style. Unfortunately, he then deposited them randomly through the shelves." Closing the book she had been studying, she looked up at her husband. "This one had best go with the medicinal works. That group by the sofa table."

She smiled as Jason came up and squatted to lift the heavy book from her lap. Catching her eye, he grimaced as he hefted the volume. "It escapes my comprehension why you cannot work at a desk like any reasonable being."

Having already won this argument the previous day,

Lenore smiled up at him. "I'm much more comfortable down here," she said, reclining against the cushions piled at her back. "Besides, the light is much better here than at the desk." She had made a thick Aubusson rug just inside one of the long windows her area of operations, lounging on its thick pile to examine the books as each section of the library shelves was emptied. Given that many of the volumes were ancient and heavy, her "office" in the gallery was out of the question. Until yesterday, Melrose, a young footman, had helped her unload and sort the tomes. Yesterday morning, after his ride, her husband had arrived and, dismissing Melrose, had offered himself as substitute.

"I'll move your damned desk." Jason grumbled, turning to do her bidding.

Her lips twisting in an affectionate smile, Lenore watched as he duly delivered the book on herbs to its fellows. His sudden interest in her endeavours was disarming. Despite being excessively well-read, he did not share her love of books. Quite what his present purpose was, she had yet to divine. She watched him return to her side, his expression easy, his long limbed body relaxed. He carried a small volume bound in red leather in his hand.

Before she could point out the next book she wished to examine, Jason sat down on the rug beside her. Reclining so that his shoulder pressed against the cushions at her back, he propped on one elbow and, stretching his long legs before him, opened the red book. "I found this amid your stacks. It must have fallen and been forgotten."

"Oh?" Lenore leaned closer to see. "What is it?"

"A collection of love sonnets."

Lenore sat back. Her heart started to thud. Drawing her lists towards her, she pretended to check them.

Jason frowned, flicking through the pages. Every now and then, he stopped to read a few lines. When he paused on one page, clearly reading the verse, Lenore risked a glance through her lashes.

And very nearly laughed aloud. Her husband's features were contorted in a grimace which left very little doubt as to his opinion of the unknown poet.

Abruptly, Jason shut the book and laid it aside. "Definitely not my style."

Turning to Lenore, he reached one large hand to her hip and drew her down, her morning gown slipping easily over the silk cushions and soft carpet.

"Jason!" Lenore managed to mute her surprised squeal. One look at her husband's face, grey eyes shimmering, was enough to inform her he had lost interest in books. Eyes wide, she glanced over his shoulder at the door.

Jason smiled wickedly. "It's locked."

Lenore was caught between scandalised disapproval and insidious temptation. But her fear of revealing the depths of her feelings while making love had receded. She had discovered that her husband was as prone to losing himself in her every bit as much as she lost herself in him. But in the library? "This is not—" she got out before he kissed her "—what you are supposed—" another kiss punctuated her admonition "—to be helping me with."

Having completed her protest, Lenore wriggled her arms free and draped them about his neck. Without further objection, she suffered a long-drawn-out kiss that made her toes curl and the lacings of her bodice seem far too tight. Her husband, luckily, seemed aware of her difficulties.

Raising his head to concentrate on the laces of her

gown, Jason's eyes held hers. "I'm sick of handling dusty tomes. I'd rather handle you—for an hour or two."

The laces gave way. His fingers came up to caress her shoulders, slipping her gown over and down. As his head bent, Lenore let her lids fall. An hour or two?

With a shuddering sigh, she decided she could spare him the time.

In the days that followed their return to the Abbey, Jason tried by every means possible to break down the constraint, subtle but still real, that existed between himself and his wife. The last barrier. He had come a long way since propounding his "reasons for marriage". Not only could he now acknowledge to himself that he was deeply in love with Lenore, but he wanted their love to be recognised and openly accepted by them both.

And that was the point where he continued to stumble.

Seated astride his grey hunter, he surveyed the vale of Eversleigh, his fields laid like a giant patchwork quilt over the low hills. He had come to the vantage point on the escarpment in the hope that the distance and early morning peace would give him a clearer perspective on his problem.

He had joined in his wife's pastimes, as far as could be excused, working in the library by her side, taking her for gentle walks about the rambling gardens and nearby woods. Mrs. Potts now looked on him with firm approval. And Lenore gladly accepted his escort, his help, his loving whenever it was offered. But she made no demands, no indication that she desired his attentions.

Yet she did. Of that he was convinced. No woman could pretend to the depths of loving intimacy, the heights of passion that Lenore effortlessly attained— not for so long. No woman could conjure without fail the welcoming smiles she treated him to every time he approached. Her reactions came from her heart, he was sure.

The grey sidled, blowing steam from his great nostrils. Leaning forward to pull the horse's ears, Jason looked down on his home, the grey stone pale in the weak morning light. A strange peace had enveloped him since returning to the Abbey, as if for years he had been on some journey and had finally found his way home. *This*, he now knew, was what he had searched for throughout the last decade, a decade filled with balls and parties and all manner of *ton*-ish pursuits. This was where he wished to remain, here, on his estates, at his home, with Lenore and their children. And he owed the discovery and his sense of deep content to Lenore.

However, no matter how hard he tried to show her, his stubborn wife refused to see. He loved her—how the devil was he to convince her of that?

Until he succeeded, she would continue as she was, eager for his company but never showing it, pleased as punch when he elected to stay by her side but frightened of suggesting it, even obliquely. No matter her task, she would never ask for his help, fearing to step over the line of what could reasonably be expected from a conventional spouse.

He had no intention of being a conventional spouse, nor of settling for a conventional marriage. Not now he knew he could have so much more. With a snort of derision Jason hauled on the grey's reins and set the beast down the track for the stables. Agatha had been right— he was a fool beyond excuse for having recited his reasons for marriage. But that was the past; he needed to secure the future—their future.

Thwarted by her reticence, he had attempted, first to

encourage, then to entrap her into admitting her love, hoping to use the opportunity to assure her of his. Remembering the scene, Jason grimaced. Unfortunately, his wife was one of those rare women who could, if pushed, out do him in sheer stubborn will. He was powerless to cajole, much less force her to reveal her secrets. She remained adamantly opposed to uttering the very words he dreamed of hearing her say—for the simple reason that he had led her to believe he would never want to hear them.

"Damn it—*why* is it that only women are allowed to change their minds?"

The grey tossed his head. With a frustrated sigh, Jason turned him on to the wide bridle path at the bottom of the hill and loosened the reins.

There was only one solution. He would have to convince her that, against all expectations, he did indeed love her. As the steep roof of the stables rose above the last trees, Jason acknowledged that mere words were unlikely to suffice. Actions, so the saying went, spoke louder.

Moonlight streamed in through the long uncurtained windows, bathing Lenore's bedroom in silvery light. Thoroughly exhausted, courtesy of her husband's amorous games, Lenore lay deeply asleep. Beside her, Jason was wide awake, listening for the sounds that would herald Moggs and his surprise. A full week had passed since his visit to the escarpment. It had taken that long to devise, then execute his plan. Tonight was the final stage, for which he had had to enlist Moggs's support.

Eyes wide in the dim light, Jason had time to pray that his valet would, as with most other matters, keep silent on this night's doings. The notion of facing his servants after they had heard of his latest touch of idiocy did not appeal. Quite how he and Moggs were going to conceal the evidence afterwards, he had not yet considered but he would think of some ploy. Unbidden, Frederick Marshall's image floated into his mind. Jason grinned wryly. If Frederick ever heard of this episode, he would cut him without compunction. Recalling his friend's absorption with Lady Wallace, Jason's grin broadened. On the other hand, it was entirely possible that Frederick might need advice on a similar problem someday soon.

A soft click heralded Moggs's arrival. Raising his head, Jason saw his valet's diminutive form glide into the room. Moggs moved about the large chamber, arranging his surprise as directed. Keeping count as Moggs went back and forth, Jason slowly eased from the warmth of his wife's bed and, finding his robe on the floor, shrugged into it. Padding noiselessly across the floor, he joined his redoubtable henchman as Moggs settled the last of his cargoes on the carpet.

"Thank you, Moggs." Jason kept his words to a whisper.

Silent as ever, Moggs bowed deeply and withdrew, drawing the door shut behind him and easing the latch back so that it did not even click.

Alone with his sleeping wife, Jason turned and surveyed Moggs's handiwork. Then, reaching into the deep pocket of his robe, he drew forth a stack of white cards. For a moment, he stood silently regarding them, and the words inscribed in his own strong hand upon their smooth surfaces. If this didn't work, Lord only knew what else he could do.

Like a ghostly shadow, Jason circled his wife's chamber, depositing the cards in their allotted places. Finally, with a sigh and a last prayer for success, he slid into bed beside his wife.

LENORE WOKE very early. The muted light of pre-dawn suffused the room, slanting in through the long windows on either side of the bed. It was, she was well aware, anticipation that brought her to her senses thus early in the day. She was facing away from Jason; without turning, she let her senses stretch. His body was relaxed and still, heavy in the bed behind her, his breathing deep and regular. Deciding she could do with a doze before he woke her up, she was about to snuggle deeper under the eiderdown when the outline of something caught her eye.

Something that should not have been there. Raising her head, Lenore blinked through the dimness, waiting for her eyes to adjust. In the grey light she made out the shape of a pedestal placed a few feet from the window, a vase of flowers—were they roses?—atop.

Frowning, she glanced to the right and saw another pedestal, the twin of the first. Slowly easing up until she was sitting, Lenore saw a third and a fourth—in fact, a large semi-circle of pedestals supporting vases of roses surrounded her bed.

They couldn't be roses. It was November.

Propelled by curiosity, Lenore slipped from her bed, shivering as the chill air reminded her of her nakedness. Suppressing a curse, she grabbed up her nightgown from the floor where Jason had thrown it and dragged it over her head. Seconds later, she was standing by the first pedestal, staring through the poor light at the flowers in the vase. They looked like roses—perhaps made of silk? Lenore rubbed a velvety petal between two fingers. Real roses. As far as she could tell in the odd light, golden ones.

Turning to study the display, she counted fifteen pedestals, each vase sporting twenty or so beautiful blooms. Such extravagance would have cost a small fortune. No need to ask from whom they came.

Slanting a glance at the bed, she saw that the large lump that was her husband had not stirred. Looking back at the vase, she noticed a small card propped by the base, overhung by a spray of roses. Picking it up, she held it to the light. "Dear" was inscribed upon the pristine surface in her husband's unmistakable scrawl. Nothing more.

Glancing at the next pedestal, Lenore saw it, too, held a card. That one said "Lenore".

Faster and faster, Lenore flitted from vase to vase, collecting cards until she stood on the other side of the bed, by the other window and, hardly daring to believe the message they held, forced herself to shuffle them and read it again.

Dear Lenore, I had to do something to convince you I love you. Do you love me?

Her heart in her mouth, Lenore looked up, straight into her husband's grey eyes. He was very much awake, propped on the pillows, his arms crossed, tense, behind his head, watching her. The shadows of the bed hid his expression.

When she simply stood, his painstakingly inscribed cards carrying a message he had sweated blood over in her hands, and said nothing, Jason inwardly grimaced. "Well, my dear?" he prompted, as gently as he was able.

Lenore did not know where to start. Struggling to

command her voice, she waved at him. "Come here if you want my answer."

Slowly expelling the breath he had been holding, Jason sat up and swung his legs over the side of the bed. Did she have to make this quite so difficult? He was on tenterhooks, more nervous than he had ever been in his life. Reaching for his robe, he stood and shrugged into it, belting it loosely before crossing the few yards to stand before her.

Fingers clutching the white cards she could not yet believe were real, Lenore waited until he towered over her before asking, her voice a shaky whisper, "Do you *really* love me?"

Her throat had constricted; tears were not far away.

Jason's heart stopped. Desperately, his eyes searched her face, trying to discover what she meant by her question, what further assurance it was in his power to give her. From his heart came the answer. Without thinking, he went down on one knee before her, capturing one small hand in his. "Lenore, I arranged our marriage for all the wrong reasons but I never *asked* you to marry me. *Will* you marry me, my dear, not for all my rational reasons, but for the right reason—because you love me—and I love you?"

Tears obliterated Lenore's vision. "Oh, Jason!" she sobbed.

Immediately, Jason was on his feet but before he could do anything, Lenore threw herself into his arms, clinging to him, the white cards scattering like confetti about them.

Bemused, Jason closed his arms about his sobbing wife, burying his face in her golden hair. "Sweetheart, I didn't mean to make you cry."

"It's—" Lenore sniffed, then gulped. "It's just *too*

beautiful," she wailed, as a fresh flood threatened. "Oh," she said, struggling to wipe her eyes on his sleeve. "This is *dreadful*. I'm not a watering pot, truly."

"Thank God for that," Jason replied. The fact that, despite her unconventional response, he had got the answer he wanted was slowly sinking in. The relief was enormous. Wrapping his arms about his snuffling wife, he lifted her and carried her back to their bed.

Snuggling back beneath the eiderdown, Lenore wiped her eyes with the lace edge of the coverlet. Her thoughts were whirling, a disjointed jumble of emotions buffeted her. She blinked at her husband as he climbed back into bed beside her, stretching out on his back, his head on the pillows. He shut his eyes, as if worn out. "You really do love me?" she asked, her voice rather small.

Exasperated, Jason groaned. "Lenore—no man in his right mind makes a cake of himself as I have over you without a *bloody good reason*. Now for God's sake come and put me out of my misery and convince me my reason was, in truth, the very best."

He reached for her. Lenore gave a last watery giggle and, without further ado, devoted herself to convincing her arrogant rake of a husband that she did indeed love him.

Beyond all reason.

* * * * *

THE WEDDING PARTY

CHAPTER ONE

WAS HE GOING TO KISS HER? He very often looked at her as if he wanted to kiss her. He had kissed her, to seal their betrothal.

But that had been a month ago. More precisely, thirty-two days, ten hours and some minutes ago. There were no clocks in the gardens, of course, but she was fairly certain of at least the hour.

You'd really have to think it was more than time he kissed her again—if you thought of this sort of thing. Which Alana Wallingford did.

Almost constantly.

Not that he hadn't kissed her hand, every day, rather than to simply bow over her fingertips, as he'd done before their betrothal. And he'd kissed her cheek, at least twice. And, granted, he hadn't been constantly in her presence since that marvelous, never-to-be-forgotten moment when he'd told her he loved her and asked her to become his wife, which was what she had wanted to hear from him since the very moment they met.

But then he'd left. There had been his mother to visit, to give her the happy news. He'd said he'd be gone for a week, but it had stretched beyond two. There had been something about overseeing the closing off of a room because of the damp, or a fallen-in roof, or some such thing. As he'd said, "The estate house is ancient, and huge, and falling down around our ears. But you'll love it, I swear!"

Bailey Armstrong, at the moment the Viscount Netherfield, but heir to the Earl of Whitcomb, had been excru-
ciatingly honest about his fortune, or rather his sad lack
of fortune. But that was all right, too, because she was
odiously wealthy, or at least that's what Kate had once
told her. "You're quite odiously wealthy, you know."

Alana couldn't wait to see Bailey's home. Not that
she'd be the lady of the manor, not yet, but she could
certainly enjoy watching her fortune refurbish the estate
Bailey clearly loved so much.

They talked about it, incessantly. Alana didn't much
care for moving about in Society, and neither did Bailey.
They would ship his mother and sisters off to London,
which was where they wanted to be in any case. His
father already resided in their town house, when he was
not shooting, fishing or gaming…mostly gaming, always
losing. With the family where it wanted to be, and themselves where they wanted to be, the world would be a
lovely place. Alana daydreamed about her soon-to-be
married life all the time.

Except when she was daydreaming about Bailey's betrothal kiss, and wondering if there existed some sort
of unspoken rule about not kissing her on the mouth
again until they were married. She'd ask Kate, but if
Kate laughed, or was shocked, well, Alana would simply
expire of embarrassment.

"Alana? You don't care for blue? It doesn't have to be
blue. It probably has been blue for fifty years. It's just
that we've always called it the blue room. But we can
change that."

She blinked, realizing her mind had taken her away
from the moment, and the conversation. That had probably happened when Bailey, sitting beside her on the
stone bench, had taken her hands in his and then…well,

and then nothing. He'd gone back to speaking about their plans for the drawing room at Netherfield, and she'd tried to do her best not to grab him by the ears and kiss him square on the mouth. His warm, sweet, lovable mouth.

"Excuse me?" she asked, feeling her cheeks growing hot. "I'm afraid I wasn't attending."

He smiled that special smile that melted her knees and leaned in to kiss her cheek. "I don't blame you. It's boring stuff, most of it, isn't it?"

Three kisses on the cheek. Alana added it to her tally.

"Oh, no, not really. I suppose I was thinking about… about Sunday."

He squeezed her hands. "Our wedding day." And then he frowned. "It isn't too soon, Alana? Gideon assured me, since it will be only a simple, family affair, there was no need to—well, he said no reason to drag the bloody business out, but I'm sure he didn't mean it that way."

Alana smiled. "Yes, he did. Gideon has been my guardian these past three years, and he's never been comfortable with riding herd on me. After Sunday, I'm your worry, as he explained it to me. Gideon is a wonderful man, Bailey, honest, and caring. He…he just hides it well."

"Ah, my betrothed is a mistress of understatement," Bailey said, and then he kissed her cheek again.

Four.

"I love you, Alana." He let go of her hands and slipped an arm around her shoulder, drawing her into his side. She rested her head on his shoulder. Sighed. This was nice. Very nice.

"I love you, too," she said quietly.

They probably made quite the lovely picture, sitting there on the stone bench in the sunshine. Even romantical.

She could wait until Sunday. She really could.

She just wished Bailey couldn't...

ELSEWHERE AT REDGRAVE MANOR, another young female was not quite so reticent about expressing her feelings.

"You idiot!"

Valentine Redgrave looked up from his frowning inspection of a small smudge he'd somehow collected on his buckskins. "Gone nearly a full year, far from the loving bosom of my family, and yet so little has changed. Including me, I suppose. I'm still an idiot? I've only been home a little above an hour, Kate—so how can you tell?"

Lady Katherine Redgrave, who in truth had sorely missed her brother, shot back, "I know, you blockhead, because I happened to walk into the morning room to see that pernicious cat Sylvia Wise perched on Trixie's favorite chair. And when I got over my shock and asked her how she came to be here, she informed me that you were kind enough to have invited her to come along with you. You idiot."

Valentine got to his feet and took hold of Kate's shoulders, which put a stop to her angry pacing. "But she asked very prettily. Something about her new carriage not being delivered on time and not wishing to miss the nuptials of her dear friend Alana. That took me by surprise, let me tell you. You could have told a person, you know."

Kate pushed him away. "A *person* could have told a family that he had returned from Paris and was about to descend on his unsuspecting family. An *idiot* just shows up like some unannounced prodigal son, having invited sure disaster to trip off along home with him." Kate cocked her head to one side as she glared at him. "You do perceive the difference?"

"Much as I loathe disappointing you, no, I don't. Is there something havey-cavey about the thing? The nuptials, I mean. Will Gideon be marching the groom to the altar with a pistol stuck to his spine?"

Kate pressed her fingertips to her temples, attempting to keep her brains from exploding. "We did write to you. The letter is in Paris by now, while you're here, ruining everything. The wedding is to be strictly a family affair. Or at least it was."

Valentine sat down beside his sister. "No, sorry, I'm still not seeing it. But wait, allow me a guess. Miss Wise is *not* a bosom chum of our Alana?"

"She barely knows her," Kate said, chewing on her full bottom lip. "It's Bailey she's after."

"Bailey? Bailey Armstrong? Alana's getting bracketed to the Old Bailey? Sorry, that's a weak joke, but it's funnier if you're half in your cups when you call him that."

"Oh, yes, very amusing. Please excuse me if I wait until I'm alone to indulge in unladylike sniffs and snorts of hilarity. But back to the point. Yes, Bailey. The thing is, he and Miss Wise were all but declared to each other when Bailey met Alana at the book repository and the two of them took one look at each other and tumbled into love. Quite romantic, when you think about it, I suppose, which I try not to do because I find it all rather soppy."

"And Lord knows we Redgraves are never soppy. Scandalous, but never soppy. Absurd. Reckless. Notorious. But never soppy."

"Never mind that now. Mark my words, Valentine, Sylvia Wise is the spurned woman, and sure as check she wangled her way here to make mischief. We have to get rid of her. And since you brought her, it's up to you to take her away again."

Valentine sprang to his feet. "Well, why didn't you just

say so? I'll simply nip off downstairs, toss her over my shoulder and tote her out to the coach—done and done."

"You're not amusing, although I'd give a five pound note to watch you do it. And I suppose she's brought her mother along with her? Lady Wise, best known for her utter lack of sensibility."

"Oh, good, I thought it was just me thinking that. Rather, um, rough around the edges for the widow of a baron, wouldn't you say?"

"Common as a dirt floor. That's what Trixie would say—and *will* say if those two women are still here when she arrives on Friday, Lord help us."

Mention of their grandmother, Lady Beatrix, the dowager countess of Saltwood and one of the most outspoken women in the history of the ton, was enough to elicit both a smile and a small shiver of apprehension from Valentine.

"You're right. I'm no coward, but we've got to get the ladies gone. I mean, once she's done with them, she'll most naturally turn on me, because I brought them. Let's put our heads together."

Valentine plunked himself down beside his sister, shoulder to shoulder, their chins rather resting on their chests, their legs raised to prop their feet on the low marble-topped table.

The Redgraves rarely stood on ceremony, and they believed very much that one should be allowed to be comfortable in one's own home—and anywhere else they were, if they took it into their heads to do so. Because they were Redgraves, and who was going to gainsay them? That was the one good thing about being known for being outrageous and shockingly scandalous creatures—you could continue to be shockingly outrageous and scandalous whenever the spirit moved you. In fact,

Society very nearly expected you to be and, for reasons only Society could explain, rather delighted in watching the show.

So the siblings reclined low on their spines with their feet resting on the tabletop. They both, at the same time, crossed their ankles, and then sighed. They stared at the fireplace for some moments. When Valentine next spoke, it was to inquire about Alana, who he liked very much.

"So Alana loves Bailey?"

"With all of her tender, soppy heart, yes."

"And he loves her?"

Kate realized she was pleating her skirt into wrinkles and stopped, folding her hands together in her lap. "I'm convinced he does."

"Then, other than the business about dirt floors, I really don't see a problem there, at least."

Kate shifted on the cushion. "Listen carefully. Sylvia Wise is one generation away from the shop. In her case, her mama's father made some incredible fortune in coal, or peat, or some sort of fuel, not that it signifies, and then married her off to the baron—old and fairly deaf and probably the only person who would have her, no matter how large her fortune or dire their need of funds. Rumor has it Sylvia's no more the baron's daughter than she's Prinney's, but we'll never know if it was the ancient fortune hunter or his valet who did the deed."

"God, but we're a cruel bunch, aren't we?"

"There's that tender heart of yours again, Valentine. It will bring you to disaster one of these days. But I'm only being honest. Yes, Society is cruel. However, as we both well know, we ignore it at our peril when the case is serious enough. At least we do if we care a rap what anyone thinks, which we Redgraves don't happen to do very often, thank God."

"Yes, and how is our brother Gideon?" Valentine asked, and then raised his hand to rub away his words. "I know, I know, it's over, and we don't talk about it. There may still be whispers, but that's all. Water off our backs, as Trixie says, and damn everyone else."

"But that's *us*, Valentine. Alana's different. She wouldn't care about Society, I don't mean that. But in this instance, she'd *care*. In her heart. Now, if I might continue?"

"You're asking my permission? Have you ever done that before? I don't seem to remember any such occasion."

"*That* I will ignore. Now, the baron promptly cocked up his toes just after Sylvia was born, and the man's courtesy title died with him, which well it should have, as he'd only gotten it, rumor has it, thanks to some nefarious thing he did to benefit one of the royal princes many years ago."

Valentine smiled at her. "I'm impressed. I had no idea you were so well versed in gossip."

"You're forgetting Trixie. She keeps me knee-deep in the stuff, even when I beg her to stop. Now, Sylvia is passably pretty, odiously wealthy, ruthlessly ambitious, and she and her mother are hell-bent on marrying her off to a title that doesn't expire upon death, for one thing, and that is connected with an old and respected family. Like Bailey's."

"Respected? The earl is a drunk and a wastrel, and locked up for debt at least twice, I think." Valentine's eyebrows rose even as he said those last words. "Oh, now I see. Or at least I think I do. Miss Wise was chasing a title, and Bailey, poor bastard—and I mean that in the God-help-the-poor-bastard sense—was chasing a fortune."

"Exactly. He was gritting his teeth and doing his duty. Until he and Alana chanced to meet. Now do you understand?"

Valentine got to his feet and began to pace back and forth in front of the fireplace. "I think I'm beginning to, yes. Alana, wonderful as she is, is also the orphaned heiress to her late father who amassed his fortune in—what was that again?"

"Textiles," Kate supplied quietly, happy her brother had at last seen the point, and wouldn't have to be led by the nose through an entire sordid explanation.

"And you—and Gideon, I'd suppose, since he's her guardian—are certain Bailey didn't just change horses in the middle of a race for solvency, or some such thing?"

"Our brother isn't a fool, Val. When he took on guardianship of Alana he did so with every intention of managing her finances and protecting her well-being. I was in the room when he interrogated Bailey—and there is no better word to describe that uncomfortable hour. Bailey knows how it must look, as if he'd simply changed horses—ladies—while retaining his motive for marriage. But he truly loves Alana."

"Not her money."

"I doubt he'll dispense it all to the poor in order to prove that love, but no. He is not marrying Alana for financial gain. Nor, might I point out, is she marrying him in order to one day be the countess, as that knife cuts both ways, remember. Not," she continued, "that the world will probably believe that any more than if Miss Wise and Bailey were to have wed. Society will see a mutually beneficial exchange of money for title. However, if our sweet, love-struck Alana were to think as much, even for a moment, if even a kernel of any notion that Bailey might have proposed to her inheritance and not to her should enter her sweet, innocent head?"

She closed her eyes and sighed. "Oh, Valentine, get that woman and her encroaching mama out of here before the dinner gong goes. Please."

Valentine drew himself up to attention and shot his sister a jaunty salute. "I will do as ordered, Captain Kate. I'm off, nipping down the stairs to the morning room, ma'am, to Do My Duty."

"And Trixie complains that country life is boring," Kate said quietly as she got to her feet in order to follow her brother. "This should be fun to watch."

She'd taken no more than a few steps before she heard the dogs barking at the head of the stairs, followed by Valentine's cheerful words of greeting to Duke and Major and his own favorite, the fat and fairly stupid aged spaniel, Tubby.

"Val, grab Tubby," she warned as the younger dogs crowded out the spaniel, backing him toward the top step. "The old fool is going to topple back down the stairs!"

Tubby yelped in panic. Valentine cursed and made a grab for the dog…and a moment later Tubby and Kate were standing at the top of the staircase, watching as Valentine and the two hounds went tumbling head over heels together down the wooden staircase before coming to rest on the half landing.

The hounds got to their feet unhurt, shook themselves, and ran off, seeming to suddenly remember they were not allowed upstairs. But Valentine didn't move.

"Valentine! Are you all right? Answer me! For God's sake, *say something*!"

He did.

And Kate, who had been raised in the company of

three older brothers and a more than slightly irascible grandmother, was surprised to realize there were still some utterances that could make her clap her hands over her ears.

CHAPTER TWO

ALANA WALLINGFORD KNEW everyone thought her to be sweet and gentle, pleasant of disposition and possessing not a single bad word to say about anyone. And truth be told, everyone was probably correct in that assessment.

Or they had been, until Bailey had come into her life.

Now, Alana decided, she had become small and petty...and very, very vulnerable.

It had been two days since Valentine Redgrave had unexpectedly returned to the bosom of his family. Two days since he had taken that unfortunate tumble down the stairs and broken his leg, so that he was now confined to his chambers, where he was, at the last she'd heard, scribbling an ode to the glories of laudanum.

Two days since Alana had come down to dinner to see Miss Sylvia Wise and her monstrosity of a mother ensconced in the drawing room, the former smiling up at Bailey, the latter inspecting the underside of a lovely silver dish as if considering placing an offer on it.

Kate had rushed over to her, quickly explaining that Miss Wise and her mother were at Redgrave Manor at the impulsive invitation of Valentine. He'd taken a romantic interest in Miss Wise, silly man that he was, and now was unable to take them away again after riding all the way from London with them, a journey that had sufficed to change his always quixotic mind on that particular head. Gideon, once he returned from Dover in two days' time, would certainly make other arrangements, but for now there really was nothing else for it. The ladies were their guests, although they'd certainly be gone before the nuptials on Sunday (her brother Max was going to offer, but Kate had rather sensed that her ladyship would expect the earl to do the honors, and who only knew what Max might say during the trip, since Maximillian Redgrave was not exactly known for his tactfulness when he believed himself to be in the company of fools).

"And that's all right, isn't it, Alana?" Kate had ended rather nervously, squeezing her friend's hands.

Of course that had been all right with Alana. She would never say otherwise. She would never look her dear friend in the eye and say, "Pull my other leg, Kate, it's got bells on." She would never then go on to point out that Miss Wise and Bailey had been considered a sure match by the gossips until only a mere six weeks ago, even if everyone, including herself, pretended that she didn't know that. She wouldn't think to put forth the mean-spirited opinion that Miss Wise had somehow tricked Valentine into bringing her to Redgrave Manor. The words, "She's here for Bailey," would never pass her lips.

But she would think them. She'd been thinking them. Every minute of those past two days and nights.

And Bailey? Oh, Bailey. He had been so attentive, even more attentive than usual. He rarely left her side. He was constantly solicitous, more gentle with her than she could bear, as if he thought she might at any moment dissolve in tears or some such ridiculous thing, just because Miss Sylvia Wise was here to ruin her happiness.

Or was it more than that? Was Bailey feeling somehow guilty? And if he was—for what reason? He'd sworn his love for her. On bended knee, which had been rather delicious to watch. So why was he acting so strangely? Was he having second thoughts now that his former... former love was under the same roof? Was he looking for some way to break off the betrothal without causing a scene?

Or did he just think she was a big, stupid baby who needed to be constantly coddled and reassured—which, when she got right down to it, would be the worst thing of all. She wasn't a child. She didn't wish to be thought of as a child, treated as a child. She was a woman. Or at least, she thought, feeling her cheeks grow hot, she would be by Monday morning.

"It's because of how I look that everyone treats me like a child, even Bailey," Alana said aloud as she sat in the garden, having decided that Redgrave Manor, all seventy-two rooms of it, was too small to contain both her and Miss Sylvia Wise at the same time. "I am a Lilliputian in a land of giants."

She loved the Redgraves, she really did. Gideon, the earl of Saltwood, had taken her in three years previously when her parents had perished in that horrible accident— which hadn't been Gideon's fault, no matter what anyone said!—and she had instantly been clasped to the collective Redgrave bosom, as it were. She was a delicate rose among the thistles, or so Kate said, petite and blonde and well-mannered, as opposed to her new family, which was collectively tall and hearty and boisterous—and at times even a bit hey-go-mad.

And she had felt protected, cosseted. Loved. Perhaps at times overwhelmed, but definitely loved. From the moment she'd bumped into Bailey at the book repository—literally bumped into him, so that he'd quickly grabbed at her shoulders so she wouldn't fall—he had made her feel the same way.

She barely came up to his shoulder, and she liked that. She could step into his embrace and all but disappear into his solid, sheltering arms. Bailey liked that, too. He'd told her so when they'd kissed that single time. He said she made him feel strong and powerful, and that he was certain he had been put on this earth expressly to always take care of her, and to love her all the days of his life.

When Alana had told Kate what he'd said, she'd rolled her eyes comically and groaned as if in pain, but that was all right. Alana already knew that the Redgraves were the least romantical family in all of England. It was enough that she felt sure she had been put on this earth expressly to be with Bailey, and to love him all the days of her life.

Or so she'd believed until she'd seen the look on his face two nights ago, when he'd turned away from Miss Wise to see his betrothed standing in the drawing room, probably looking very much like a stunned kitten.

Was she out in the gardens because she wished to avoid Miss Wise? Or was she hiding out here because she wished to avoid Bailey? Was she now not only small and petty—and what was that last one? Oh, yes, very, very vulnerable—or had she also overnight become suspicious and distrusting of this man she loved so much?

Alana swiped at her damp eyes with her handkerchief before quickly replacing it in her pocket when she heard footsteps on the path. "Alana? What are you doing sitting out here alone? I've been looking all over for you, sweetheart."

"And now you've found me," she said as brightly as possible as Bailey sat down beside her on the stone bench. What a mess she was—she couldn't even hide properly! "I thought you'd gone out riding with Max."

"Nobody rides with Maximillian Redgrave, Alana. They eat the dust that black monster of his kicks up until they decide there are more pleasant ways to spend a lovely afternoon." Bailey lifted Alana's hand to lightly touch his lips to her fingertips. "Like being with you."

Oh, how smooth he was, Alana thought, wondering where that particular revelation had come from. Never at a loss for something to say; making all the right moves, tossing off compliments with such ease.

He was so handsome. Blond as was she, but his eyes were such a deep and lovely green to her own pale blue shade. His smile could melt stone, his manners were impeccable, and although he was quite tall, like the Redgraves, he was much more gentle-natured; his heart touched by a pretty verse, his voice never raised, his temperament even, no matter the situation.

Her wonderful, dependable rock. Her safe harbor. He was everything she'd ever hoped for, everything she wanted him to be.

Had he also been everything Sylvia Wise had wanted him to be?

"Alana? Is something wrong? You're…well, you're looking at me as if I may have just grown an extra head."

"I am? Oh, yes, I suppose I am," she answered, hating herself for her terrible thoughts. "Bailey? May I ask you a question?"

He took her hands in his, nearly destroying her resolve. "You can ask me anything, sweetheart. I can see something's troubling you."

She took a deep breath and asked her question. "If… if you and I had not met that day…would you have proposed to Miss Wise?"

His grip momentarily tightened on her fingers. "Would I…*what*? Would I have married her, exchanged my title for her fortune? Is that what you're asking me, Alana?"

She lowered her head, no longer able to look into his eyes. "No, I don't think it is. I think I already know you would have married her in order to repair your family's fortune. That is your duty as the heir, isn't it? I'm…I'm not a complete goose."

Bailey let go of her hands and got to his feet, clearly not able to sit still any longer. He knifed his fingers through his hair, leaving those smooth golden locks looking adorably disheveled and eminently touchable, which she would do her best to ignore.

"There's another term for that besides doing my duty, Alana. And that's fortune hunter."

"Yes, I suppose that's true," she said, adding hastily, "but I fully understand that you had little choice. I mean, there's the matter of your mother, and your three dowerless sisters all needing successful Seasons in a few years. And then there's the estate, and all those who work there—I know you feel responsible for them as well. My fortune will solve all of those problems for you."

"God," Bailey said, looking at her as if now perhaps she'd grown a second head. "I had no idea you were thinking things like that. You think I proposed marriage to you in order to take control of your inheritance?"

Alana got to her feet. He was tall enough when she stood beside him, but when she had to look up at him while she was seated, she could easily develop a crick in her neck. "I'm sorry, Bailey, I'm not saying this correctly. I suppose what I want to know is this—if you were prepared to marry Sylvia Wise for her fortune, how do you know you aren't marrying me for mine?"

For a moment he looked as if she'd just physically slapped him, and she wanted to die, just die. But she had to know.

"How do I know, or how do you know? Is that it, Alana? You're doubting my affection for you?"

Being closer to him wasn't helping, so she sat down again. "Miss Wise took me aside yesterday, Bailey. I tried to avoid her—I've been trying very diligently to avoid her—but she…she cornered me in the music room. She told me she felt sorry for me."

Bailey muttered something pithy concerning Miss Wise, and probably best reserved for times he was in strictly male company. At any rate, it didn't sound like a very pretty word.

"Yes, I think you're right. She's not a nice person," Alana agreed, still keeping her gaze directed down at her tightly clasped hands. "But she did explain why she convinced Valentine to bring her here. She said she felt it only fair to warn me that I am heading for heartbreak if I believe anything you say about…about having feelings for me."

"I do have feelings for you, Alana. Very deep feelings. Feelings I thought we shared."

She blinked back tears. "Thank…thank you. Miss Wise doesn't love you, by the way. She made herself very clear on that point. She, um, she said she was just happy you were fairly young, and presentable, and that you had no bad habits such as…oh, dear…such as belching in public."

"No, she leaves that party trick to her mother," Bailey said, dropping to one knee in front of the bench, so that at last the two of them were seeing eye to eye, at least physically. "Alana, Sylvia is here to make mischief between us. You have to know that."

Alana extracted her handkerchief from her pocket and tried her best to blow her nose daintily—sadly, a talent she had never quite mastered. "I know she didn't wangle her way to Redgrave Manor to give us her blessing, Bailey. Give me some credit."

Oh, dear. That had sounded more sharp than she'd intended, and not at all like her. But, then, she hadn't been sleeping at all well, so perhaps she could be excused.

"What else did she say to you? Let's get this over with, sweetheart, so that we can put it, and Miss Wise, behind us."

"Very well, I suppose we should. I think you can most probably imagine what else she said. She doesn't love you, you don't love her, but you'd discussed the mutual advantages of your...your union. You were even going to send her mother on a lengthy voyage to Greece, I believe it was."

"In the hope the ship would sink somewhere along the way, yes. Pirates would have been too much to hope for."

"Oh, Bailey," Alana said, very nearly smiling. "But the point is, you were all but declared to her, weren't you?"

He didn't speak for several nerve-shredding seconds, and then sighed deeply before admitting, "Yes. Yes, Alana, I was fully prepared to declare for her. I didn't see that I had a choice. But, if there is any credit in the thing for me, and there isn't much, at least I was honest with Sylvia."

"Honesty is a virtue, Bailey." Alana sniffed, or sniffled, she supposed, although sniffled sounded more delicate. "I can almost forgive Miss Wise for coming here. You greatly disappointed her, you know."

"I believe she'll survive. I'm not the only penniless peer in the realm."

"I suppose," Alana said, rather glad she didn't have to feel badly that she didn't feel badly for Miss Wise and her dashed matrimonial hopes.

Perhaps she should stop now, not ask the question that still burned inside her head. It could only lead to trouble.

But then she heard herself asking it anyway:

"And…and if we'd met, and…and if you'd been…attracted to me…and if I was poor as some church mouse… would you still have declared for me?"

He raised his hand to cup her cheek for a moment, and something melted inside of her. "That doesn't signify, Alana, because it isn't true."

"And yet I still would be most interested in your answer."

"I love you, Alana. With all my heart."

"That's not an answer. Because there's love, Bailey, and there is duty. So, please, tell me, and please give me the courtesy of the honesty with which you approached the subject with Miss Wise. If we'd met that day, and I was, oh, a parson's daughter, come to borrow a book, would you even now be preparing for your nuptials with Miss Wise? Much as you say you love me."

Bailey took her hands in his and looked deeply into her eyes. "I can't answer that, Alana, because I didn't have to make that choice."

I shouldn't have asked…I shouldn't have asked. Now look what I've done.

She disengaged her hands from his grip and got to her feet. "On the contrary, Bailey. I think you did answer my question, simply by refusing to answer it. Thank you for being honest."

And then she was off, running down the path to the house, her handkerchief clasped hard against her mouth to help stifle her sobs.

CHAPTER THREE

"HONOR'S A REAL BASTARD, isn't it?" Maximillian Redgrave asked as he handed out glasses of wine to his friend Bailey and his brother Valentine. "As younger sons, Val here and I don't have to tax our heads about it overmuch, do we, Val? No, don't answer. We already know you don't worry your head about anything. Miss Wise's presence downstairs speaks sufficiently to your brainpower."

"I told you, Max, I thought I was doing the damned woman a favor. Can I help it that she lied to me?"

"You'll do one favor too many one day, Val, and end up hanged, or worse," Max prophesied as he sat down beside Bailey, who had long since given up paying attention to anything the brothers said to each other.

He'd heard that there were seven levels of Hell, and he believed he'd visited each and every one of them since he'd bungled his answer to Alana's quite reasonable question. Except that it hadn't been reasonable, because she wasn't a parson's daughter. But she could have been. She could have been the rat catcher's daughter, damn it. And he still would have loved her with all his heart, forever.

But there was still his mother, his sisters: Mary, the eldest, was already a full year overdue to make her Come Out. The hundreds of workers on the estate. He had a responsibility to all of them. There was love, and there was duty. Alana had asked him a reasonable yet impossible question. But he should have had an answer.

"How could I have not answered her?" he asked the room at large now. "I knew what she wanted to hear. That I'd have tossed aside my mother, my sisters, the estate—everything—for love of her. That's what I should have said, that's what she needed to hear."

"So why didn't you say it?" Valentine asked from his bed of pain (which wasn't half so painful today, not that he'd tell anyone, or they wouldn't continue being so nice to him). "It certainly was simple enough. 'Yes, Alana, my dearest darling girl—I still would have married you cap over the windmill if you were poorer than a church mouse, and we would have lived together in abject yet glorious poverty as the estate crumbled all around us. Unless, of course, I'm clapped up in the Fleet for my inherited debts, at which time I would only ask that I could lower my basket down the outside wall each morning and you would fill it with whatever crusts of stale bread you might find in our humble larder.' See? That wasn't so difficult, was it?"

"I could smother him with one of his pillows, if you'd like," Max offered, not all that helpfully. "Tell me again, why is the woman still here? Not to mention the mother, and nobody in his right mind would wish to mention that nasty piece of work."

"Gideon arrives late tonight from Dover," Bailey explained, "before heading off again tomorrow morning to gather up your grandmother for the nuptials, remember? It would have seemed too much as if we—I—was afraid to have Sylvia and Alana under the same roof if we were to boost her out of here before then. At least that's what Kate said."

"Ah, yes, our lovable old Tartar of a grandmother,"

Max said, wincing. "And we're all certain she wants to leave London in the midst of the Season? Surely she hasn't managed to insult everyone in the ton already."

"Gideon's the only one who can handle her. I didn't even bother stopping off to say hello during the few days I was there. She asks such embarrassing questions of a person, you know," Valentine told Bailey. "In any event, if Gideon can handle Trixie, he won't have any trouble escorting the ladies back to Mayfair. Kate thinks like a general, you know. Very good at strategy. Maybe you should apply to her for help now, Bailey? Clearly we're not of much use to you."

"Not if lying to Alana is your only suggestion, no," Max said, looking at Bailey. "Could you at least try not to look so maudlin, old fellow? You could put a man off his drink."

"I'm sorry," Bailey said, getting to his feet. "You're right. I should talk to Kate. As confidants, you two are pretty worthless, you know."

"Not as if we didn't tell you that," Valentine pointed out happily. "Women are by nature more devious, and much better suited to whatever it is you're going to have to do, whatever that turns out to be. But if you fancy a hand of whist later, we'll be here."

Bailey thanked the brothers and went off in search of Lady Katherine, running her down in the music room, where she was attacking a tune on the pianoforte with much more enthusiasm than expertise.

"Oh, good, a reason to cut my practice short," she said, rising from the bench at the same time she gestured toward a pair of chairs near the fireplace, inviting him to sit down. "Although I did manage to roust Miss Wise and her mother with my joyful noise, as Trixie would term it, so we shouldn't term the thing a total loss.

Where's Alana? I had assumed you two were hiding together somewhere."

Five minutes later, Kate's smile had completely disappeared, and her posture had stiffened somewhat, as if she might be girding her loins for battle, if Valentine's description of his sister was to be believed. Lady Katherine was a striking woman, her tall, dark beauty quite singular in a world filled mostly by petite blonde misses of pale skin and blue eyes. But the late countess had been Spanish, and all four Redgrave offspring had been influenced in looks and spirit by that woman's heated Iberian blood.

Not that Alana's looks were ordinary. She might possess the coloring (and, compared with Lady Katherine, at least, the petite stature of most Englishwomen), but her sweet, loving nature shone from her like a beacon, making her more than merely beautiful.

His mind retreated from the music room, traveling back to that quite ordinary Tuesday that had somehow turned into the most glorious day of his life.

He'd gone into the book repository because it was the closest open door when London's always precarious weather had turned wet. He'd been idly inspecting the spines of books in the Modern History section, backing his way down the narrow aisle, when he'd inadvertently stepped on the hem of someone's gown, turned about sharply to apologize, and nearly knocked Alana off her feet.

He'd immediately dropped the book in his hands and took hold of her shoulders to steady her, prepared to apologize. But he couldn't find the words. All he could do was look at her. She was the sun on a rainy day. She was an angel somehow come to earth.

He should have let her go. Immediately. He should

have apologized, bowed and asked if he could present his compliments to her mother or whoever had accompanied her to the book repository, so that they could be formally introduced. He should have done any number of things.

Instead, still holding on to her shoulders, looking down into her huge blue eyes with his heart shining in his own, he'd said, "I'm Bailey."

"I'm Alana," she'd answered, demurely lowering her eyelids, but then looking up at him again through her dark lashes, at which time Bailey had felt fairly sure his legs were going numb.

It had been Fate. That's what it had been. The rain, the book repository, all of it. Nothing planned, nothing premeditated, for God's sake. Love wasn't like that…and this was love. He'd known it from that first instant…and thought Alana had as well.

Bailey shook himself from his thoughts, allowed time to grow thanks to Kate's unnerving silence, when she at last spoke.

"Well? Have you come up with an answer, because I believe I'd like to hear it as well? Would you be about to marry my good and dear friend this coming Sunday if she were to come to you without a groat to her name?"

He thought about repeating what he'd said to Alana, but one look at General Kate, and he decided that wouldn't be a good idea. "I don't know," he said at last, hating himself. Truly loathing himself.

"All right," Kate said consideringly. "At least you're being honest now. You have been raised to do your duty, haven't you? Not by your spendthrift father, I'm assured, but by your mother, who has drummed it into your head that you and you alone are responsible for your sisters and, indeed, everything and everyone connected with the Armstrong name and the title of Earl of Sandling that will one day be yours. Hopefully soon, before your father can ruin you all beyond salvation."

"Knowing that I was seriously pursing Sylvia Wise is answer enough to that question, isn't it?"

"God, yes. That doesn't simply smack of desperation—it all but shouts it from the rooftops." She looked at him sorrowfully. "You poor thing."

"Max says honor's a bastard," Bailey said, beginning to believe he was on the verge of sliding into a sad decline, which was not at all like him. Or at least he had never considered himself the melodramatic sort.

"Ah, yes. And said, I'm quite certain, with all the fervor of a younger son, who doesn't have to worry about such things. So Alana is crushed, I'll assume?" she added, again surprising Bailey with her candor.

He hadn't blinked when she'd mentioned his father, but it was rather amazing to know that others felt as he did; his father was a total loss. He'd lived his life determined to never do a single thing his father had done. He'd always considered himself an upright man, doing his duty. And as his reward, the gods had smiled on him, and sent him Alana.

He spared a moment to wonder who had sent him Sylvia Wise.

"Yes, I'm certain she is." Bailey looked into his wineglass and then put it down without tasting its contents. "I can't say that I blame her. Why should she believe I love her?"

"Pity there aren't any fire-breathing dragons about for you to slay. To save her, you understand, with some grand bit of derring-do," Kate said, and then gnawed on her lower lip for a moment. "I mean, the closest thing we have to a fire-breathing dragon is my grandmother, and she adores Alana, so that wouldn't work."

Bailey looked at her levelly. "Max and Valentine said you'd help. That doesn't sound like help."

"No, but it does give me an idea. We should think of what Trixie would do." Then she frowned.

"What?" Bailey leaned closer, rather like a drowning man reaching for a bit of floating straw.

"No, you can't do that. I can't even say it." Then Kate waved her words away. "Well, I could certainly say it. I'm not missish, for pity's sake. And it could work. I mean, it should work. The way I've heard it, in one way or another it has worked for a thousand years."

"Kate…"

"Oh, all right, don't glower. Alana loves you because you're sweet and wonderful and kind and all sorts of other laudable attributes that make my teeth itch, but to each his own, I say."

"Thank you," Bailey said, fairly certain he wasn't feeling all that sweet or kind at the moment.

"You're welcome," Kate said absently, or perhaps the proper term would be obliviously. "Now promise me you didn't hear this from me, because I'd deny it in any case. Remember that. It's Trixie. She's…she's speaking through me. Yes, that's the way of it. You'll never say I was the one to suggest such a thing."

"I'll swear that on your family Bible, if you just tell me where it is. For God's sake, Kate, tell me. I love Alana. I'd do anything to make her see that."

Kate didn't blush. It wasn't in her nature, but she did say the words rather quietly. Still, they seemed to echo all around the room, bouncing back from the walls as Bailey sat there, rather stunned.

"Bed her, Bailey. That's what Trixie would say. If you truly love her, *show* her."

JUST AS THE LARGE CLOCK in the grand foyer was striking ten the following morning, Kate entered Alana's bedchamber. She carried with her a tray holding two china cups and a squat ceramic teapot, the favorite receptacle for Redgrave hot chocolate for the past decade…replacing the pot that had been the favorite before that, thanks to Trixie having tossed that one at Valentine's head for one reason or another.

"Alana? You're not still asleep, are you?" she asked, squinting into the dimness in the general direction of the bed. "Up you get, slugabed, I've brought hot chocolate. And biscuits."

There was some slight rustling of bedclothes and then Alana raised her sleep-mussed blond head from beneath the covers as she pushed herself back against the headboard. She wanted to be alone. She'd ask Kate to leave if she thought her friend would obey her, but since she already knew Kate obeyed no one, she didn't bother. "I'm not hungry, thank you. Or thirsty."

"Good, more for me," Kate said, sliding the tray onto a low table and seating herself on one of a pair of facing chairs placed in front of the fireplace. "Do you know what's wrong with Bailey?" she asked as she poured two cups of the steaming chocolate. "I saw him downstairs just now in the breakfast room, and if his chin got any lower, he'd be dragging it along the ground when he walks."

What had she said about Bailey? All right, so perhaps she didn't want to be alone. Alana turned back the covers and carefully aimed her feet toward the floor. The beds at Redgrave Manor were all built for giants. "He is? I mean, it is?"

"Hmm?" Kate asked, looking up from her pouring. "Oh, we're talking about Bailey, aren't we? Never mind. I'm sure I was mistaken. The man's to be married in a few days. He can't be anything but happy. You're happy, aren't you, sweetheart?"

Alana slipped her arms into the sleeves of her dressing gown and sat down on the facing chair, wrapping the soft white material around her. "Brides are always happy," she replied, going on her guard. Kate wasn't the sort for idle chatter.

"Oh, I seriously doubt that. Her Royal Highness Princess Caroline certainly wasn't, or so it's said. I doubt any of King Henry Tudor's wives were happy, always wondering how long it would be before their heads were separated from their shoulders. Then there's—"

"In general," Alana said quickly. "I was speaking of brides in general. As...as a species."

Kate looked at her and smiled. "Brides are a species? What a singular idea. In any event, you're happy, and that's all that concerns me."

At which point, Alana burst into tears.

But that was all right. That was probably very good. She'd wanted to speak with someone about what had happened the day before in the gardens. Needed to speak with someone. She loved Bailey, and she had hurt him. She had asked him a question she should not have thought, let alone asked, and now she didn't know how to fix what she very well knew was her obligation to correct.

Kate was her best friend in the entire world. Who better to unburden herself on, who better to advise her as to what she should do now that she'd made such a horrible muddle of things?

Because there had to be a way to make things right, there just had to be, or else she would simply die. She had to find some way to convince Bailey that she understood the great pressure he was under to rescue his family, and how he would not wish her to spend her life in perilous poverty simply because he loved her, and that she shouldn't have asked a question that had no basis in reality in the first place. Because, in the second place, she was wealthy, and he did love her, and she did love him, and what was wrong with any of that, for pity's sake? But how could she convince Bailey she understood all of that now…now that she'd made such a muddle of things?

"I think I'm feeling the beginnings of a headache," Kate said some half hour of such muddled and at times tearful statements later, rubbing at her left temple as she stared into her empty cup. "But I think I have a solution for you. Well, not precisely me, but you know how brilliant Trixie is, and I think I know just what she would say to do. But perhaps not. It's—it's rather, well…no, I probably shouldn't say."

Alana leaned forward in her chair. "Yes? Please, Kate, don't hesitate now. Tell me."

That was just before her innocent blue eyes got wide as saucers.

"But first, Alana, I think you need to speak with somebody else," Kate said when Alana at last recovered enough to reach for a biscuit. Not that she was hungry; she might never eat again. But she had to do something, or else Kate might repeat herself, or worse, go into embarrassing detail.

"I scarcely think I should go from person to person,

presenting your solution for their opinions," she said, and then took another large bite of biscuit.

"That wasn't what I meant, but all right," Kate said, shrugging her shoulders as she got to her feet, clearly having decided this conversation was over. "You aren't me, and I'm not you. I'm probably even mean. But if I *were* you, I'd get dressed, go downstairs and put a flea in Sylvia Wise's ear before Gideon comes to take her away, at the very least. Just to make myself feel better."

Kate's final words on the subject repeated themselves in Alana's ears (both of them) as she bathed and dressed and made her way downstairs an hour later.

She went first to the main drawing room, and then to the breakfast room, and finally to the music room—not that she was actively looking for Sylvia Wise. She was simply wandering about aimlessly, a lady of leisure, a—oh, all right, she admitted to herself. She was hunting, and all that was missing was enlisting one of the Redgrave hounds to help point the way to her quarry.

And there she was, sitting like Little Miss Muffet, all snug on her tuffet…or at least looking very much at her ease on the settee.

"Good morning, Miss Wise," Alana said with more confidence than she felt.

Sylvia Wise slowly turned her head to smile at Alana. "How wonderful of you to join me, Miss Wallingford. I had so feared I might have abused your sensibilities with my candor of the other day. I'm being banished, you know, even though my intentions were entirely honorable."

"Oh, they were not," Alana said, quickly losing her discomfort as she mentally took off her gloves, more than ready for some plain speech. "Bailey chose me over you, and you wanted to get some of your own back for the slight by making me feel terrible and perhaps even withdrawing from the betrothal. Did you really think he'd then come running back to you?"

Sylvia's startlingly blue eyes narrowed as she slowly got to her feet and faced Alana across the expanse of carpet. "Come running back to me? You foolish little girl. He's never left me. I…*do* things for him you could never do. Your fortune is larger, that's all. But we have an understanding, your betrothed and I. I even prefer it, as marriage is my mother's idea, not mine. I enjoy my freedom, and a variety of lovers, each with his own talents.

"Indeed, your marriage is to my benefit, as long as Bailey continues to pleasure me when I call for him. I admit to some worry, initially, but having seen you for myself, pasty-faced little innocent that you are, I'm no longer concerned that we won't simply continue on as we began so many months ago."

This was it: the moment. The moment when Alana would either crumble or soar, the moment when what she wanted to believe and what she believed would war with each other, with only one feeling emerging the victor.

She blinked a time or two.

She smiled.

And then she laughed. Laughed in real amusement, and not a small portion of relief.

Sylvia Wise's cheeks turned an angry red. "It's true! Every word! What are you laughing at, you silly twit?"

Alana sobered, not without effort. "You," she said frankly. "I'm laughing at you, Miss Not-So-Wise. And myself, for ever being so silly as to think you were anything Bailey could ever care for, even if you were covered in gold and your teeth were made out of diamonds. He never proposed marriage to you because he couldn't love you, much as he loves his family. I doubt he even much likes you; I know I certainly don't. Good day to you, madam, I've wasted more than enough time on you."

"Wait! You can't—"

Alana turned back to the woman. "Oh, and one thing more. You will kindly complain of illness and take to your chamber until such time as my guardian boosts you on your way back to London, you and your mother both. Because you won't care for the public stagecoach, which is where you will find yourself if I see you again. Understood?"

Alana didn't wait for the woman's answer, because she didn't need to hear it, but only lifted her chin and walked out of the room, slowly and deliberately...before all but skipping down the hallway to the French doors leading out to the gardens.

Sunday evening she would become a woman, yes, but she believed she might already be halfway there.

CHAPTER FOUR

BAILEY HADN'T REALIZED how uncomfortable he'd been with Sylvia Wise and her mother in residence until they'd gone. He knew he hadn't been *happy*, but never had a leave-taking made him feel more ebullient. He wondered how Sylvia would feel if she knew how much she brightened a room just by leaving it.

Gideon Redgrave had been and gone, but not before delivering a pithy, ear-burning bedside lecture to his brother Valentine on the merits of his mouth consulting with his brain before it opened, especially when it was a beautiful woman seeking his assistance. He'd then imperiously—Gideon was brilliant at being imperious—gathered up Sylvia Wise and her reluctant mother, and surprised everyone by ordering one of the lesser coaches for them, saying that he'd planned to travel to London by horseback in any case, and then escort his grandmother to Redgrave House in her own coach.

So much for any of Lady Wise's possible thoughts about bracketing her Sylvia to the infamous Earl of Saltwood (she'd actually said she never believed those rumors about him murdering people anyway, or at least not enough to toss away the chance to be mother to a countess).

In any event, this outstanding tactical maneuver on Gideon's part prompted Max to say in some awe as he stood at the window and watched the earl ride off,

"That's why it's so convenient that he's the earl. He thinks of things. All I could think was how I'd have been stuck inside the coach with those two all the way back to Mayfair, and how I was going to make Valentine pay for that indignity the moment his leg was mended. Still, we should have thought of something like that."

"We shouldn't have had to," Kate responded, at which point she and Max and Bailey turned to stare at Valentine, who was pretending a great interest in the bit of orange marmalade slowly sliding off his piece of toast and heading for his nightshirt.

In any case, Sylvia Wise was halfway to the city by now, and while Bailey wasn't breathing all that easily, he at least no longer felt as if a noose was slowly tightening around his neck.

And in just a few days' time, he and Alana would be wed, and the unfortunate interlude with Sylvia Wise would be a thing of the past.

Unless Kate was wrong, and Alana was about to ask him to release her from their engagement.

Unless Kate was wrong, and Alana was in no mood to be spoken to, let alone...seduced.

And how in bloody blazes did a person go about seducing someone in the first place?

Bailey was young, only four and twenty, but he wasn't some wet-behind-the-ears looby. He'd bedded his share of women. Granted, the evenings all ended with coins leaving his pocket to reside in the woman's purse, but still—he wasn't inexperienced.

It was just that Alana was...different. She was young, only just nineteen, and innocent. He'd written her poems. He'd brought her flowers. He'd kissed her fingertips. They'd shared only one brief, chaste betrothal kiss. He...

he cherished her. Yes, that was the word: *cherish*. She was a lady. Innocent. Virginal.

In point of fact, he'd been more than a little concerned that their wedding night might prove something of a shock to her.

Her mother had died just as Alana had left the schoolroom; she was scarcely a woman of the world. The only female influence she'd encountered before entering her first Season had come from the Dowager Countess and Kate. Bailey felt certain Kate wouldn't have educated Alana in the way of wives, and he could only pray the dowager hadn't.

He, her husband, would be cast in that role. Teacher. He'd planned to be gentle. *Seduction* wasn't a word that went well with gentle. One didn't have a gentle seduction. Seduction was wild, impetuous, fraught with impatience and heavy breathing…and often indulged in sans bed.

While the notion appealed to him very much—he had to be honest with himself and admit that—Alana had never experienced real, womanly desire, he was certain, and his prenuptial ardor might frighten her.

"It's the only way," Kate had told him again just that morning. "Saying you love her is one thing. But those are just words. Anyone can say the words. Saying you would have tossed away her fortune is nothing but mouthing words that even I find hard to believe, considering your circumstances. It doesn't matter how you found each other, things like fortune don't matter when there's real love—I do truly believe that. What matters is that you did find each other."

"I know, I understand," Bailey had told her, hoping she'd stop talking, as they were in the hallway outside the breakfast room when she caught up to him, and someone could come along and overhear them.

"Now you have to *show* her you can't exist without her, that she is the sun and the moon and the stars and all of that nonsense to you. That's probably been the problem all along, you know, Bailey. You've been treating Alana as if she's made of crystal. She would never have questioned your love for her if you'd—well, you know what I mean. At least I dearly hope so, or we're all lost."

He'd been lectured by a woman, a young, unmarried woman at that, nearly five years his junior. And the bleeding pity of it had been that she was right.

How many nights had he left Alana at the Redgrave mansion and then walked the streets of Mayfair, unable to sleep for wanting her? How many times had he longed to pull her into his arms, kiss her the way a man kisses the woman he loves. Touch her. Teach her. Take her.

Now he wasn't simply being encouraged to do all of those things—he'd been ordered to.

"And yet you've been sitting here running your mind in circles, instead of hunting up Alana," he told himself as he left the others and went off in search of his betrothed. "Maybe you are a looby."

ALANA HAD BEEN WALKING the lower gardens for what seemed like hours, pretending an interest in the flowers and topiaries that was shallow at best, wondering how long it would take for Bailey to find her. Kate had promised to position herself in the drawing room and then steer him in the correct direction if he should ask where she was. But perhaps he hadn't asked.

She wouldn't blame him. She'd conducted herself abominably and then avoided him whenever possible. She'd known then that she'd behaved badly, but it had taken Kate to truly open her eyes to what she had done.

Of course Bailey hadn't wanted to answer her. How

could he have tossed his family aside—three dowries to be found, not to mention fixing the leaking roofs on the estate, paying off all his father's duns and other creditors—all for love? That would have been selfish of him in the extreme.

Worse, or so Kate had explained the thing, he would at the same time be asking the woman he loved to share his penury, and that he would never do. He was a man, and therefore too proud to ask such a sacrifice of her. Men could be so unreasonably starchy and honorable that way. Kate had told her.

She never should have asked the question. She never should have thought it. The question had been romantic and silly and unworthy of a person who longed to call herself woman, wife.

And she'd thought of one thing more, the question Bailey had not asked of her and most certainly would have been justified in putting to her: *If I were not heir to an earldom, but only a poor man with no prospects, would you have married me?*

In her mind, she'd said vehemently, *Of course I would have!* But then she'd thought about Gideon's sure protests to such a union, and what her mother's reaction would have been were she still alive, as Bailey's mother was. Yes, she would still have said that she would marry him. But it would not have been easy, and she would have hesitated before answering, just as Bailey had done.

She may even have protested that there was no reason to answer, because that was not the case for them.

Love wasn't grand. It was stupid. And it made a person say things a person should not say. *Climb this mountain for me. Slay this dragon if you love me.*

Maybe she didn't really know what love was. Maybe she didn't deserve someone as wonderful as Bailey.

Oh, but when he looked at her… When he touched her hand and something warm and almost hungry came to life deep inside of her… When he smiled and she could only watch his mouth, and her toes curled in her shoes as she thought about that glorious mouth closing over hers…

But there had only been that one kiss. Just that one. Sometimes she had longed to grab him by the lapels of his coat and pull him against her so that he'd stop treating her as if she might break if he did more than compliment her eyes, her gown.

He said he loved her. He said it often, and that was very nice. But if he truly, truly loved her, shouldn't he have done more than say the words? Shouldn't he, couldn't he, have ever shown her?

And if he had, would she have even thought to ask him that stupid, stupid question?

"Alana?"

She turned quickly at the sound of Bailey's voice, nearly toppling as her skirts seemed to tangle about her feet. Or so she'd let him think.

He caught her to him, rather as he'd done that first day at the book repository. It felt so good. So right.

So…frustrating.

"You nearly fell," he said, his hands on her upper arms as he steadied her.

She looked up into his concerned eyes. Moistened her lips. Dared to say, "But you wouldn't let me fall."

"Alana, I—"

"Bailey, I—"

"No, you first," he said, gently putting her away from him.

He'd let her go. He'd had the perfect opportunity to kiss her, and he'd let her go. She'd thought she'd been rather daring, even blatant. Maybe she hadn't done it right?

"I…I just wanted to tell you that it was horribly unfair of me to ask you what I asked you. And I apologize."

"No, it was a valid question. I should have answered you."

"But I don't want you to."

"I should."

Honestly, how could she save him from himself, if he didn't let himself be saved? "I know you love me, and that's enough. Please, Bailey. Miss Wise is gone—"

"And good riddance," he interrupted with a smile. "We think she and her mother only stayed so long so that Sylvia could take a dead set at Gideon during the ride to London."

That information served to divert Alana. "Gideon? I would imagine he dashed those expectations soon enough."

"Yes, it's a true measure of my love for you that I didn't escape to the wilds of America halfway through his questions regarding my intentions toward you. He's not an easy man. Shall we walk?"

Now it was she who had a perfect opportunity—in her case, to tell him what she'd done, how she'd all but cornered Sylvia Wise in the music room, and what the woman had said to her. But was that really necessary? It was much too pleasant a day to speak of the woman. In fact, it could be sleeting and freezingly cold, and it still would be too pleasant a day to speak of the woman. No, not everything had to be said, shared. And the past was the past—it was the future she was interested in now. The very *near* future.

So she only nodded, and he held out his arm so that she could take it, and they turned down the path Alana had been haunting this past quarter hour...the one leading to that lovely, vine-covered gazebo and the comfortable, softly cushioned chaise tucked inside it.

The path looked different now. The flowers had more color, the neatly trimmed greenery seemed more whimsical.

She curled her arm about his more securely, allowed her body to brush up against his as they navigated the uneven stone path. She lifted her other hand and placed it on his forearm as well, and smiled up into his face as he told her that his mother and sisters would be arriving the morning of the wedding, having made arrangements to stay with one of his mother's friends at an estate not five miles from Redgrave Manor.

"Will they like me?" Alana asked, as she'd yet to meet any of the Armstrong family other than Bailey.

"How could they not?" he said at once, and then rather winced at his own words. "That was too glib, wasn't it?"

"Perhaps," she admitted, wondering how he knew.

"My sisters are too excited about the idea of each of them having a well-financed Season," he told her then, "and my mother is only anxious that the marriage take place before you can realize you've been cold-bloodedly wooed for your fortune."

"And now perhaps too honest," Alana told him. "But thank you. Shall we make a pact to never speak about any of this again?"

"Or think about it?" he asked her as a turning in the path revealed the gazebo in all its isolated glory, surrounded by tall yew trees, completely invisible from the house.

She decided to be daring. At least she hoped he would consider her daring and teasing, and not quarrelsome.

"As long as you don't believe I said yes to your proposal in order to one day be a countess."

Bailey stopped on the path, so that she had to as well. "That never occurred to me," he said in some shock. "I never thought of our marriage as some sort of trade. I should have, shouldn't I? I certainly thought about it almost constantly when I was wooing Sylvia's fortune. But not with you. Never with you. Perhaps that's why your question took me so by surprise."

He turned her toward him and put his hands on her waist. "When I think of you, and I always think of you, I think of how wonderful you are, how good, how sweet and gentle and—"

"I'm not sweet and gentle!" Alana burst out, actually stamping one small foot on the cobblestone path. She lowered her voice, shocked at her own outburst. "I'm not, Bailey. Really. I may not have realized that until that awful woman showed up here, but it's true. I'm not nice."

He tipped up her chin with his fingertip and smiled down into her face. "Of course you are. Why else do you think I fell in love with you? I couldn't help myself. You're everything precious I could ever hope for. Your goodness all but beams from you."

"Well, I don't want it to," Alana said mulishly, knowing she was fairly close to making an utter fool of herself, yet unable to stem her words. "Most of all, I'm heartily sick of being good. I want to be bad, Bailey. I want to be adventuresome, and…and dangerous…and…and shocking. Yes, that's it, shocking. I want to shock you."

"Me?" Bailey couldn't have looked more surprised if she'd just reached into her pocket and pulled out a fat white rabbit. "You want to shock me? How? Why?"

Her burst of bravado, or hysterics, faded as quickly as

it had bloomed. "I don't know," she admitted in a quiet voice. "I…I have these thoughts…these feelings. About… things…about you. And when I saw Sylvia Wise in the drawing room, leering up at you that way, I wanted to go over to her and tear her hair straight off her head. I did, Bailey, I really did. But…but that wouldn't have been sweet, or gentle, or ladylike. Or good. You would have been appalled!"

"Once I got done applauding, yes, probably. Alana, I don't mean to be dense, but what are you trying to say to me?"

"I don't *know*! Can't you understand that, Bailey? I don't know exactly what I'm saying. Everybody thinks I do, or at least Kate does. But I don't. Nobody ever really *told* me how to go about what I'm desperately trying to go about—and, yes, I know I'm making no sense at all. I just know that I'm not what everybody thinks I am. I'm not what you think I am, and if I am, then I'm heartily sick of being who you think I am, but you should know that now because then maybe I won't be the person you thought I was and you won't love me because I'm really not this…this *paragon* you keep rattling on about as if it was wonderful to be so sickeningly nice. I just…I just— oh, here!"

She grabbed at his wrists and pressed his hands against her breasts.

Alana had once read somewhere—probably in one of those marble-backed novels Kate scoffed at—that there are moments when time stands still. It stops, just stops for several moments. And then it moves on….

Bailey cupped his palms around her softness. Slowly. Gently.

She watched his chest rise and fall, her own breaths

equally shallow, her heart—part of the world that had *stopped*—beginning to beat at an alarmingly rapid rate.

She felt something seem to tighten between her legs, and not in an uncomfortable way. It felt rather good, actually. Not good as in how the world thought she was good, but good in a way that might be deliciously bad. Better than good ever was or could be.

"Alana," Bailey breathed softly, not moving his hands. Except for his thumbs, which now were for some unknown reason stroking back and forth across her nipples that, for reasons of their own, she supposed, began to feel tight and hard. And quite good.

There was that word again. *Good.* Perhaps good wasn't so bad.

But now they were just standing there. Like statues. With Bailey's hands still on her.

Oh, dear. Wasn't *that* awkward?

Wasn't he going to do anything else? At the very least, *say* something?

"Alana...I didn't know," he said at last, his voice rather thick. "I'd hoped...but when you've got the sun and the moon, as I have in you, it would be greedy to ask for the stars as well."

His hands left her breasts, and she had to fight back a moan of protest, but he'd only moved them so that he could draw her closer, so he could raise up her chin, so he could press his mouth against hers.

Their betrothal kiss had been nice. Good. But now he was urging her lips apart and insinuating his tongue between them, and he was probing at her, drawing sensation from her, somehow making the tightening between her legs turn to a warm tingling void that seemed to be asking for something, some sort of attention to be paid to it.

She slid her hands up the front of his coat, and then wrapped her arms around his neck, pressing her breasts against his chest. She didn't know why she was doing any of these things; she simply let her body do what it seemed to know to do on its own.

He moaned low in his throat and then insinuated his thigh between hers, pressing up against her as if he'd known about the tingle. That was good; he seemed to know about a lot of things, things he could teach her. Dare she tell him she thought she would make a very apt pupil?

Bailey broke the kiss at last, pulling her against him, his breath rather shaky close against her ear.

"I'd slay dragons for you," he told her, sounding quite romantic and serious, which for some strange reason caused a giggle to escape her lips. And then they were both laughing. Laughing, and holding on to each other, and probably looking very silly to Maximillian Redgrave, who, because the gods weren't always kind, had chosen that exact moment to make use of the lower garden as a shortcut back from the stables.

"Oops—forgot I wasn't to come this—that is, oh, good. Made it up between you I see," he said. "Kate's a genius, almost as brilliant as our grandmother. Just don't tell her, please. She's smug enough as it is. Well, I'm off! See you both at dinner…or whenever."

He'd just about passed them by when Bailey called out, "Wait a moment, Max. What did you mean? You weren't supposed to come this way? Was that it? And Kate's a genius?"

Max stopped, seemed to realize he'd soon be facing his sister's wrath. He might be six years her senior, but Kate was a force to be reckoned with, and all her brothers knew it. "What? Oh, that. She said you two love

each other and you'd figure that out and make it up between you. That's all. Wagered me five pounds it would
be today, as a matter of fact. I said not until tomorrow.
Sorry for thinking you such a slow-top, Bailey. Now I'm
off to clean up my dirt before dinner."

By now Alana had not only managed to step clear of
Bailey, who'd seemed to have forgotten he was holding
on to her, but she was wondering why he was looking
so...well, so guilty.

Or maybe she thought he looked guilty because she
was feeling guilty?

Because she doubted either one of them believed
Max's story about a wager. Because he had not only
looked guilty, but had sounded it as well. And then there
was that business about being warned not to come back
to the house via the lower garden.

"Bailey?" Alana asked when her betrothed finally
turned to look at her as if attempting to see into her head,
discern what she was thinking. Which, by her quick reck-
oning, would be a disaster. "Is...is something wrong?"

"I don't know. Alana, why were you here? In the lower
garden, I mean. I'd been looking for you, to—well, in any
case, when I couldn't find you, Kate told me you were
here." He looked toward the gazebo as if it might provide
some sort of answer, but then asked again, "Why were
you here?"

She took refuge in a question of her own. "Why were
you looking for me?"

"Why would you ask that? You weren't hiding from
me, were you?"

Oh, this wasn't going well! If he was avoiding answering her, and she was avoiding answering him, they'd
never get anywhere. Not that Alana was sure she wanted
to go anywhere, not when she was beginning to think

Lady Katherine Redgrave was behind whatever it was Bailey didn't want to tell her as well as behind what she didn't want to tell him.

But there was nothing else for it. One of them had to say something, and since she was the one who'd taken his hands and—well, she'd done what she'd done, hadn't she? So it was up to her to answer Bailey's question.

"I never should have asked you that horrible question," she told him by way of preliminary...or trying to drag out the inevitable as long as possible. "I mean, it's one thing for my inheritance to be...convenient for you. And it's another thing for the fact that my parents had always hoped I'd marry into Society. But...but the important thing is that I love you. And you love me. Isn't it?"

"No," Bailey said after spending a few moments obviously trying to decipher what she'd said. "The important thing is that we know we love each other for ourselves, and not for fortune or social station. Because that really was your question, at the heart of it. Wasn't it?"

"Yes! Yes, that was exactly it. And even though I should never have asked, never have questioned, once I had, it seemed imperative that I...that I show you how I feel about you. Be-before the wedding."

"I see," Bailey said rather stiffly. "And—" he put out his index fingers and rather *twirled* them in front of her breasts "—doing what you did was by way of being in aid of *showing* me? Let me hazard a guess here. It was Kate's idea, wasn't it? She set you on me, like a hound on the fox."

She felt the heat of abject embarrassment rushing into her cheeks. "You don't have to be crude, Bailey."

"Yes, you're right. That was uncalled for. If not a bit cold-blooded on your part," he added, and then winced.

"No, I didn't mean that. We all make mistakes. Not that what you did was a mistake," he amended quickly. "Or me, either. Made a mistake, that is. Damn it all, Alana, I don't know what I'm saying anymore."

Now his cheeks were looking rather pink. "Bailey? Why were you looking for me? Max seemed to know to stay away from this area of the gardens, and yet Kate directed you here."

"Yes," he said slowly, as if speaking might have suddenly become painful. "About that…"

And then, as surely as the sun Bailey had compared her to rose in the east, everything became suddenly and horrifyingly clear. Alana's hands flew to her own cheeks as the realization hit her. She looked toward the gazebo, and then back at Bailey, who now was looking rather *strangled*. "Kate! Oh, my God! You came here to *seduce* me! Didn't you? On…on orders from *Kate*!"

"It wasn't so much an order as a suggestion." Bailey took her hands in his, which wasn't an easy feat, because she didn't want him to hold her hands, didn't want him to look at her the way he was looking at her. She wanted to be angry. She certainly was embarrassed—horribly so. "And I have to admit that, at least until Max showed up, a fairly good one."

As it was time—past time—to be honest, Alana nodded her agreement. "We were being stupid, weren't we? I mean, I know I was. Allowing Sylvia Wise to put doubts in my mind the way she did. I should have trusted you more…trusted myself more." She looked up into his wonderful face. "I do love you, Bailey. Very much. And I trust you. I'll never doubt you again."

He took her in his arms again, and they kissed, sealing their love, committing to each other wholly and completely, and Alana was once more at home, safe and protected in Bailey's arms, which was, after all, where she wanted to spend the rest of her life. She was willing, more than willing—even eager—to put the past few days behind them and get on with their lives.

And that should have been the end of it. They would marry on Sunday and live happily ever after.

But of course that couldn't be the end of it. Not when dealing with the Redgraves.

Bailey broke the kiss and put his hands on her shoulders, pushing her slightly away from him. "Alana? Has it occurred to you that—the fact that her plan worked out so wonderfully well for the two of us to one side—at this very moment, Kate is sitting in the drawing room, licking cream off her whiskers?"

"What?" she asked in confusion. But then she realized what he meant. She turned her head to look toward the gazebo, and then jerked her head back around to look goggle-eyed at Bailey. "She thinks we're...that we're... and she's—oh!"

"Yes. Oh. I don't know about you, sweetheart, but it seems to me, her aforementioned good intentions notwithstanding, we might not wish to have to spend the rest of our lives with Kate thinking she'd tricked us into seducing each other out here this afternoon."

"Oh, God." Alana nearly groaned the words. "I don't want her to spend so much as the rest of the afternoon thinking she'd tricked us into...you know, what you said. How could we possibly face her at dinner?"

"She'd probably wink at us," Bailey said, beginning to smile.

"She would, wouldn't she," Alana said, feeling her stomach sink to her toes at the thought. "And Max, Bailey. Max knows as well, doesn't he? And if Max knows—"

"Valentine knows. None of them will tell Gideon, they're not fools enough to do that, but the dowager countess will have it out of one of them by tomorrow night. I can see her now, Alana, giving me a hearty slap on the back and saying *Good on you* or some such thing. Or worse. Maybe something more along the lines of *It took you long enough,* or *Needed a push in the right direction, did you*?"

Alana bit her lip as she nodded her agreement. "That last one, I think. The dowager is very…forthright. We can't let this happen, Bailey. But what are we going to do?"

"I think I know. Are you willing to follow where I lead, sweetheart?"

"Anywhere you go, yes." She held out her hand to him, and he took it, raised it to his lips. "But, um, where are we going?"

"To the drawing room. To ruin Kate's afternoon."

Alana thought about that for the space of five seconds; two of them spent remembering that Kate's intentions had all been of the best, and three contemplating the knowing smile on her friend's face if they'd shown up just before dinner, looking flushed and guilty. "Good. I think that's an excellent idea."

Bailey pressed a short, hard kiss on her mouth, and then they were off, holding hands until they reached the terrace.

"I love you," he told her.

"And I love you," she responded, knowing she had never meant the words more.

And then they stepped inside the drawing room to see Lady Katherine sitting there as if waiting for some sort of *report*, for goodness sake. Kate glanced at the mantel clock and then at Bailey and Alana. "Back so soon? I thought you were…that is, is it coming on to rain?"

"No," Bailey answered evenly, "the weather remains fine. Alana and I just wanted to thank you, Kate."

She smiled rather proudly, and waved away his words. "Oh, there's no need to do that. I was just—"

"Because," Bailey went on before she could finish, "thanks to you, and a few uncomfortable moments in the gardens upon which I'm sure you would not wish me to dwell, Alana and I have realized we would not suit. I have granted Miss Wallingford's wish to terminate our engagement."

"Ter-*terminate*?" Kate's eyes went wide as she looked from Bailey to Alana. "You… But that's not what was supposed to— Alana?"

Alana loved the Redgraves. Truly she did. But Bailey by her side or not, she knew she was still the Lilliputian in the land of the giants. Or a loved and cosseted pet to these wonderful, wild, teasing, sometimes reckless and even scandalous Redgraves. They were never mean, no, never, but they were a bit *much* sometimes for a person born with a quieter nature. In the three years she had been Gideon's ward, she had never once managed to give as good as she got, or surprise them in any way.

Until now. With Bailey beside her, she could dare anything. And dare she would!

"It's true, Kate," she said, looking her friend fully in the eye. "I find I'm not…enamored of…of certain aspects of the married life. The, um, more intimate aspects. This is no fault of Bailey's, but something I have worried about for some months. I'm really very much relieved. In fact, I have all but decided to enter a nunnery."

"A…a— *What!*"

"I'm sure you can appreciate that I'd like to be alone

now with...with my prayers. If you could please arrange a dinner tray to be brought up to me later, Kate? Just something simple. I'm fairly certain there are no fine sauces at the convent." Alana turned to curtsy to Bailey. "And thank you again for your kindness and consideration, my lord," she said. "I am so happy!"

"God speed, Miss Wallingford," he said with all seriousness, bowing to her in his turn, and then rather slyly winked at her as he offered his arm. "I'll walk you to the stairs. If I might say a final farewell later, before I ride off to inform my mother?"

"You are too kind."

And so they went their separate ways, Alana to her chambers (locking the door behind her to assure her privacy) and Bailey to the stables so that he might avoid the Redgraves, planning to take his dinner at a nearby tavern...leaving Lady Katherine in the drawing room to mutter under her breath, "But...but...they *thanked* me? Wait until the others find out what a disaster I've made of things. Oh, Lord, I'll never hear the end of this...."

CHAPTER FIVE

THE CLOCKS IN THE LARGE, rambling Redgrave Manor were all in various stages of chiming out the hour of midnight when Bailey eased open the unlocked door to Alana's chambers and slipped inside.

He'd pressed a note into Alana's maid's hand earlier about the door and the time, but it wasn't until the latch had moved so easily beneath his hand that he expelled the breath he may have been holding for hours. She'd sounded so convincing with that business about the convent.

Well, not after tonight!

"Alana?" he whispered, waiting for his eyes to adjust to the near darkness. "Where are you?"

"Over here," she answered just as quietly, and still from some distance away. "In...in bed. Do you mind that I didn't light many candles?"

He turned toward the sound of her voice. "No, no, of course not," he said, and then bit his lip as the toes of his right foot came in sharp contact with a chair leg. He stepped around the chair and, now able to make out the outline of the four-poster bed, headed in that direction. Only more cautiously.

And then he saw her, sitting propped against several pillows, her glorious blond hair undone and falling to her nearly bare shoulders, as she was clad in some sort of sheer, snowy-white confection that completed her quite virginal yet heart-stoppingly welcoming look.

"You're the most beautiful woman in the world, Alana. You humble me."

She dipped her chin slightly. "Thank you. Are…are you coming to bed? That is…I thought we'd… But I realize now that you never *said*…"

"Alana," he told her as her voice trailed off in clear confusion, "I want this more than I have ever wanted anything in my life. I love you more than life itself. But we can wait, if you wish. It's only a few more days."

"Oh," she said, pulling the coverlet a little higher across her breasts.

Bailey smiled. "You didn't let me finish. I said we could wait. That didn't mean I wanted to wait."

She lifted her head and returned both his smile and his candor. "I was hoping you'd say that. Is that bold of me?"

"It's honest of you," Bailey said, reaching for the buttons of his shirt, as he had come to her in his shirtsleeves, seeing no need to waste time shedding himself of his jacket, waistcoat and cravat. "We're to be married, sweetheart, and if the vows of honesty and trust aren't in the marriage ceremony, we'll just have to recite them here, tonight, between the two of us."

His buttons were open now, and he began pulling the tail of his shirt free of his pantaloons.

Even in the dim light from the bedside candles, he could see Alana's eyes growing wide as he finished stripping to his waist, tossing the shirt to the floor. He put his hands to the buttons at the front of his pantaloons and then hesitated.

"Yes, that would seem to be a splendid idea. I'll go first. I, Alana Elizabeth Wallingford, do hereby vow before God and man to be always honest with and trusting of you, Bailey Richard Armstrong." And then she added, "Now I shall be completely honest by saying that, intrigued as I will admit to being, I would greatly appreciate it if you'd please blow out that candle before you remove any more of your clothing."

Bailey's bark of laughter could have betrayed them, were Redgrave Manor not such an enormous old pile. He then quickly did what Alana asked, even as she turned to use the snuffer on the candle on her side of the bed.

Her side of the bed. As opposed to his side of the bed. Their bed. From this day forward. They would never sleep apart, as his own parents did, as most couples who could afford separate chambers did. No, never.

He'd add that to his list of vows when he recited them for Alana.

But not right now.

Right now he was much more interested in ridding himself of the rest of his clothing and sliding beneath the covers and, now that the room was lit only by thin moonlight coming in through one of the high windows, convincing Alana that neither of them needed clothing for what they were about to do.

But he wasn't about to rush her. So thinking, he propped himself against pillows he'd moved closer to hers, and made sure the coverlet concealed him to his waist before turning to press a soft kiss against her temple.

She sighed audibly, and didn't flinch at all when he then slid his arm across her waist.

"I spent the hours since we made our announcement to Kate thinking over everything you'd said to me this afternoon, sweetheart. I don't know how to do anything but ask you outright—do you know what's supposed to go on here tonight? Did your mother, or Kate perhaps, tell you?"

She shook her head. "No, not either of them. But I...I'm not entirely stupid, Bailey. And the dowager took me aside right after you and I were betrothed," she told him. "She was...most explicit."

Bailey barely suppressed a groan.

Alana hurried into speech. "Oh, no, it's all right, Bailey, really. I still had some questions but...well, I thought she'd told me enough to go on with. Besides, according to the dowager, it isn't so bad if you do it wrong, but if you do it right, it's glorious. She meant you, Bailey, not me. Doing, you know...the doing. So...so I'm trusting you to...you know."

"Do it right," he grumbled. "Wonderful."

He almost asked her if she had a decanter of wine in her chambers, but knew she wouldn't, and besides, that would be cowardly. But the *dowager* had explained things to her? If rumor was to be believed, the woman had entertained more than one man in her bed over the years since the late earl died. All in all, just from the little Bailey knew of the lady who preferred to be called Trixie, she could have spent half her life tipped back on her heels. Good Lord, what had she said to Alana? Had she sketched her pictures?

"Come here," he said at last, as Alana had begun twisting the coverlet in her hands. "I have an idea. Let's learn together."

Her eyes went wide. "Together? You mean you don't—"

Bailey cut off her question with his kiss, having also decided that they'd talked enough for a while.

He knew himself to be young, eager and very much in love, which was why he carefully tamped down the *eager* part of the equation that was Bailey in their antic-ipation-of-marriage bed.

He kissed Alana, again and again; softly, deeply, teas-ingly. He kissed her hair, her cheek, her throat, her heart-breakingly sweet mouth. He took his signals from her, advancing when she seemed to melt against him, hold-ing her close when she would stiffen slightly in his arms before beginning again with the patient kisses, the ever more intimate touches that had her relaxing into him once more.

Her nightrail was gone now, not ripped from her in one frustrated tug, as the carnal side of Bailey wished, but kissed down and away from her body, inch by tanta-lizing inch, until Alana actually kicked it the rest of the way off herself.

He worshipped her with his mouth, his hands, trail-ing his lips down over the curve of her breast, capturing her nipple in his mouth even as his fingertips skimmed across her lower belly. He pressed his palm against her just above the sweet nest of curls, and she responded by lifting her hips slightly, her body signaling that what he was doing was good…but the placement of his hand per-haps could be better.

"I know, sweetings, I know," he whispered against her breast, and then continued his journey of discovery, placing kisses against her soft, heated skin, dipping the tip of his tongue into her navel, being encouraged by the way her hands reached down to touch him, but not to stop him.

"So nice…so good…"

"Yes, sweetings, I know," he repeated. "But there's so much more. Just relax, Alana, let me give you more." He cupped his hand over her sex, although her thighs remained firmly closed against him. "Let me in, sweetings. Let me touch you. Let me take you where your body longs to go. Please, Alana. Trust me."

She whimpered, turning her head side to side, her breathing rapid and shallow as he claimed her nipple once more, dragged his tongue across it as it sprang to instant hardness. She was close, so close.

He moved his hand, pressing his fingers against her, stroking at her, hinting of what could be if she'd give over, give in, open to him.

"Oh, God…" he moaned against her as slowly, while her body seemed to relax, she spread her legs for him.

She was silk and fire, and so warm and tight. So maidenly and modest, yet equally eager to feel, to know, to experience.

Once again he went slowly, kissing her, coaxing her, as he dared each new intimacy, until at last he felt encouraged enough to rise up over her, take her mouth once more, and strip away the last barrier keeping them apart.

"I love you, Alana. I love you so much. Forgive me, but the pain will only be a moment," he said, and then plunged home.

She stiffened against him, but then the moment was over and he was deep inside her, holding her close, kissing her and kissing her, again and again, until her bones seemed to turn to liquid and she cried out his name in mingled joy and confusion.

She was his sun and moon, and now, together, they had flown to the stars.

EPILOGUE

"THE DOWAGER TOLD you *that*?"

Alana snuggled more closely into Bailey's arms, still unable to rid her face of the smile it had been wearing this past hour or more. Every time she thought she could say with conviction that she loved Bailey Armstrong with all of her heart, she found herself loving him more. That she had just shocked him by relating something the dowager countess had told her delighted her...and now she was wondering if she would ever dare to take the woman's words and put them into action.

She felt fairly confident she could. And would. Perhaps even tonight. She was fairly certain Bailey, for all he'd sounded faintly stunned just now, wouldn't protest.

"Oh, yes. She explained that and a lot more. But she failed to mention how good this feels. Lying here in your arms. I think I may like this part even more than anything else. Just...just being here. With you. I love you so much."

"And I love you," Bailey said, pressing a kiss against her hair. "Will you do me the great honor of marrying me this Sunday, Miss Wallingford?"

"I would, sir, yes, thank you. I do believe I've quite given up any thought of the convent—oh, Lord!" She pushed her hand against his belly, nearly knocking his breath from him as she sat up, looking into his eyes, her own gone very wide. "Kate!" she exclaimed, and Bailey quickly looked toward the door, clearly thinking the woman had actually just magically appeared. "No, no, not here. But—when are we going to tell her the truth, Bailey? She was only trying to be helpful. Although she really didn't have to look quite so *smug* when we first entered the drawing room, did she? As if we were puppets, with her holding all the strings. Still, poor Kate."

"Yes, having to face her brothers tomorrow morning with the mess she thinks she made rather than the triumph she thought she'd managed."

"Oh, but that's *awful*. Max and Valentine will tease her unmercifully once they know we tricked her. We really must get dressed and go wake her now, and tell her."

"Now?" Bailey asked, rolling her onto her back so that he could begin blazing a trail of kisses down her throat, onto her bare shoulder and lower. "Do we really?"

Alana closed her eyes and tipped back her head, enjoying the sensation his touch provoked. "Yes. Really. Although she did seem to be enjoying herself entirely too much, or at least she was at first, believing her plan had been so brilliant."

"We'd never have heard the end of that brilliance," he reminded her just before he licked her nipple, and then he closed his mouth around her, drawing her in.

"You're right. But still, we have… We really should…"

Bailey slipped his hand between her thighs, his fingers doing delicious things to her.

"Well," Alana breathed, lifting herself to him, "perhaps not just *now*...."

* * * * *

UNLACED

To editor extraordinaire Emily Ohanjanians,
who knows how to dig into the souls of my
characters and has great taste in music.
Nudge, nudge
Thank you for sending Jason Mraz my way.
"If It Kills Me" allowed this story to bloom.

PROLOGUE

London, England
23rd of April, 1819—afternoon
The Kent House

EVERYTHING WHISPERED her name.

When had it not?

Mark Jacob Danford, the fourth earl of Thornton, slowly pulled out one of the two cane chairs at the chess table of the quiet study, as he did every Tuesday afternoon. Drawing in a calming breath, he sat before the game.

Everything was set and waiting, looking no different than it had last week and the week before that and all the weeks and years they'd been doing this. The usual decanter of brandy and two crystal glasses were already lined atop the oak sideboard beside the chess table to accommodate their mutual drink of choice.

Mark leaned forward and nudged all of his black pieces back into their set rows opposite Magdalene's own ivory pieces. He sighed.

In truth, he loathed chess.

From pawn to bishop to rook to knight to king to queen.

But she loved it. And so…he played.

And yet, for him, the game was becoming less and

less about chess and more and more about the way he felt about Magdalene.

Shifting in his chair, he eyed the empty seat opposite his own and shifted again. Jesus. One would think he was a bachelor of twenty, not a widower of forty with three young children to boot.

Reaching out, he grabbed up the crystal decanter, removing the stopper, and poured the amber liquid into each glass. He filled hers and then his to the rim so that it lasted throughout their entire session, then set aside the decanter and placed the stopper back atop.

Let the game of her obliviousness begin. Yet again.

The clicking of heels echoed from down the corridor, drifting toward him through the open double doors of the study.

He leaned back against the chair and hissed out a breath, adjusting his morning coat, which he hoped looked decent. Draping an arm across the side of the chair, he extended a trouser-clad leg, trying to exude casualness. Trying.

Within moments, his beautiful Dowager Countess of Kent, Magdalene Evelyn Ryder, appeared.

He dug his fingers into the wood of the chair to keep his breath and mind steady. "Magdalene."

"Thornton." She grinned, that left cheek dimpling as the edges of her sultry dark eyes crinkled, hinting at her own age of forty. She swept toward him, hips swaying, her alabaster gown flowing ravishingly against the elegant movements of her shapely body. Her curling, chestnut hair, though pinned up in its usual gathered fashion, had an exquisite new addition of white silk flowers, delicately woven through those tresses to match the shade of her morning gown.

She never dressed like that.

By God. It was as if the woman had donned a whole new fashion just for him.

He rose in greeting, unable to do much of anything but stare. "You look…stunning. If I may say. Might I ask what occasion you appear to be celebrating today?"

"The fact that you are here, of course." She paused before him, that incredible scent of powder and chamomile—a scent he'd breathed in longingly for so, so long—teasing his senses. She extended her bare hand to his, still playfully grinning up at him. "You know Tuesdays never come soon enough for me."

He bit back a smile. "Nor me." He reached out and squeezed the warmth of her soft hand in greeting, reveling in that touch.

She squeezed his palm in turn, but quickly drew her hand away.

He fisted his hand, attempting to keep her warmth in it, and lowered it back to his side. He cleared his throat, refocusing. "I have been meaning to ask about Charles."

"Oh?"

"I haven't seen that boy about the club lately. Not even for a meal. Is everything all right?"

Her grin faded at hearing about her grown son. "Ah, you know him." She rounded the chess table and seated herself across from him with a disgruntled sigh. "He prefers to define himself outside of everything known as London society."

"You make that sound so bad." Mark sat, settling in. "Now that he is of age and officially head of the estate, he *should* be defining himself outside the hours of some crusty club. I was simply worried when I hadn't seen him at all."

She leaned over and retrieved the glass of brandy he had poured for her off the sideboard. "Bless you for inquiring." She sipped at the brandy and paused. "In truth, the club agitates him, right along with pretending that he cares to socialize with anyone at all. I can tell he only does it to appease me." With a shake of her head, she brought the glass to her lips and fully tilted it back, swallowing the rest of the brandy he'd filled to the rim with overly large gulps that were anything but refined.

It was something he'd never seen her do. Ever. He blinked. "What was that?"

She smirked, as if amused by the look on his face, and set aside the empty glass on the sideboard with a *chink*. "That was me in dire need of a new life. I have tried and tried to make that boy step outside his way of thinking. Do you know he just invested in a whole new set of sketchbooks and announced he intends on spending all of his mornings and afternoons engraving half the city?" She rolled her eyes and leaned toward Mark and the chessboard. "One of these days, my son is going to draw himself a pretty girl, rip her out of his own sketchbook and marry the parchment. I just know it. I'll have paper dolls for grandchildren."

He let out a gruff laugh. "'Tis better than no grandchildren. Give him time. At one and twenty, he has his whole life ahead of him."

"I suppose." Magdalene huffed out a breath. "Forgive my rants pertaining to Charles. They bore even me."

Sensing that she was saddened by this talk about her son, he knew it was up to him to put a smile on that beautiful face. He shifted toward her. "Do you like tomatoes?"

She paused. "I...yes. Why?"

"So do I. By God, are they not incredible? I dread wondering what our lives would be like without them. Can you imagine how utterly tasteless our soups and sauces and main courses would be? Even the French would agree with me on this. Tomatoes are the crown jewel of the kitchen."

She blinked. "Is there a point to this?"

He lifted a knowing brow. "Yes, of course there is. You are now thinking about tomatoes instead of Charles."

She burst into laughter, rolling her eyes. "Only you can put a smile on my face when I least expect it." Still grinning, she shook her head and reset her pieces before meeting his gaze again. "So. How are the girls? Good?"

He nodded, tracing his gaze from those gorgeous eyes that now shined to those full lips that now smiled and back to those eyes again. "Uh…very good. They send wet kisses and the likes."

She smiled, that cheek dimpling again. "Tell them I will be calling on them this Friday. Charles spent the last two weeks drawing their portraits on my request. They are absolutely stunning. Life-size."

"We ardently look forward to seeing it and you."

"Wonderful. Oh, and I forgot to ask—did they receive the dolls this morning?" She searched his face excitedly. "You know, the ones with the fur hats, braids and ribbons? When I saw them in the shop yesterday afternoon, I knew I had to get them. I hope you don't mind."

He smiled, remembering each and every clap and squeal those open boxes had elicited. "Mind? God, no. Less shopping on my part." Her unannounced gifts were becoming a family event at his house that further edged him into not only falling on a knee but proclaiming his love until he turned into the very sop he swore he'd never be. The only thing keeping him from doing it was his fear of being rejected by a woman who had endured far,

far worse at the hands of her dead spouse than he had at the hands of his.

He caught her gaze. "Elizabeth, Francine and Sarah about ran out into the street and under a carriage out of glee. In my opinion, you really need to cease spoiling them or I will permanently drop them off at your house." He paused and theatrically added, "Not that you would mind."

She laughed and endearingly teased back, "One of these days, Thornton, those girls will realize who their real mother is and we might as well create a scandal and move in together."

He savagely rolled the palm of his hand on the edge of his chair, trying to calm the damn fluttering inside of him with a painful sensation, wishing Magdalene *had* been the woman he'd had children with. He honestly didn't know how much longer he could go on without—

She tapped the side of the board. "Are you ready to lose your queen? *Again?*"

How fitting a remark. He puffed out a breath. Maybe he should just be a man about this, fling her onto the board and checkmate. "I suggest you go first. That will give me time to better strategize." *Whilst I suffer.*

She lifted a brow, lowered her gaze and, using the tips of slim fingers, moved a knight. Heatedly holding his gaze for a long moment, she asked, "Is everything all right, Thornton? You appear a touch distracted. Not to mention unusually somber. Is something weighing on your thoughts?"

He paused, noting the way her voice had seductively dipped in concern and how intently she held his gaze. He lowered his shaven chin, his pulse roaring against his own ears. Maybe *now* was the time, finally, to tell her what he'd been unable to say last time. Or the time before that. Or the time before that.

Without breaking her gaze or caring which damn pawn he used, he moved a piece. "Actually, yes. Something has been weighing on my thoughts. I simply haven't wanted to burden you with it, is all."

She countered his move, intently holding his gaze, in turn. "Burden me with it? Nonsense. You know you can tell me anything. Is it serious?"

He wet his lips and leaned closer toward her and the board. What if she didn't feel the same? He would be destroying everything that he had come to savagely love and depend upon. Including these stupid Tuesday afternoon chess games. "I suppose it depends on its outcome. It could be a very good thing or it could be a very bad thing."

She eyed him. "That sounds rather vague. Even for you. You aren't in some sort of trouble, are you?"

He swiped his face in exasperation. Yes, he most certainly was in some sort of trouble. Because he couldn't do this. Leaning away from the board, he moved another pawn and shrugged. "No. 'Tis nothing really. Investments." *So to speak.*

"Investments?" A bubble of a laugh escaped her. "Oh, how utterly droll for you to worry about something like that. I suggest you hire a better secretary and a better bookkeeper. In fact, have mine. Both are beyond exceptional and are always looking to acquire new accounts."

She surveyed the board and paused. "I never know what to expect from you during a play. 'Tis so odd, really, given we've been doing this for so long. Sometimes, I think you are actually getting worse at this. Not better." She moved a piece, claiming the pawn he'd just moved. Setting it aside, she drew in a large breath and let it out.

Dropping his gaze to those full breasts swelling in response to that lofty breath, he paused. The décolletage of her lace-trimmed gown appeared lower than usual, those lush rounded tops pushing up in a way he'd never had the pleasure of seeing. Tightening his jaw, he snapped his gaze to her face, trying to focus on *her*, not her breasts.

Magdalene's startled dark eyes met his. She searched his face in awkward astonishment, clearly aware that he had just been openly admiring her breasts like fresh cross buns on display at the local bakery.

Shit.

Her features not only stilled, but flushed to an unfamiliar hue, acknowledging something he thought that she, as a woman, never would. That he, Mark Jacob Danford, the fourth earl of Thornton, was *more* than just a friend. That he was, in fact, a…*man*.

They stared at each other wordlessly.

He swallowed hard. She had never looked at him like this before. It was as though she was waiting for something to happen. She was waiting for him to do something. She was waiting for him to kiss her.

Without thinking, he leaned over the chess table, rising slightly from his chair, and closed the remaining space between them, knocking over a few of his pieces with his vest. His pulse thundered as his mouth edged toward hers. He paused, just beyond the heat of those full lips, and brushed them softly with his own.

The room spun and fell over on its side.

Her hands jumped to his face and held him lovingly in place, as if sensing he might fall over. Their lips parted in unison and the heat of their wet tongues connected and moved, the taste of brandy from her mouth overwhelming his senses.

He'd never known anything like it.

His mind blanked realizing she was kissing him. With her tongue. Christ, she was actually submitting to *everything* he had felt these past four years but had not seized for fear of rejection, of distrust, of eliminating all that they were to each other.

At first, their kiss was searingly slow and teasing and rhythmic and delectable. And then, it turned into a pulsing mess of savage need that made his very lips sting from the devastating pressure they both applied. Without breaking their moving mouths, they both scrambled around the chess table in an unspoken effort not to knock it and themselves over.

Still kissing and kissing her, he yanked her fiercely against himself, crushing her softness in place until those breasts pressed against his chest. He bit back an anguished groan as she erotically sucked on his tongue.

Why the hell had he waited four years? Why?

Her hands clambered up to his cravat. To his hazed, dazed astonishment, she unraveled the silk with expert haste as she continued to kiss him. May he never wake. Magdalene was undressing him. *Him.*

Soft, warm hands found his pulsing throat and pushed their way down into his shirt, frilling across his chest. His cock grew so hard, he almost staggered trying to hold on to her.

She suddenly froze. Jerking her lips from his, she wrenched herself out of his grasp.

His arms dropped heavily to his sides in a gloried glow. She loved him. That kiss and touch said it all. His chest heaved in an effort to remain calm as he reopened his eyes. "Magdalene."

She stared up at him, beautifully flushed from lip to cheeks to throat. Glancing toward his exposed throat and half-hanging cravat, her astounded features twisted into what he could only define as anguish. "How could you? Thornton, how could you—" Her hand jumped up, smacking his face so hard his head snapped toward his shoulder.

He blinked rapidly in disbelief, the sting against his shaven cheek overshadowing the reality that she had just hit him.

His gaze lurched to hers.

She stepped back, covering her mouth with a hand.

The look in those haunting, dark eyes and in that face told him everything he needed to know. It was over. Whatever had induced her to step outside their friendship for that one brief moment, to kiss him and downright strip his cravat, was gone. Maybe it had never been there at all.

The sudden denial was an all-too-familiar ache. It felt as though he were married to Anne all over again.

He half nodded, acknowledging the very thing he had feared, reaffixed his clothing and turned away, wrapping his cravat back into place and tying it. Without a word, he left.

CHAPTER ONE

A month later—late evening
The Kent House

A GROUP OF TITLED YOUNG MEN, barely at an age to be
called men, really, lingered within an elbow's reach of
her just beyond the crowds. They paused in between low,
conspiratorial tones, their gazes drifting from the faces
of passing women to their cleavages and back again with
the stealth of spiders planning an ambush. Several of
them inclined their heads toward unsuspecting victims,
wishing to make their presence known.

This, from her own son's peers.

And it didn't even include the rest of male society.

Dowager Countess of Kent, Magdalene Evelyn Ryder,
sidled herself closer toward the main entrance of the ballroom, angling herself out of view. At what age did men
mature? If ever? And at what age did a woman cease
having to deal with men acting as if they owned the right
to lustfully indulge in a woman, be it with his eyes or
hands?

There was more to a woman than a womb and breasts.

Drawing in a breath, Magdalene let it out, trying to
focus on her guests. Countless individuals from every
level of aristocratic society whisked forward and back
across the dance floor, advertising their extravagant coifs
and lavish ensembles. Refined smiles and glances flitted

across those flushed faces as they elegantly turned and paired off one by one for the quadrille, floating effortlessly to the strains of the violin.

Knowing there was only one dance left before the night found its end—thank God—Magdalene restlessly turned her attention back to her son's tall figure. He jutted well above the squat men alongside the far wall where he lingered in solitude near the open doors of the garden.

She paused as he dug into his evening coat pocket and pulled out a small, leather-bound sketchbook. Those refined features remained unflinchingly calm amidst the blur of gaiety as he dabbed the tip of his graphite stick against his tongue, lowered his dark gaze and used the quick stroke of a hand to draw what appeared to be his interpretation of ballroom life. It was very much like Charles to sketch at a time when sketching was simply not an option.

He hadn't danced once. As usual. Nor did he appear to have an interest in *any* of the women in attendance, unlike the rest of his virile little friends. Whatever set of introductions she had provided in the hopes of sparking his curiosity or conversation had been endured with typical edged politeness. She didn't expect him to marry quite yet, and she supposed she should be happy that he didn't ogle young ladies the way his peers did, but she did expect him to acknowledge people and converse. Or at the very least look at them. The rules of society demanded it, and yet he had no interest in following societal rules.

Shaking her head, she considered going over and speaking to him, when an astonishingly well-built gentleman with coal-black hair, garbed in dark, dashing evening attire, casually leaned against the wall beside Charles and began conversing with him.

Charles grinned, slapping his sketchbook shut, and tucked everything back into his pocket as he turned to the man with unprecedented enthusiasm. It was an exceptional interest he only ever showed one man.

Thornton.

Her stomach flipped and then flopped realizing that the man with Charles was, in fact, none other than Thornton himself.

Her new nemesis. Of sorts.

They had actually once been neighbors, and though Thornton had long since moved to a different square, they had remained the best of friends for years. They had a lot in common. They were both parents, widows, had been miserable in their respective marriages, and neither of them were interested in getting involved with the opposite sex ever again. They even cheekily toasted to it twice a year, on the anniversary of each of their spouses' deaths.

Until one afternoon, whilst playing chess and having their brandies, he heatedly scanned her breasts with a searing enthusiasm she'd never seen, leaned across the board and kissed her. At first, she hadn't known what to do. And then, she'd known *exactly* what to do and, much to her dismay, it involved her own tongue.

In a blur she could only blame on brandy, she'd whipped off his cravat and pushed open his shirt beneath his vest. That was when she realized their friendship, which she cherished beyond all else, was at an end and was giving way to meaningless lust. Or rather, harmful lust, which had only maimed her in life thus far. So, despite her attraction to him, she'd panicked and smacked him for introducing the kiss in the first place. She had smacked him a bit harder than she'd intended, and of course, without a word, he'd left.

He'd been avoiding her ever since.

Even though she'd written him countless letters apologizing for her behavior and had invited him to every event she had hosted, hoping to rekindle their friendship, he hadn't responded. Not once. Not even so much as to tell her *When Hell descends*, which she would have preferred over piercing silence. So why had he come tonight? And so late? And so unannounced? To wage a war she wasn't prepared to fight?

God, did she ever need a brandy.

She paused, noting that the crowded ballroom surrounding her had become unusually…*smoky*. She sniffed, wrinkling her nose against the acrid stench. It was as if a chute within one of the chimneys had been left closed. She glanced toward the large double doors beside her and froze.

Her gaze drifted upward, toward a hazy, gray-black smoke that wisped through the upper-top of her white Grecian archway. Her eyes widened. Had the chef gone mad with one too many bushels of charcoal in the stove?

Servants suddenly appeared beyond that same archway, each hoisting enormous wooden buckets. Several guests paused from their lively conversations to watch as the servants bustled past the entryway, one by one, splashing and trailing water across the marble floor of the corridor. The servants disappeared, all heading with said buckets toward the direction of the parlor.

Oh, no. She hurried toward the doorway, her breath hitching.

A bewigged footman in red livery and white silk stockings appeared and darted toward her. He skidded to a halt, keeping her from entering the main corridor.

"My lady." He leaned in and rasped, "Someone set fire to the parlor."

She gasped. "As in, on purpose?"

"Not exactly."

She glanced toward the corridor beyond them where the smoke plumed, her heart pounding. "Dearest God. Should we be evacuating people?"

He intently met her gaze and offered with austere gravity, "It would be best."

"Move everyone out at once."

"Yes, my lady." He disappeared out into the corridor and returned with a gaggle of footmen. They all barreled into the ballroom, darting left and right through the crowds, yelling over the still-playing orchestra. Their reverberating shouts soon penetrated the entire room. *"Fire!"* they boomed, one by one by one. "Move out! Everyone please move out toward the direction of the garden!"

The instruments petered off. There was a momentary lapse of stillness, followed by the rapid scrambling of booted and slippered feet and a most unnecessary echoing slew of *"Fire!"*

Oh, for heaven's sake!

Panicked screams of women, young and old, and the escalating shouts of men trying to guide others filled the ballroom as everyone turned in chaotic unison toward the only entrance left in the room that wasn't emitting smoke: the verandah. Amidst the frenzy of blurred faces and shoving coats and gowns, she momentarily glimpsed Thornton shoving Charles out through the open doors beside them, which led into the garden.

Thank God they were safe.

Though she tried to weave through the crush of bodies toward them, she found herself unable to. Magdalene coughed against the now biting, hazy air as the resistance of the crowd bobbed her more backward than forward. Smoke snaked its way from the ornate main corridor across sections of the high Grecian ceiling, making her lips part in horror. More than a settee was burning.

Gritting her teeth, she tried to wedge past the surrounding wall of bodies, only to stumble. She was going to die. On her own dance floor!

"Magdalene." Thornton jumped toward her, his sharp green eyes capturing hers amidst the clamor. His rugged features tightened as he grabbed her waist, startling her with not only his presence but the strength of his hold. Turning her toward the direction of the terrace, he commenced guiding her forcefully through the throng of people.

She glanced up at him, her heart pounding but blissfully happy knowing he thought her worthy of rescuing. "Thornton."

Someone violently shoved her in a desperate effort to move past, breaking their hold. She gasped and tumbled to the floor, her body instantly swallowed by a mass of swarming, pushing limbs. Booted feet now kicked and stepped and climbed over her without pause, and though she tried to scramble up amidst panicked breaths, too many people kept rushing past and none of them seemed to care if she lived or died.

"Magdalene!" Thornton thrust people aside and jumped toward her through the torrent of bodies. He grabbed her by the arms and yanked her up and off the floor with unprecedented strength. "These people are mad. If the fire doesn't kill us, they will."

He savagely tucked her against his towering frame, the scent of sandalwood faintly wafting through the acrid, smoky air. Those muscled arms tightened around her, mashing her cheek against his chest as he veered them through the crowd with his body.

Magdalene clung to his embroidered waistcoat as he hurried them forward and onto the crowded terrace. People rushed out into the darkened gardens beyond, their shouts echoing all around and lifting up to the cloudless, starry night sky above.

Despite the fray, a sense of strange serenity descended upon her knowing that Thornton was not only back in her life but in her arms. She could now openly admit to herself that, yes, the month without him had been torturous and beyond lonely. She had stared at their unfinished chess game for hours thinking about him and that kiss and how confused she was knowing that she had wanted him naked all along. Such had been the case for quite some time, much to her consternation, but she had taken sweet refuge knowing that he would never overstep the bounds of their cherished friendship by making her face it.

She'd been wrong.

Her throat tightened as she glanced up at him. His shadowed profile remained intently focused on the path before them as he strategically moved them left and right and left again, rounding others. She shouldn't have smacked him. He wasn't a man to be feared, as her late husband had been. Thornton had always been a good friend. One of the few she'd had in life.

A cool gust of night air slapped her heated face, sweeping her back into the reality that her house was on fire. Scrambling against Thornton's strong hold, she wrenched herself loose to look back at the house, stumbling on the edge of the stone steps that led out into the garden. The open doors of the ballroom held an eerie stillness as a thick haze dimmed the brightness of the chandeliers and muted the appearance of the bright honey walls to a yellow-gray.

"Stay here," Thornton said as he dodged past her and jogged back up the stairs, making his way back into the smoke-filled house.

She pivoted toward the direction he'd gone. "Thornton!" Her heart pounded as she watched his large frame disappear back into the wavering haze of the ballroom. She frantically headed after him. *"Thornton!"*

A hand hooked her arm and yanked her back toward the terrace. "Mother." Charles jerked her around, grabbed her hands and squeezed them hard.

She hissed out a breath. "Charles. Are you all right?"

"Yes. Thornton pushed me straight out before I even knew what was happening. I haven't seen him since."

Her stomach roiled as she whipped toward the house, realizing that Thornton still hadn't come back out. Oh, God. Gathering her skirts, she hurried back inside.

"Mother, what— *Where the hell are you going?*" he shouted from outside. "The house is on fire!"

"I know! Believe me, *I know*! Stay there!" she shouted back and dashed on.

CHAPTER TWO

THICK SMOKE STUNG MAGDALENE'S watering eyes as she bounded toward the direction of the fire. Coughing spastically against the sooty air that crawled into her throat, she pushed onward, chanting to herself to grab Thornton and get out.

Male shouts drifted from beyond. She hurried toward them and skidded to an abrupt halt upon reaching the foyer that led toward the parlor. A cool, welcoming breeze gushed past through the entrance doors which had been pushed wide open, revealing the moonlit, starry night beyond.

"*Faster!* Move those buckets faster!" Thornton's harsh command echoed all around her.

To her astonishment, Thornton and all of her servants, footmen, coachmen, stable hands, the steward and the butler alike, stood in a single, regulated line that impressively extended from the kitchen all the way to the hazy parlor.

Bucket after bucket of water was passed from hand to hand down the length of the corridor toward Thornton whose muscled frame stood waiting within the entrance of the parlor. Having tossed his evening coat to the marble floor, he now wore only an embroidered vest and white linen shirt that grew increasingly transparent as water splashed out of the bucket and repeatedly soaked his sleeves. That shirt indecently clung to muscled arms as he savagely tossed more water out onto a smoking carpet before handing back the empty bucket and grabbing a new one.

She edged back against the wall, watching Thornton in a half daze. There were so many times she had secretly wished her son would become just like him. Strong, valiant and reliable.

She worried for the thousandth time that she hadn't done enough for Charles during his upbringing, and that she was the reason why he hadn't become the man she now wished he could be. Of course…at one and twenty, he was still young. There was still time for him to grow, though, in truth, she feared he would never be more than he already was: flippant toward society and his duties as earl. He was a wonderful son to her, caring and kind, but it was as if he didn't care if his name or the estate crumbled. If it didn't involve his sketching or her, he simply didn't care.

Handing off the last wooden bucket, Thornton hissed out a breath, swiping cascading strands of black hair out of his eyes. "Enough." He stepped back, scanning the parlor.

She scrambled forward. "'Tis contained?"

The butler turned and called out, "That it is, my lady."

"For now," Thornton added, not bothering to turn. "Your settee, the Persian rug and some of the chairs weren't quite as fortunate."

She stared awkwardly at that broad back. "I am indebted to you, Thornton. Thank you."

He glanced at her from over his shoulder, those green eyes meeting her gaze for a long, searing moment. "What happened?"

Heat splashed her entire body, realizing they were

facing each other in sudden stillness for the first time since… "I don't know."

"Mother?" Charles skidded to a halt beside her. He shook her, his face ablaze with emotion. "What the hell were you thinking running back into a flame-ridden house?"

She assuredly squeezed his arms. "Cease yelling. I'm fine. Everything is fine."

Releasing her with a breath, Charles glanced toward the obscure parlor and staggered. "Jesus bloody Christ." He scrubbed his hair, mussing his dark tonic hair. "What…how did the fire even start?"

Mr. Beagle, the footman, rounded them, gesturing in exasperation toward the parlor. "The butler caught a young woman rifling through the writing desk. She attempted to flee and knocked over one of the lamps. We've detained her up in the garret. She had the audacity to insist that Lord Kent himself had stolen something and that she was merely looking to retrieve it."

Magdalene jerked toward Charles. "What?"

He gaped. "Mother, I didn't—" He eyed her, edging back. "I just… I—" He winced and averted his dark gaze, falling into a silence he usually retreated to when overwhelmed.

She lowered her chin, sensing something wasn't quite right. Moving toward him, she touched his arm and asked in a tone she hoped would assure him that she wasn't angry. Yet. "Charles? What are you not telling me?"

He pushed her arm away. "I would rather we not…" He swiped his face. "You would never understand."

She? Not understand?

All but a breath ago she had considered her relationship with him to be unbreakable. He was the only child out of four to have survived birth and had been her greatest comfort through the black woes of a twelve-year marriage to his father. Charles had been the only reason she had survived.

Despite fleeing with him into the night on many occasions, only to be dragged back by her husband again and again and again, that little hand would lovingly touch her bruised face and whisper with childlike staid assurance, "Mama, maybe tomorrow he won't be angry." That promise had miraculously come true when Adam had been found dead in the water closet one morning, his trousers still slung around his booted feet. His heart had stopped in the middle of his business.

It was a morbid victory and a well-deserved ending.

Despite desperately trying to erase everything that her poor Charles had endured during the first twelve years of his life by introducing to him every known happiness a child deserved, and consistently showing him love and support, this was what it had all amounted to. Him thinking she wouldn't understand.

Magdalene pushed out a breath, trying to fight the tears burning her eyes. "Charles. Whatever this is, surely you know that you can always—"

"No. Not this." He shook his head and kept shaking it, his gaze withdrawn. He eyed the small crowd surrounding them and stalked back toward the ballroom, disappearing from sight.

The servants lingered, right along with Thornton.

All of them no doubt thought the worst of Charles.

She couldn't bear it. London whispered enough about him.

Setting her chin, she coolly announced to the servants, "Ensure that no one is hurt and that the carriages commence lining up for all the guests. Have them use the side entrance, as opposed to this one. We will address the parlor later. Now go."

The servants bobbed in respect of the command, grabbed up all the buckets and disbanded one by one.

She turned to the butler just as he was veering away. Knowing she had no choice but to face what Charles clearly didn't want to, she demanded, "Where is this woman in question? Is she still up in the garret?"

The butler's tufts of gray brows flickered. "That she is, my lady." Digging into his soot-covered vest pocket, he produced a brass key and held it up. "Shall I—"

"No." Magdalene took the garret key. "I will do it. Go."

The butler inclined his head and departed.

She paused, realizing she stood alone with Thornton in the lingering fog of smoke. How fitting that they stand in diminishing embers.

His flat, stoic expression prolonged the moment. He eventually shifted his shaven jaw and provided, "You raised him well. Whatever this is, he isn't to blame. You do know that, yes?"

A part of Magdalene's soul melted and dripped into a pool at his feet. It was very much like Thornton to be a friend when she needed it most. It was the very thing she didn't want to lose and why she had panicked that afternoon in the study. Because she didn't want to lose the only man she had ever come to adore to the stupid passion that only ever ruined everything between a man and a woman. "Thank you, Thornton. I really needed to hear that."

He half nodded. "I suggest you let me talk to him."

She nodded, knowing Charles would, in fact, prefer it. She had an annoying tendency to coddle Charles and treat him like the child he no longer was. She couldn't help it. Guilt over his wretched upbringing always brought out the worst in her. "If you could. A bit of man-to-man."

"Of course. I'll give him some time to himself first before I wander over. No man likes being cornered or chased." He strode over to his evening coat and swiped it up. Draping it over his broad shoulders, he slid his arms into it and readjusted the coat back over his frame, covering his vest and linen shirt. He smoothed the lapels and eyed her.

It was as if he were reliving the way she had undressed him and then smacked him. She swallowed in awkwardness.

Shoving his hands into his coat pockets, he departed with long, steady strides, momentarily stepping out through the open doors of the main entrance and into the night. He lingered, still making his presence known to her, that strong frame blurring within the shadows.

She sighed, sensing that he wanted to talk before wandering over to Charles but was too proud to be the first to do it. She slowly made her toward him. "'Tis good to see you."

"And you." His wry tone indicated otherwise.

"It's been a hard month for me," she confided.

"Has it?"

"Yes." Not seeing Francine, Elizabeth and Sarah had been as equally unbearable as not seeing him. Whenever his girls gathered about her on her visits, one by one, all chipper and cheeky with radiant green eyes that matched his, she often forgot they weren't even hers. They represented each and every child she had lost and the family she wished she'd always had.

Drawing in a shaky breath, she added, "I missed you."

"I bet you have. I still have the mark to prove it."

She cringed. "I'm sorry."

"If you were sorry you wouldn't have done it."

He was making this so difficult. "Why did you come tonight, Thornton? To push this pitchfork into my side? I feel guilt-ridden enough as it is. As I have written in each and every letter I sent, you didn't deserve it. Nor should I have perpetuated the situation. 'Tis my hope we can move past this. 'Tis my hope we can return to what we had."

He said nothing.

"Thornton?"

He still said nothing.

"Thornton, say something."

He still said nothing, merely lingered in the darkness.

She nodded. "This is but one of the many reasons as to why I panicked. I knew it would change everything between us. And it has."

He huffed out a breath. "Do you know what I realized tonight? Shortly after I arrived and before the fire disbanded everyone?"

She hesitated, dreading what he was about to say. "What?"

"Men like you. Young, old, they are drawn to your presence and everything you are. The trouble is, you don't like men. Every look and every glance they give you, you ignore like a nun on a Sunday. Perhaps you are not even aware of it, but I have a problem with it all the same, especially given that I myself am a man."

Oh, now, that was white-knuckle-fisted male pride talking. Not common sense. "I don't think I need to stand here and justify what my view on men is. 'Tis no different than your view of women. 'Tis why you and I have always got along so well. We never saw each other as a threat. And now you seek to change that? Why? I thought we were friends. *Real* friends capable of seeing past meaningless physicality."

Silence pulsed between them.

"Magdalene?" he suddenly said in a strained, husky tone.

She swallowed. "Yes?"

He turned and strode out of the darkness toward her, pausing at a distance she knew was best kept between them. Without meeting her gaze, he said in a troubled voice, "Fool that I am, after receiving all of your rambling letters of apologies that gave me hope, I came tonight, not to rekindle our friendship, but to ask you to marry me. That is all I want out of this, and that is all I am willing to settle for."

Her eyes widened. She gripped shaky hands together, the brass key to the garret biting into her palms. Her hands quaked beyond anything she'd ever experienced, knowing that she had already lost him. She had lost her closest friend to all the things they had both sworn to stay away from. "Please don't do this to me. You and I both swore we would never go down this path. With *anyone.* We took the…the *oath* of 'I've already been married and I'm not doing that again.' Remember? You also still have three children to raise. Those girls need you. *I* don't."

His face went grim. "My understanding in this is that by giving myself more, I give my daughters more. They need a good mother and I need a good wife. Pardon me for assuming you were ever capable of being both."

Her heart squeezed. He said it as if he meant it…as if he truly loved her and was looking for more than a mother to his children and more than a companion for his bed.

He stepped toward her and leaned in, inching his face

close enough that the seductive heat of his breath frilled hers. "What are you afraid of? Is it the intimacy? Or is it me?"

Her legs quaked. Everything did. "I don't want to lose what we have to something as stupid as lust and passion that will only last in between breaths."

"Nothing is going to change between us."

"But it already has! You aren't even looking at me the same."

His gaze softened as he searched her face. "Magdalene." Lifting his hand, he grazed the back of his finger against her cheek, his warmth penetrating her skin. "I have looked at you the same way for years. You have just never noticed it."

She held that soft gaze and swallowed in effort to ease the anxious fluttering overtaking her body and soul. It reminded her of the way he had looked at her before he leaned in across that chess table and kissed her. It was a tenderness she had never seen in Adam's face when he'd grabbed for her, stripped her and rode her until she climaxed in an effort to make her forget that he had just beat her. Lust, pleasure and pain in combination were Adam's forte, and needless to say, she'd been avoiding all three ever since.

Thornton's eyes trailed down to her lips and lingered. "Say something." His finger softly slid its way down from her cheek to her exposed throat.

She fought against swaying from that touch. "Passion is a very dangerous game, Thornton. If we lose playing it, we lose everything, including each other, and I'm not willing to risk it. Lines blur fast. Adam taught me that much. His *passion* became my prison. He didn't know whether to bed me or fist me."

His features grew taut and derisive. "Don't abase me,

Magdalene, by comparing me to that prick. Allow me to resolve this. After tonight, we never see each other again. 'Tis best. Not only for you but me."

Magdalene edged toward him, eyes widening. "You don't actually mean that."

"I do."

She pressed a hand against her cheek in angst. "Why are you doing this to me? To us? Are we not worth more than a fleeting need to pursue intimacy that will never be as rewarding as the friendship we share?"

"Fleeting?" His expression stilled. "Given that you wish to categorize me with a dead man, I am asking that you not complicate my life by calling on me or my girls anymore, making us feel as if we are a family, when in fact, we are anything but. I also ask that you don't send them any more of those damnable weekly trinkets that they've come to depend upon, waiting by the door like dogs. It isn't fair to them and it isn't fair to me."

A part of her soul shattered knowing that he meant it. This was him never looking back. She could see it in that face and in those eyes.

She stepped toward him. "Thornton—"

"No." He shook his head, avoiding her gaze. "You and I have been doing this for five years, and I'm not doing it for another day knowing that I have been madly in love with you for at least *four* of those goddamn years. I had actually thought that the worst of this was you not noticing. But now I'm realizing that the worst part is that even now that you *do* know, you just don't bloody care." He rounded her, popping up both of his hands in disgust. "I am done. *We* are done, and I have nothing more to say. I am going to talk to Charles. He needs me. Whilst you, apparently, don't." He stalked down the corridor and into the ballroom.

Magdalene staggered, unable to breathe. Thornton loved her? Dear God, he…loved her? So all of this was, in fact, *more* than base attraction?

Upon her soul. Love was something she had never thought possible between them. Thornton had always merrily scoffed at everything pertaining to love and romance, which he believed only blinded one from seeing the death arrows pointed at one's head and heart. He scoffed at flower arrangements. He scoffed at poetry. He scoffed at flirtations. He scoffed at picnics in the park and boat rides on the lake. He even scoffed at the waltz because it involved too much touching.

Clearly, his days of scoffing were over.

What a mess. She glanced down at the key in her trembling hand. It was going to be a *very* long night, and she only hoped poor Charles was in a better place than she was.

CHAPTER THREE

GATHERING HER EMBROIDERED satin gown from around her slippered feet, Magdalene hurried up the large staircase. Drifting past her own private suites, she made her way farther up toward the servants' quarters at the very top level of the house, toward the garret. She eventually paused before a closed, paneled door.

Lanterns on wrought-iron hooks lit the quiet space.

She fingered the brass key, wondering if it was wise to open the door. Perhaps she should speak to the woman first and open the door last. She knocked. "Miss?"

"Do what you will," a woman choked out from beyond. "Call the authorities. I earned it."

Magdalene pressed a hand against the closed door. The woman sounded as if she'd been crying.

Magdalene hesitated then offered, "What is your name?"

"I hardly think it matters."

"It matters to me."

There was a shifting of weight behind the door. "And who are you?"

"Dowager Lady Kent. This here is my home." She paused and added, "Whatever is left of it, that is."

There was a groan and a penetrating moment of silence followed by a surprisingly gracious, "I'm so sorry about the parlor. My name is Miss Emma Vance. Daughter of Mr. Vance, the chemist. Though mind you, he's been dead for a year."

"Miss Vance, forgive me for not understanding the situation, and why you felt the need to trespass and rifle through my belongings, but—"

"All you need understand," the woman interrupted, "is that your son, Lady Kent, is a scoundrel of the worst sort, and I not only want him out of my life, but I want those sketches he did of me back."

Sketches? Magdalene drew in an astonished breath. "What are you referring to? What did he do?"

There was a momentary pause. "Do you know a man by the name of Mr. Royce?"

Magdalene paused. Shaking her head slowly from side to side, she supplied, "No. That I do not."

A loud thud reverberated from within the garret. "Of course you don't. 'Tis an alias of his. Calls himself Mr. Royce about town and is known to be quite the artist. Is very celebrated for his honest and realistic depiction of people. I met him in passing whilst he was sitting over at the docks, sketching. He wanted to draw me and even paid me for it. Only…I haven't been able to get rid of him since."

A diffident boy seeking anonymity while depicting the world for what it was. How utterly Charles. Despite him being a misfit who always ran about town instead of tending to estate matters, he was an honest, respectable boy. While his fellow peers debauched women in the name of England and a good time, he couldn't even bring himself to talk to them. For a while, she'd actually wondered if he preferred men. Though clearly, he didn't.

"Might I…open the door, Miss Vance? Can I trust you to—"

"I won't slit your throat, if that is what concerns you."

"Good. I am pleased to know that you and I have an understanding." Magdalene pushed the key into the lock, turning it. She pulled the door open, bracing herself for what lay beyond.

The lanterns within the corridor filtered into the darkness, displaying uneven wooden planks, overturned buckets, brooms and the figure of a woman who remained hidden in the shadows. The figure drifted into the wavering light of the corridor.

Magdalene's lips parted.

A pale but strikingly beautiful and youthful face appeared. She couldn't have been older than nineteen. Thick tendrils of curling blond hair cascaded out from a lopsided chignon as the saddest, bluest eyes she'd ever seen met hers. Though her azure cotton gown was simple in its fabric and stitching, whispering of a merchant class, there was an unspoken sophisticated elegance to this girl. It was the way she held her chin despite having emerged from a dark space. Those hands flattened her loose gown against her sides. "Though I have yet to show, I am with child. Given that you are his mother, I thought you should know."

Magdalene staggered and placed a shaky hand to her lips, to keep herself from gasping. She could feel the pulsing within her own hand and lips and throat as she continued to stand there, unable to believe that Charles would do this. "Are you certain we are referring to the same man, Miss Vance?"

The woman lowered her chin and pursed her lips. "Tall? Astonishingly tall, actually. Dark hair? Brown eyes? Has a dimple on his left cheek when he smiles? Has a fancy for Latin words? Carries a leather-bound sketchbook that he makes use of at the oddest of times? Is that not him?"

Oh, but it was. "It is indeed him." She swallowed in disbelief. "Have you informed him of your…condition, Miss Vance?"

"Yes. When he visited me last. Four days ago. He hastily gave me all the money from his pockets and left."

Charles was going to be a father.

And the mother was the daughter of a chemist.

Heaven help her and the world itself, the boy had unknowingly followed the path of his father by impregnating a lower class woman. "Miss Vance. I apologize for not being more responsive. I am a bit overwhelmed at the moment."

A gargled laugh escaped her lips. "You are overwhelmed?" Her voice now wavered, despite that chin still jutting out. "This tale has yet to end. Whilst I was going about my business, not even two days after I announced all of this to him, I was astounded to see Mr. Royce himself stepping out of a crest-emblazoned carriage on Regent Street. And he wasn't wearing his usual wool and cap. He was wearing clothes meant to blow the whistle off a woman. So I paid a hackney to follow him about town. Imagine my surprise when I find he's an aristo living all fancy here on Park Lane!"

With a flare of her nostrils, Miss Vance seethed on. "He'd been making a fool of me. *All along.* And the worst of it? He has dozens of nude sketches of me. Sketches I know could ruin what is left of me. Which isn't much. So I snuck in to try to find them and burn them, going from room to room, and that's when it all went to the pot. The butler caught me, and in an effort to get out, I knocked over one of the large lamps in the parlor. It shattered, sprayed oil and with the flame already burning in the lamp, it…" She winced. "I'm ever so sorry."

Magdalene knew this was her fault. She swallowed

back the need to vomit. Few had the patience to love Charles for what he was. Everyone saw his constant sketching, during Parliament proceedings, church and the dinner table alike, as a sign of flip oddity, superiority and disrespect. What no one knew was that those sketches in his bound book were a part of his soul and an internal expression of private images he shared with no one. Not even her.

It was a world she had unknowingly introduced him to. Whenever she had locked them both away for long periods of time to avoid his father, she would thrust pieces of parchment into his small hands and insist that he draw the world, not for what it was, but what he wanted it to be and that, one day, it would be.

He'd been doing it ever since.

Only he wouldn't be able to sketch his way out of this one. Though she had tried and tried to immerse Charles in countless social settings after the death of her husband to assist him in overcoming his distrust of the world, in the end, she hadn't done enough. He had turned that distrust toward his own understanding of women. And her.

She could either be a good mother and do right by what her son clearly wanted for himself but was too afraid to step forth and grab, or she could turn away from everything her son was in the name of superficial societal mores, rules and rank. Those superficial societal mores, rules and rank hadn't saved her from beatings. In fact, they had added to her agony. Which was why she was going to save her son from this beating. Because he deserved more. Because he *was* more.

She had always wanted him to step outside the solitary world of his sketching. It was a knee-bending blessing to know that he finally had. "Miss Vance."

The young woman folded her hands and set her chin

in a distinguished manner as if fully accepting of whatever punishment Magdalene had in mind. A loose tendril of blond hair fell across that cheek. She tossed her head to the side, sending the hair away, and locked her gaze with Magdalene's.

Magdalene let out a calming breath, submitting gallantly to what she was about to do. "Given that Lord Kent is my son, I ask that you answer all of my questions in earnest so we might resolve this without having to involve the authorities."

Her tone softened. "I will do my best."

"Good. How old are you?"

"Twenty, my lady."

"Twenty. Certainly old enough to know that trespassing and setting fire to the estate of an aristocratic peer of the realm is equivalent of suicide. Whatever the reason."

She said nothing.

"Are you known for trouble?" Magdalene pressed.

"I've never set fire to a house before, if that's what you're insinuating."

Magdalene bit back a smile. She liked this girl. She had a quick mind, which Charles needed. "Have you ever been arrested?"

"No," she replied in agitation, now holding her gaze. "Prior to meeting Lord Kent, I considered myself to be a respectable citizen. I paid my taxes, even when I couldn't afford to, and showed respect to my king by following the laws of the land." She smoothed her gown against her hips again. "Sadly, my lady, the laws of the heart are a bit more involved. Though I have nothing to my name, I don't deserve to be disrespected. Not by anyone and most certainly not by a man who had actually claimed to love me."

Well, at least the girl appeared to have her bricks in

a row despite a momentary lapse of judgment. For, yes, the heart had a tendency to lead even the best astray.

Magdalene should know.

It had been her greatest downfall as a woman knowing she had ever loved a man like Adam at all, because he had never loved her. He had only ever truly lusted for her. "My son is a good man, Miss Vance. Know that."

Miss Vance tartly observed her. "Oh, yes. When he isn't collecting nude sketches and pretending to be something that he isn't."

Magdalene inwardly winced. "What do you know about him? Separate from this mess?"

She glanced away. "I don't know where his deception began or where it ended. So I can't say."

"I see." The girl deserved as much of the truth as possible. "Not to give him any excuses, but he had a most tragic upbringing, having had to watch his own mother beaten at the hands of his father. Sad though it is, he has always felt trapped between wanting to know happiness yet fearing it doesn't exist. Sketching is a big part of his life. It is who he is and who he has always been. If you think he is the sort of man who lures unsuspecting women for his own gain, Miss Vance, in that you are wrong. He doesn't really associate with women. If at all. In fact, and pardon my being so forward, you may be the first...*nude* he has ever drawn."

Miss Vance glanced toward her, her lips parting. "What?"

"'Tis true. I should probably also add, and by no means do I wish to disrespect you by saying this, but men of his status don't associate with women like you. I imagine that had a lot to do with his deception. It would seem he feared disappointing me and the rest of our society, although I never would have believed that of him before now. I imagine he also feared disappointing you once the deception had been cast."

Miss Vance blinked rapidly. "Had he told me the truth, I wouldn't have rejected him. 'Tis I who is well below his station," she uttered in the most heartbreaking way. "I love him. Despite everything, I still do."

Magdalene's chest tightened. Love. Sweet love. Did it, in fact, still exist? That anguished, pretty young face whispered that it not only did but that nothing had changed since she herself was a woman of twenty. The only good in this was that Charles was a dear, dear angel worthy of being loved by someone other than his mother. It was obvious this girl still yearned for him. And Charles's apparent fears of marrying below his station should not stand in their way. "Is there anything you wanted to know, Miss Vance? Anything that might change your view on this and him? For I wish to assure you that he, of all men, is deserving of your love."

Miss Vance pinched the fabric of her gown above her knee, and after a moment of silence asked, "Is he as endearing as he had made me believe?"

Magdalene smiled at all the memories that suddenly flooded her of her dear Charles over the years. "Endearing doesn't even begin to define him. If you ever wanted a star, he will not only draw it for you, but he will ensure that the ceiling is removed so you might never be wanting of a star again."

A muffled laugh escaped the young woman as she continued pinching and playing with the fabric of her gown, watching her own fingers. "I suppose a part of me wants to believe that our moments spent together were real, is all."

Magdalene leaned in, searching that pretty face, and tapped her cheek. "Then I would venture to say, yes.

Yes, they were real. No one knows him more than I. He is ever loving, he is ever protective and above all, he is ever genuine."

Much like...Thornton.

Magdalene swallowed and lowered her hand, knowing she had openly rejected him with a smack similar to the ones she had received throughout the years. It was unforgivable. Especially when all she had ever wanted to do, if she were honest with herself, was love him for everything he was in the best way she could. But the old way wasn't best anymore, was it? He and she were well beyond that best.

Miss Vance glanced toward Magdalene, tears welling within those large eyes. "What am I to do? Given that I am with child?"

This was a wedding waiting to happen.

Everyone in her circle was going to hang the last of her, that much she knew. But after the supposedly respectable marriage she had endured, they could all hang themselves. At worst, there was always Germany or France. "I ask that you wait downstairs in the servants' quarters, Miss Vance," she eventually offered, gesturing toward the corridor behind them. "I would like to speak to my son. Rest assured, you and he will be settling this on your own. It will be whatever you both decide, though I genuinely hope your love for him and his love for you will prevail. Especially with there being a child. My grandchild."

Miss Vance blinked.

"Now go," Magdalene prodded, hoping the girl didn't start blubbing on her, lest she make her blub knowing she was going to be a forty-year-old *grandmother.*

"Thank you, my lady. Thank you for being so... Thank you." Miss Vance nodded in what appeared to be a half daze and hurried past, disappearing around the corner, her skirts dancing about her slippered feet. Those quick, eager feet thudded down, down the corridor until they faded, leaving Magdalene to realize that everyone's path to a happily-ever-after wasn't always the same. Nor could it ever be personified or defined by the realm of the ton.

I hank God.

There was something profoundly touching about that moment. It made her realize that facing life for what it was and opening one's self to one's true heart as opposed to one's fear gave way to unexpected and beautiful things. It was a lesson she had needed to relearn.

It would seem her own stupid, stubborn fears had been as equally unfounded as her son's, given Thornton's unexpected admission of love for her. It hadn't been mere lust or a fancy that had compelled him to kiss her. It had been love. It was a love she had yet to fully grasp and kiss and cradle. Because Thornton, her dear beloved Thornton, deserved more of a chance than she'd been willing to give him. The man had already won her heart long ago. He just didn't know she'd been squirreling it away, burying it should everything go to hell, as she was accustomed to. In truth…she now knew there were worse things than hell.

Such as living without Thornton for the rest of her life.

CHAPTER FOUR

BLOWING OUT A RAGGED breath in an effort to remain focused, Mark strode out onto the eerie, lonely stillness of the verandah, long emptied of the crowds that had earlier swarmed in frenzy. Moonlight blanketed the sweeping stone stairwell leading out into the shadows of the provincial garden.

He paused. There, sitting on the stairs, was none other than Charles himself, his dark head resting on a forlorn hand. His leather-bound sketchbook had been tossed beside him, pages and pages ripped out, scenes of drawn London life rebelliously strewn everywhere.

And Mark thought he had problems.

He strode over and sat beside Charles. Setting his forearm on his knee, he eventually offered, "Know that I'm not going anywhere."

Charles glanced toward him, those soulful dark eyes hauntingly reminding him of Magdalene. He looked away. Shifting against the stair they sat on, he fingered a graphite stick. "Ever since I could remember," Charles confided, "I only ever wanted to sketch the goddamn moon and make it my own. Even knowing it could never fit on any page, let alone in my mind or my life. And now, because of it, *this* is my life. *This.* A mess beyond anything I can fix."

Oh, to be young again and full of that much spirit to even bother with the moon. Sadly, Mark hadn't made use of his youth all that well, either. He should have rebelled against his status more, and married a woman of his own choice, as opposed to a titled beauty who made his inherited estate look good. He had spent seven miserable years married to a duke's daughter who, as it turned out, had fallen in love with another man of a lesser station, but whose parents had denied the union to insist upon *him.* And devil take them all, he hadn't known about it until *after* the wedding.

Though he never doubted Anne's loyalty, he sensed that secretly, she hated him and blamed him for the happiness her parents had denied her. Despite repeated attempts to connect with her, she always put him at a distance. Their conversations were one-sided, and the sex was at times awkward. She kept her eyes closed, more often than not, as if envisioning someone else. He simply couldn't compete with a love she had already given to another and eventually…he just stopped trying. The only good to have come of the union were his three girls. He'd been monstrously bitter about Anne and women and his lot until…Magdalene. Damn her.

Both he and Charles sat in grudging silence.

Mark knew better than to say anything or push the boy into saying more. Charles didn't like being rushed into talking. In that way, they were alike.

Charles puffed out a breath. "Are women really as complicated as they seem?"

Mark muttered, "Yes. They like to think we are the only ones complicating everything, but in truth, it is an infinite circle of mutual offenses. Sadly, no one ever wins until both sides admit defeat. Which is rare."

Charles rubbed his chin with the back of his hand. "This is where I will admit that I did something rather… *fatuus.*"

Charles and his Latin. "English, please."

"Stupid," he obliged. "I did something stupid."

"Welcome to my world." He eyed the boy. "What did you do?"

Charles lowered his dark gaze and winced, that one-and-twenty-year-old face taking on the guise of a thousand-year-old sinner. He eventually leaned in. "I fell in love with a woman I shouldn't have. A woman so far below my station, I can't even see the bottom." He half nodded. "And that isn't the worst part." He was quiet for a moment. "I got her pregnant."

Mark sighed. There wouldn't be any paper grandchildren for Magdalene. She was getting the real thing whether she wanted it or not. "Ah. So this woman who ventured into the parlor and accidentally—"

"Yes. I don't know any other women. I never *wanted* to know any other women prior to her."

"Ah." It was about all he could say in that moment.

Charles scrubbed his hair and groaned. "God, am I ever an ass. An ass who... I just...I don't know what to do. I want to marry her and do what is right by the way I feel, but in doing so I would be ostracizing my mother and everything she wants for me. I already disappoint her at every turn."

"No, you don't."

"I do. As an artist, I see it all. I see things for what they are. Sadly, sometimes seeing is a curse. Because you wait for things to happen that never do. Like you and my mother. You should have been married to one another by now."

Mark froze. "She and I aren't—"

Charles snorted. "Aren't what? 'Tis obvious you are both madly in love with each other, yet neither of you is willing to step beyond your gilded little frames to admit to it. You both prefer watching as opposed to doing."

Mark swallowed. "It would seem the artist has painted us well." He set a hand on Charles's back. "You need to talk to your mother about all of this. Not to me. I mean…you can always talk to me…what I meant to say is that I want you to tell your mother everything you just told me about yourself and this girl."

Charles shook his head and kept shaking it. "She and every last person in London with half a name will shred me and Emma apart."

"Hey, hey." He elbowed him hard to let him know he was serious. "All of London I will agree with, Charles, yes, but not this nonsense about your mother. She loves you. Trust in that. She will always put you before all else. That is what a good mother does."

His shadowed features remained somber. "Do you honestly think she would even support my pursuit of matrimony to a girl well below my station? Given *her* experience in matrimony and all that she has endured?"

Mark shifted his jaw. "I suppose you have a mild point. She can't even swallow the word without spitting."

The rustling of a gown behind them made him pause. "It would seem neither of you know me as well as you should," Magdalene's voice penetrated the silence. "And it saddens me."

Both he and Charles scrambled up in astonishment toward her lingering frame in the shifting shadows of the terrace. Dread soaked every last inch of his body as those dark eyes met his. As if she didn't hate him enough.

She trailed a calculating gaze to Charles.

Charles set his shoulders. "Mother." Striding toward her with what appeared to be newfound confidence, he announced in a strained tone, "There is something I must tell you."

"I already know. I spoke to Miss Vance."

Charles froze and met her gaze.

She lifted a chiding brow. "Collecting nude sketches appears to be a relatively new interest for you, I would say."

Mark blinked. *Nude* sketches? Oh, now, bravo, Charles. *That* was real art.

Magdalene sighed with the shake of her head. "You should have told me about her. You should have told me about this entire situation well before it escalated to this."

Charles hissed out a long breath. He squeezed his eyes shut, tapping his fingers rigidly against his forehead. "I knew nothing could ever come of it given who she was and given who I was, but I was so damn…*desperate* to step outside of everything relating to the ton that I—" He reopened his eyes and dropped his hand to his side. He stoically stood there, looking anguished and lost and without hope.

If it had been anyone else in the ton that boy was pleading to, his cause would have been lost with the lop of a guillotine. But Magdalene, sweet Magdalene—damn her—grabbed her son's chin gently and rattled it. "This is but the beginning of your journey known as life." She released him. "Do right by this girl and the child she carries. Marry her. I thought her to be utterly deserving and charming."

Mark drew in a slow, astounded breath. She never ceased to amaze him. He knew she would have never turned against her own boy, but actually seeing it was as profound a moment as any.

Charles gaped. *"I can marry her?"*

She heaved out a sigh. "Not that you need it, Charles, but I give you full permission to be happy. That is all I ever wanted for you since you were placed in my arms. And if marrying this girl will make you happy, then marry her you must."

As if Mark didn't love the woman enough, she had to go do *that*.

Charles grabbed her and pressed her savagely against himself. "I'm so sorry. I'm so sorry for all of this."

"Now, now," she murmured against his shoulder, nestling her chin against it. "Go right this. She is waiting for you over in the servants' quarters."

Charles pulled away. "She is?"

A knowing smile touched those full lips. "She is, and it is fairly obvious that if you want a wedding, there will be one."

Charles grabbed her face and kissed it not once, not twice, but thrice. "I don't know why I ever doubted you. After everything we have been through together... I should have never..." He paused. "I have to go." Jerking away, Charles dodged around her and disappeared into the ballroom, leaving Mark and Magdalene to stand alone in complete silence in the shadows of the terrace.

"Thornton." Charles skid back into view, startling him, and pointed. *"You* are going to be the damn groomsman. Not to mention godfather to the babe. And anything else you want to be!"

Mark inclined his head. "I would be honored."

Charles grinned and darted off.

Silence pulsed again, reminding Mark that it was time to go.

His gaze momentarily met Magdalene's soulful dark

eyes, which always made his breath hitch in the most annoying way.

She lingered, the candlelight from the chandeliers beyond illuminating her gathered chestnut hair in the softest of ways. He'd always been in awe of that glorious hair, which held barely a single wisp of gray despite her lavish year of forty. Unlike his own hair that was beginning to silver at the temples. There were so many times he wished he could have met her in his youth and in hers, before life had bloody—

He was digressing.

It was time to go.

He rounded her.

Magdalene stepped toward him. "Thank you for speaking to him, Thornton. He sees you as the father he never had. You do realize that, yes?"

He nodded, but started walking, refusing to skewer the last of himself in the name of a woman who, sadly, would never be able to step beyond the wrongs committed against her. No matter how much time, love, patience and hope he offered.

It was indeed Anne all over again.

Only this hurt more. Because he had expected more from Magdalene given all that she was. Instead, she had given in to victimizing herself and him.

Which was why it was time to rise above her. It was time to cease settling for women who just couldn't see beyond themselves. He had a life. It wasn't perfect, but it was good. More importantly, he had his girls. He would never settle for anything less than *everything* for them, and that was why he wasn't going to bloody settle for anything less than *everything* for himself. Not ever again. At least Magdalene had taught him that much.

He inclined his head toward her one last time. "Good night." And off he strode, knowing he was never going to see her again.

CHAPTER FIVE

THOUGH MAGDALENE HAD ALWAYS believed matrimony was but a form of imprisonment that permitted a man to legally do with his wife's body and soul as he pleased, one she had sworn to *never* submit herself to again, this was Thornton. The one and only man she had ever come to trust and adore and love in her forty years, who had carried every imaginable burden she had ever placed upon him without fail.

Even when she had failed him.

And she was not about to fail him again. She already knew how it felt to live without him and his girls. This past month had been beyond torturous, and she wasn't doing that again. God save her, she was about to jump off a ledge in the hopes that he'd be there to catch her before her brains scattered across the pavement.

Gathering her skirts, she darted after his stalking figure, which had veered past her on the terrace and through the open doors leading into the ballroom. "Thornton—"

"There is no need to say anything. In fact, I prefer the chirping of crickets. I prefer—"

"Marry me."

He jerked to a halt and swung toward her, his burning green eyes intently holding hers in the wavering candle-light.

Her heart lurched as that steady gaze pried into her soul in a way she'd never experienced.

He searched her face but still said nothing.

When the silence made her feel as if her very chest might burst, she blurted up at him in complete exasperation, "Well, say something. I just agreed to be your wife."

He swung away and kept walking. Only faster.

"Thornton?" she called.

Still walking at a fast, rigid pace, he tossed out over his broad shoulder, "I decline your offer and ask we never return to the subject again."

She gasped and scurried after him in an effort to keep up. "I just asked you to marry me!"

He headed straight for the double doors leading to the main corridor of the foyer beyond the ballroom. "Such flippant submission is not the sort of relationship I want, Magdalene. Which is why I am declining your offer."

"But I…" Her breath hitched. He was throwing out a saber and expecting her to parry back. "All right." She hurried after him. "What sort of relationship did you want?"

"Don't insult me. If you don't know the sort of relationship I want out of you, and have no expectations for yourself, then damn you, woman, you don't have what I want."

"Oh, dearest God. And I thought I had insecurities."

He came to halt just within the opening of the ballroom. Turning, he caught her gaze. "I didn't have any insecurities until I met you. Anne left me wounded, yes. But you, Magdalene, *you* up and left me for dead when I laid my very self in your hands. You expect me to forgive that? With the mere toss of a marriage proposal from your lips? I want more than that. 'Tis obvious, however, that you don't have *more* than that, or you would have already offered it to me."

Now that hurt. And yes, she did deserve it for submitting to her fears as opposed to trusting the last man who would ever seek to hurt her. She drew in a shaky breath and let it out, making her way toward him. "I'm sorry. I'm sorry I didn't know how to go about this then, and I'm sorry I don't know how to go about this now."

He adjusted his coat around his frame with a solid tug, avoiding her gaze. "Four years. Four years of me waiting for you to—" He bared his teeth.

Her throat tightened. She'd been hurting him all along without knowing it.

"I spent *years* trying to prove my worth to Anne only to find it was never good enough. I don't deserve this. I don't. Not from you, not from anyone."

He was referring to his wife. A woman who had given him everything but her love. "Thornton—"

"Good night." Without deigning her a glance, he disappeared, leaving her to wonder how her life had ever become so complicated. Her chest ached miserably. It was clearly up to her to salvage whatever was left between them. And she was frightened out of her wits knowing it. She'd forgotten what it was like to be involved with a man in *that* way. But drat it all, if Charles could take on the world and his dreams, risking it all in the name of love, so could she.

WOMEN.

Stalking down the corridor, Mark made his way into the main section of the house, toward the entrance hall. That front door sure as hell wasn't where it needed to be.

"Thornton," Magdalene called after him.

"For God's sake, don't say anything. Don't." He *re-*

fused to settle for anything less than her heart, and it was something, goddamn her, she hadn't even bothered to offer him throughout her merry charade of tossing out the concept of matrimony.

The heels of her slippers *click-click-clicked* as she trotted alongside him. She reached out and tapped the side of his arm. "Life is full of surprises, isn't it? Whoever thought my son would marry the daughter of a chemist? And whoever thought that you and I would *ever* find each other attractive? I would have gagged if you had told me any of this when we first met."

Bloody brilliant. Now she was being downright insulting. "I have to get back to the girls." He yanked open the entrance door.

She jumped in front of him, causing him to skid to a halt.

"Thornton." Angling herself better between him and the entrance, she slowly closed the door leading to Park Lane and latched it. She hesitated. "I'm sorry. It's been so long since I even wanted to be involved with a man in that way. In truth, what happened between us that afternoon paralyzed me. I thought I knew how I felt about men and…you. But I didn't. Obviously. I mean, I did know how I felt about you all along, I just… Stupid as it was, I thought you were giving in to a fancy. All you need know, though, is this—I cannot imagine living my life without you after having met you. And that is why I not only want to be your wife but need to be your wife. Because you are, and have always been, more than a friend to me. You are my everything and I have loved you, Thornton, for as many years as you claim to have loved me. My heart tamped it all down but it was there. So in that, our suffering has been the same. We both suffered, loving each other in silence out of fear it wasn't real. When in fact…it was."

A raw heat tightened his entire body as he stared down at her astounded. All this time. All this time and she— "Why the devil didn't you tell me? Magdalene, why didn't you—"

"Why didn't you tell *me*?" she tossed right back, throwing up both hands and rattling them. "I wasn't sure what it was I was feeling, but you… All I needed and wanted to know was that it was love you felt, not— not…*lust* that can fade within a breath. Attraction is one thing, drat you, but *love* is quite another! Adam gave me more than enough lust and passion and angst to last me a lifetime. What I wanted and needed is love, damn you. *Love!*"

He groaned. They were both so stupid. They had both been so blinded by their own insecurities, it took away four goddamn years of their lives.

"Thornton." She leaned in, that divine scent of powder and chamomile entrancing the last of him. She lifted her eyes from his chest to his face in what he could only describe as Persephone submitting to her fate. "I thought unlacing my heart after Adam would never be possible. But thank God you came along to prove me wrong. Thank God there was you. Please don't give up on me. Please give me another chance."

It took every breath left within him not to grab her and make love to her there on the marble floor of the foyer. "You know what I want for us, Magdalene?" he confided. "More than anything?"

She was quiet for a moment. "What?"

"To be able to start anew." He reached up and outlined that pretty, oval face with the tip of his finger. "Court me. Court me for a few weeks in front of all of London before we make our way down that cathedral aisle."

She pulled in her chin. "Court you? Whatever do you mean? As if I were some...*debutante* in her first Season?"

"Yes."

"Off with you."

"Magdalene. Neither of us were equals to our spouses in our last marriage. I say we not only rise above that, but change it. I say we change everything that made us first come together."

She blinked. "And what is your definition of...*courting*, exactly?"

"Carriage rides, picnics in the park, a boat on the lake. You know, the things we never got to do because we were always too busy griping about our dead spouses and thinking the worst of what in the end was actually the best? We deserve to swallow and know bliss."

Their eyes locked.

The glittering awareness in her dark stare hit him with the strength of a bamboo rod.

She'd never looked at him that way before. Not ever.

Edging toward her, he drew in a calming breath and leaned in toward those incredible full lips, needing to make this real.

She leaned away, lifting a reprimanding brow. "You and I are not doing this here."

He leaned back, squelching his disappointment.

She grabbed his hand. "We will do this *elsewhere*. And you had better be ready to pull off those trousers, given that I have been shamelessly eyeing them for years."

His stomach flipped as he savagely squeezed her hand, submitting to the frenzied idea that... Oh, God.

He tried not to panic. It had been far too long.

She steadily walked them past the charred parlor and past the main stairwell and sconces whose candles had burned halfway to their stubs. Her gaze remained intently focused on the path before them, whispering of exotic possibilities he couldn't even begin to comprehend.

She veered them to the left, into the silence of her candlelit study. Releasing his hand to slide the double doors shut, she latched them and grabbed his hand again, guiding them over to the chess table beside the drawn curtains of the study.

In dazed exasperation, he watched her pull out the cane chair he always sat in. This wasn't exactly—

"What are we doing?"

She grabbed him by the shoulders, turning him, and pushed him down into the chair. "We never finished the game."

His throat tightened as he glanced at the chess pieces before him. They had all been left untouched since... that afternoon when he had lost the last of his rational mind by giving in to the one thing he had wanted to do for years: kiss her. Some of the pieces were still knocked over from his attempt.

Rounding over to her side of the table, she elegantly alighted into her chair, arranging her verdant satin gown about herself. Letting out a delicate breath, she shifted and lowered her gaze to the board, taking on that pensive look of concentration she assumed to slay him at chess.

He stared. "You can't be serious."

"Play."

"Why? I thought—"

"Just play."

Feeling as if he'd been punched in the gut, he hissed

out a breath. And here he thought she had had some sort of revelation that included a lot of kissing and a bed. He just couldn't win, could he? "I should probably confess something to you here and now. Before another minute passes."

"And what would you like to confess, Thornton dear? Hmm?"

"I hate chess. *Loathe* it, actually. With a passion. I always have. So there. Now you know everything there is to know about me. And I don't want to play. I have something else in mind for us. Something that involves you, me, brandy and a bed. Because *this* simply doesn't meet my level of approval. *At all.*"

She smirked, keeping her dark eyes locked on the board, leaned in and said matter-of-factly, "This is where you lean over the board, Thornton, and kiss me. And this time, I promise not to smack you. Not even for disliking what I consider to be the best game known to humanity." She hesitated and added, "So play. Play knowing that all you have to do is kiss the queen to, uh...*checkmate.*" She eyed him. "You do know how to checkmate, don't you? Or has it been too long for you to remember...*how*?"

A knot rose in his throat as the air of the study seemed to grow hot. Everything he had ever wanted had miraculously become his in a single night.

There was no more Anne.

There was no more Adam.

There were no more regrets of what could have or should have or might have been. There was just this. Them. Friends turned lovers and soon to be husband and wife.

He leaned over the chess table, rising slightly from his chair, and closed the remaining space between them. His pulse thundered as she strategically angled her mouth toward his. His mouth edged toward hers and their lips connected.

Yet again, the room spun and fell over on its side.

Her hands jumped to his face and held him in place. Yet again. Their lips instantly parted and the heat of their wet tongues connected. As before, it was slow and teasing and rhythmic and delectable. And as before, it turned into a pulsing mess and savage need that made his very lips sting from the eager pressure they both applied.

His cock swelled with a vengeance.

Checkmate. And how.

Knocking over the entire chess table with a solid sweep of his arm, he grabbed her. He yanked her against his body, molding the heat of that softness against his arms and chest.

They kissed harder and harder, without taking any breaths, until it turned into a blur.

Her hands slid up his chest and paused at his throat. Unknotting his cravat, in between kisses, she whipped it aside. She unbuttoned his vest. Button by button by button.

He released his hold on her body and lips and shrugged off his evening coat, letting it drop to the floor. She pushed off his vest with it and then jerked his linen shirt out of his trousers.

Grabbing each other to kiss again, they stumbled over to the large writing desk set off to the side and hit its edge hard. His hands jumped to her face to steady her and himself as he sucked on that tongue, pulling it deeper into his own mouth.

Releasing her mouth so he could look at her and assure himself that this was real, he slowly pushed his fingers up into her gathered hair.

Her eyes fluttered open, revealing those smoky eyes.

He drew in a shaky breath and gently tugged at her coif, causing pins and ribbons to cascade out of it, and dug his fingers in and out, in and out, unraveling as much of her hair as he could. It cascaded down onto her shoulders, framing her face in a way he'd never had the pleasure of seeing.

He couldn't breathe. She was so beautiful.

Her hands wedged between them, her fingers furiously unbuttoning the flap of his trousers. Her warm hands pulled his hard length out. He groaned in anguished bliss as she moistened her hand with her own tongue and stroked him.

Her sultry eyes never once left his.

She seductively and erotically and masterfully stroked him. His chest tightened in disbelief as he pushed his hips toward her hand, demanding more. He rippled beneath his skin, pushing toward climax.

He grabbed her hands, overwhelmed. In between ragged breaths he managed, "We need to stop. This is going far beyond—"

"I'm not exactly a virgin, Thornton."

He swallowed again, his entire body pulsing. As much as he wanted this and her, he couldn't help feeling as if he were going about this wrong. "We were supposed to court… You deserve a wedding night. Not…this."

She turned toward the desk behind them and swept off papers. "I did it traditionally the first time and there is no need for me to do it again. I'm going about this the way I want to, Thornton. I'm done living with regret. And so are you." She leaned over the desk, pushing out her backside toward him and planted both hands on the wood surface. Glancing back at him from over her slim shoulder, she met his gaze.

He let out a whistle, realizing that this woman was

about to make up for all the years he'd gone without it. "You mean you actually want to—"

She pushed away from the desk, turning toward him. She let out an awkward laugh and fidgeted with her hands as if realizing she was nervous.

Grabbing her hard by the waist, he spun her around back toward the desk and jerked up her skirts. "I intend to take this seriously. Very seriously." His hands plunged beneath the cascading fabric and slid up the bare sides of her smooth thighs. He draped away the fabric, exposing her entire backside to him and ground his hard length against her bum.

He leaned in from behind and in between tongue strokes against the smooth curve of her extended throat, said, "You may want to hold on to something, love."

She drew in a notable breath and bent forward, setting her hands back upon the desk.

He nudged her legs apart and trailed the tips of his fingers from her outer thighs to her bum and then in between her thighs, eliciting a gasp from her. He rubbed and rubbed her, making her ride his hand. Soft pants escaped her as he rubbed and flicked at her faster. She rode his hand, pushing her backside against him with choked moans. He leaned into her and kept intently fingering her until she quaked within his arms.

He couldn't believe he was actually touching her like this. He couldn't believe he was about to consummate every last emotion he'd ever felt for her.

He shifted his tight jaw, slipping his arm around her waist and used his other hand to position himself. She pushed back against him, her wet softness digging into the tip of his erection. His breath quickened. He savagely grabbed hold of her waist and plunged deep into her wetness.

A gasp escaped them both.

He slowly slid in and out of her, letting her adjust to his length. He pressed, then retreated. Pressed, then retreated. Hissing out breaths, he stroked faster and faster in and out of that slick passage until he was so damn hard, he thought he'd burst from the next stroke.

She threw back her head, rocking forward and backward against him. He held her firmly in place, and ground deeper, making her gasp when he hit the resistance of her womb. Gritting his teeth against the pleasure rippling through him, his mind blanked. He just pounded.

He heard her cry out his name.

He felt her shuddering.

It made him want her all the more.

Thrusting one last time, he gave in to a climax, his seed spurting into her with the buck of his hips. He groaned in anguished disbelief, trying to hold himself up. Eventually, he collapsed against her as the last of his pleasure subsided.

Magdalene.

With his chest still heaving, he nuzzled against her, brushing away her long hair and murmured, "You amaze me."

She was quiet for a moment, her cheek still resting against the desk in what appeared to be dazed exhaustion. "And you amaze me," she murmured back in a dreamy tone.

They remained there half draped on the desk for some time. He didn't want to pull out. He wanted this to last indefinitely.

She eventually shifted against him, forcing him to give up his claim. "Thornton?"

"Hmm?"

"I want a wedding."

He lifted his head from her shoulder and bit back a laugh. "Did you doubt there would be one? I'm not letting you out of this. I have three girls and a reputation to uphold."

She reached up and poked him with a finger. "No. I just...I want this to be special. For all of us. And for Charles, too. We can dress up the girls in lace and satin and make it bigger than people usually do. We deserve it."

"Bigger. I see. And I imagine you will want flowers?"

"Lots of flowers. Naturally."

"And music?"

"Music to melt the soul."

"And monkeys?"

She paused. "Monkeys?"

He nipped her shoulder and drawled, "I will be sure not to invite them."

She laughed. Rolling onto her back and out of his arms, she propped herself up on an elbow on the desk, her hair cascading around her shoulders. "'Tis good to know that absolutely *nothing* has changed." She shook her head and smiled.

It was a glorious, glorious smile that whispered to him of never-ending friendship and a delectable, crazy and seductive love that was his. At long bloody last, it was *his*.

* * * * *

SPECIAL EXCERPT FROM

HARLEQUIN®

HISTORICAL

From Bronwyn Scott comes the incredible new quartet
RAKES WHO MAKE HUSBANDS JEALOUS, featuring two
fantastic full-length Harlequin Historical novels and two
very sexy Harlequin Historical Undone! ebooks. Read on
for a sneak preview of our first hero, Nicholas D'Arcy…
the talk of the ton *for all the wrong reasons!*

"I'm going swimming. How about you?"

Annorah drew her knees up and hugged them. She used to love to swim, but that was before she grew up and swimming was ruled as something ladies didn't do. A lady couldn't very well swim in her clothes, which made the activity lewd *and* public. "The water will make my skirts too heavy."

Nicholas grinned wickedly. "Then take them off."

He was going to have to debate with her about it. Nicholas heard the regret in her voice, as if she was merely making the appropriate answer. Well, he'd see what he could do about that. He rose from the blanket and shrugged out of his shirt. It was perhaps not as gracefully done as it might have been. The shirt was wet and it stuck to him. He threw it on a hanging branch and his hands went to the waistband of his trousers.

"What are you doing?" Annorah's voice barely disguised a gasp of excitement mixed with trepidation.

"I'm taking off my trousers. I don't mean to swim in them," he called over his shoulder.

"What *do* you mean to swim in?"

"In my altogether. You could swim in your chemise if you preferred," he suggested.

"I couldn't." Annorah hesitated, biting her lip.

"Then take it off, too." He pushed his trousers past his hips and kicked them off, leaving only his smalls—a concession to her modesty. He turned around and Annorah blushed, her gaze looking everywhere but at him.

"Don't tell me you're embarrassed by my natural state." Nick spread his arms wide from his sides and sauntered toward her. He couldn't resist having a bit of fun. If he'd learned one thing about her this afternoon, it was that she could be teased—the wildness inside was very much alive once she let down her guard. He rather enjoyed getting past that guard, as he had in the river.

"It's not that."

"It isn't? Then is it perhaps that you're embarrassed about your natural state? I think your natural state would be quite lovely." He reached a hand down to her and tugged, letting the teasing fade from his voice. "Come on, Annorah. It's just the two of us. You've been eyeing that swimming hole since we got here. You know you want to." *You want to do more than swim, and if you'd look at me, you'd know I do, too.*

He had her on her feet and then he had her in his arms, kissing her—her throat, her neck, her lips. She tasted like wine, her body all compliance beneath his mouth. A soft moan escaped her. His hands worked the simple fastenings of her gown. He hesitated before pushing the dress down her shoulders, giving her one last chance to back out. If she resisted now, he'd let her. But she didn't. He smiled to himself. Sometimes all a person needed was a nudge.

Don't miss
SECRETS OF A GENTLEMAN ESCORT
available from Harlequin® Historical January 2014

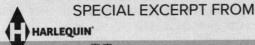
Next month, don't miss TO TEMPT A VIKING,
the incredible second book in
Michelle Willingham's FORBIDDEN VIKINGS duet.
Elena Karlsdotter lays siege to
Ragnar Olafsson's battle-hardened heart in this
passionate tale of illicit temptation…

"I was dreaming of you," she confessed. "That night in the tent when I made you touch me. It shouldn't have happened and I'm sorry for what I did."

His dark green eyes fixed upon her, as if he couldn't believe what he was hearing. She half expected him to move away from her in disgust. Instead, he took her face between his hands, remaining silent. And she knew, without him speaking a single word, that he'd desired her, too.

Elena covered his hands with her own, drinking in the touch of his palms. The heat of this moment sank beneath her skin, conjuring up the lost feelings she'd put aside. She remembered how his lips had felt beneath hers and a sudden longing flushed through her skin.

It was as if a part of her had been brought back to life, resurrected in this man's touch. She wasn't used to feeling so strongly, or yearning for something she couldn't have.

Finally, he took his hands away and regarded her. "I believe that Styr is alive and that you'll go back with him. I kept my word to protect you and I promise to keep you safe until the day I have to let you go."

The words were a stark reminder that nothing would

happen between them. No matter how much she might want to take comfort from his touch.

But though his hands were no longer upon her, he was still staring at her with unbridled longing. "If you were my wife at this moment, I'd kiss you now," he said. "I'd taste your sweetness and run my tongue over your lower lip."

The words flowed through her, pushing the forbidden feelings to the surface.

She closed her eyes, trying not to envision it.

"I'd use my mouth all over your skin," he continued. "Your neck…your bare breasts, and then I'd go lower," he said huskily. "Until you're craving me inside you."

Just like the night she'd dreamed of him, her body went soft, imagining him. He shouldn't be speaking such words, tempting her in such a way. She could hardly bear it and her face was flushed.

It didn't matter what had happened these past few days. No matter that she'd grown so close to him. She was a woman of honor and would never be disloyal to her husband. "I can't be yours, Ragnar," she whispered. "I belong to him."

The tension in his hands was palpable as he drew them back. "Don't fear, Elena. I'll never touch you again. Whatever I might desire, I'll never do anything to act upon it. He won't know."

"He can't," she whispered. "I won't be disloyal to him."

Yet all she could think was that Styr had never affected her in that way. And Ragnar hadn't laid a hand upon her.

TO TEMPT A VIKING
available from Harlequin Historical February 2014